THE PARIS APARTMENT

THE PARIS APARTMENT

A NOVEL

LUCY FOLEY

WM
WILLIAM MORROW
An Imprint of HarperCollinsPublishers

FOR AL, FOR EVERYTHING.

THE PARIS APARTMENT. Copyright © 2022 by Lost and Found Books Ltd. All rights reserved. Printed in the United States of America. No part of this book may be used or reproduced in any manner whatsoever without written permission except in the case of brief quotations embodied in critical articles and reviews. For information, address HarperCollins Publishers, 195 Broadway, New York, NY 10007.

HarperCollins books may be purchased for educational, business, or sales promotional use. For information, please email the Special Markets Department at SPsales@harpercollins.com.

Published in 2022 by HarperFiction, an imprint of HarperCollins UK.

FIRST U.S. EDITION

Designed by Bonni Leon-Berman

Library of Congress Cataloging-in-Publication Data has been applied for.

ISBN 978-0-06-300305-7 (hardcover)
ISBN 978-0-06-322792-7 (international edition)

22 23 24 25 26   LSC   10 9 8 7 6 5 4 3 2 1

Ben

HIS FINGERS HOVER OVER THE keyboard. Got to get it all down. This: this is the story that's going to make his name. Ben lights another cigarette, a Gitane. Bit of a cliché to smoke them here but he does actually like the taste. And fine, yeah, likes the way he looks smoking them too.

He's sitting in front of the apartment's long windows, which look onto the central courtyard. Everything out there is steeped in darkness, save for the weak greenish glow thrown by a single lamp. It's a beautiful building, but there's something rotten at its heart. Now he's discovered it he can smell the stench of it everywhere.

He should be clearing out of here soon. He's outstayed his welcome in this place. Jess could hardly have chosen a worse time to decide to come and stay. She barely gave him any notice. And she didn't give much detail on the phone but clearly something's up; something wrong with whatever crappy bar job she's working now. His half sister has a knack for turning up when she's not wanted. She's like a homing beacon for trouble: it seems to follow her around. She's never been good at just *playing the game.* Never understood how much easier it makes life if you just give people what they want, tell them what they want to hear. Admittedly, he did tell her to come and stay "whenever you like," but he didn't really mean it. Trust Jess to take him at his word.

When was the last time he saw her? Thinking about her always makes him feel guilty. Should he have been there for her more, looked out for her . . . ? She's fragile, Jess. Or—not fragile exactly, but vulnerable in a way people probably don't see at first. An "armadillo": softness beneath that tough exterior.

Anyway. He should call her, give her some directions. When her phone rings out he leaves a voicenote: "Hey Jess, so it's number twelve, Rue des Amants. Got that? Third floor."

His eye's drawn to a flash of movement in the courtyard beneath the windows. Someone's passing through it quickly. Almost running. He can only make out a shadowy figure, can't see who it is. But something about the speed seems odd. He's hit with a little animal spike of adrenaline.

He remembers he's still recording the voicenote, drags his gaze from the window. "Just ring the buzzer. I'll be up waiting for you—"

He stops speaking. Hesitates, listens.

A noise.

The sound of footsteps out on the landing . . . approaching the apartment door.

The footsteps stop. Someone is there, just outside. He waits for a knock. None comes. Silence. But a weighted silence, like a held breath.

Odd.

And then another sound. He stands still, ears pricked, listening intently. There it is again. It's metal on metal, the scrape of a key. Then the clunk of it entering the mechanism. He watches the lock turn. Someone is unlocking his door from the outside. Someone who has a key, but no business coming in here uninvited.

The handle begins to move downward. The door begins to open, with that familiar drawn-out groan.

He puts his phone down on the kitchen counter, voicenote forgotten. Waits and watches dumbly as the door swings forward. As the figure steps into the room.

"What are you doing here?" he asks. Calm, reasonable. Nothing to hide. Not afraid. Or not yet. "And why—"

Then he sees what his intruder holds.

Now. Now the fear comes.

Jess

FOR CHRIST'S SAKE, BEN. ANSWER your phone. I'm freezing my tits off out here. My Eurostar was two hours late leaving London; I should have arrived at ten-thirty but it's just gone midnight. And it's cold tonight, even colder here in Paris than it was in London. It's only the end of October but my breath smokes in the air and my toes are numb in my boots. Crazy to think there was a heatwave only a few weeks ago. I need a proper coat. But there's always been a lot of things I need that I'm never going to get.

I've probably called Ben ten times now: as my Eurostar pulled in, on the half hour walk here from Gare du Nord. No answer. And he hasn't replied to any of my texts. Thanks for nothing, big bro.

He said he'd be here to let me in. "Just ring the buzzer. I'll be up waiting for you—"

Well, I'm here. Here being a dimly lit, cobblestoned cul-de-sac in what appears to be a seriously posh neighborhood. The apartment building in front of me closes off this end, standing all on its own.

I glance back down the empty street. Beside a parked car, about twenty feet away, I think I see the shadows shift. I step to the side, to try and get a better look. There's . . . I squint, trying to make out the shape. I could swear there's someone there, crouched behind the car.

I jump as a siren blares a few streets away, loud in the silence. Listen as the sound fades away into the night. It's different from

the ones at home—"nee-naw, nee-naw," like a child's impression—
but it still makes my heart beat a little faster.

I glance back at the shadowy area behind the parked car. Now
I can't make out any movement, can't even see the shape I thought
I glimpsed before. Maybe it was just a trick of the light, after all.

I look back up at the building. The others on this street are
beautiful, but this one knocks spots off them all. It's set back
from the road behind a big gate with a high wall on either side,
concealing what must be some sort of garden or courtyard. Five
or six stories, huge windows, all with wrought-iron balconies. A
big sprawl of ivy growing all over the front of it which looks like a
creeping dark stain. If I crane my neck I can see what might be
a roof garden on the top, the spiky shapes of the trees and shrubs
black cut-outs against the night sky.

I double-check the address. Number twelve, rue des Amants.
I've definitely got it right. I still can't quite believe this swanky
apartment building is where Ben's been living. He said a mate
helped sort him out with it, someone he knew from his student
days. But then Ben's always managed to fall on his feet. I suppose
it only makes sense that he's charmed his way into a place like
this. And charm must have done it. I know journalists probably
earn more than bartenders, but not by this much.

The metal gate in front of me has a brass lion's head knocker:
the fat metal ring held between snarling teeth. Along the top
of the gate, I notice, is a bristle of anti-climb spikes. And all
along the high wall either side of the gate are embedded shards
of glass. These security measures feel kind of at odds with the
elegance of the building.

I lift up the knocker, cold and heavy in my hand, let it drop.
The clang of it bounces off the cobblestones, so much louder than
expected in the silence. In fact, it's so quiet and dark here that

it's hard to imagine it's part of the same city I've trundled across this evening from Gare du Nord: all the bright lights and crowds, people spilling in and out of restaurants and bars. I think of the area around that huge cathedral lit up on the hill, the Sacré-Coeur, which I passed beneath only twenty minutes ago: throngs of tourists out taking selfies and dodgy-looking guys in puffer jackets sharking between them, ready to nick a wallet or two. And the streets that I walked through with the neon signs, the blaring music, the all-night food, the crowds spilling out of bars, the queues for clubs. This is a different universe. I look back down the street behind me: not another person in sight. The only real sound comes from a scurry of dead ivy across the cobblestones. I can hear the roar of traffic at a distance, the honking of car horns—but even that seems muffled, like it wouldn't dare intrude on this elegant, hushed world.

I didn't stop to think much, pulling my case across town from the station. I was mainly concentrating on not getting mugged, or letting the broken wheel of my suitcase stick and throw me off balance. But now, for the first time, it sinks in: I'm here, in Paris. A different city, a different country. I've made it. I've left my old life behind.

A LIGHT SNAPS on in one of the windows up above. I glance up and there's a dark figure standing there, head and shoulders in silhouette. Ben? If it were him, though, he'd wave down at me, surely. I know I must be lit up by the nearby streetlamp. But the figure at the window is as still as a statue. I can't make out any features or even whether they're male or female. But they're watching me. They must be. I suppose I must look pretty shabby and out of place with my broken old suitcase trying to bust open despite the bungee cord wrapped around it. A strange feeling, knowing they can see me but I can't see them properly. I drop my eyes.

Aha. To the right of the gate I spot a little panel of buttons for the different apartments with a lens set into it. The big lion's head knocker must just be for show. I step forward and press the one for the third floor, for Ben's place. I wait for his voice to crackle through the intercom.

No answer.

Sophie

SOMEONE IS KNOCKING ON THE front door to the building. Loud enough for Benoit, my silver whippet, to leap to his feet and let out a volley of barks.

"*Arrête ça!*" I shout. "Stop that."

Benoit whimpers, then goes quiet. He looks up at me, confusion in his dark eyes. I can hear the change in my voice as well—too shrill, too loud. And I can hear my own breathing in the silence that follows, rough and shallow.

No one ever uses the door knocker. Certainly, no one familiar with this building. I go to the windows on this side of the apartment, which look down into the courtyard. I can't see onto the street from here, but the front door from the street leads into the courtyard, so if anyone had come in I would see them there. But no one has entered and it must have been a few minutes since the knocking. Clearly it's not someone the concierge thinks should be admitted. Fine. Good. I haven't always liked that woman, but I know I can trust her in this at least.

In Paris you can live in the most luxurious apartment and the scum of the city will still wash up at your door on occasion. The drug addicts, the vagrants. The whores. Pigalle, the red-light district, lies just a little way away, clinging to the coattails of Montmartre. Up here, in this multi-million-euro fortress with its views out over the city's rooftops, all the way to the Tour

Eiffel, I have always felt comparatively safe. I can ignore the grime beneath the gilt. I am good at turning a blind eye. Usually. But tonight is . . . different.

I go to check my reflection in the mirror that hangs in the hallway. I pay close attention to what I see in the glass. Not so bad for fifty. It is partly due to the fact that I have adopted the French way when it comes to maintaining my *forme*. Which essentially means always being hungry. I know that even at this hour I will be looking immaculate. My lipstick is flawless. I never leave the apartment without it. Chanel, "La Somptueuse": my signature color. A bluish, regal color that says: "stand back," not "come hither." My hair is a shining black bob cut every six weeks by David Mallet at Notre Dame des Victoires. The shape perfected, any silver painstakingly concealed. Jacques, my husband, made it quite clear once that he abhors women who allow themselves to go gray. Even if he hasn't always been here to admire it.

I am wearing what I consider my uniform. My armor. Silk Equipment shirt, exquisitely-cut dark slim trousers. A scarf—brightly patterned Hermès silk—around my neck, which is excellent for concealing the ravages of time to the delicate skin there. A recent gift from Jacques, with his love of beautiful things. Like this apartment. Like me, as I was before I had the bad grace to age.

Perfect. As ever. As expected. But I feel dirty. Sullied by what I have had to do this evening. In the glass my eyes glitter. The only sign. Though my face is a little gaunt, too—if you were to look closely. I am even thinner than usual. Recently I have not had to watch my diet, to carefully mark each glass of wine or morsel of croissant. I couldn't tell you what I ate for breakfast this morning; whether I remembered to eat at all. Each day my waistband hangs looser, the bones of my sternum protrude more sharply.

I undo the knot of my scarf. I can tie a scarf as well as any born and bred Parisian. By it you know me for one of them, those chic moneyed women with their small dogs and their excellent breeding.

I look at the text message I sent to Jacques last night. **Bonne nuit, mon amour. Tout va bien ici.** *Good night, my love. Everything is fine here.*

Everything is fine here. HA.

I don't know how it has come to this. But I do know that it started with him coming here. Moving into the third floor. Benjamin Daniels. He destroyed everything.

Jess

I PULL OUT MY PHONE. Last time I checked Ben hadn't replied to any of my messages. One on the Eurostar: **On my way!** And then: **At Gare du Nord! Do you have an Uber account?!!!** Just in case, you know, he suddenly felt generous enough to send a cab to collect me. Seemed worth a shot.

There is a new message on my phone. Only it's not from Ben.

You stupid little bitch. Think you can get away with what you've done?

Shit. I swallow past the sudden dryness in my throat. Then I delete it. Block the number.

As I say, it was all a bit last minute, coming here. Ben didn't sound that thrilled when I called him earlier and told him I was on my way. True, I didn't give him much time to get used to the idea. But then it's always felt like the bond between us is more important to me than it is to my half brother. I suggested we hang out last Christmas, but he said he was busy. "Skiing," he said. Didn't even know he could ski. Sometimes it even feels like I'm an embarrassment to him. I represent the past, and he'd rather be cut loose from all that.

I had to explain I was desperate. "Hopefully it'll only be for a month or two, and I'll pay my way," I said. "Just as soon as I get on my feet. I'll get a job." Yeah. One where they don't ask too many questions. That's how you end up in the places I've worked at—there aren't that many that will take you when your references are such a shitshow.

Up until this afternoon I was gainfully employed at the Copacabana bar in Brighton. The odd massive tip made up for it. A load of wanker bankers, say, down from London celebrating some Dick or Harry or Tobias' upcoming nuptials and too pissed to count the notes out right—or maybe to guys like that it's just so much loose change anyway. But, as of today, I'm unemployed. Again.

I press the buzzer a second time. No answer. All the building's windows are dark again—even the one that lit up before. Christ's sake. He couldn't have turned in for the night and totally forgotten about me . . . could he?

Below all the other buzzers there's a separate one: *Concierge*, it reads in curly script. Like something in a hotel: further proof that this place is seriously upmarket. I press the button, wait. No answer. But I can't help imagining someone looking at the little video image of me, assessing, then deciding not to open up.

I lift up the heavy knocker again and slam it several times against the wood. The sound echoes down the street: someone must hear it. I can just make out a dog barking, from somewhere deep inside the building.

I wait five minutes. No one comes.

Shit.

I can't afford a hotel. I don't have enough for a return journey to London—and even if I did there's no way I'm going back. I consider my options. Go to a bar . . . wait it out?

I hear footsteps behind me, ringing out on the cobblestones. Ben? I spin round, ready for him to apologize, tell me he just popped out to get some ciggies or something. But the figure walking toward me isn't my brother. He's too tall, too broad, a parka hood with a fur rim up over his head. He's moving quickly and there's something purposeful about his walk. I grip the handle of my suitcase a little tighter. Literally everything I own is in here.

He's only a few meters away now, close enough that by the light of the streetlamp I can make out the gleam of his eyes under the hood. He's reaching into his pocket, pulling his hand back out. Something makes me take a step backward. And now I see it. Something sharp and metallic, gleaming in his hand.

Concierge

THE LOGE

I WATCH HER ON THE intercom screen, the stranger at the gate. What can she be doing here? She rings the buzzer again. She must be lost. I know, just from looking at her, that she has no business being here. Except she seems certain that this is the place she wants, so determined. Now she looks into the lens. I will not let her in. I cannot.

I am the gatekeeper of this building. Sitting here in my *loge*: a tiny cabin in the corner of the courtyard, which would fit maybe twenty times into the apartments above me. But it is mine, at least. My private space. My home. Most people wouldn't consider it worthy of the name. If I sit on the pull-down bed, I can touch nearly all the corners of the room at once. There is damp spreading from the ground and down from the roof and the windows don't keep out the cold. But there are four walls. There is a place for me to put my photographs with their echoes of a life once lived, the little relics I have collected and which I hold onto when I feel most alone; the flowers I pick from the courtyard garden every other morning so there is something fresh and alive in here. This place, for all its shortcomings, represents security. Without it I have nothing.

I look again at the face on the intercom screen. As the light catches her just so I see a familiarity: the sharp line of the nose and jaw. But more than her appearance it is something about the way she moves, looks around her. A hungry, vulpine quality that reminds me of another. All the more reason not to let her in. I don't like strangers. I don't like change. Change has always been dangerous for me. He proved that: coming here with his questions, his charm. The man who came to live in the third-floor apartment: Benjamin Daniels. After he came here, everything changed.

Jess

HE'S COMING STRAIGHT FOR ME, the guy in the parka. He's lifting his arm. The metal of the blade gleams again. Shit. I'm about to turn and run—get a few yards on him at least—

But wait, no, *no* . . . I can see now that the thing in his hand isn't a blade. It's an iPhone, in a metallic case. I let out the breath I've been holding and lean against my bag, hit by a sudden wave of tiredness. I've been wired all day, no wonder I'm spooking at shadows.

I watch as the guy makes a call. I can make out a tinny little voice at the other end; a woman's voice, I think. Then he begins to talk, over her, louder and louder, until he's shouting into his handset. I have no idea what the words mean exactly but I don't need to know much French to understand this isn't a polite or friendly chat.

After he's got his long, angry speech off his chest he hangs up and shoves the phone back in his pocket. Then he spits out a single word: "*Putain.*"

I know that one. I got a D in my French GCSE but I did look up all the swear words once and I'm good at remembering the stuff that interests me. *Whore*: that's what it means.

Now he turns and starts walking in my direction again. And I see, quite clearly, that he just wants to use the gate to this building. I step aside, feeling a total idiot for having got so keyed up over nothing. But it makes sense; I spent the whole Eurostar journey looking over my shoulder. You know, just in case.

"*Bonsoir*," I say in my best accent, flashing my most winning smile. Maybe this guy will let me in and I can go up to the third floor and hammer on Ben's apartment door. Maybe his buzzer's simply not working or something.

The guy doesn't reply. He just turns to the keypad next to the gate and punches in a series of numbers. Finally he gives me a quick glance over his shoulder. It's not the *most* friendly glance. I catch a waft of booze, stale and sour. Same breath as most of the punters in the Copacabana.

I smile again. "Er . . . *excuse moi?* Please, ah—I need some help, I'm looking for my brother, Ben. Benjamin Daniels—"

I wish I had a bit more of Ben's flair, his charm. "Benjamin Silver-Tongue," Mum called him. He's always had this way of getting anyone to do what he wants. Maybe that's why he ended up a journalist in Paris while I've been working for a bloke affectionately known as The Pervert in a shithole bar in Brighton serving stag dos at the weekends and local lowlifes in the week.

The guy turns back to face me, slowly. "Benjamin Daniels," he says. Not a question: just the name, repeated. I see something: anger, or maybe fear. He knows who I'm talking about. "Benjamin Daniels is not here."

"What do you mean, he's not here?" I ask. "This is the address he gave me. He's up on the third floor. I can't get hold of him."

The man turns his back on me. I watch as he pulls open the gate. Finally he turns round to face me a third time and I think: maybe he is going to help me, after all. Then, in accented English, very slowly and loudly, he says: "Fuck off, *little girl*."

Before I even have time to reply there's a clang of metal and I jump backward. He's slammed the gate shut, right in my face. As the ringing fades from my ears I'm left with just the sound of my breathing, fast and loud.

But he's helped me, even though he doesn't know it. I wait a moment, take a quick look back down the street. Then I lift my hand to the keypad and punch in the same numbers I watched him use only a few seconds ago: 7561. Bingo: the little light flickers green and I hear the mechanism of the gate click open. Dragging my case after me, I slip inside.

Mimi

MERDE.

I just heard his name, out there in the night. I lift my head, listening. For some reason I'm on top of the covers, not under them. My hair feels damp, the pillow cold and soggy. I shiver.

Am I hearing things? Did I imagine it? His name . . . following me everywhere?

No: I'm sure it was real. A woman's voice, drifting up through the open window of my bedroom. Somehow I heard it four stories up. Somehow I heard it through the roar of white noise inside my head.

Who is she? Why is she asking about him?

I sit up, pulling my bony knees tight against my chest, and reach for my childhood *doudou*, Monsieur Gus, a scraggy old penguin stuffed animal toy I still keep beside my pillow. I press him against my face, try to comfort myself with the feel of his hard little head, the soft, shifting scrunch of the beans inside his body, the musty smell of him. Just like I did as a little girl when I'd had a bad dream. You're not a little girl any longer, Mimi. He said that. Ben.

The moon is so bright that my whole room is filled with a cold blue light. Nearly a full moon. In the corner I can make out my record player, the case of vinyls next to it. I painted the walls in here such a dark blackish-blue that they don't reflect any light at all but the poster hanging opposite me seems to glow. It's a Cindy Sherman; I went to her show at the Pompidou last year. I got completely obsessed with how raw and freaky and intense her work is: the kind of thing I try to do with my painting. In the poster, one of the Untitled Film Stills, she's wearing a short black wig and she stares out at you like she's possessed, or like she might be about to eat your soul. "*Putain!*" my flatmate Camille laughed, when she saw it. "What happens if you bring some guy back? He's gonna have to look at that angry bitch while you're screwing? That'll put him off his rhythm." As if, I thought at the time. Nineteen years old and still a virgin. Worse. A convent-school-educated virgin.

I stare at Cindy, the black bruise-like shadows around her eyes, the jagged line of her hair which is kind of like my own, since I took a pair of scissors to it. It feels like looking in a mirror.

I turn to the window, look down into the courtyard. The lights are on in the concierge's cabin. Of course: that nosy old bitch never misses a trick. Creeping out from shadowy corners. Always watching, always there. Looking at you like she knows all your secrets.

This building is a U-shape around the courtyard. My bedroom is at one end of the U, so if I peer diagonally downward I can see into his apartment. Nearly every evening for the last two months he sat there at his desk working late into the night, the lights on. For just a moment I let myself look. The shutters are open but the lights are off and the space behind the desk looks more than empty, or like the emptiness itself has a kind of depth and weight. I glance away.

I slide down from my bed and tiptoe out into the main part of the apartment, trying not to trip over all the stuff Camille leaves scattered around like it's an extension of her bedroom: magazines and dropped sweaters, dirty coffee cups, nail varnish pots, lacy bras. From the big windows in here I've got a direct view of the front entrance. As I watch, the gate opens. A shadowy figure slips through the gap. As she comes forward into the light I can make her out: a woman I have never seen before. No, I say silently. No no no no no. Go away. The roar in my head grows louder.

"Did you hear that knocking?"

I spin around. *Putain*. Camille's lounging there on the couch, cigarette glowing in her hand, boots up on the armrest: faux-snakeskin with five-inch heels. When did she get in? How long has she been lurking there in the dark?

"I thought you were out," I say. Normally, if she goes clubbing, she stays till dawn.

"*Oui*." She shrugs, takes a drag on her cigarette. "I've only been back twenty minutes." Even in the gloom I see how her eyes slide away from mine. Normally she'd be straight into some story about the crazy new club she's been at, or the guy whose bed she's just left, including an overly detailed description of his dick or exactly how skilled he was at using it. I've often felt like I'm living vicariously through Camille. Grateful someone like her would choose to hang out with me. When we met at the Sorbonne she told me she likes collecting people, that I interested her because I have this "intense energy." But when I've felt worse about myself I've suspected this apartment probably has more to do with it.

"Where have you been?" I ask, trying to sound halfway normal.

She shrugs. "Just around."

I feel like there's something going on with her, something she's not telling me. But right now I can't think about Camille. The roaring in my head suddenly feels like it's drowning out all my thoughts.

There's just one thing I know. Everything that has happened here happened because of him: Benjamin Daniels.

Jess

I'M STANDING IN A SMALL, dark courtyard. The apartment building proper wraps around it on three sides. The ivy has gone crazy here, winding up almost to the fourth floor, surrounding all the windows, swallowing drainpipes, a couple of satellite dishes. Ahead a short path winds between flowerbeds planted with dark shrubs and trees. I can smell the sweetish scent of dead leaves, fresh-turned earth. To my right there's a sort of cabin structure, only a bit bigger than a garden shed. The two windows seem to be shuttered. On one side a tiny chink of light shows through a crack.

In the opposite corner I make out a door, which seems to lead into the main part of the building. I head that way along the path. As I do a pale face looms suddenly out of the darkness on my right. I stop short. But it's the statue of a nude woman, life-size, her body wound about with more black ivy, her eyes staring and blank.

The door in the corner of the courtyard has another passcode, but it clicks open with the same set of numbers, thank God. I step through it into a dark, echoing space. A stairwell winds upward into deeper darkness. I find the little orange glow of a light switch on the wall, flick it. The lights hum on, dimly. A ticking sound: some sort of energy-saving timer maybe. I can see now that there's a dark reddish carpet beneath my feet, covering a stone floor then climbing up the polished wooden staircase. Above me the bannister coils around on itself and inside the staircase there's a lift shaft—a tiny, ancient, rickety-looking capsule that might be as old as the apartment itself, so ancient-looking I wonder if it's actually still in use. There's a trace of stale cigarette smoke on the air. Still, all pretty posh, all a long, long way from the place I've been crashing at in Brighton.

There's a door to the left of me: *Cave*, it says. I've never let a closed door stay closed for long: I suppose you could say that's my main problem in life. I give it a push, see a flight of steps leading down. I'm hit by a waft of cold underground air, damp and musty.

I hear a noise then, somewhere above me. The creak of wood. I let the door swing shut and glance up. Something moves along the wall several flights up. I wait to see someone appear around the corner, in the gaps between the bannisters. But the shadow stops, as though waiting for something. And then suddenly everything goes dark: the timer must have run out. I reach over, flick it back on.

The shadow's gone.

I walk over to the lift in its metal cage. It's definitely on the antique side, but I'm too exhausted to even think about lugging my stuff up those stairs. There's barely room for me and the suitcase inside. I close the little door, press the button for the third floor, put a hand against the structure to steady myself. It gives under the pressure of my palm; I hastily pull my hand away. There's a bit of a shudder as the lift sets off; I catch my breath.

Up I go: each floor has one door, marked with a brass number. Is there only one apartment per floor? They must be pretty big. I imagine the sleeping presence of strangers behind those doors. I wonder who lives in them, what Ben's neighbors are like. And I find myself wondering which apartment the dickhead I met at the gate lives in.

The lift judders to a halt on the third floor. I step out onto the landing and drag my suitcase after me. Here it is: Ben's apartment, with its brass number 3.

I give it a couple of loud knocks.

No answer.

I crouch down and look at the keyhole. It's the old-fashioned kind, easiest in the world to pick. Needs must. I take out my hoop earrings and bend them out of shape—the convenience of cheap jewelry—leaving me with two long, thin pieces of metal. I make my rake and my pick. Ben actually taught me this when we were little so he can hardly complain. I got so good at it I can unpick a simple pin tumbler mechanism in less than a minute.

I wiggle the earrings back and forth in the lock until there's a click, then turn the handle. Yes—the door begins to open. I pause. Something about this doesn't feel right. I've had to rely on my instincts quite a lot over the years. And I've also been here before. Hand clasped around the door handle. Not knowing what I'm going to find on the other side—

Deep breath. For a moment it feels like the air contracts around me. I find myself gripping the pendant of my necklace. It's a St. Christopher: Mum gave us both one, to keep us safe—even if that was her job, not something to be outsourced to a little metal saint. I'm not religious and I'm not sure Mum was either. All the same, I can't imagine ever being parted with mine.

With my other hand I push the handle down. I can't stop myself from squeezing my eyes shut tight as I step into the space.

It's pitch-black inside.

"Ben?" I call out.

No answer.

I step farther inside, grope about for a light switch. As the lights come on the apartment reveals itself. My first thought is:

Christ, it's huge. Bigger even than I expected. Grander. High-ceilinged. Dark wooden beams up above, polished floorboards below, huge windows facing down onto the courtyard.

I take another step into the room. As I do something lands across my shoulders: a blunt, heavy blow. Then the sting of something sharp, tearing into my flesh.

Concierge

THE LOGE

A FEW MINUTES AFTER THE knocking I watched through the windows of my lodge as the first figure entered the courtyard, his hood pulled up. Then I saw a second figure appear. The newcomer, the girl. Clattering that huge suitcase across the cobbles of the courtyard, making enough noise to wake the dead.

I watched her on the intercom screen until the buzzer stopped ringing.

I am good at watching. I sweep the residents' hallways, I collect their post, I answer the door. But also, I watch. I see everything. And it gives me a strange kind of power, even if I'm the only one who's aware of it. The residents forget about me. It's convenient for them to do so. To imagine that I'm nothing more than an extension of this building, just a moving element of a large machine, like the lift that takes them up to their beautiful apartments. In a way I have become part of this place. It has certainly left its mark on me. I am sure the years of living in this tiny cabin have caused me to shrink, hunching into myself, while the hours spent sweeping and scrubbing the corridors and stairs of the apartment building have winnowed my flesh. Perhaps in another life I would have grown plump in my old age. I have not had that luxury. I am sinew and bone. Stronger than I look.

I suppose I could have gone and stopped her. Should have done. But confrontation is not my style. I have learned that watching is the more powerful weapon. And it had a feeling of inevitability, her being here. I could see her determination. She would somehow have found her way in, no matter what I did to try and prevent her.

Stupid girl. It would have been far, far better if she'd turned and left this place and never returned. But it's too late now. So be it.

Jess

MY HEART IS BEATING DOUBLE-TIME, my muscles tensed.

I look down at the cat as it weaves its way between my legs, purring, a blur of movement. Slinky, black, a white ruff. I put a hand down the back of my top. My fingers come away with a sheen of blood. *Ouch.*

The cat must have jumped onto my back from the counter next to the door, digging its claws in for grip when I fell forward. It looks up at me now through narrowed green eyes and gives a squawk, as though asking me what the hell I think I'm doing here.

A cat! Jesus Christ. I start laughing and then stop, quickly, because of the strange way the sound echoes around the high space.

I didn't know Ben had a cat. Does he even like cats? It suddenly seems crazy that I don't know this. But I suppose there's not all that much I do know about his life here.

"Ben?" I call out. Again the sound of my voice bounces back at me. No answer. I don't think I expected one: it feels too silent, too empty. There's a strange smell, too. Something chemical.

I suddenly really need a drink. I wander into the little kitchen area to my right and start raiding the cupboards. First things first. I come up with half a bottle of red wine. I'd prefer something with more of a kick, but beggars can't be choosers and that might as well be the motto for my whole bloody life. I slosh some into a glass. There's a pack of cigarettes on the side too, a bright blue box: Gitanes. I didn't know Ben still smoked. Typical of him to favor some fancy French brand. I fish one out, light up, inhale, and cough like I did the first time a fellow foster kid gave me a drag: it's strong, spicy, unfiltered. I'm not sure I like it. Still, I push the rest of the pack into the back pocket of my jeans—he owes me—and take my first proper look around the place.

I'm . . . surprised, to say the least. I'm not sure what I imagined, but this isn't it. Ben's a bit creative, a bit cool (not that I'd ever describe him that way to his face), and in contrast this whole apartment is covered in antique-looking old-lady wallpaper, silvery with a floral pattern. When I put out a hand and touch the nearest wall I realize it's not paper after all: it's a very faded silk. I see brighter spots where there were clearly once pictures hanging, small rusty age spots on the fabric. From the high ceiling hangs a chandelier, curls of metal holding the bulbs. A long strand of cobweb swings lazily back and forth—there must be a breeze coming from somewhere. And maybe there were once curtains behind those window shutters: I see an empty curtain rail up above, the brass rings still in place. A desk plumb in front of the windows. A shelf holding a few ivory-colored books, a big navy French dictionary.

In the near corner there's a coat stand with an old khaki jacket on it; I'm sure I've seen Ben wearing it before. Maybe even the last time I saw him, about a year ago, when he came down to Brighton and bought me lunch before disappearing back out of my life again without a backward glance. I reach into the pockets and draw out a set of keys and a brown leather wallet.

Is it a bit strange that Ben's gone but left these behind?

I open the wallet: the back pocket's stuffed with a few euro notes. I take a twenty and then, for good measure, a couple of tens. I'd have asked to borrow some money if he was here anyway. I'll pay it back . . . sometime.

A business card is stuffed into the front of the section that holds credit cards. It reads: **Theo Mendelson. Paris editor,** *Guardian.*

And scribbled on it, in what looks like Ben's handwriting (some-times he remembers to send me a birthday card): *PITCH STORY TO HIM!*

I look at the keys next. One of them's for a Vespa, which is odd as last time I saw him he was driving an old eighties Mercedes soft top. The other's a large antique-looking thing that looks like it might be for this place. I go to the door and try it: the lock clicks.

The uneasy feeling in the pit of my stomach grows. But he might have another set of keys. These could be spares, the set he's going to lend me. He probably has another key for the Vespa, too: he might even have gone off on it somewhere. As for the wallet, he's probably just carrying cash.

I find the bathroom, next. Nothing much to report here, other than the fact that Ben doesn't appear to own any towels at all, which seems bizarre. I step back out into the main room. The bedroom must be through the closed pair of French double doors. I walk toward them, the cat following, pressing close as a shadow. Just for a moment, I hesitate.

The cat squawks at me again as if to ask: what are you waiting for? I take another long slug of wine. Deep breath. Push open the doors. Another breath. Open my eyes. Empty bed. Empty room. No one here. Breathe out.

OK. I mean, I didn't really think I was going to find anything like that. That's not Ben. Ben's sorted; I'm the fuck-up. But when it's happened to you once—

I drain the dregs from my glass, then go through the cupboards in the bedroom. Not much by way of clues except that most of my brother's clothes seem to come from places called Acne (why would you wear clothes named after a skin condition?) and A.P.C.

Back out in the main room I pour the remainder of the bottle into the glass and neck it back. Drift over to the desk by the large windows, which look down onto the courtyard. There's nothing on the desk beyond a ratty-looking pen. No laptop. Ben seemed surgically attached to it when he took me for lunch that time, getting it out and typing something while we waited for our order. I suppose he must have it with him, wherever he is.

All at once I have the definite feeling that I'm not alone, that I'm being watched. A prickle down the back of my neck. I spin around. No one there except the cat, which is sitting on the kitchen counter. Perhaps that's all it was.

The cat gazes at me for a few moments, then turns its head on one side like it's asking a question. It's the first time I've seen it sit still like this. Then it raises a paw to its mouth and licks. This is when I notice that both the paw and the white ruff at its throat are smeared with blood.

Jess

I'VE GONE COLD. WHAT THE—

I reach out to the cat to try to get a closer look, but it slinks out from under my hand. Maybe it's just caught a mouse or something? One of the families I fostered with had a cat, Suki. Even though she was small she could take down a whole pigeon: she came back once covered in blood like something out of a horror film and my foster parent Karen found the headless body later that morning. I'm sure there's some small dead creature lying around the apartment, just waiting for me to step on it. Or maybe it killed something out there in the courtyard—the windows are open a crack, which must be how it gets in and out of this place, walking along the guttering or something.

Still. It gave me a bit of a jolt. When I saw it for a moment I thought—

No. I'm just tired. I should try and get some sleep.

Ben will turn up in the morning, explain where he's been, I'll tell him he's a dick for leaving me to basically break in and it'll be like old times, the *old* old times, before he went to live with his shiny rich new family and got a whole new way of speaking and perspective on the world and I got bounced around the care system until I was old enough to fend for myself. I'm sure he's fine. Bad stuff doesn't happen to Ben. He's the lucky one.

I shrug off my jacket, throw it onto the sofa. I should probably take a shower—I'm pretty sure I stink. A bit of B.O. but mainly of vinegar: you can't work at the Copacabana and not reek of the stuff, it's what we use to sluice the bar down after every shift.

But I'm too tired to wash. I think Ben might have mentioned something about a camp bed, but I don't see any sign of one. So I take a throw from the sofa and lie down in the bedroom on top of the covers in all my clothes. I give the pillows some thumps to try and rearrange them. As I do something slithers out of the bed onto the floor.

A pair of women's knickers: black silk, lacy, expensive-looking. *Ew.* Christ, Ben. I don't want to think about how those got here. I don't even know if Ben has a girlfriend. I feel a little pang of sadness, in spite of myself. He's all I've got and I don't even know this much about him.

I'm too tired to do much more than kick the knickers away, out of sight. Tomorrow I'll sleep on the sofa.

Jess

A SHOUT RIPS THROUGH THE silence. A man's voice. Then another voice, a woman's.

I sit up in bed listening hard, heart kicking against my ribs. It takes a second for me to work out that the sounds are coming from the courtyard, filtering through the windows in the main room. I check the alarm clock next to Ben's bed. 5 A.M.: morning, just, but still dark.

The man is shouting again. He sounds slurred, like he's been drinking.

I creep across the main room to the windows and crouch down. The cat pushes its face into my thigh, mewing. "Shh," I tell it—but I quite like the feel of its warm, solid body against mine.

I peer into the courtyard. Two figures stand down there: one tall, one much smaller. The guy is dark-haired and she's blonde, the long fall of her hair silver in the cool light of the courtyard's one lamp. He's wearing a parka with a fur rim that looks familiar, and I realize it's the guy I "met" outside the gate last night.

Their voices get louder—they're shouting over one another now. I'm pretty sure I hear her say the word "police." At this his voice changes—I don't understand the words but there's a new hardness, a threat, to his tone. I see him take a couple of steps toward her.

"*Laisse-moi!*" she shouts, sounding different now, too—scared rather than angry. He takes another step closer. I realize I'm pressed so close to the window that my breath has misted up the glass. I can't just sit here, listening, watching. He raises a hand. He's so much taller than her.

A sudden memory. Mum, sobbing. *I'm sorry, I'm sorry*: over and over, like the words to a prayer.

I lift my hand to the window and slam it against the glass. I want to distract him for a few seconds, give her a chance to move away. I see both of them glance up in confusion, their attention caught by the sound. I duck down, out of sight.

When I look back out again it's just in time to see him pick something up from the ground, something big and bulky and rectangular. With a big petulant shove he throws it toward her—at her. She steps back and it explodes at her feet: I see it's a suitcase, spilling clothes everywhere.

Then he looks straight up at me. There's no time to crouch down. I understand what his look means. *I've seen you. I want you to know that.*

Yeah, I think, looking right back. *And I see you, dickhead. I know your sort. You don't scare me.* Except all the hairs on the back of my neck are standing to attention and the blood's thumping in my ears.

I watch as he walks over to the statue and shoves it viciously off its plinth, so that it topples to the ground with a crash. Then he makes for the door that leads back into the apartment building. I hear the slam echoing up the stairwell.

The woman is left on her knees in the courtyard, scrabbling around for the things that have fallen out of the suitcase. Another memory: Mum, on her knees in the hallway. Begging . . .

Where are the other neighbors? I can't be the only one who heard the commotion. It's not a choice to go down and help: it's something I have to do. I snatch up the keys, run down the couple of flights of stairs and out into the courtyard.

The woman starts as she spots me. She's still on her hands and knees and I see that her eye make-up has run where she's been crying. "Hey," I say softly. "Are you OK?"

In answer she holds up what looks like a silk shirt; it's stained with dirt from the ground. Then, shakily, in heavily accented English: "I came to get my things. I tell him it's over, for good. And this—this is what he does. He's a . . . a son-of-a-bitch. I never should have married him."

Jesus, I think. This is why I know I'm better off single. Mum had exceptionally terrible taste in men. My dad was the worst of all of them though. Supposedly a good guy. A real fucking bastard. Would have been better if he'd disappeared off into the night like Ben's dad did before he was born.

The woman's muttering under her breath as she shovels clothes into the suitcase. Anger seems to have taken over from fear. I go over and crouch down, help her pick up her things. High heels with long foreign names printed inside, a black silk, lacy bra, a little orange sweater made out of the softest fabric I've ever felt. "*Merci*," she says, absent-mindedly. Then she frowns. "Who are you? I've never seen you here before."

"I'm meant to be staying with my brother, Ben."

"*Ben*," she says, drawing out his name. She looks me up and down, taking in my jeans, my old sweater. "He's *your* brother? Before him I thought all Englishmen were sunburnt, no elegance, bad teeth. I did not know they could be so . . . so beautiful, so *charmant*, so *soigné*." Apparently there aren't enough words in English for how wonderful my brother is. She continues shoveling clothes into the suitcase, a violence to her movements, scowling every so often at the door into the apartment building. "Is it so strange I got bored of being with a stupid fucking . . . loser *alcoolique*? That I wanted a little flirtation? And, *d'accord*, maybe

I wanted to make Antoine jealous. Care about something other than himself. Is it such a surprise I started to look elsewhere?"

She tosses her hair over her shoulder in a shining curtain. It's quite impressive, being able to do that while crouched down picking your lacy underwear out of a gravel path.

She looks toward the building and raises her voice, almost as though she wants her husband to hear. "He says I only care about him because of his money. Of *course* I only care about him because of his money. It was the only thing that made it—how do you say—worthwhile? But now . . ." she shrugs, "it's not worth it."

I pass her a silky, electric blue dress, a baby pink bucket hat with JACQUEMUS printed across the front. "Have you seen Ben recently?" I ask.

"*Non*," she says, raising an eyebrow at me like I might be insinuating something. "*Pour quoi*? Why do you ask?"

"He was meant to be here last night, to let me in, but he wasn't—and he hasn't been answering my messages."

Her eyes widen. And then, under her breath, she murmurs something. I make out: "*Antoine . . . non. Ce n'est pas possible . . .*"

"What did you say?"

"Oh—*rien*, nothing." But I catch the glance she shoots toward the apartment building—fearful, suspicious, even—and wonder what it means.

Now she's trying to clip shut her bulging suitcase—brown leather with some sort of logo printed all over it—but I see that her hands are trembling, making her fingers clumsy.

"*Merde*." Finally it snaps closed.

"Hey," I say. "Do you want to come inside? Call a cab?"

"No way," she says, fiercely. "I'm never going back in there. I have an Uber coming . . ." As if on cue, her phone pings. She checks it and gives what sounds like a sigh of relief. "*Merci. Putain*, he's here. I have to go." Then she turns and looks up at the apartment building. "You know what? Fuck this evil place." Then her expression softens and she blows a kiss toward the windows above us. "But at least one good thing happened to me here."

She pulls up the handle of the little case then turns and begins stalking toward the gate.

I hurry after her. "What do you mean, evil?"

She glances at me and shakes her head, mimes zippering her lips. "I want my money, from the divorce."

Then she's out onto the street and climbing into the cab. As it pulls away, off into the night, I realize I never managed to ask whether what she had with my brother was ever more than a flirtation.

I TURN BACK toward the courtyard and nearly jump out of my skin. Jesus Christ. There's an old woman standing there, looking at me. She seems to glow with a cold white light, like something off *Most Haunted*. But after I've caught my breath, I realize it's because she's standing beneath the outdoor lamp. Where the hell did she appear from?

"*Excuse-moi?*" I say. "*Madame?*" I'm not even sure what I want to ask her. *Who are you*, maybe? *What are you doing here?*

She doesn't answer. She simply shakes her head at me, very slowly. Then she's retreating backward, toward that cabin in the corner of the courtyard. I watch as she disappears inside. As the shutters—which I see now must have been open—are quickly drawn closed.

Nick

SECOND FLOOR

I LEAN FORWARD ONTO THE handlebars of the Peloton bike, standing up in the saddle for the incline. There's sweat running into my eyes, stinging. My lungs feel like they're full of acid, not air, my heart hammering so hard it feels like I might be about to have a heart attack. I pedal harder. I want to push beyond anything I've done before. Tiny stars dance at the edges of my vision. The apartment around me seems to shift and blur. For a moment I think I'm going to pass out. Maybe I do—next thing I know I'm slumped forward over the handlebars and the mechanism is whirring down. I'm hit by a sudden rush of nausea. I force it down, take huge gulps of air.

I got into spinning in San Francisco. And bulletproof coffee, keto, Bikram—pretty much any other fad the rest of the tech world was into, in case it provided any extra edge, any additional source of inspiration. Normally I'd sit here and do a class, or listen to a Ted Talk. This morning wasn't like that. I wanted to lose myself in pure exertion, push through to a place where thought was silenced. I woke just after five A.M., but I knew I wasn't going to sleep, especially during that fight in the courtyard, the latest—and worst—of many. Getting on the bike seemed like the only thing that made sense.

I climb down from the saddle, a little unsteadily. The bike is one of the few items in this room besides my iMac and my books. Nothing up on the walls. No rugs on the floor. Partly because I like the whole minimal aesthetic. Partly because I still feel like I haven't really moved in, because I like the idea that I could up and leave at any moment.

I pull the headphones out of my ears. It sounds like things have quieted down out there in the courtyard. I walk over to the window, the muscles in my calves twitching.

I can't see anything at first. Then my eye snags on a movement and I see there's a girl down there, opening the door to the building. There's something familiar about her, about the way she moves. Difficult to put my finger on, but my mind gropes around as if for a forgotten word.

Now I see the lights come on in the apartment on the third floor. I watch her move into my line of sight. And I know that she has to be something to do with him. With my old mate and—as of very recently—neighbor, Benjamin Daniels. He told me about a younger sister, once. Half sister. Something of a tearaway. Bit of a problem case. From his old life, however much he'd tried to sever himself from all that. What he definitely didn't tell me was that she was coming here. But then it wouldn't be the first time he's kept something from me, would it?

The girl appears briefly at the windows, looking out. Then she turns and moves away—toward the bedroom, I think. I watch her until she's out of sight.

Jess

MY THROAT HURTS AND THERE'S an oily sweat on my forehead. I stare up at the high ceiling above me and try and work out where I am. Now I remember: getting here last night . . . that scene in the courtyard a couple of hours ago. It was still dark out so I got back into bed afterward. I didn't think I'd be able to sleep but I must have drifted off. I don't feel rested though. My whole body aches like I've been fighting someone. I think I *was* fighting someone, in my dream. The kind you're relieved to wake up from. It comes back to me in fragments. I was trying to get into a locked room but my hands were clumsy, all fingers and thumbs. Someone—Ben?—was shouting at me not to open the door, *do not open the door*, but I knew I had to, knew I didn't have any other choice. And then finally the door was opening and all at once I knew he was right—oh why hadn't I listened to him? Because what greeted me on the other side—

I sit up in bed. I check my phone. Eight A.M. No messages. A new day and still no sign of my brother. I call his number: straight to voicemail. I listen to the voicenote he left me again, with that final instruction: "Just ring the buzzer. I'll be up waiting for you—"

And this time I notice something strange. How his voice seems to cut off mid-sentence, like something has distracted him. After this there's a faint murmur of sound in the background—words, maybe—but I can't make anything out.

The uneasy feeling grows.

I walk out into the main living space. The room looks even more like something from a museum in the light of day: you can see the dust motes hanging suspended in the air. And I've just spotted something I didn't see last night. There's a largish, lighter patch on the floorboards just a few feet before the front door. I walk toward it, crouch down. As I do the smell—the strange smell I noticed last night—catches me right at the back of the throat. A singe-the-nostrils chemical tang. Bleach. But that's not all. Something's caught here in the gap between the floorboards, glinting in the cold light. I try to wiggle it out with my fingers, but it's stuck fast. I go and get a couple of forks from the drawer in the kitchen, use them together to pry it loose. Eventually, I work it free. A long gilt chain unspools first, then a pendant: an image of a male saint in a cloak, holding a crook.

Ben's St. Christopher. I reach up and feel the identical texture of the chain around my neck, the heavy weight of the pendant. I've never seen him without it. Just like me, I suspect he never takes it off, because it came from Mum. Because it's one of the few things we have from her. Maybe it's guilt, but I suspect Ben's almost more sentimental about stuff like that than me.

But here it is. And the chain is broken.

Jess

I SIT HERE TRYING NOT to panic. Trying to imagine the rational explanation that I'm sure must be behind all this. Should I call the police? Is that what a normal person would do? Because it's several things now. Ben not being here when he said he would and not answering his phone. The cat's blood-tinged fur. The bleach stain. The broken necklace. But more than any of this it's the way it all . . . feels. It feels wrong. *Always listen to your inner voice*, was Mum's thing. *Never ignore a feeling.* It didn't work out so well for her, of course. But she was right, in a way. It's how I knew I should barricade myself in my bedroom at night when I fostered with the Andersons, even before another kid told me about Mr. Anderson and his preferences. And way before that, before foster care even, it's how I knew I shouldn't go into that locked room—even though I did.

I don't want to call the police, though. *They might want to know things about you*, a little voice says. *They might have questions you don't want to answer.* The police and I have never got on all that well. Let's just say I've had my share of run-ins. And even though he had it coming, what I did to that arsehole is, I suppose, technically still a crime. Right now I don't want to put myself on their radar unless I absolutely have to.

Besides, I don't really have enough to tell them, do I? A cat that might just have killed a mouse? A necklace that might just have been innocently broken? A brother who might have just fucked off, yet again, to leave me to fend for myself?

No, it's not enough.

I put my head in my hands, try to think what to do next. At the same moment my stomach gives a long, loud groan. I realize I can't actually remember the last time I ate anything. Last night I'd sort of imagined I'd get here and Ben would fix me up some scrambled eggs or something, maybe we'd order a takeaway. Part of me feels too queasy and keyed up to eat. But perhaps I'll be able to think more clearly with some food in my belly.

I raid the fridge and cupboards but besides half a pack of butter and a stick of salami they're bare. One cupboard is different from all the rest: it's some sort of cavity with what looks like a pulley system, but I can't work out what it's for at all. In desperation I cut off some of the salami with a very sharp Japanese knife that I find in Ben's utensil pot, but it's hardly a hearty breakfast.

I pocket the set of keys I found in Ben's jacket. I know the code now, I've got the keys: I can get back into this place.

The courtyard looks less spooky in the light of day. I pass the ruins of the statue of the naked woman, the head separated from the rest, face up, eyes staring at the sky. One of the flowerbeds looks like it has recently been re-dug, which explains that smell of freshly turned earth. There's a little fountain running, too. I look over at the tiny cabin in the corner and see a dark gap between the closed slats of the shutters; perfect for spying on anything that's going on out here. I can imagine her watching me through it: the old woman I saw last night, the one who seems to live there.

I take in the strangeness of my surroundings as I close the apartment's gates, the foreignness of it all. The crazily beautiful buildings around me, the cars with their unfamiliar number-plates. The streets also look different in daylight—and much busier when I get away from the hush of the apartment building's cul-de-sac. They smell different, too: moped fumes and cigarette smoke and roasted coffee. It must have rained in the night as the cobbles are gleaming wet, slippery underfoot. Everyone seems to know exactly where they're going: I step into the street out of the way of one woman walking straight at me while talking on her phone and nearly collide with a couple of kids sharing an electric scooter. I've never felt so clueless, so like a fish out of water.

I wander past shop fronts with their grilles pulled down, wrought-iron gates leading onto courtyards and gardens full of dead leaves, pharmacies with blinking neon green crosses—there seems to be one on every street, do the French get sick more?—doubling back on myself and getting lost a couple of times. Finally, I find a bakery, the sign painted emerald green with gold lettering—BOULANGERIE—and a striped awning. Inside the walls and the floor are decorated with patterned tiles and it smells like burnt sugar and melted butter. The place is packed: a long queue doubles back on itself. I wait, getting hungrier and hungrier, staring at the counter which is filled with all sorts of things that look too perfect to be eaten: tiny tarts with glazed raspberries, eclairs with violet icing, little chocolate cakes with a thousand very fine layers and a touch of what looks like actual gold on top. People in front of me are putting in serious orders: three loaves of bread, six croissants, an apple tart. My mouth waters. I feel the rustle of the notes I nicked from Ben's wallet in my pocket.

The woman in front of me has hair so perfect it doesn't look real: a black, shining bob, not a strand out of place. A silk scarf tied around her neck, some kind of camel-colored coat and a black leather handbag over her arm. She looks rich. Not flashy rich. The French equivalent of posh. You don't have hair that perfect unless you spend your days doing basically nothing.

I look down and see a skinny, silver-colored dog on a pale blue leather lead. It looks up at me with suspicious dark eyes.

The woman behind the counter hands her a pastel-colored box tied with a ribbon: "*Voilà, Madame Meunier.*"

"*Merci.*"

She turns and I see that she's wearing red lipstick, so perfectly applied it might be tattooed on. At a guess she's about fifty—but a very well-preserved fifty. She's putting her card back into her wallet. As she does something flutters to the ground—a piece of paper. A banknote?

I bend down to pick it up. Take a closer look. Not a banknote, which is a shame. Someone like her probably wouldn't miss the odd ten euros. It's a handwritten note, scribbled in big block capitals. I read: *double la prochaine fois, salope.*

"*Donne-moi ça!*"

I look up. The woman is glaring at me, her hand outstretched. I think I know what she's asking but she did it so rudely, so like a queen commanding a peasant, that I pretend not to understand.

"Excuse me?"

She switches to English. "Give that to me." And then finally, as an afterthought, "please."

Taking my time about it, I hold out the note. She snatches it from my hand so roughly that I feel one of her long fingernails scrape at my skin. Without a thank you, she marches out through the door.

"*Excusez-moi? Madame?*" the woman behind the counter asks, ready to take my order.

"A croissant, please." Everything else is probably going to be too expensive. My stomach rumbles as I watch her drop it into the little paper bag. "Two, actually."

On the walk back to the apartment through the cold gray morning streets I eat the first one in big ravenous bites and then the second slower, tasting the salt of the butter, enjoying the crunch of the pastry and the softness inside. It's so good that I could cry and not much makes me cry.

Back at the apartment building I let myself in through the gate with the code I learned yesterday. As I cross the courtyard I catch the scent of fresh cigarette smoke. I glance up, following the smell. There's a girl sitting there, up on the fourth-floor balcony, cigarette in her hand. A pale face, choppy dark hair, dressed in head-to-toe black from her turtleneck to the Docs on her feet. I can see from here that she's young, maybe nineteen, twenty. She catches sight of me looking back at her, I can see it in the way her whole body freezes. That's the only way I can describe it.

You. You know something, I think, staring back. And I'm going to get you to tell me.

Mimi

FOURTH FLOOR

SHE'S SEEN ME. THE WOMAN who arrived last night, who I watched this morning walking around in his apartment. She's staring straight at me. I can't move.

In my head the roar of static grows louder.

Finally she turns away. When I breathe out my chest burns.

I WATCHED HIM arrive from here, too. It was August, nearly three months ago, the middle of the heatwave. Camille and I were sitting on the balcony in the junky old deckchairs she'd bought from a *brocanter* shop, drinking Aperol Spritzes even though I actually kind of hate Aperol Spritz. Camille often persuades me to do things I wouldn't otherwise do.

Benjamin Daniels turned up in an Uber. Gray T-shirt, jeans. Dark hair, longish. He looked famous, somehow. Or maybe not famous but . . . special. You know? I can't explain it. But he had that thing about him that made you want to look at him. *Need* to look at him.

I was wearing dark glasses and I watched him from the corner of my eye, so it didn't seem like I was looking his way. When he opened the boot of the car I saw the stains of sweat under his arms and, where his T-shirt had ridden up, I also saw how the line of his tan stopped beneath the waistband of his jeans, where the paler skin started, an arrow of dark hair descending. The muscles in his arms flexed when he lifted the bags out of the trunk. Not like a jacked-up gym-goer. More elegant. Like a drummer: drummers always have good muscles. Even from here I could imagine how his sweat would smell—not bad, just like salt and skin.

He shouted to the driver: "Thanks, mate!" I recognized the English accent straightaway; there's this old TV show I'm obsessed with, *Skins*, about all these British teenagers screwing and screwing up, falling in love.

"Mmm," said Camille, lifting up her sunglasses.

"*Mais non*," I said. "He's really old, Camille."

She shrugged. "He's only thirty-something."

"*Oui*, and that's old. That's like . . . fifteen years older than us."

"Well, think of all that *experience*." She made a vee with her fingers and stuck her tongue out between them.

I laughed at that. "Beurk—you're disgusting."

She raised her eyebrows. "*Pas du tout*. And you'd know that if your darling papa ever let you near any guys—"

"Shut up."

"Ah, Mimi . . . I'm kidding! But you know one day he's going to have to realize you're not his little girl any longer." She grinned, sucked up Aperol through her straw. For a second I wanted to slap her . . . I nearly did. I don't always have the best impulse control.

"He's just a little . . . protective." It was more than that, really. But I suppose I also never really wanted to do anything to disappoint Papa, tarnish that image of me as his little princess.

I often wished I could be more like Camille, though. So chill about sex. For her it's just another thing she likes doing: like swimming or cycling or sunbathing. I'd never even had sex, let alone with two people at the same time (one of her specialties), or tried girls as well as boys. You know what's funny? Papa actually approved of her moving in here with me, said living with another girl "might stop you from getting into too much trouble."

Camille was in her smallest bikini, just three triangles of pale crocheted material that barely covered anything. Her feet were pressed up against the ironwork of the balcony and her toenails were painted a chipped, Barbie-doll pink. Apart from her month in the South with friends she'd sat out there pretty much every hot day, getting browner and browner, slathering herself in La Roche-Posay. Her whole body looked like it had been dipped in gold, her hair lightened to the color of caramel. I don't go brown; I just burn, so I sat tucked in the shade like a vampire with my Francoise Sagan novel, wearing a big man's shirt.

She leaned forward, still watching the guy getting his cases out of the car. "Oh my God, Mimi! He has a cat. How *cute*. Can you see it? Look, in that carry basket. *Salut minou!*"

She did it on purpose, so he would look up and see us—see her. Which he did.

"Hey," she called, standing up and waving so hard that her *nénés* bounced around in her bikini top like they were trying to escape. "*Bienvenue*—welcome! I'm Camille. And this is Merveille. Cute pussy!"

I was so embarrassed. She knew exactly what she was saying, it's the same slang in French: *chatte*. Also, I hate that my full name is Merveille. No one calls me that. I'm Mimi. My mum gave me that name because it means "wonder" and she said that's what my arrival into her life was: this unexpected but wonderful thing. But it's also completely mortifying.

I sank down behind my book, but not so much that I couldn't still see him over the top of it.

The guy shielded his eyes. "Thanks!" he called. He put up a hand, waved back. As he did I saw again that strip of skin between his T-shirt and jeans. "I'm Ben—friend of Nick's? I'm moving into the third floor."

Camille turned to me. "Well," she said, in an undertone. "I feel like this place has just got a *lot* more exciting." She grinned. "Maybe I should introduce myself to him properly. Offer to look after the pussy if he goes away."

I wouldn't be surprised if she's fucking him in a week's time, I thought to myself. It would hardly be a surprise. The surprising thing was how much I hated the thought of it.

SOMEONE'S KNOCKING ON the door to my apartment.

I creep down the hall, look through the peephole. *Merde*: it's her: the woman from Ben's apartment.

I swallow—or try to. It feels like my tongue is stuck in my throat.

It's hard to think with this roaring in my ears. I know I don't have to open the door. This is my apartment, my space. But the *knock knock knock* is incessant, beating against my skull until I feel like something in me is going to explode.

I grit my teeth and open the door, take a step back. The shock of her face, close up: I see him in her features, straightaway. But she's small and her eyes are darker and there's something, I don't know, hungry about her which maybe was in him too but he hid it better. It's like with her all the angles are sharper. With him it was all smoothness. She's scruffy, too: jeans and an old sweater with frayed cuffs, dark red hair scragged up on top of her head. That's not like him either. Even in a gray T-shirt on a hot day he looked kind of . . . pulled-together, you know? Like everything fit him just right.

"Hi,' she says. She smiles but it's not a real smile. "I'm Jess. What's your name?"

"M—Mimi." My voice comes out as a rasp.

"My brother—Ben—lives on the third floor. But he's . . . well, he's kind of disappeared on me. Do you know him at all?"

For a crazy moment I think about pretending I don't speak English. But that's stupid.

I shake my head. "No. I didn't know him—don't, I mean. My English, sorry, it's not so good."

I can feel her looking past me, like she's trying to see her way into my apartment. I move sideways, try to block her view. So instead she looks at me, like she's trying to see into *me*: and that's worse.

"This is your apartment?" she asks.

"*Oui.*"

"Wow." She widens her eyes. "Nice work if you can get it. And it's just you in here?"

"My flatmate Camille and me."

She's trying to peer into the apartment again, looking over my shoulder. "I was wondering if you'd seen him lately, Ben?"

"No. He's been keeping his shutters closed. I mean—" I realize, too late, that wasn't what she was asking.

She raises her eyebrows. "OK," she says, "but do you remember the last time you saw him generally about the place? It would be so helpful." She smiles. Her smile is not like his at all. But then no one's is.

I realize she's not going to go unless I give her an answer. I clear my throat. "I—I don't know. Not for a while—I suppose maybe a week?"

"*Quoi? Ce n'est pas vrai!*" *That's not true!* I turn to see Camille, in just a camisole and her *culotte*, wandering into the space behind me. "It was yesterday morning, remember Mimi? I saw you with him on the stairs."

Merde. I can feel my face growing hot. "Oh, yes. That's right." I turn back to the woman in the doorway.

"So he *was* here yesterday?" she asks, frowning, looking from me to Camille and back. "You *did* see him?"

"Uh-huh," I say. "Yesterday. I must have forgotten."

"Did he say if he was going anywhere?"

"No. It was only for a second."

I picture his face, as I passed him on the stairs. *Hey Mimi. Something up?* That smile. No one's smile is like his.

"I can't help you," I say. "Sorry." I go to close the door.

"He said he'd ask me to feed his kitty if he ever went away," Camille says and the almost flirtatious way she says "kitty" reminds me of her "Cute pussy!" on the day he arrived. "But he didn't ask this time."

"Really?" The woman seems interested in this. "So it sounds like—" Maybe she's realized I'm slowly closing the door on her because she makes a movement like she's about to step forward into the apartment. And without even thinking I slam the door in her face so hard I feel the wood give under my hands.

My arms are shaking. My whole body's shaking. I know Camille must be staring at me, wondering what's going on. But I don't care what she thinks right now. I lean my head against the door. I can't breathe. And suddenly I feel like I'm choking. It rushes up inside me, the sickness, and before I can stop it I'm vomiting, right onto the beautifully polished floorboards.

Sophie

PENTHOUSE

I'M COMING UP THE STAIRS when I see her. A stranger inside these walls. It sends such a jolt through me that I nearly drop the box from the boulangerie. A girl, snooping around on the penthouse landing. She has no business being here.

I watch her for a while before I speak. "*Bonjour,*" I say coolly.

She spins around, caught out. Good. I wanted to shock her.

But now it's my turn to be shocked. "You." It's her from the boulangerie: the scruffy girl who picked up the note I dropped.

Double la prochaine fois, salope. *Double the next time, bitch.*

"Who are you?"

"I'm Jess. Jess Hadley. I'm staying with my brother Ben," she says, quickly. "On the third floor."

"If you are staying on the third floor then what are you doing up here?" It makes sense, I suppose. Sneaking around in here as though she owns the place. Just like him.

"I was looking for Ben." She must realise how absurd this sounds, as though he might be hiding in some shadowy corner up here in the eaves, because she suddenly looks sheepish. "Do you know him? Benjamin Daniels?"

That smile: a fox entering the henhouse. The sound of a glass smashing. A smear of crimson on a stiff white napkin.

"Nicolas's friend. "Yes. Although I've only met him a couple of times."

"Nicolas? Is that 'Nick'? I think Ben might have mentioned him. Which floor's he on?"

I hesitate. Then I say: "The second."

"Do you remember when you last saw him about?" she asks. "Ben, I mean? He was meant to be here last night. I tried asking one of the girls—Mimi?—on the fourth floor, but she wasn't too helpful."

"I don't recall." Perhaps my answer sounds too quick, too certain. "But then he keeps so much to himself. You know. Rather—what's the English expression?—reserved."

"Really? That doesn't sound anything like Ben! I'd expect him to be friends with everyone in this building by now."

"Not with me." That at least is true. I give a little shrug. "Anyway, maybe he went away and forgot to tell you?"

"No," she says. "He wouldn't do that."

COULD I REMEMBER the last time I saw him? Of course I can.

But I am thinking now about the first time. About two months ago. The middle of the heatwave.

I did not like him. I knew it straightaway.

The laughter, that's what I heard first. Vaguely threatening, in the way male laughter can be. The almost competitive nature of it.

I was in the courtyard. I had spent the afternoon planting in the shade. To others gardening is a form of creative abandon. To me it is a way of exerting control upon my surroundings. When I told Jacques I wanted to take care of the courtyard's small garden he did not understand. "There are people we can pay to do it for us," he told me. In my husband's world there are people you can pay for anything.

The end of the day: the light fading, the heat still oppressive. I watched from behind the rosemary bushes as the two of them entered the courtyard. Nick first. Then a stranger, wheeling a moped. Around the same age as his friend, but he seemed somehow older. Tall and rangy. Dark hair. He carried himself well. A very particular confidence in the way he inhabited the space around him.

I watched as Nick's friend plucked a sprig of rosemary from one of the bushes, tearing hard to wrench it free. How he crushed it to his nose, inhaled. There was something presumptuous about the gesture. It felt like an act of vandalism.

Then Benoit was running over to them. The newcomer scooped him up and held him.

I stood. "He doesn't like to be held by anyone but me."

Benoit, the traitor, turned his head to lick the stranger's hand.

"*Bonjour* Sophie," Nicolas said. "This is Ben. He's going to be living here, in the apartment on the third floor." Proud. Showing off this friend like a new toy.

"Pleased to meet you, Madame." He smiled then, a lazy smile that was somehow just as presumptuous as the way he'd ripped into that bush. *You will like me*, it said. *Everyone does.*

"Please," I said. "Call me Sophie." The Madame had made me feel about a hundred years old, even though it was only proper.

"Sophie."

Now I wished I hadn't said it. It was too informal, too intimate. "I'll take him, please." I held out my hands for the dog. Benoit smelled faintly of petrol, of male sweat. I held him at a little distance from my body. "The concierge won't like that," I added, nodding at the moped, then toward the cabin. "She hates them."

I had wanted to assert myself, but I sounded like a matron scolding a small boy.

"Noted," he said. "Cheers for the tip. I'll have to butter her up, get her on side."

I stared at him. Why on earth would he want to do that?

"Good luck there," Nick said. "She doesn't like anyone."

"Ah," he says. "But I like a challenge. I'll win her over."

"Well watch out," Nick said. "I'm not sure you want to encourage her. She has a knack for appearing round corners when you least expect it."

I didn't like the idea of it at all. That woman with her watchful eyes, her omnipresence. What might she be able to tell him if he did "win her over"?

When Jacques got home I told him I had met the new inhabitant of the third–floor apartment. He frowned, pointed to my cheekbone. "You have dirt, there." I rubbed at my cheek—somehow I must have missed it when I had checked my appearance . . . I thought I had been so careful. "So what do you make of our new neighbor?"

"I don't like him."

Jacques raised his eyebrows. "I thought he sounded like an interesting young man. What don't you like?"

"He's too . . . charming." That charm. He wielded it like a weapon.

Jacques frowned; he didn't understand. My husband: a clever man, but also arrogant. Used to having things his way, having power. I have never acquired that sort of arrogance. I have never been certain enough of my position to be complacent. "Well," he said. "We'll have to invite him to drinks, look him over."

I didn't like the sound of that: inviting him into our home.

The first note arrived two weeks later.

I know who you are, Madame Sophie Meunier. I know what you really are. If you don't want anyone else to know I suggest you leave €2000 beneath the loose step in front of the gate.

The "Madame": a nasty little piece of faux formality. The mocking, knowing tone. No postmark; it had been hand-delivered.

My blackmailer knew this building well enough to know about the loose step outside the gate.

I didn't tell Jacques. I knew he would refuse to pay, for one thing. Those who have the most money are often the most close-fisted about handing it over. I was too afraid not to pay. I took out my jewelry box. I considered the yellow sapphire brooch Jacques had given me for our second wedding anniversary, the jade and diamond hair clips he gave me last Christmas. I selected an emerald bracelet as the safest, because he never asked me to wear it. I took it to a pawnbroker, a place out in the *banlieues*, the neighborhoods outside the *peripherique* ring road that encircles the city. A world away from the Paris of postcards, of tourist dreams. I had to go somewhere no one could possibly recognize me. The pawnbroker knew I was out of my depth. I think he could sense my fear. Little did he know it was less to do with the neighborhood than my horror at finding myself in this situation. The debasement of it.

I returned with more than enough cash to cover it—less than I should have got, though. Ten €200 notes. The money felt dirty: the sweat of other hands, the accumulated filth. I slid the wedge of notes into a thick envelope where they looked even dirtier against the fine cream card and sealed them up. As though it would somehow make the fact of the money less horrific, less demeaning. I left it, as directed, beneath the loose step in front of the apartment building's gate.

For the time being, I had covered my debts.

"PERHAPS YOU'LL WANT to return to the third floor now," I tell the strange, scruffy girl. His sister. Hard to believe it. Hard, actually, to imagine him having had a childhood, a family at all. He seemed so . . . discrete. As though he had stepped into the world fully formed.

"I didn't catch your name," she says.

I didn't give it. "Sophie Meunier," I say. "My husband Jacques and I live in the penthouse apartment, on this floor."

"If you're in the penthouse apartment, what's up there?" She points to the wooden ladder.

"The entrance to the old *chambres de bonne*—the old maids' quarters—in the eaves of the building." I nod my head in the other direction, toward the descending staircase. "But I'm sure you'll want to get back to the third floor now."

She takes the hint. She has to walk right by me to go back down. I don't move an inch as she passes. It is only when my jaw begins to ache that I realize how hard I have been gritting my teeth.

Jess

I CLOSE THE APARTMENT DOOR behind me. I think of the way Sophie Meunier looked at me just now: like I was something she'd found on the sole of her shoe. She might be French, but I'd know her type anywhere. The shining black bob, the silk scarf, the swanky handbag. The way she stressed "penthouse." She's a snob. It's not exactly a new feeling, being looked at like I'm scum. But I thought I sensed something else. Some extra hostility, when I mentioned Ben.

I think of her suggestion that he might have gone away. "It's not a great time," he'd said, on the phone. But he wouldn't just up and go without leaving word . . . would he? I'm his family—his *only* family. However put out he was, I don't think he would abandon me.

But then it wouldn't be the first time he's disappeared out of my life with little more than a backward glance. Like when suddenly he had some shiny new parents ready to whisk him away to a magical new life of private schools and holidays abroad and family Labradors and *sorry but the Daniels are only looking to adopt one child. Actually it can be best to separate children from the same family, especially when there has been a shared trauma.* As I said, my brother's always been good at getting people to fall in love with him. Ben, driving away in the back seat of the Daniels' navy blue Volvo, turning back once and then looking forward, onward to his new life.

No. He left me a voicenote giving me directions, for Christ's sake. And even if he did have to leave for some reason, why isn't he answering any of my calls or texts?

I keep coming back to the broken chain of his St. Christopher. The bloodstains on the cat's fur. How none of Ben's neighbors seem prepared to give me the time of day—more than that, seem actively hostile. How it just feels like something here is *wrong*.

I search Ben's social media. At some point he seems to have deleted all his socials except Instagram. How have I only just realized this? No Facebook, no Twitter. His Instagram profile picture is the cat, which right now is sitting on its haunches on the desk, watching me through narrowed eyes. There isn't a single photo left on his grid. I suppose it's just like Ben, master of reinvention, to have got rid of all his old stuff. But there's something about the disappearance of all his content that gives me the creeps. Almost like someone's tried to erase him. I send him a DM, all the same. **Ben, if you see this: answer your phone!**

My mobile buzzes: **You have only 50MB of Roaming Data remaining. To buy more, follow this link . . .**

Shit. I can't even get by on the cheapest plan.

I sit down on the sofa. As I do I realize I've sat on Ben's wallet, I must have tossed it here earlier. I open it and pull out the business card stuck in the front. **Theo Mendelson, Paris editor,** *Guardian*. And scribbled on the card: PITCH STORY TO HIM! Someone Ben's working for, maybe, someone he might have been in touch with recently? There's a number listed. I call but it rings out so I fire off a quick text:

Hi. It's about my brother Ben Daniels. Trying to find him. Can you help?

I put the phone down. I just heard something odd.

I sit very still, listening hard, trying to work out what the noise is. It sounds like footsteps passing down a flight of stairs. Except the sound isn't coming from in front of me, from the landing and the staircase beyond the apartment's entrance. It's behind my head. I stand up from the sofa and study the wall. And it's now, looking properly, that I see something there. I run my hands over the faded silk wall covering. There's a break, a gap in the fabric, running horizontally above my head and vertically down. I step back and take in the shape of it. It's cleverly hidden, and the sofa's pushed in front of it, so you wouldn't notice it at all unless you were looking pretty closely. But I think it's a door.

Sophie

PENTHOUSE

BACK IN THE APARTMENT I reach into my handbag—black leather Celine, ferociously expensive, extremely discreet, a gift from Jacques—take out my wallet and am almost surprised to find the note hasn't burnt a hole through the leather. I cannot believe I was so clumsy as to drop it earlier. I am never normally clumsy.

Double the next time, bitch.

It arrived yesterday morning. The latest in the series. Well. It has no hold over me now. I rip it into tiny pieces and scatter them into the fireplace. I pull the tasseled cord set into the wall and flames roar into life, instantly incinerating the paper. Then I walk quickly through the apartment, past the floor-to-ceiling windows with their view out over Paris, along the hallway hung with its trio of Gerhard Richter abstracts, my heels tapping briefly over the parquet then silenced on the silk of the antique Persian runner.

In the kitchen I open the pastel box from the boulangerie. Inside is a quiche Lorraine, studded with lardons of bacon, the pastry so crisp it will shatter at the slightest touch. The dairy waft of the cream and egg yolk briefly makes me want to gag. When Jacques is away from home on one of his business trips I usually exist on black coffee and fruit—perhaps the odd piece of dark chocolate broken from a Maison Bonnat bar.

I did not feel like going out. I felt like hiding in here away from the world. But I am a regular customer and it is important to stick to the usual routines.

A couple of minutes later, I open the door to the apartment again and wait a few moments listening, looking down the staircase, making sure no one's there. You cannot do anything in this building without half-expecting the concierge to appear from some dark corner as if formed from the shadows themselves. But for once it isn't her that I'm concerned about. It's this newcomer, this stranger.

When I am certain I am alone, I walk across the landing to the wooden stairs that lead up to the old *chambres de bonne*. I am the only one in the building with a key to these old rooms. Even the concierge's access to the public spaces of this building ends here.

I fasten Benoit to the bottom rung of the wooden steps with his leash. He wears a matching set in blue leather from Hermès: both of us, with our expensive Hermès collars. He'll bark if he sees anyone.

I take the key out of my pocket and climb the stairs. As I put the key into the lock my hand trembles a little; it takes a couple of attempts to turn.

I push the door open. Just before I step inside I check, again, that I am not being watched. I can't afford to be too careful. Especially not with her here now, snooping around.

I spend perhaps ten minutes up here, in the *chambres de bonne*. Afterward I lock the padlock again just as carefully, pocket the little silver key. Benoit is waiting for me at the bottom of the steps, looking up at me with those dark eyes. My secret-keeper. I put a finger to my lips.

Shh.

Jess

I GRAB HOLD OF THE sofa, drag it away from the wall. The cat jumps down from the desk and trots over, maybe hoping I'm going to reveal a mouse or some creepy crawlies. And yes, here it is: a door. No handle but I get a hold of the edge, wedge my fingers into the gap and pull. It swings open.

I let out a gasp. I don't know what I'd expected: a hidden cupboard, maybe. Not this. Darkness greets me on the other side. The air as cold as if I'd just opened a fridge. There's a smell of musty old air, like in a church. As my eyes adjust to the gloom I make out a stone staircase, spiraling up and down, dark and cramped. It couldn't be more different from the grand sweeping affair beyond the apartment's main door. I suppose from the looks of it this was probably some kind of servants' staircase, like the maids' rooms Sophie Meunier told me about upstairs.

I step inside and let the door swing closed behind me. It's suddenly very dark. But I notice a chink of light showing through the door, slightly lower than head-height. I crouch and put my eye to it. I can see into the apartment: the living area, the kitchen. It looks like some kind of homemade spy hole. I suppose it could always have been here, as old as the building itself. Or it could have been made more recently. Someone could have been watching Ben through here. Someone could have been watching *me*.

I can still hear the footsteps heading downward. I turn on my phone's flashlight and follow, trying not to trip over my own feet as the steps twist tightly round on themselves. This staircase must have been made for a time when people were smaller: I'm not exactly large, but it still feels like a tight squeeze.

A second of hesitation. I have no idea where this might lead. I'm not sure this is the best idea. Could I even be heading toward some sort of danger?

Well. It's not like that's ever stopped me before. I carry on downward.

I come to another door. Here, too, I spot another little spy hole. I press my eye to it quickly, look in. No sign of anyone about. I'm feeling a little disorientated but I suppose this must be the second-floor apartment: Ben's friend Nick's place. It looks like it might be pretty much the same layout as Ben's, but it's all whitewashed walls with nothing on them. Beyond the giant computer in the corner, some books, and what looks like a piece of exercise equipment it's practically empty, with about as much character as a dentist's surgery. It seems Nick has barely moved in.

The footsteps below me continue, urging me to follow. I carry on down, the light from my phone bouncing in front of me. I must be on the first floor now. Another apartment and there it is: another spy hole. I look through. This place is a mess: stuff everywhere, empty sharing-size crisp packets and overflowing ashtrays, side tables crowded with bottles, a standing lamp lying on its side. I take an involuntary step back as a figure looms into view. He's not wearing his parka but I recognize him instantly: the guy from the gate, from that fight in the courtyard. Antoine. He appears to be swigging from a bottle of Jack Daniel's. He drains the last dregs then lifts up the bottle. Jesus: I jump as he smashes it against the side table.

He sways on the spot, looking at the jagged stump like he's wondering what to do with it. Then he turns in my direction. For a horrible moment it feels like he's staring directly at me. But I'm peering through a chink only a few millimeters wide . . . there's no way he could possibly see me here. Right?

I'm not going to hang around to find out. I hurry on down. I must be passing the ground floor level, the entrance hall. A further flight of steps: I think I'm underground now. The air feels heavier, colder; I can imagine the earth surrounding me. Finally the staircase leads me to a door, swinging on its hinges—whoever I'm following has just stepped through it. My pulse quickens, I must be getting closer. I push through the door and even though it's still just as dark on the other side I have the impression of having stepped into a wide, echoing space. Silence. No sound of footsteps. Where can they have gone? I must only be moments behind.

It's colder down here. It smells of damp, of mold. My phone throws only a very weak beam into the darkness but I can see the orange glow of a light switch across from me. I press it and the lights come on, the little mechanical timer clicking down: *tick tick tick tick tick*. I've probably only got a couple of minutes before it goes dark again. I'm definitely in the basement: a wide, low-ceilinged space easily double the size of Ben's apartment; several doors leading off it. A rack in the corner that holds a couple of bikes. And leaning against one wall there's a red moped. I walk over to it, take out the set of keys I found in Ben's jacket, fit the Vespa one into the ignition and turn. The lights hum on. It hits me: so Ben can't be away on his bike somewhere. I must have been leaning against it because it tilts under me. It's now that I see that the front wheel is flat, the rubber completely shredded. An accident? But there's something about the total decimation that feels intentional.

I turn back to the basement. Perhaps whoever it was has disappeared behind one of those doors. Are they hiding from me? A shiver of unease as I realize I may now be the one being watched.

I open the first door. A couple of washing machines—one of which is on, all the clothes whizzing around in a colorful jumble.

In the next room I smell the bins before I see them, that sweetish, rotten scent. Something makes a scuffling sound. I shut the door.

The next is some sort of cleaning cupboard: mops and brooms and buckets and a pile of dirty-looking rags in the corner.

The next one has a padlock on the door but the door itself is open. I push inside. It's stuffed full of wine: racks and racks of it, floor to ceiling. There might be well over a thousand bottles in here. Some of them look seriously old: labels stained and peeling, the glass covered in a layer of dust. I pull one out. I don't know much about wine. I mean, I've worked in plenty of bars but they've been the sort of place where people ask for "a large glass of red, love" and you get the bottle thrown in for an extra couple of quid. But this, it just *looks* expensive. Whoever's keeping this stuff down here clearly trusts their neighbors. And probably won't notice if just one little bottle goes missing. Maybe it'll help me think. I'll pick something that looks like it's been down here for ages, something that they'll have forgotten about. I find the dustiest, most cobweb-covered bottles on the bottom racks, search along the rows, pull one out a little way. *1996*. An image of a stately home picked out in gold. Château Blondin-Lavigne, the label reads. That'll do.

The lights go out. The timer must have run down. I look for a light switch. It's so dark in here; I'm immediately disorientated. I step to the left and brush up against something. Shit, I need to be careful: I'm basically surrounded by teetering walls of glass.

There. Finally I spot the little orange glow of another light switch. I press it, the lights hum back on.

I turn to find the door. That's odd, I thought I left it open. It must have swung shut behind me. I turn the handle. But nothing happens when I pull. The door won't budge. What the hell? That can't be right. I try it again: nothing. And then again, putting everything into it, throwing all my weight against it.

Someone's locked me in. It's the only explanation.

Concierge

AFTERNOON AND ALREADY THE LIGHT seems to be fading, the shadows growing deeper. A rap on the door of my cabin. My first thought is that it's him, Benjamin Daniels. The only one who would deign to call on me here. I think of the first time he knocked on my door, taking me by surprise:

"*Bonjour Madame*. I just wanted to introduce myself. I'm moving in on the third floor. I suppose that makes us neighbors!" I assumed, at first, that he was mocking me, but his polite smile said otherwise. Surely he had to know there was no world in which we were neighbors? Still, it made an impression.

The knock comes again. This time I hear the authority in it. I realize my mistake. Of course it isn't him . . . that would be impossible.

When I open the door, there she stands on the other side: Sophie Meunier. Madame to me. In all her finery: the elegant beige coat, the shining black handbag, the gleaming black helmet of her hair, the silk knot of her scarf. She's part of the tribe of women you see walking the smarter streets of this city, with shopping bags over their arms made from stiff card with gilded writing, full of designer clothes and expensive *objets*. A little pedigree dog at the end of a lead. The wealthy husbands with their *cinq-à-sept* affairs, the grand apartments and white, shuttered holiday homes on the Île de Ré. Born here, bred here, from old French money—or at least so they would like you to believe. Nothing gaudy. Nothing *nouveau*. All elegant simplicity and quality and heritage.

"*Oui Madame?*" I ask.

She takes a step back from the doorway, as though she cannot bear to be too close to my home, as though the poverty of it might somehow infect her.

"The girl," she says simply. She does not use my name, she has never used my name, I am not even sure she knows it. "The one who arrived last night—the one staying in the third-floor apartment."

"*Oui Madame?*"

"I want you to watch her. I want you to tell me when she leaves, when she comes back. I want to know if she has any visitors. It is extremely important. *Comprenez-vous?*" *Understand?*

"*Oui Madame.*"

"Good." She is not much taller than I am but somehow she manages to look down at me, as though from a great height. Then she turns and walks away as quickly as possible, the little silver dog trotting at her heels.

I watch her go. Then I go to my tiny bureau and open the drawer. Look inside, check the contents.

She may look down upon me but the knowledge I have gives me power. And I think she knows this. I suspect, even though she would never think to admit it, that Madame Meunier is a little afraid of me.

Funny thing: we share more than meets the eye. Both of us have lived in this building for a long time. Both of us, in our own way, have become invisible. Part of the scenery.

But I know just what sort of woman Madame Sophie Meunier really is. And exactly what she is capable of.

Jess

"HELLO?" I SHOUT. "CAN ANYONE hear me?"

I can feel the walls swallowing the sound, feel how useless it is. I shove at the door with all my strength, hoping the weight of my body might break the lock. Nothing: I might as well be ramming myself against a concrete wall. Panicking now, I pummel the wood.

Shit. *Shit.*

"Hey!" I shout, desperately now. "HEY! HELP ME!"

The last two words. A sudden flashback to another room. Shouting at the top of my lungs, shouting until my voice went hoarse, but it never felt loud enough . . . there was no one coming. *Help me help me help me someone help she's not . . .*

My whole body is trembling.

And then suddenly the door is opening and a light flashes on. A man stands there. I take a step back. It's Antoine, the guy I just watched casually smashing a bottle against a side table—

No . . . I can see now that I'm wrong. It was the height, maybe, and the breadth of the shoulders. But this guy is younger and in the weak light I can see that his hair is lighter, a dark golden color.

"Ça va?" he asks. Then, in English: "Are you OK? I came down to get my laundry and I heard—"

"You're British!" I blurt. As British as the Queen, in fact: a proper, plummy, posh-boy accent. A little like the one Ben adopted after he went to live with his new parents.

He's looking at me like he's waiting for some kind of explanation. "Someone locked me in here," I say. I feel shivery now that the adrenaline's wearing off. "Someone did this on purpose."

He pushes a hand through his hair, frowns. "I don't think so. The door was jammed when I opened it. The handle definitely seems a bit sticky."

I think of how hard I threw myself against it. Could it really just have been stuck? "Well, thanks," I say weakly.

"No worries." He steps back and looks at me. "What are you doing here? Not in the *cave*, I mean: in the apartment?"

"You know Ben, on the third floor? I'm meant to be staying with him—"

He frowns. "Ben didn't tell me he had anyone coming to stay."

"Well it was kind of last minute," I say. "So . . . you know Ben?"

"Yeah. He's an old friend. And you are?"

"I'm Jess," I say. "Jess Hadley, his sister."

"I'm Nick." A shrug. "I—well, I'm the one who suggested he come and live here."

Nick

I SUGGESTED JESS COME UP to my place, rather than us chatting in the chilly darkness of the *cave*. I'm slightly regretting it now: I've offered her a seat but she's pacing the room, looking at my Peloton bike, my bookcases. The knees of her jeans are worn, the cuffs of her sweater frayed, her fingernails bitten down to fragments like tiny pieces of broken shell. She gives off this jittery, restless energy: nothing like Ben's languor, his easy manner. Her voice is different too; no private school for her, I'm guessing. But then Ben's accent often changed depending on who he was speaking to. It took me a while to realize that.

"Hey," she says, suddenly. "Can I go splash some water on my face? I'm really sweaty."

"Be my guest." What else can I say?

She wanders back in a couple of minutes later. I catch a gust of Annick Goutal Eau de Monsieur; either she wears it too (which seems unlikely) or she helped herself when she was in there.

"Better?" I ask.

"Yeah, much, thanks. Hey, I like your rain shower. That's what you call it, right?"

I continue to watch her as she looks around the room. There's a resemblance there. From certain angles it's almost uncanny. . . . But her coloring's different from Ben's, her hair a dark auburn to his brown, her frame small and wiry. That, and the curious way she's prowling around, sizing the place up, makes me think of a little fox.

"Thanks for helping me out," she says. "For a moment I thought I'd never get out."

"But what on earth were you doing in the *cave*?"

"The what?"

"*Cave*," I explain, "it means 'cellar' in French."

"Oh, right." She chews the skin at the edge of her thumbnail, shrugs. "Having a look around the place, I suppose." I saw that bottle of wine in her hand. How she slipped it back into the rack when she didn't think I was looking. I'm not going to mention it. The owner of that cellar can afford to lose a bottle or two. "It's huge down there," she says.

"It was used by the Gestapo in the war," I tell her. "Their main headquarters was on Avenue Foch, near the Bois de Boulogne. But toward the end of the Occupation they had . . . overspill. They used the *cave* to hold prisoners. Members of the Resistance, that kind of thing."

She makes a face. "I suppose it makes sense. This place has an atmosphere, you know? My mum was very into that sort of thing: energy, auras, vibrations."

Was. I remember Ben telling me about his mum. Drunk in a pub one night. Though even drunk I suspect he never spilled more than he intended to.

"Anyway," she says, "I never really believed in that stuff. But you can feel something here. It gives me the creeps." She catches herself. "Sorry—didn't mean to offend—"

"No. It's fine. I suppose I know what you mean. So: you're Ben's sister." I want to work out exactly what she's doing here.

She nods. "Yup. Same mum, different dads."

I notice she doesn't say anything about Ben being adopted. I remember my shock, finding out. But thinking that it also made sense. The fact that you couldn't pigeonhole him like you could the others in our year at university—the staid rowing types, the studious honors students, the loose party animals. Yes, there was the public school accent, the ease—but it always felt as though there was some other note beneath it all. Hints of something rougher, darker. Maybe that's why people were so intrigued by him.

"I like your Gaggia," Jess says, wandering toward the kitchen. "They had one like that in a café I used to work in." A laugh, without much humor in it. "I might not have gone to a posh school or uni like my brother but I do know how to make a mean microfoam." I sense a streak of bitterness there.

"You want a coffee? I can make you one. I'm afraid I've only got oat milk."

"Have you got any beer?" she asks, hopefully. "I know it's early but I could really do with one."

"Sure, and feel free to sit down," I say, gesturing to the sofa. Watching her prowl around the room, combined with the lack of sleep, is making me feel a little dizzy.

I go to the fridge to get out a couple of bottles: beer for her, kombucha for me—I never drink earlier than seven. Before I can offer to open hers she's taken a lighter out of her pocket, fitted it between the top of her index finger and the bottom of the cap and somehow flipped the lid off. I watch her, amazed and slightly appalled at the same time. Who is this girl?

"I don't think Ben mentioned you coming to stay," I say, as casually as I can. I don't want her to feel like I'm accusing her of anything—but he definitely didn't. Of course we didn't speak much the last couple of weeks. He was so busy.

"Well, it was kind of last minute." She waves a hand vaguely. "When did you last see him?" she asks. "Ben?"

"A couple of days ago—I think."

"So you haven't heard from him today?"

"No. Is something the matter?"

I watch as she tears at her thumbnail with her teeth, so hard it makes me wince. I see a little bead of blood blossom at the quick. "He wasn't here when I arrived last night. And I haven't heard from him since yesterday afternoon. I know this is going to sound weird, but could he have been in some sort of trouble?"

I cough on the sip I've just taken. "Trouble? What kind of trouble?"

"It just . . . feels all wrong." She's fidgeting with the gold necklace around her neck now. I see the metal saint come free; it's the same as his. "He left me this voicenote. It . . . kind of cuts out halfway through. And now he isn't answering his phone. He hasn't read any of my messages. His wallet and his keys are still in the apartment—and I know he hasn't taken his Vespa because I saw it in the basement—"

"But that's just like Ben, isn't it?" I say. "He's probably gone off for a few days, chasing some story with a couple of hundred euros in his back pocket. You can get the train to most of Europe from here. He's always been like that, since we were students. He'd disappear and come back a few days later saying he'd gone to Edinburgh 'cause he fancied it, or he'd wanted to see the Norfolk Broads, or he'd stayed in a hostel and gone hiking in the Brecon Beacons."

The rest of us in our little bubble, hardly remembering—some of us wanting to forget—that there was a world outside it. It wouldn't have occurred to us to leave. But off he'd go, on his own, like he wasn't crossing some sort of invisible barrier. That hunger, that drive in him.

"I don't think so," Jess says, cutting into these memories. "He wouldn't do that . . . not knowing I was coming." But she doesn't sound all that certain. She sounds almost as though she's asking a question. "Anyway, you seem to know him pretty well?"

"We hadn't seen much of each other until recently." That much, at least, is true. "You know how it is. But he got in touch with me when he moved to Paris. And meeting back up . . . it felt like it had been no time at all, really."

I'm drawn back to that reunion nearly three months ago. My surprise—shock—at finding the email from him after so long, after everything. A sports bar in Saint-Germain. A sticky floor and sticky bar, signed French rugby shirts tacked to the wall, moldy-looking chunks of charcuterie with your beer and French club rugby playing on about fifteen different screens. But it felt nostalgic; almost like the kind of place we would have gone to as students nursing pints and pretending to be real men.

We caught up on the missed decade between us: my time in Palo Alto; his journalism. He got out his phone to show me his work.

"It's not exactly . . . hard-hitting stuff," he said, with a shrug. "Not what I said I wanted to do. It's fluff, let's be honest. But it's tough right now. Should have gone the tech route like you."

I coughed, awkwardly. "Mate, I haven't exactly conquered the tech world." That was putting it mildly. But I was almost more disappointed by his lack of success than my own. I'd have expected him to have written his prize-winning novel by now. We'd met on a student paper but fiction always seemed more his thing, not the factual rigors of journalism. And if anyone was going to make it I'd been so sure it would be Ben Daniels. If he couldn't, what hope was there for the rest of us?

"I feel like I'm really hunting around for scraps," he said. "I get to eat in some nice restaurants, a free night out once in a while. But it's not exactly what I thought I'd end up doing. You need a big story to break into that, make your name. A real coup. I'm sick and tired of London, the old boys' club. Thought I'd try my luck here."

Well, we both had our big plans, back when we'd last seen each other. Even if mine didn't involve much more than getting the fuck away from my old man and being as far away from home as possible.

A sudden clatter brings me back into the room. Jess, on the prowl again, has knocked a photograph off the bookshelf: one of the rare few I've got up there.

She picks it up. "Sorry. That's a cool boat, though. In the photo."

"It's my dad's yacht."

"And this is you, with him?"

"Yes." I'm about fifteen in that one. His hand on my shoulder, both of us smiling into the camera. I'd actually managed to impress him that day, taking the helm for a while. It might have been one of the only times I've ever felt his pride in me.

A sudden shout of laughter. "And this one looks like something out of Harry Potter," she says. "These black cloaks. Is this—"

"Cambridge." A group of us after a formal, standing on Jesus Green by the River Cam in the evening light, wearing our gowns and clutching half-drunk bottles of wine. Looking at it I can almost smell that green, green scent of the fresh-cut grass: the essence of an English summer.

"That's where you met Ben?"

"Yup, we worked on *Varsity* together: him in editorial, me on the website. And we both went to Jesus."

She rolls her eyes. "The names they give those places." She squints at it. "He's not in this photo, is he?"

"No. He was taking it." Laughing, getting us all to pose. Just like Ben to be the one behind the camera, not in front of it: telling the story rather than a part of it.

She moves over to the bookcases. Paces up and down, reading the titles. It's hard to imagine she ever stops moving. "So many of your books are in French. That's what Ben was doing there, wasn't it? French studies or something."

"Well, he was doing Modern Languages at first, yes. He switched to English Literature later."

"Really?" Something clouds her face. "I didn't—I didn't know that about him. He never told me."

I recall the fragments that Ben told me about her while we were traveling. How she had it so much harder than him. No one around to pick up the pieces for her. Bounced around the care system, couldn't be placed.

"So you're the friend that helped him out with this place?" she asks.

"That's me."

"IT SOUNDS INCREDIBLE," he'd said, when I suggested it the day we met up again. "And you're sure about that, the rent? You reckon it would really be that low? I have to tell you I'm pretty strapped for cash at the moment."

"Let me find out," I told him. "But I'm pretty sure, yes. I mean, it's not in the best shape. As long as you don't mind some slightly . . . antique details."

He grinned. "Not at all. You know me. I like a place with character. And I tell you, it's a hell of a lot better than crashing on people's sofas. Can I bring my cat?"

I laughed. "I'm sure you can bring your cat." I told him I'd make my inquiries. "But I think it's probably yours if you want it."

"Well . . . thanks mate. I mean . . . seriously, that sounds absolutely amazing."

"No problem. Happy to help. So that's a yes, you're interested?"

"It's a hell yes." He laughed. "Let me buy you another drink, to celebrate."

We sat there for hours with more beers. And suddenly it was like we were back in Cambridge with no time having passed between us.

He moved in a couple of days later. That quick. I stood there with him in the apartment as he looked around.

"I know it's a little retro," I told him.

"It's certainly . . . got character," he said. "You know what? I think I'll keep it like this. I like it. Gothic."

And I thought how great it was, having my old buddy back. He grinned at me and for some reason I suddenly felt like everything might be OK. Maybe more than OK. Like it might help me find that guy I had been, once upon a time.

"CAN I USE your computer?"

"What?" I'm jolted out of the memory. I see Jess has wandered over to my iMac.

"Those bloody roaming charges are a killer. I just thought I could check Ben's Instagram again, in case something's happened to his phone and he's messaged me back."

"Er—I could give you my Wifi code?" But she's already sitting down, her hand on the mouse. I don't seem to have any choice in the matter.

She moves the mouse and the screen lights up. "Wait—" she leans forward, peering at the screensaver, then turns around to me. "This is you and Ben, isn't it? Jeez, he looks so young. So do you."

I haven't switched on my computer in several days. I force myself to look. "I suppose we were. Not much more than kids." How strange, to think it. I felt so adult at the time. Like all the mysteries of the world had suddenly been unlocked to me. And yet we were still children, really. I glance out of the windows. I don't need to look at the photo; I can see it with my eyes shut. The light golden and slanting: both of us squinting against the sun.

"Where were you, here?"

"A group of us went interrailing, the whole summer after our finals."

"What, on trains?"

"Yes. All across Europe . . . it was amazing." It really was. The best time of my life, even.

I glance at Jess. She's gone quiet; seems lost in her own thoughts. "Are you OK?"

"Yeah, sure." She forces a smile. A little of her energy seems to have evaporated. "So . . . where was this photo taken?"

"Amsterdam, I think."

I don't think: I know. How could I forget?

Looking at that photo, I can feel the late July sun on my face, smell the sulphur stink of the warm canal water. So clear, that time, even though those memories are over a decade old. But then everything on that trip seemed important. Everything said, everything done.

Jess

"I'VE JUST REALIZED," NICK SAYS, looking at his watch. "I've actually got to get going. Sorry, I know you wanted to use the computer."

"Oh," I say, a little thrown. "No worries. Maybe you could lend me your code? I'll see if I can get on the Wifi from up there."

"Sure."

He suddenly looks very eager to be gone; maybe he's late for something. "What is it," I ask, "work?"

I've been wondering what he does for a living. Everything about this guy says money. But whispers it rather than shouts it. As I've been looking around his place I've noticed some very swanky-looking speakers (Bang & Olufsen, I'll look it up later but I can just tell they're expensive), a fancy camera (Leica), a massive screen in the corner (Apple) and that professional-looking coffee machine. But you have to really look to see the wealth. Nick's are the possessions of someone who is loaded but doesn't want to boast about it . . . might even be a little embarrassed by it. But they tell a story. As do the books on his shelves—the titles that I can understand, anyway: *Fast Forward Investing, The Technologized Investor, Catching a Unicorn, The Science of Self-Discipline.* As did the stuff in his bathroom. I spent about three seconds splashing my face with cold water and the rest of the time having a good root through his cabinets. You can learn a lot about someone from their bathroom. I learned this when I was taken to meet prospective foster families. No one's ever going to stop you if you ask to use the toilet. I'd go in there, poke around— sometimes nick a lipstick or a bottle of perfume, sometimes explore the rooms on the way back—find out if they were concealing anything scary or weird.

In Nick's bathroom I found all the usual: mouthwash, toothpaste, aftershaves, paracetamol, posh toiletries with names like "Aesop" and "Byredo" and then—interesting—quite a large supply of oxycodone. Everyone has their poison, I get that. I dabbled with some stuff, back in the day. When it felt like it might be easier to stop caring about anything, to just kind of slip out the back door of life. It wasn't for me, but I get it. And I guess rich boys feel pain, too.

"I'm—well, between jobs at the moment," Nick says.

"What were you doing before?" I ask, reluctantly moving away from the desk. I'm fairly certain his last job didn't involve working in a dive with inflatable palm trees and flamingos dangling from the ceiling.

"I was in San Francisco for a while. Palo Alto. Tech start-ups. An Angel, you know?"

"Er . . . no?"

"An investor."

"Ah." It must be nice to be so casual about looking for work. Clearly "between jobs" doesn't mean that he's scrabbling for cash.

He squeezes past me to get to the doorway; I've been blocking his way and being a nice posh English boy he's probably too polite to ask me to budge. I smell his cologne as he does: smoky and expensive and delicious, the same one I had a spray of in his bathroom.

"Oh," I say. "Sorry. I'm holding you up."

"It's OK." But I get the impression he's not as relaxed as he sounds: something in his posture, perhaps, a tightness about his jaw.

"Well. Thanks for your help."

"Look," he says. "I'm sure it's nothing to worry about. But I'm still keen to help. Anything I can do, any questions I can answer—I'll try to."

"There is one thing," I say. "Do you know if Ben's seeing anyone?"

He frowns. "Seeing anyone?"

"Yeah. Like a girlfriend, or something more casual."

"Why do you ask?"

"Just a hunch." It's not like me to be prudish, but there's something in me that gets the ick at describing the knickers I found in Ben's bed.

"Hmm . . ." He puts a hand up to his hair and runs his fingers through it, which only makes his curls stand out more messily. He's beautiful. Yes, all my focus is on finding Ben but I'm also not blind. I've always had a stupid weakness for a polite posh boy; I'm not saying I'm proud of it. "Not that I know of," he says, finally. "I don't *think* he has a girlfriend. But I suppose I don't know everything about his life here in Paris. I mean, we'd kind of fallen out of touch before he arrived here."

"Yeah." I know how that is.

But that's just like Ben, isn't it? Nick had said, just before. *He's always been like that, since we were students.* And all I could think was: *is* he? *Has* he? And if he was always rushing off at the drop of a hat when he was at Cambridge, how did he not find more time to come and see me? He was always saying he was "so busy with essays" or "I can't miss any of my tutorials. You know how it is." But I didn't, of course. He knew I didn't. One of the only times he came to see me—I was fostering in Milton Keynes at the time—was when I suggested a trip to Cambridge. I had an inkling that the threat of his scuzzy foster-kid sister turning up and damaging his image might work. Thinking about it, I feel a little spike of something that I hope is anger, not hurt. Hurt is the worst.

"Sorry not to be more use," Nick says, "but if you need me, I'm right here. Just one floor down."

Our eyes meet. His are a very dark blue, not the brown I'd taken them for. I try to see past the little tug of attraction. Can I trust this guy? He's Ben's mate. He says he's keen to help. The problem is I'm not good at trusting people. I've been used to fending for myself for too long. But Nick could be useful. He knows Ben—apparently better than I do, in some ways. He clearly speaks French. He seems like a decent guy. I think of weird, jumpy Mimi and frosty Sophie Meunier: it's nice to think someone in this building might be a useful ally.

I watch as he pulls on a smart navy wool coat, wraps a soft-looking gray scarf around his neck.

He goes to the door and opens it for me. "It's nice to meet you, Jess," he says, with a small smile. He looks like a painting of an angel. I don't know where the thought comes from—maybe it's because he used the word himself just now—but I know that it's right; perfect even. A fallen angel. It's the dark gold curls, those purple shadows under his navy eyes. Mum had a thing about angels, too, she was always telling me and Ben we all have one looking out for us. Shame hers didn't seem up to the job. "And, look," Nick says. "I'm sure Ben will turn up."

"Thanks. I think so too." I try to believe it.

"Here, let me give you my number."

"That would be great." I give him my phone: he puts his details in.

As I take it from him our fingers brush, and he quickly drops his hand.

BACK UP IN Ben's apartment I'm relieved to find I can get onto Nick's Wifi using the password he gave me. I head to Ben's Instagram and look for "Nick Miller"—the name he's put in my phone—but I can't see him among Ben's followers. I try a more general search and get Nick Millers from all over the place: the

States, Canada, Australia. I look through them until my eyes sting. But they're too young, too old, too bald, from the wrong country. Google is useless, too: there's some fictional guy called Nick Miller from a TV show which fills all the Google results. I give up. Just as I'm about to put it back in my pocket my phone vibrates with a text. And for a moment I think: *Ben*. It's from Ben! How amazing would that be, after all this—

It's from an unknown number:

Got your message about Ben. Haven't heard from the guy. But he'd promised me a couple of pieces of work and a pitch. I'm working at the Belle Epoque café next to the Jardin du Luxembourg all day. You can meet me here. T.

I'm confused for a moment, then I scroll up to my message above and I realize it's the guy I texted earlier. I take Ben's wallet out of my back pocket to remind me of his full name. Theo Mendelson, Paris editor, *Guardian*.

I'm coming now, I text back.

Just before I slide the card back into the wallet, I notice another one sitting behind it. It catches my eye because it's so simple, so unusual. Made from metal, it's a dark midnight blue with an image like an exploding firework, picked out in gold. No text or numbers or anything. Not a credit card. Not a business card either, surely. Then what? I hesitate, feel the surprising weight of it in my palm, then pocket it.

When I open the door that leads onto the courtyard I realize it's already starting to get dark, the sky the color of an old bruise. When did that happen? I haven't noticed the hours passing. This place has swallowed time, like something from a fairytale.

As I walk through the courtyard I hear a sound close by, a rasping: *scritch, scritch, scritch*. I turn and start as I see a small, stooped figure standing only a couple of meters away to my right. It's the old woman, the one I saw last night. She wears a scarf tied about her gray hair, and some sort of long shapeless cardigan over an apron. Her face is all nose and chin, hollow eye-sockets. She could be anything from seventy to ninety. She's holding a broom, which she's using to sweep dead leaves into a heap. Her eyes are fixed on me.

"*Bonsoir,*" I say to her. "Um. Have you seen Ben? From the third floor?" I point up to the windows of the apartment. But she just keeps on sweeping: *scritch, scritch, scriiiitch,* all the while watching me.

Then she steps even closer. Her eyes on me the whole time, barely even blinking. But just once, quickly, she looks up at the apartment building, as though checking for something. Then she opens her mouth and speaks in a low hiss, a sound not un- like the rasping of those dead leaves: "*There is nothing for you here.*"

I stare at her. "What do you mean?"

She shakes her head. And then she turns and walks away, goes back to her sweeping. It all happened so quickly I could almost believe I imagined the whole thing. Almost.

I stare after her stooped, retreating figure. For Christ's sake: it feels like everyone I meet in here is speaking in riddles—except Nick, maybe. I have this sudden, almost violent urge to run up to her and, I don't know, shake her or something . . . force her to tell me what she means. I swallow my frustration.

When I turn to open the gate I'm sure I can feel her gaze across my shoulder blades, definite as the touch of fingertips. And as I step onto the street I can't help but wonder: was that a warning or a threat?

Concierge

THE LOGE

THE GATE CLANGS SHUT BEHIND the girl. She thinks that she's staying in a normal apartment building. A place that follows ordinary rules. She has no idea what she has got herself into here.

I think of Madame Meunier's instructions. I know that I have no option but to obey. I have too much at stake here not to cooperate. I will tell her that the girl has just left, as she asked me to do. I will tell her when she comes back, too. Just like the obedient member of staff I am. I do not like Madame Meunier, as I have made clear. But we have been forced into an uneasy kind of alliance by this girl's arrival. She has been sneaking around. Asking questions of those that live here. Just like he did. I can't afford to have her drawing attention to this place. He wanted to do that too.

There are things here that I have to protect, you see. Things that mean I can never leave this job. And up until recently I have felt safe here. Because these are people with secrets. I have been too deep into those secrets. I know too much. They can't get rid of me. And I can never be rid of them.

He was kind, the newcomer. That was all. He noticed me. He greeted me each time he passed in the courtyard, on the staircase. Asked me how I was. Commented on the weather. It doesn't sound like much, does it? But it felt like such a long time since someone had paid any attention to me, let alone shown me kindness. Such a long time since I had even been noticed as a human being. And soon afterward he began asking his questions.

"How long have you worked here?" he inquired, as I washed the stone floor at the base of the staircase.

"A long time, Monsieur." I wrung out my mop against the bucket.

"And how did you come to work here? Here—let me do that." He carried the heavy bucket of water across the hallway for me.

"My daughter came to Paris first. I followed her here."

"What did she come to Paris for?"

"That was all a very long time ago, Monsieur."

"I'm still interested, all the same."

That made me look at him more closely. Suddenly I felt I had told him enough. This stranger. Was he *too* kind, *too* interested? What did he want from me?

I was very careful with my answer. "It isn't a very interesting story. Perhaps some other time, Monsieur. I have to get on with my work. But thank you, for your help."

"Of course: don't let me hold you up."

For so many years my insignificance and invisibility have been a mask I can hide behind. And in the process I have avoided raking up the past. Raking up the shame. As I say, this job may have its small losses of dignity. But it does not involve shame.

But his interest, his questions: for the first time in a very long time I felt seen. And like a fool, I fell for it.

And now this girl has followed him here. She needs to be encouraged to leave before she is able to work out that things are not what they seem.

Perhaps I can *persuade* her to go.

Jess

IT'S STRANGE TO BE BACK among people, traffic, noise, after the hush of the building. Disorientating, too, because I still don't really know where I am, how all the roads around here connect to one another. I check the map on my phone quickly, so as not to burn too much more data. The café where I'm meeting this Theo guy turns out to be all the way across town on the other side of the river so I decide to take the Metro, even though it means I'll have to break another of the notes I nicked from Ben.

It feels like the further I move away from the apartment the easier I can breathe. It's like a part of me has smelled freedom and never wants to go back inside that place, even though I know I have to.

I walk along cobbled streets, past crowded pavement cafés with wicker chairs, people chatting over wine and cigarettes. I pass an old wooden windmill erupting from behind a hedge and wonder what on earth that's doing in the middle of the city, in someone's garden. Hurrying down a long flight of stone steps I have to climb around a guy sleeping in a fort of soggy-looking cardboard boxes; I drop a couple of euros into his paper cup. A little way on I cut through a couple of smart-looking squares that look almost identical, except in the middle of one there are these old guys playing some kind of *boules* and in the other a merry-go-round with a candy-striped top, kids clinging onto model horses and leaping fish.

When I get to the more crowded streets around the Metro stop there's an odd, tense feeling, like something's about to happen. It's like a scent in the air—and I have a good nose for trouble.

Lo and behold, I spot three police vans parked in a side street. I glimpse them sitting inside wearing helmets, stab vests. On instinct, I keep my head down.

I follow the stream of people underground. I get stuck in the turnstile because I forget to take the little paper ticket out; I don't know how to unlatch the doors on the train when it arrives so a guy has to help me before it pulls away without me. All of it makes me feel like a clueless tourist, which I hate: clueless is dangerous, it makes you vulnerable.

As I stand in the crowded, smelly, too-warm crush of bodies on the train I get the feeling I'm being watched. I glance around: a cluster of teenagers hanging from the rails, looking like they've stepped out of a nineties skate park; a young woman in a leather jacket; a few elderly women with tiny dogs and grocery trollies; a group of bizarrely dressed people with ski goggles on their heads and bandannas round their necks, one of them carrying a painted sign. But nothing obviously suspicious and when we get to the next stop a man playing an accordion steps on, blocking half the carriage from view.

Up out of the Metro the quickest way seems to be through a park, the Jardin du Luxembourg. In the park the light is purple, shifting, not quite dark. On the path leaves crunch under my feet where they haven't been swept into huge glowing orange pyramids; the branches of the trees are nearly bare. There's an empty bandstand, a shuttered café, chairs stacked in piles. Again I have that feeling of being watched, followed: certain I can feel someone's gaze on me. But every time I turn back no figure stands out.

Then I see him. *Ben.* He flashes right by me, jogging alongside another guy. What the hell? He must have seen me: why didn't he stop?

"Ben!" I shout, quickening my step, "Ben!" But he doesn't look back. I start to jog. I can just about make him out, disappearing into the dim light. Shit. I'm lots of things but I'm not a runner. "Hey, Ben! For fuck's sake!" He doesn't turn around, though several other runners glance at me as they pass. Finally I'm just behind him, breathing hard. I reach out, touch his shoulder. He turns around.

I take a step backward. It isn't Ben. His face is totally wrong: eyes too close together, weak chin. I see Ben's raised eyebrow, clear as if he really were standing in front of me. *You mistook me for that guy?*

"*Qu'est-ce que tu veux?*" the stranger asks, looking irritated, then: "What do you want?"

I can't answer, partly because I can't breathe and talk at once but mainly because I'm so confused. He makes a little "crazy" gesture to his mate as they jog off.

Of course it wasn't Ben. As I watch him move away, I can see everything's wrong—he runs clumsily, his arms loose and awkward. There's never been anything awkward about Ben. I'm left with the same feeling I had when he ran by me. It was like seeing a ghost.

THE CAFÉ BELLE EPOQUE has a kind of festive look to it, glimmering red and gold, light spilling onto the pavement. The tables outside are crowded with people chatting and laughing and the windows are steamy with condensation from all the bodies crowded around tables inside. Round the corner, where they haven't turned on the heat-lamps, there's one guy on his own hunched over a laptop; somehow I just know this is him.

"Theo?" I feel like I'm on a Tinder date, if I bothered going on those anymore and it wasn't all catfishers and arseholes.

He glances up with a scowl. Dark hair long overdue a cut and the beginnings of a beard. He looks like a pirate who's decided to dress in ordinary clothes: a woolen sweater, frayed at the neck-line, under a big jacket.

"Theo?" I ask again. "We texted, about Benjamin Daniels—I'm Jess?"

He gives a curt nod. I pull out the little metal chair opposite him. It sticks to my hand with cold.

"Mind if I smoke?" I think the question's rhetorical, he's already pulled out a crumpled pack of Marlboro Reds. Everything about him is crumpled.

"Sure, I'll have one thanks." I can't afford a smoking habit but I'm feeling jittery enough to need one—even if he didn't actually offer.

He spends the next thirty seconds struggling to light his cigarette with a crappy lighter, muttering under his breath: *"Fuck's sake"* and *"Come on, you bastard."* I think I detect a slight accent as he does.

"You're from East London?" I ask, thinking that maybe if I ingratiate myself he'll be more willing to help. "Whereabouts?"

He raises a dark eyebrow, doesn't answer. Finally, the lighter works and the cigarettes are lit. He draws on his like an asthmatic on an inhaler, then sits back and looks at me. He's tall, uncomfortable-looking in the little chair: one long leg crossed over the other knee at the ankle. He's kind of attractive, if you like your men rough around the edges. But I'm not sure I do—and I'm shocked at myself for even thinking about it, in the circumstances.

"So," he says, narrowing his eyes through the smoke. "Ben?" Something about the way he says my brother's name suggests there's not that much love lost there. Maybe I've found the one person immune to my brother's charm.

Before I can answer a waiter comes over, looking pissed off at having to take our order, even though it's his job. Theo, who looks equally pissed off at having to talk to him and speaking French with a determined English accent, orders a double espresso and something called a Ricard. "Late night, on a deadline," he tells me, a little defensively.

Mainly to warm up I ask for a *chocolat chaud*. Six euros. Let's assume he's paying. "I'll have the other thing too," I tell the waiter.

"*Un Ricard?*"

I nod. The waiter slouches off. "I don't think we served that at the Copacabana," I say.

"The what?"

"This bar I worked in. Until a couple of days ago, actually."

He raises a dark eyebrow. "Sounds classy."

"It was the absolute worst." But the day The Pervert decided to show his disgusting little dick to me was the day I'd finally had enough. Also the day I decided I'd get the creep back for all the times he'd lingered too long behind me, breath hot and wet on the back of my neck, or "steered" me out of the way, hands on my hips, or the comments he'd made about the way I looked, the clothes I wore—all those things that weren't quite "things" except were, making me feel a little bit less myself. Another girl might have left then and never come back. Another might have called the police. But I'm not that girl.

"Right," Theo says—clearly he has no time for further chit-chat. "Why are you here?"

"Ben: does he work for you?"

"Nah. No one works for anyone these days, not in this line of work. It's dog eat dog out there, every man for himself. But, yeah, sometimes I commission a review from him, a travel piece. He's been wanting to get into investigative stuff. I guess you know that." I shake my head. "He's due to deliver a piece on the riots, in fact."

"The riots?"

"Yeah." He peers at me like he can't believe I don't know. "People are seriously fucked off about a hike in taxes, petrol prices. It's got pretty nasty . . . tear gas, water cannons, the lot. It's all over the news. Surely you've seen something?"

"I've only been here since last night." But then I remember: "I saw police vans near the Pigalle Metro stop." I remember the group with the ski goggles on the train. "And maybe some protestors."

"Yeah, probably. Riots have been breaking out all over town. And Ben's meant to be writing me a piece on them. But he was also going to tell me about a so-called 'scoop' he had for me—this morning, in fact. He was very mysterious about it. But I never heard from him."

A new possibility. Could that be it? Ben dug too deep into something? Pissed off someone nasty? And he's had to . . . what? Do a runner? Disappear? Or—I don't want to think about the other possibilities.

Our drinks come; my hot chocolate thick and dark and glossy in a little jug with a cup. I pour it out and take a sip and close my eyes because it may be six euros but it is also the best fucking hot chocolate I have had in my life.

Theo pours five sachets of brown sugar into his coffee, stirs it in. Then he takes a big glug of his Ricard. I give mine a sip—it tastes of licorice, a reminder of all the sticky shots of Sambuca I've done behind the bar, bought for me by punters or snuck from the bottle on a slow evening. I down it. Theo raises his eyebrows.

I wipe my mouth. "Sorry. I needed that. It's been a really shitty twenty-four hours. You see, Ben's disappeared. I know you haven't heard from him, but you don't have any idea where he might be, do you?'

Theo shrugs. "Sorry." I feel the small hope I'd been holding onto fizzle and die. "How do you mean disappeared?"

"He wasn't in his apartment last night when he said he would be. He's not answering any of my calls or even reading my messages. And there's all this other stuff . . .' I swallow, tell him about the blood on the cat's fur, the bleach stain, the hostile neighbors. As I do I have a moment where I think: how has it come to this? Sitting here with a stranger in a strange city, trying to find my lost brother?

Theo sits there dragging on his cigarette and squinting at me through the smoke and his expression doesn't change at all. The guy has a great poker face.

"The other strange thing," I say, "is he's been living in this big, swanky building. I mean, I can't imagine Ben makes that much from writing?" Judging by the state of Theo's outfit, I suspect not.

"Nope. You certainly don't get into this business for the money."

I remember something else. The strange metal card I took from Ben's wallet. I slide it out of the back pocket of my jeans.

"I found this. Does it mean anything to you?"

He studies the gold firework design, frowning. "Not sure. I've definitely seen that symbol. But I can't place it right now. Can I take it? I'll get back to you." I hand it over, a little reluctantly, because it's one of the few things I have that feels like a clue. Theo takes it from me and there's something about the way he grabs it that I don't like. It suddenly seems too eager, despite the fact he's told me he doesn't know Ben all that well and doesn't seem all that concerned for his welfare. He doesn't exactly give off a Good Samaritan vibe. I'm not sure about this guy. Still, beggars can't be choosers.

"There's one other thing," I say, remembering. "Ben left this voicenote for me last night, just before I got into Gare du Nord."

Theo takes my phone. He plays the recording and Ben's voice sings out. "Hey Jess—"

It's strange hearing it again like this. It sounds different from the last time I listened, somehow not quite like Ben, like he's that much further out of reach.

Theo listens to the whole thing. "It sounds like he says something else, at the end. Have you been able to work out what?"

"No—I can't hear it. It's too muffled."

He puts up a finger. Hang on. Then he reaches into the rucksack by his chair—as crumpled as everything else about him—and pulls out a tangled pair of headphones. "Right. Noise-canceling and they go really loud. Want one?' He holds out a bud to me.

I stick it in my ear.

He dials up the volume to the max and presses play on the voicenote again.

We listen to the familiar part of the recording. Ben's voice: "Hey Jess, so it's number twelve, rue des Amants. Got that? Third floor" and "Just ring the buzzer. I'll be up waiting for you—" His voice seems to cut off mid-sentence, just like every time I've listened to it before. But now I hear it. What sounded like a crackle on the voicemail is actually a creaking of wood. I *recognize* that creak. It's the hinges of the door to the apartment.

And then I hear Ben's voice at a distance, quiet but still much clearer than what had been only a mumble before: "What are you doing here?" A long pause. Then he says: "What the fuck . . . ?"

Next there's a sound: a groan. Even at this volume it's difficult to tell if it's a person making the sound or something else—a floorboard creaking? Then: silence.

I feel even colder than I did before. I find myself taking hold of my necklace, reaching for the pendant, gripping it hard.

Theo plays the recording again. And finally a third time. Here it is. Here's the proof. Someone was there in the apartment with Ben, the night he left this voicenote.

We each remove an earbud. Look at each other.

"Yeah," Theo says. "I'd say that's a little fucking weird."

Mimi

SHE'S NOT IN THE APARTMENT right now. I know because I've been watching from my bedroom window. All the lights are off on the third floor, the room in darkness. But for a moment I actually think I see him; appearing out of the shadows. Then I blink and of course there's no one there.

But it would be like him. He had this habit of showing up un-announced. Just like he did the second time I met him.

I'd stopped by this old vinyl store on my way back from the Sorbonne: Pêle-Mêle. It was so hot. We have this expression in French, *soleil de plomb*, for when the sun feels as heavy as lead. That was what it was like that day—hard to imagine now, when it's so cold out. It was horrible: exhaust fumes and sweaty sun-burnt tourists crammed together on the pavements. I always hate the tourists but I hate them most of all in the summer. Bumbling around, hot and angry that they came to the city rather than the beach. But there were no tourists in the store because it looks so gloomy and depressing from the outside, which is exactly why I like it. It was dark and cool, like being underwater, the sounds from outside muted. I could spend hours in there in my own little bubble, hiding from the world, floating between the stacks of vinyl and listening to record after record in the scratched glass booth.

"Hey."

I turned around.

There he was. The guy who'd just moved in on the third floor. I saw him most days, wheeling his Vespa across the courtyard or sometimes moving around in his apartment: he always left the shutters open. But close up, it was different. I could see the stubble on his jaw, the coppery hairs on his arms. I could see he wore a chain around his neck, disappearing beneath the neckline of his T-shirt. I wouldn't have expected that, somehow: he seemed too preppy. Up close I could catch the tang of his sweat, which sounds kind of gross—but it was a clean peppery smell, not the fried onion stink you get on the Metro. He was kind of old, like I'd said to Camille. But he was also kind of beautiful. Actually, he took my breath away.

"It's Merveille, isn't it?"

I nearly dropped the record I was holding. He knew my name. He'd remembered. And somehow, even though I hate my name, on his lips it sounded different, almost special. I nodded, because I didn't feel like I could speak. My mouth tasted of metal; maybe I'd bitten my tongue. I imagined the blood pooling between my teeth. In the silence I could hear the ceiling fan, *whoomp, whoomp, whoomp*, like a heartbeat.

Finally, I managed to speak. "M—most people call me Mimi."

"Mimi. Suits you. I'm Ben." His English accent; the bluntness of it. "We're neighbors: I moved into the apartment on the third floor, a few days ago."

"*Je sais*," I said. It came out like a whisper. *I know*. It seemed crazy that he thought I might not know.

"It's such a cool building. You must love living there." I shrugged. "All that history. All those amazing features: the *cave*, the elevator—"

"There's a dumbwaiter, too." I blurted it out. It's one of my favorite things in the building. I wasn't sure why, but I suddenly wanted to share it with him.

He leaned forward. "A dumbwaiter?" He looked so excited; I felt a warm glow that I'd been the cause of it. "Really?"

"Yeah. From back when the building was a proper *hôtel particulier*—it belonged to this countess or something and there was a kitchen down in the *cave*. They'd send food and drink up in it and the laundry would come back down."

"That's amazing! I've never actually seen one of those in real life. Where? No, wait—don't tell me. I'm going to try and find it." He grinned. I realized I was smiling back.

He pulled at the collar of his T-shirt. "Christ it's hot today."

I saw the small pendant on the end of the chain come free. "You wear a St. Christopher?" Again, I just kind of blurted it out. I think it was the surprise at seeing it, recognizing the little gold saint.

"Oh." He looked down at the pendant. "Yeah. This was my mum's. She gave it to me when I was small. I never take it off—I kind of forget it's there." I tried to see him as a child and couldn't. Could only see him tall, broad, the tanned skin of his face. He had lines, yes, but now I realized they didn't make him look old. They just made him seem more interesting than any of the guys I knew. Like he'd been places, seen stuff, done stuff. He grinned. "I'm impressed you recognized it. You're a Catholic?"

My cheeks flamed. "My parents sent me to a Catholic school." A Catholic girls' school. *Your papa really hoped you'd turn out a nun*, Camille said. *The closest thing he could find to a chastity belt.* Most kids I know, like Camille, went to big lycées where they wore their own clothes and smoked cigarettes and ate each other's faces in the street at lunch break. Going to a place like the Soeurs Servantes du Sacré Coeur makes you into a total freak. Like something out of the kids' book *Madeline*. What it means is you get stared at in your uniform by a certain kind of creep on the Metro and ignored by all the other guys. Makes you unable to talk to them like a normal human being. Which is probably exactly why Papa chose it for me.

Of course, I didn't stay the whole time at the SSSC. They had some trouble with a teacher there, a young man: my parents thought it best I leave and for the last few years I had a private tutor, which was even worse.

I saw Benjamin Daniels looking at the record I was holding. "Velvet Underground," he said. "Love them." The design on the front of the vinyl sleeve—by Andy Warhol—was a series of pictures showing wet red lips opening to suck soda from a straw. Suddenly it seemed somehow dirty and I felt my cheeks grow warm again.

"I'm getting this," he said, holding up his record. "The Yeah Yeah Yeahs. You like them?"

I shrugged. "*Je ne sais pas.*" I'd never heard of them. I'd never listened to the Velvet Underground record I'd picked up, either. I'd just liked the Warhol design; had planned to copy it in my sketchbook when I got home. I go to the Sorbonne, but what I'd really like to do (if it were left up to me) is art. Sometimes, when I've got a stick of charcoal or a paintbrush in my hand, it feels like the only time I'm complete. The only way I can speak properly.

"Well—I've got to run." He made a face. "Got a deadline to meet." Even that sounded kind of cool: having a deadline. He was a journalist; I'd watched him working late into the night at his laptop. "But you guys are on the fourth floor, right? Back at the apartment? You and your flatmate? What's her name—"

"Camille." No one forgets Camille. She's the hot one, the fun one. But he'd forgotten her name. He'd remembered mine.

* * *

A FEW DAYS later a note was pushed under the apartment door.

I found it!

I couldn't work out what it meant at first. Who had found what? It didn't make any sense. It had to be something for Camille. And then I remembered our conversation in the record store. Could it be? I went to the cupboard that contained the dumbwaiter, pulled out the hidden handle, cranked it to bring the little cart upward. And I saw there was something in it: the Yeah Yeah Yeahs record he'd bought in the store. A note was attached to it. *Hey Mimi. Thought you might like to try this. Let me know what you think. B x*

"Who's that from?" Camille came over, read the note over my shoulder. "He lent it to you? Ben?" I could hear the surprise in her voice. "I saw him yesterday," she said. "He told me he'd love it if I could feed his kitty, if he ever goes away. He's given me his spare key." She flipped a lock of caramel-colored hair behind one ear. I felt a little sting of jealousy. But I reminded myself he hadn't left *her* a note. He hadn't sent *her* a record.

There's this expression in French. *Être bien dans sa peau.* To feel good in your own skin. I don't feel that way often. But holding that record, I did. Like I had something that was just mine.

NOW, I LOOK at the cupboard that has the dumbwaiter hidden inside it. I find myself drifting over to it. I open the cupboard to expose the pulleys, crank the handle, just like I did that day in August. Wait for the little cart to come into view.

What?

I stare. There's something inside it. Just like when he sent me the record. But this isn't a record. It's something wrapped in cloth.

I reach down to pick it up and, as I close my hand around it, I feel a sting. Hold my hand up and see blood beading from my palm. *Merde.* Whatever is inside here has cut me, biting through the fabric. I drop it and the cloth spills its contents onto the ground.

I take a step back. Look at the blade, crusted with something that looks like rust or dirt but isn't, something that's also streaked all over the cloth it was wrapped in.

And I start to scream.

Jess

I CAN'T STOP THINKING ABOUT how Ben sounded at the end of that message. The fear in his voice. "What are *you* doing here?" The emphasis. Whoever was there in the room, it sounded like he knew them. And then the "What the fuck?" My brother, always so in control of any situation. I've never heard him like that. It hardly even sounded like Ben.

There's a sick feeling in the pit of my stomach. It's been there all along, really, growing since last night. But now I can't ignore it any longer. I think something happened to my brother last night, before I arrived. Something bad.

"Are you going to go back to that place?" Theo asks. "After hearing that?"

I'm kind of struck by his concern, especially as he doesn't seem the sensitive sort.

"Yeah," I say, trying to sound more confident than I feel, "I need to be there."

And I do. Besides—I don't say this—I don't have anywhere else to go.

I DECIDE TO walk back instead of taking the Metro—it's a long way but I need to be out in the air, need to try and think clearly. I look at my phone to check my route. It buzzes:

You have used nearly all your Roaming Data! To buy more, follow this link . . .

Shit. I put it back in my pocket.

I pass little chi-chi shops painted red, emerald-green, navy blue, their brightly lit windows displaying printed dresses, candles, sofas, jewelry, chocolates, even some special bloody meringues tinted pale blue and pink. There's something for everyone here, I suppose, if you've got the money to spend. On the bridge I push through crowds of tourists taking selfies in front of the river, kissing, smiling, talking and laughing. It's like they're living in a different universe. And now the beauty of this place feels like so much colorful wrapping hiding something evil inside. I can smell things rotting beneath the sweet sugary scents from the bakeries and chocolate shops: fish on the ice outside a fishmonger's leaving stinking puddles collecting on the pavement, the reek of dog shit trodden into the pavement, the stench of blocked drains. The sick feeling grows. What happened to Ben last night? What can I do?

There have been times in my life when I've been pretty desperate. Not quite sure how I'm going to make the rent that month. Times I've thanked God I have a half brother with deeper pockets than me. Because, yeah, I might have resented him in the past, for having so much more than I ever did. But he has got me out of some pretty tight spots.

He came and collected me from a bad foster situation once in the Golf his parents had bought him, even though it was in the middle of his exams:

"We have to stick together, us orphans. No: worse than orphans. Because our dads don't want us. They're out there but they don't want us."

"You're not like me," I told him. "You've got a family: the Daniels. Look at you. Listen to how you talk. Look at this frigging car. You've got so much of everything."

A shrug. "I've only got one little sister."

Now it's my turn to help him. And even though every part of me recoils from calling the police, I think I have to.

I take out my phone, search the number, dial 112.

I'm on hold for a few moments. I wait, listening to the engaged tone, fiddling with my St. Christopher. Finally someone picks up: "*Comment puis-je vous aider?*" A woman's voice.

"Um, *parlez-vous anglais?*"

"*Non.*"

"Can I speak to someone who does?"

A sigh. "*Une minute.*"

After a long pause another voice—a man's. "Yes?"

I begin to explain. Somehow the whole thing sounds so much flimsier out loud.

"Excuse me. I do not understand. Your brother left you a voice message. From his apartment? And you are worried?"

"He sounded scared."

"But there was no sign of a break-in in his home?"

"No, I think it was someone he knew—"

"Your brother is . . . a child?"

"No, he's in his thirties. But he's disappeared."

"And you are certain he has not, for example, gone away for a few days? Because that seems like the likeliest possibility, *non?*"

I have this growing feeling of hopelessness. I don't feel like we're getting anywhere here. "I'm fairly certain, yeah. It's all pretty fucking weird—sorry—and he's not answering his phone, he's left his wallet, his keys."

A long pause. "OK, Mademoiselle. Give me your name and your address, I will make a formal record and we will come back to you."

"I—" I don't want to be on any formal record of anything. What if they compare notes with the UK, run my name? And the way he says, "formal record," in that bored flat voice, sounds like—yeah, we'll think about doing something in a couple of years after we've done all the stuff that actually matters and maybe a bit of the stuff that doesn't.

"Mademoiselle?" he prompts.

I hang up.

That was a total waste of time. But did I really expect anything else? The British police have never helped me before. Why did I think their French counterparts would be any different?

When I look up from my phone I realize I've lost my bearings. I must have been wandering aimlessly while I was on the call. I go to the map on my phone but it won't load. As I try to get it to work my phone buzzes and a notification pops up:

You have used up all of your Roaming Data. To buy more, follow this link . . .

Shit, shit . . . It's getting darker, too and somehow this only makes me feel more lost.

OK. Pull yourself together Jess. I can do this. I just need to find a busier street, then I can find a Metro station and a map.

But the streets get quieter and quieter until I can hear just one other set of footsteps, a little way behind me.

There's a high wall on my right and I realize, glimpsing a little plaque nailed to it, that I'm skirting a cemetery. Above the wall I can just make out the taller tombs, the wing tips and bent head of a mourning angel. It's almost completely dark now. I stop.

The footsteps behind me stop, too.

I walk faster. The footsteps quicken.

Someone is following me. I knew it. I round the curve of the wall so I'll be out of sight for a few seconds. Then, instead of carrying on I stop and press myself back against the wall on the other side. My heart's beating hard against my ribs. This is probably really fucking stupid. What I should be doing is running away, finding a busy street, surrounding myself with other people. But I have to know.

I wait until a figure appears. Tall, a dark coat. My chest is burning: I realize I've been holding my breath. The figure turns, slowly—looking around. Looking for me. They're wearing a hood, and for a moment I can't see their face.

Then they take a sudden step back; I know they've seen me. The hood falls down. I can see their face now in the light from the streetlamp. It's a woman: young, beautiful enough to be a model. Dark brown hair cut in a sharp fringe, a mole on her high cheekbone, like a piece of punctuation. A hoodie under a leather jacket. She's staring at me in surprise.

"Hello," I say. I take a cautious step toward her, the shock ebbing away, especially now I can see she's not the threatening figure I'd imagined. "Why were you following me?" She backs away. It feels like I have the upper hand now. "What do you want?" I ask, more insistently.

"I—I'm looking for Ben." A strong accent, not French. Eastern European, maybe—the thick sound of the "I." "He isn't answering. He told me—only if it's very important—to come to the apartment. I heard you asking about him last night. In the street."

I think back to when I first arrived at the building, when I thought for a moment I saw a figure crouched in the shadows behind a parked car. "Was that you? Behind the car?"

She doesn't say anything, which I suppose is as much of an answer as I'm going to get. I take another step toward her. She takes a step back.

"Why?" I ask her. "Why are you looking for Ben? What's important?"

"Where is Ben?" is all she says. "I must speak with him."

"That's exactly what I'm trying to work out. I think something's happened. He's disappeared."

It happens so quickly. Her face goes white. She looks so scared that I suddenly feel pretty scared myself. Then she swears in another language—it sounds like "*koorvah.*"

"What is it?" I ask her. "Why are you so frightened?"

She's shaking her head. She takes a few more steps backward, almost tripping over her feet. Then she turns and begins walking, quickly, in the other direction.

"Wait," I say. And then, as she gets farther away, I shout it: "Wait!" But she starts running. I hurry after her. Shit, she's fast—those long legs. And I'm skinny but not fit. "Stop—please!" I try calling.

I chase her down onto a busier street—people are turning to look at us. At the last minute she veers off to the left and clatters down the stairs of a Metro station. A couple walking up the steps, arm in arm, break apart in alarm to let her through.

"Please," I call, pounding down the stairs behind her, gasping for breath, feeling like I'm moving in slow motion, "wait!"

But she's through the barrier already. Luckily there's an out-of-order gate that's been left open: I charge through after her. But as I get to a junction, the right fork leading to eastbound trains and the left to westbound, I realize I have no idea which way she's gone. I've got a fifty percent chance, I suppose: I choose right. Panting, I make it down to the platform to find her standing on the opposite side of the tracks. Shit. She's staring back at me, white-faced.

"Please!" I shout, trying to catch my breath, "please, I just want to talk to you—"

People are turning to stare at me, but I don't care.

"Wait there!" I shout. There's a big rush of warm air, the thunder of an approaching train down the tunnel. I sprint up the stairs, up over the bridge that leads to the other platform. I can feel the rumble of the train passing beneath me.

I clatter down the other side. I can't see her. People are piling onto the train. I try to get on but it's full, there are too many bodies packed in there, people are stepping back down onto the platform to wait for the next train. As the doors close I see her face, pale and scared, staring out at me. Now the train's pulling away, *clackety-clacking* its way into the tunnel. I glance at the board displaying the route: there are fifteen stations before the end of the line.

A link to Ben, a lead—finally. But I've got no chance of working out where she's going, where she might get off. Or, most likely, of ever seeing her again.

Jess

THE APARTMENT IS AS BRIGHT as I can make it. I've turned on every single lamp. I've even put a vinyl on Ben's posh record player. I'm trying not to panic and it seemed a good idea to have as much noise and light as possible. It was so quiet when I entered the building just now. Too quiet, somehow. Like there was no one behind the doors I passed. Like the place itself was listening, waiting for something.

It's totally different now, being here. Before, it was just a feeling I couldn't put my finger on. But now I've heard the end of the voicenote. Now I know that the last time I heard from Ben he was afraid, and that there was someone in this apartment with him.

I think about the girl, too. The look on her face when I said I thought something had happened to Ben. She was scared but it also seemed like she'd somehow been expecting it.

Suddenly I'm very aware of how, if you looked across from the right spot in any of the other apartments, you'd be able to see me sitting here, lit up like I'm onstage. I go to the windows and slam all the big wooden shutters closed. Better. There were definitely curtains here once: I notice that the rings on the rail are all broken, as though at some point they've been pulled down.

I can't just sit here and run through everything in my head over and over. There must be something else I'm missing. Something that will provide a clue as to what might have happened.

I tear through the apartment. I crouch down to look under the bed, rip through the shirts in Ben's wardrobe, hunt through the kitchen cabinets. I yank his desk away from the wall. Bingo:

something falls out. Something that had been trapped between the wall and the back of the desk. I pick it up. It's a notebook. One of those posh leather ones. Just the kind Ben would use.

I flick it open. There are a few scribbled notes that look like they're for restaurant reviews, that kind of thing. Then, on a page near the back, I read:

LA PETITE MORT
Sophie M knows.
Mimi: how does she fit in?
The Concierge?

La Petite Mort. Even I can translate that: *the little death.*

Sophie M—it has to be Sophie Meunier, the woman who lives in the penthouse apartment. *Sophie M knows.* What does she know? Mimi, that's the girl on the fourth floor, the one who looked like she was going to hurl her breakfast when I asked about Ben. How *does* Mimi fit in? What *is* the concierge's connection? Why was Ben writing in his notebook about these people, about "little deaths"?

I flip through the rest of the notebook, hoping to discover more, only to find it's blank after this. But this does tell me something. There is something strange going on with the people in this building. Ben was keeping notes about them.

I drink more of Ben's wine, waiting for it to take the edge off my nerves but it doesn't seem to be helping. It only starts to make me feel groggy. I put the wine glass down because I have an urge to stay awake, to keep watch, to keep thinking. I don't want to fall asleep here. Suddenly it doesn't feel safe.

When my eyes start closing of their own accord I realize I don't have a choice. I have to sleep. I need the energy to keep going. I drag myself into the bedroom and fall onto the bed. I know I can't do any more today, not while I'm this knackered. But as I turn out the light I realize that a whole day has now passed without word from my brother and the feeling of dread grows.

MY EYES SNAP open. It feels like no time has passed, but the neon numbers on Ben's alarm clock read: 3:00. Something woke me. I know it, even if I'm not sure what. Could it have been the cat, knocking something over? But no, it's here at the end of the bed, I can feel the weight of its body against my feet and, as my eyes adjust to the dark, I can make it out more clearly in the green glow of the alarm clock. It's sitting up, alert, ears pricked and twitching like radars trying to catch a signal. It's listening to something.

And then I hear it. A creak, the sound of a floorboard giving under someone's foot. Someone's here, in the apartment with me, just the other side of the French doors.

But . . . could it be Ben? I open my mouth to call out. Then I hesitate. Remember the voicenote. There's no light beneath the French doors: my visitor is moving around in the dark. Ben would have switched on the lights by now.

Suddenly I'm wide awake. More than awake: wired. My breathing sounds too loud in the silence. I try to calm it, make it as quiet as possible. I close my eyes and fake sleep, lying as still as I can. Has someone broken in? Wouldn't I have heard the glass shattering, the door splintering?

I wait, listening to every tiny creak of the footsteps making their way around the room. It doesn't feel as though they're in any particular rush. I pull the throw up so I'm almost completely covered by it. And then, through the thundering of my own blood in my ears, I hear the doors to the bedroom begin to open.

My chest is so tight it's hard to breathe. My heart is jumping against my ribs. I'm still pretending to sleep. But at the same time I'm thinking about the lamp next to the bed, the metal base nice and heavy. I could snatch out an arm—

I wait, head pressed against the pillow, trying to decide whether to grab for the lamp now or—

But . . . now I hear the soft pad of footsteps retreating. I hear the French doors closing. And then, a few moments later, further away, the groan of the main door to the apartment opening and shutting.

They've gone.

I LIE STILL for a moment, my breathing coming in rough pants. Then I jump up, push through the French doors and run out into the main room. If I move quickly, I might catch them. But first—I rummage through the kitchen cupboards, come up with a heavy frying pan, just in case, then pull open the apartment's main door. The corridor and stairwell are dark and silent. I close the door, go to the windows instead. Maybe I'll catch someone out there in the courtyard. But it's just a dark pit: the black shapes of trees and bushes, no flicker of movement. Where did they go?

I turn on a light. The place looks completely untouched. No broken glass and the front door looks undamaged. Like they just walked right in.

I could almost believe I dreamt it. But someone was here, I'm certain. I heard them. The cat heard them. Even if, right now, it couldn't look more chilled, sprawled on the sofa, cleaning delicately between its outspread toes.

I glance at Ben's desk, and that's when I realize the notebook is gone. I search the drawers, behind the gap in the desk where I found it before. Shit. I'm an idiot. Why did I leave it out there in full view? Why didn't I hide it somewhere?

It seems so obvious now. After hearing that voicenote I should have taken extra precautions. I should have put something in front of the door. Should have known that someone might come in here, poke around. Because they wouldn't need to break in. If it's the same person Ben was speaking to on that recording, they already have a key.

Ben

EVERYTHING GOES BLACK. JUST FOR a moment. Then it all becomes terrifyingly clear. It is going to happen here, now, in this apartment. Right here, on this innocuous spot of flooring just beyond the door, he is going to die.

He understands what must have happened. Nick. Who else? But one of the others in this place might be involved . . . because of course they are all connected—

"Please," he manages, "I can explain." He has always been able to talk himself out of any situation. *Benjamin Silver-Tongue* she called him. If he can only find the words. But speech seems suddenly very difficult . . .

The next attack comes with astonishing suddenness, astonishing force. His voice is pleading, high as a child's. "No, no—please, please . . . don't—" The words tumbling out of him, he who is always so poised. No time for explanations now. He is begging. Begging for mercy. But there is none in the eyes gazing down upon him.

He sees the blood spatter onto his jeans but he doesn't understand what it is immediately. Then he watches as spots of crimson begin to fall onto the parquet floor. Slowly at first, then faster, faster. It doesn't look real: such a brilliant, intense red and there is so much of it, all at once. How can all of this have come from him? More and more every second. It must be spilling out of him.

Then it happens again, the next attack, and he is falling and on the way down his head bounces against something hard and sharp: the edge of the kitchen counter.

He should have known. Should have been less arrogant, less cavalier. Should at least have had a chain put on the door. And yet he thought he was invincible, thought that he was the one in control. He has been so stupid, so arrogant.

Now he's down on the floor and he cannot imagine ever being able to stand again. He tries to put up his hands, to beg without words, to defend himself, but his hands won't obey him either. His body is no longer within his control. With this comes a new terror: he is utterly helpless.

The shutters . . . the shutters are open. It's dark outside: which means that this whole scene must be illuminated to the outside world. If someone saw—if someone could come to help—

With a vast effort he opens his eyes, turns and begins to crawl toward the windows. It's so hard. Each time he places a hand it slips out from under him: it takes a moment for him to realize that this is because the floor is slick with his own blood. Eventually he reaches the window. He raises himself a little way above the sill, he reaches out a hand and marks a gory handprint against the pane. Is there someone out there? A face turned up toward him, caught by the light spilling from the windows, out there in the gloom? His vision is blurring again. He tries to beat his palm, to mouth the word: *HELP.*

And then the pain hits him. It is huge, more overwhelming than anything he has experienced in his life. He can't bear this, surely: it must be too much. This is where the story ends.

And his last lucid thought is: Jess. Jess will be coming tonight, and no one will be here to meet her. From the moment she arrives, she too will be in danger.

Nick

SECOND FLOOR

MORNING. I ENTER THE BUILDING'S stairwell. I've been running for hours. I have no idea how long, actually, or how far I went. Miles, probably. Normally I'd have the exact stats, would be checking my Garmin obsessively, uploading it all to Strava the second I'd got back. This morning I can't even be bothered to look. Just needed to clear my head. I only stopped because the agony in my calf began to cut through everything else—though for a while I almost enjoyed running through the pain. An old injury: I pushed a Silicon Valley quack to prescribe me oxycodone for it. Which also helped dull the sting when my investments started to go bad.

On the first floor I hesitate outside the apartment. I knock on the door once, twice—three times. Listen for the sound of footsteps inside while I take in the scuffed doorframe, the stink of stale cigarette smoke. I linger perhaps a couple of minutes but there's no answer. He's probably passed out in there in a drunken stupor. Or maybe he's avoiding me . . . I wouldn't be surprised. I have something I want—need—to say to the guy. But I suppose it'll have to wait.

Then I close the door, start climbing the stairs, my eyes stinging. I lift the hem of my sweat-soaked T-shirt to rub at them, then carry on up.

I'm just passing by the third-floor apartment when the door is flung open and there she stands: Jess.

"Er—hi," I say, pushing a hand through my hair.

"Oh," she says, looking confused. "It looked like you were going upstairs?"

"No," I say, "No . . . actually, I was coming to see how you were. I meant to say—sorry for running off yesterday. When we were talking. Did you have any luck tracking Ben down?"

I look at her closely. Her face is pale. No longer the sly little fox she seemed yesterday, now she's a rabbit in the headlamps.

"Jess," I say. "Are you all right?"

She opens her mouth but for a moment no sound comes out. I get the impression she's fighting some sort of internal battle. Finally she blurts, "Someone was in here, very early this morning. Someone else must have a key to this apartment."

"A key?"

"Yeah. They came in and crept around." Less rabbit-in-the-headlamps now. That tough veneer coming back up.

"What, *into* the apartment? Did they take anything?"

She shrugs, hesitates. "No."

"Look, Jess," I say. "It sounds to me like you should speak to the police."

She screws up her face. "I called them yesterday. They weren't any help."

"What did they say?"

"That they'd make a record," she says with an eyeroll. "But then, I don't know why I even bothered. I'm the fucking idiot who comes to Paris alone, barely able to speak the language. Why I thought they'd take me seriously . . ."

"How much French can you speak?" I ask her.

She shrugs. "Hardly anything. I can just about order a beer, but that's it. Pretty bloody useless, right?"

"Look, why don't I come with you to the *Commissariat*? I'm sure they'd be more helpful if I spoke to them in French."

She raises her eyebrows. "That would be—well, that would be amazing. Thank you. I'm . . . look, I'm really grateful." A shrug. "I'm not good at asking for favors."

"You didn't ask—I offered. I told you yesterday I want to help. I mean it."

"Well, thanks." She tugs at the chain of her necklace. "Can we go soon? I need to get out of this place."

Jess

WE'RE OUT ON THE STREET, walking along in silence. My thoughts are churning. That voicenote made me feel like I shouldn't trust anyone in the building—including Ben's old uni mate, friendly as he might be. But on the other hand, Nick's the one who suggested going to the police. Surely he wouldn't do that if he had something to do with Ben's disappearance?

"This way," Nick takes hold of my elbow—my arm tingles slightly at his touch—and steers me into an alleyway, no, more like a kind of stone tunnel between buildings. "A cut-through," he says.

In contrast with the crowded street we left behind there's suddenly no one else in sight and it's much darker. Our footsteps echo. I don't like that I can't see the sky.

It's a relief when we pop out at the other end. But as we turn onto the street I see it ends in a police barricade. There are several guys wearing helmets and stab vests, holding batons, radios crackling.

"Fuck," I say, heart thudding.

"*Merde*," says Nick, at the same time.

He goes over and speaks to them. I stay where I am. They don't seem friendly. I can feel them looking us over.

"It's the riots," Nick says, striding back. "They're expecting a bit of trouble." He looks closely at me. "You OK?"

"Yeah, fine." I remind myself that we're literally on the way to talk to the police. They might be able to help. But it suddenly feels important to get something off my chest. "Hey—Nick?" I start, as we begin walking again.

"Yup?"

"Yesterday, when I spoke to the police, they said they wanted to take my name and address, for their records or whatever. I, er . . . I don't want to give them that information."

Nick frowns at me. "Why's that?"

Because even though he had it coming, I think, what I did to that arsehole is technically still a crime.

"I—it's not worth getting into." But because he's still looking at me oddly and I don't want him to think I'm some sort of hardened criminal, I say: "I had a little trouble at work, just before I came here."

More than a little trouble. Two days ago I walked into the Copacabana, smile on my face, as though my boss hadn't flashed his dick at me the day before. Oh, I can play along when I need to. I needed that bloody job. And then at lunch before opening, while The Pervert was taking a crap (he went in there with a dirty magazine, I knew I had a while), I went and got the little key from his office and opened the till and took everything in it. It wasn't loads; he was too wily for that, refilled it every day. But it was enough to get here, enough to escape on the first Eurostar I could book myself onto. Oh, and for good measure I heaved two kegs in front of the toilet door, one stacked on the other and the top one just under the door handle so he couldn't turn it. Would have taken him a while to get out of that one.

So no, I'm not desperate to be on any official record of anything. It's not like I think Interpol are after me. But I don't like the idea of my name in some sort of system, of the police here comparing notes with the UK. I came here for a new start.

"Nothing major," I say. "It's just . . . sensitive."

"Er, sure," Nick says. "Look, I'll give them my details as a contact. Does that work?"

"Yes," I say, my shoulders slumping with relief . . . "Thank you, that would be great."

"So," he says, as we wait at some traffic lights, "I'm thinking of what I say to the police. I'll tell them you thought there was someone in the apartment last night, of course—"

"I don't *think* there was someone," I interject, "I know."

"Sure," he nods. "And is there anything else you want me to say?"

I pause. "Well . . . I spoke to Ben's editor."

He turns to me. "Oh yes?"

"Yeah. This guy at the *Guardian*. I don't know if it's important but it sounded like Ben had an idea he was excited about, for an article."

"What about?"

"I don't know. Some big investigative piece. But I suppose if he got mixed up in something . . ."

Nick slows down slightly. "But his editor doesn't know what the piece was about?"

"No."

"Ah. That's a shame."

"And look, I found a notebook. But it was missing this morning. It had these notes in it—about people in the building. Sophie Meunier—you know the lady from upstairs? Mimi, from the fourth floor. The concierge. There was this line: *La Petite Mort.* I think it means 'the little death'—"

I see something shift in Nick's expression.

"What is it? What does it mean?"

He coughs. "Well, it's also a euphemism for orgasm."

"Oh." I'm not all that easy to embarrass but I feel my cheeks growing warm. I'm also suddenly really aware of Nick's eyes on me, how near we are to each other in the otherwise empty street. There's a long, awkward silence. "Anyway," I say. "Whoever was creeping around this morning took the notebook. So there must be something in it."

We turn into a side street. I spot a couple of ragged posters pasted to some hoardings. Pause for a moment in front of them. Ghostly faces printed in black and white stare out at me. I don't need to understand the French to know what—who—these are: Missing Persons.

"Look," Nick says, following my gaze. "It's probably going to be tough. Loads of people go missing every year. They have a certain . . . cultural issue here. There's this view that if someone goes missing, it may be for their own reasons. That they have a right to disappear."

"OK. But surely they won't think that's what's happened to Ben. Because there's more . . ." I hesitate, then decide to risk telling Nick about the voicenote.

A long pause, while he digests it. "The other person," he says. "Could you actually hear their voice?"

"No. I don't think they said anything. It was just Ben talking." I think of the *what the fuck?* "He was scared. I've never heard him like that. We should tell the police about that too, right? Play it for them."

"Yes. Definitely."

We walk in silence for a couple more minutes, Nick setting the pace. And then suddenly he stops in front of a building: big and modern and seriously ugly, a total contrast to all the fancy apartment blocks flanking it.

"OK. Here we are."

I look up at the building in front of us. COMMISSARIAT DE POLICE, it says, in large black letters above the entrance.

I swallow, then follow Nick inside. Wait just inside the front door as he speaks in fluent-sounding French to the guy on the desk.

I try to imagine what it must be like to have the confidence Nick has in a place like this, to feel like you have a right to be here. To my left there are three people in grimy clothes being held in cuffs, faces smeared with what looks like soot, yelling and tussling with the policemen holding them. More protestors? I feel like I have much more in common with them than I do with the nice rich boy who's brought me here. I jump back as nine or ten guys in riot gear burst into the reception and shove past me and out into the street, piling into a waiting van.

The guy behind the desk is nodding at Nick. I see him pick up a telephone.

"I asked to speak to someone higher up," Nick says as he comes over. "That way we'll actually be listened to. He's just calling through now."

"Oh, great," I say. Thank God for Nick and his fluent French and his posh boy hustle. I know if I'd walked in here I'd have been fobbed off again—or, worse, bottled it and left before I'd spoken to anyone.

The receptionist stands and beckons us through into the station. I swallow my unease about heading farther into this place. He leads us down a corridor into an office with a plaque that reads COMMISSAIRE BLANCHOT on the door and a man—in his late fifties at a guess—sitting behind a huge desk. He looks up. A bristle of short gray hair, a big square face, small dark eyes. He stands and shakes Nick's hand then turns to me, looks me up and down, and sweeps a hand at the two chairs in front of his desk. *"Asseyez vous."*

Clearly Nick pulled some strings: the office and Blanchot's air of importance tell me he's some sort of bigwig. But there's something about the guy I don't like. I can't put my finger on it. Maybe it's the pitbull face, maybe it's to do with the way he looked at me just now. It doesn't matter, I remind myself. I don't have to like him. All I need is for him to do his job properly, to find my brother. And I'm not so blind that I can't see I might be bringing my own baggage to all of this.

Nick starts speaking to Blanchot in French. I can barely pick up a word they're saying. I catch Ben's name, I think, and a couple of times they glance in my direction.

"Sorry," Nick turns back to me. "I realize we were talking pretty fast. I wanted to get everything in. Could you follow any of it? He doesn't speak much English, I'm afraid."

I shake my head. "It wouldn't have made much difference if you'd gone slowly."

"Don't worry: I'll explain. I've laid out the whole situation to him. And basically we're coming up against what I was telling you about before: the 'right to disappear.' But I'm trying to convince him that this is something more than that. That you—that we—are really worried about Ben."

"You've told him about the notebook?" I ask. "And what happened last night?"

Nick nods. "Yes, I went through all that."

"How about the voicenote?" I hold up my phone. "I have it right here, I could play it."

"That's a great idea." Nick says something to Commissaire Blanchot, then turns to me and nods. "He'd like to listen to it."

I hand over the phone. I don't like the way the guy snatches it from me. *He's just doing his job, Jess*, I tell myself. He plays the voicenote through some kind of loudspeaker and, once again, I hear my brother's voice like I've never heard it before. "*What the fuck?*" And then the sound. That strange groan.

I look over at Nick. He's gone white. He seems to be having the same reaction as I did: it tells me my gut feeling was right.

Blanchot turns it off and nods at Nick. Because I don't speak French, or I'm a woman—or both—it feels like I barely exist to him.

I prod Nick. "He has to do something now, yes?"

Nick swallows, then seems to pull himself together. He asks the guy a question, turns back to me. "Yes. I think that's helped. It gives us a good case."

Out of the corner of my eye I see Blanchot watching the two of us, his expression blank.

And then suddenly it's all over and they're shaking hands again and Nick is saying: "*Merci*, Commissaire Blanchot" and I say "*Merci*" too and Blanchot smiles at me and I try to ignore the uneasiness that I know is probably less to do with this guy than everything he represents. Then we're being shown back out into the corridor and Blanchot's door is closing.

"How do you think it went?" I ask Nick, as we walk out of the front door of the station. "Did he take it seriously?"

He nods. "Yes, eventually. I think the voicenote clinched it." He says, his voice hoarse. He still looks pale and sickened by what he just heard, on the voicenote. "And don't worry—I've given myself as a contact, not you. As soon as I hear anything I'll let you know."

For a moment, back out on the street, Nick stops and stands stock-still. I watch as he covers his eyes with his hand and takes a long, shaky breath. And I think: here is someone else who cares about Ben. Maybe I'm not quite as alone in this as I thought.

Sophie

I'M SETTING UP THE APARTMENT for drinks. The last Sunday of every month, Jacques and I host everyone in our penthouse apartment. We open some of the finest vintages from the store in the cellar. But this evening will be different. We have a great deal to discuss.

I pour the wine into its decanter, arrange the glasses. We could afford staff to do this. But Jacques never wanted strangers in this apartment capable of nosing around through his private affairs. It has suited me well enough. Though I suppose if we did have staff I might have been less alone here, over the years. As I place the decanter on the low table in the sitting area, I can see him there in the armchair opposite me: Benjamin Daniels, exactly as he sat nearly three months ago. One leg crossed over the knee at the ankle. A glass of wine dangling from one hand. So at ease in the space.

I watched him. Saw him sizing the place up, the wealth of it. Or perhaps trying to find a flaw in the furnishings I had chosen as carefully as the clothes I wear: the mid-century Florence Knoll armchair, the Ghom silk rug beneath his feet. To signify class, good taste, the kind of breeding that cannot be bought.

He turned and caught me watching. Grinned. That smile of his: a fox entering the hen coop. I smiled back, coolly. I would not be wrong-footed. I would be the perfect hostess.

He asked Jacques about his collection of antique rifles.

"I'll show you." Jacques lifted one down—a rare honor. "Feel that bayonet? You could run a man straight through with it."

Ben said all the right things. Noticed the condition, the detailing on the brass. My husband: a man not easily charmed. But he was. I could see it.

"What do you do, Ben?" he asked, pouring him a glass. A hot, late summer night: white would have been better. But Jacques wanted to show off the vintage.

"I'm a writer," Ben said.

"He's a journalist," Nick said, at the same time.

I watched Jacques' face closely. "What sort of journalist?" He asked it so lightly.

Ben shrugged. "Mainly restaurant reviews, new exhibitions, that sort of thing."

"Ah," Jacques said. He sat back in his chair. King of all he surveyed. "Well, I'm happy to suggest some restaurants for you to review."

Ben smiled: that easy, charismatic smile. "That would be very helpful. Thank you."

"I like you, Ben," Jacques told him, pointing. "You remind me a little of myself at your age. Fire in the belly. Hunger. I had it too, that drive. It's more than can be said for some young men, these days."

Antoine and his wife Dominique arrived then, from the first-floor apartment. Antoine's shirt was missing a button: it gaped open, the soft flesh pushing through. Dominique, however, had made what could be described as an effort. She wore a dress made of a knit so fine that it clung to every ripe curve of her body. *Mon Dieu*, you could see her nipples. There was something Bardot-like about her: the sullen moue of her mouth, those dark, bovine eyes. I found myself thinking all that ripeness would fade, run to fat (just look at Bardot, poor cow), anathema to so many French men. Fat in this country is seen as a sign of weakness, even of stupidity. The thought gave me a nasty sort of pleasure.

I watched her look at Ben. Look up and down and *all over* him. I suppose she thought she was subtle; to me she resembled a cheap whore, touting for a fare. I saw him gaze back. Two attractive people noticing one another. That *frisson*. She turned back to Antoine. I watched her mouth curve into a smile while she talked to him. But the smile was not for her husband. It was for Ben. A carefully calculated display.

Antoine was drinking too much. He drained his glass and held it out for a refill. His breath, even from a couple of feet away, smelled sour. He was embarrassing himself.

"Does anyone smoke?" Ben asked. "I'm going to go for a cigarette. Terrible habit, I know. I wondered if I might use the roof terrace?"

"It's that way," I told him. "Past the bookcase there and to the left, out of the doorway: you'll see the steps."

"Thanks." He smiled at me, that charming smile.

I waited for the sensor lights to come on, which would be the sign that he had found his way to the roof terrace. They did not. It should have only taken him a minute or so to climb the steps.

As the others talked I got up to investigate. There was no sign of him out on the terrace, or in the other half of the room beyond the bookcase. I had that cold, creeping feeling again. The sense that a fox had entered the henhouse. I walked along the shadowed corridor that leads to the other rooms in the apartment.

I found him in Jacques' study, the lights off. He was looking at something.

"What are you doing in here?" My skin was prickling with outrage. Fear, too.

He turned in the dark space. "Sorry," he said. "I must have got confused with the directions."

"They were quite clear." It was difficult to remain civil, to suppress the urge to simply tell him to get out. "It was left," I said. "Out of the doorway. The opposite direction."

He pulled a face. "My mistake. Perhaps I've had too much of that delicious wine. But tell me, while we're here—this photograph. It fascinates me." I knew instantly which one he was looking at. A large black and white, a nude, hung opposite my husband's desk. The woman's face turned sideways, her profile dissolving into the shadows, her breasts bared, the dark triangle of her pubic hair between white thighs. I had asked Jacques to get rid of it. It was so inappropriate. So seedy.

"It belongs to my husband," I said, curtly. "This is his study."

"So this is where the great man works," he said. "And do you work, yourself?"

"No," I said. He must know that, surely. Women in my position do not work.

"But you must have done something before you met your husband?"

"Yes."

"Sorry," he said, after the pause had grown so long it felt like a physical presence in the air between us. "It's the journalist in me. I'm just . . . curious about people." He shrugged. "It's incurable, I'm afraid. Please, forgive me."

I had thought it that first time I met him: that he wielded his charm like a weapon. But now I was sure of it. Our new neighbor was dangerous. I thought of the notes. My mystery blackmailer. Could it be a coincidence that they had arrived almost at the same time—this man, with his air of knowing—and the demand for money, threatening to reveal my secrets? If so, I would not allow it. I would not let this random stranger dismantle everything I had built.

I managed to find my voice. "I'll show you to the roof terrace," I told him. Followed him until he walked through the right door. He turned around and gave me a grin, a brief nod. I did not smile back.

I went back and joined the others. A few moments later Dominique stood up, announced that she, too, was going for a cigarette. Perhaps she was embarrassed by her husband drinking himself into a stupor on the sofa. Or—I thought of the way she looked at Ben when she arrived—she was simply shameless.

Antoine's arm shot out; his hand gripped her wrist, hard. The wine glass in her hand jerked, a crimson splash landed on the pale knit of her dress. "*Non*," he said. "*Tu ne feras rien de la sorte.*"

You'll do no such thing.

Dominique glanced at me, then. Her eyes wide. Woman to woman. *See how he treats me?* I looked away. You have made your choices, *chérie*, just as I have made mine. I knew what sort of man my husband was when I married him; I'm sure it was the same for you. If not—well, you're even more of a foolish little tart than I thought.

I watched as she wrenched her hand away from her husband's grip and stalked off in the direction of the roof terrace. I imagined the two of them up there, could see the scene play out. The rooftops of Paris laid out before them, the illuminated streets like strings of fairy lights. Her bending forward as she lit her cigarette from his. Her lips brushing his hand.

They came back down a short while later. When he spotted them Antoine rose from the seat where he had been slumped. He lumbered over to Dominique. "We're going."

She shook her head. "No. I don't want to."

He leaned in very close and hissed, loud enough for all of us to hear: "We're going, you little slut." *Petite salope.* And then he turned to Ben. "Stay away from my wife, you English bastard.

Comprends-tu? Understand?" Like a final piece of punctuation he gestured with his full wine glass, and I could not tell if it was because he was drunk or if it was on purpose that it flew from his hand. An explosion of glass. Wine smattered up the wall.

Everything went very still and quiet.

Ben turned to Jacques: "I'm very sorry, Monsieur Meunier, I—"

"Please," Jacques stood. "Do not apologize." He stalked over to Antoine. "No one behaves like that in my apartment. You are not welcome here. Get out." His voice was cold, heavy with menace.

Antoine's mouth opened. I saw his teeth, stained by the wine. For a moment I thought he was about to say something unforgivable. Then he turned and looked at Ben. A long look that said more than any words could.

The silence that followed their exit rang like a tuning fork.

LATER, WHILE JACQUES took a phone call, I went and took a shower in my bathroom. I found myself almost idly directing the shower head between my legs. The image that came to my mind was of the two of them: Dominique and Ben, up in the roof garden. Of all the things that might have occurred between them while the rest of us made small talk downstairs. And as my husband barked instructions—just audible through the wall—I had a silent orgasm, my head pressed against the cool tiles. The little death, it's called. *La petite mort.* And perhaps that was only appropriate. A small part of me had died that evening. Another part had come alive.

Jess

IT'S EVENING AND I'M BACK in the apartment. Gazing out into the courtyard, looking up and down at the illuminated squares of my neighbors' windows, trying to catch a glimpse of one of them moving around.

I've texted Nick a couple of times to ask if he's heard anything from the police but I haven't had anything back yet. I know it's way too soon, but I couldn't help myself. I'm grateful for his help earlier. It's good to feel I have an ally in this. But I still don't trust the police to do anything. And I'm starting to feel itchy again. I can't just sit around waiting to hear.

I shrug on my jacket and step out of the apartment onto the landing, not knowing what I'm going to do but knowing I need to do *something*. As I pause, trying to decide what that is, I realize I can hear raised voices somewhere above me, echoing down the stairwell. I can't resist following the sound upward. I start to climb the stairs, up past Mimi's on the fourth floor, listening for a moment to the silence behind the door. The voices must be coming from the penthouse. I can hear a man speaking over the others, louder than the rest. But I can hear other voices now, too, they all seem to be talking at once. I can't make out any of the words, though. Another flight of stairs and I'm on the top landing, with the door to the penthouse apartment in front of me and to my left that wooden stepladder leading up to the old maids' quarters.

I creep toward the door of the penthouse apartment, wincing at every creak in the floorboards. Hopefully the people inside are too distracted by the sounds of their own voices to pay attention to anything outside. I get right up close to the door, then drop down and put my ear to the keyhole.

The man starts to speak again, louder than before. Crap—it's all in French, of course it is. I think I hear Ben's name and I go tense, craning to hear more. But I can't make out a single—

"*Elle est dangereuse.*"

Wait. Even I can guess what that means: *She is dangerous.* I press my ear closer to the keyhole, listening hard for anything else I might understand.

Suddenly there's the sound of barking, right up close to my ear. I stumble away from the keyhole, half-fall backward, try and scrabble my way to standing. Shit, I need to get out of here. I can't let them see—

"You."

Too late. I turn back. She stands there in the doorway, Sophie Meunier, wearing a cream silk shirt and black trousers, crazily sparkling diamonds at her earlobes—her expression so frosty that they might be tiny icicles she just sprouted there. There's a small gray dog at her feet—a whippet?—looking at me with gleaming black eyes.

"What are you doing here?"

"I heard voices, I . . ." I trail off, realizing that hearing voices behind someone else's apartment door isn't exactly a good excuse to go and eavesdrop. Silver-tongued Ben might be able to, but I can't find a way of talking myself out of this one.

She looks like she's trying to decide what to do with me. Finally, she speaks. "Well. As you are here, perhaps you will come in and join us for a drink?"

"Er—"

She's watching me, waiting for an answer. Every instinct is telling me that going inside this apartment would be a very bad idea.

"Sure," I say. "Thanks." I look down at my outfit—Converse, shabby jacket, jeans with a rip at the knee. "Am I dressed OK?"

Her expression says she thinks there's nothing remotely OK about anything I'm wearing. But she says, "You're fine as you are. Please, come with me."

I follow her into the apartment. I can smell the perfume she's wearing, something rich and floral—although really it just smells like money.

Inside, I stare. The apartment is at least double the size of Ben's, perhaps bigger. A brightly lit, open-plan space bisected by a giant bookcase. Floor-to-ceiling windows look out over the rooftops and buildings of Paris. In the darkness the illuminated windows of all the apartment buildings surrounding us make a kind of tapestry of light.

How much would an apartment like this cost? Lots, that's all I can guess. Millions? Probably. Fancy rugs on the floor, huge works of modern art on the walls: bright splashes and streaks of color, big bold shapes. There's one small painting, nearest to me, a woman holding some kind of pot, a window behind her. I spot the signature in the bottom-right corner: Matisse. OK. Holy shit. I don't know much about art but even I've heard of Matisse. And everywhere, displayed on side tables, are little figurines, delicate glass vases. I bet even the smallest would fetch me more than I earned in a whole year in that shitty bar. It would be so easy to slip one—

I'm suddenly aware of feeling watched. I look up and meet a pair of eyes. Painted, not real. A huge portrait: a man sitting in an armchair. Strong jaw and nose, gray at the temples. Kind of handsome, if a little cruel-looking. It's the mouth, maybe, the curl to it. The funny thing is, he seems familiar. I feel like I've seen his face before but I can't for the life of me think where. Could he be someone a bit famous? A politician, something like that? But I'm not sure why I'd recognize some random politician, let alone a French one: I don't know anything about that stuff. So it must be from somewhere else. But where on earth—

"My husband, Jacques," Sophie says, behind me. "He's away on business at the moment but I'm sure will be . . ." a small hesitation, "eager to meet you."

He looks powerful. Rich. Obviously rich, just frigging look at the place. "What does he do?"

"He's in wine," she says.

So that explains the thousands of bottles of wine in the cellar. The *cave* must also belong to her and her husband.

Next my eye travels to a strange display on the opposite wall. At first I think it's some kind of abstract art installation. But on second glance I see it's a display of old guns. Each with a sharp, knife-like protrusion attached to the end.

Sophie follows my gaze. "From the First World War. Jacques likes to collect antiques."

"One's missing," I say.

"Yes. It's gone for a repair. They require more upkeep than you might think. *Bon*," she says, curtly. "Come through and meet the others."

WE WALK TOWARD the bookcase. It's only now that I become aware of the presence of people behind it. As we skirt round it I see them facing each other on two cream-colored sofas. Mimi, from the fourth floor, and—oh no—Antoine from the first floor. He's staring at me as though he is exactly as pleased to see me as I am him. Surely he's the sort of neighbor you just give a wide berth and leave to their own devices? When I look back he's still staring at me. It feels like something's crawling down my spine.

It's such a random grouping of people, nothing in common

with each other beyond the fact that they live nearby: weird quiet Mimi, who can only be nineteen or twenty; Antoine, a middle-aged mess; Sophie in her silk and diamonds. What could they have been talking about just now? It didn't sound like a polite, neighborly conversation. I can feel their eyes on me, feel like they're all looking at me like I'm an unknown specimen brought into a laboratory. *Elle est dangereuse.* I'm sure I didn't mishear.

"Perhaps you would like a glass of wine?" Sophie asks.

"Oh, yeah. Thanks." She lifts the bottle and as the wine glugs out into a glass I see the gold image of the chateau on the front and realize it's familiar, the match of the bottle I picked up from the cellar downstairs.

I take a long sip of my wine; I need it. I sense three pairs of eyes watching me. They're the ones with the power in this room, the knowledge; I don't like it. I feel outnumbered, trapped. And then I think: fuck it. One of them must know something about what happened to Ben. This is my chance.

"I still haven't heard from Ben," I say. "You know, I'm really starting to think something must have happened to him." I want to shock them out of their watchful silence. So I say, "When I went to the police today—"

It happens so quickly, too quickly for me to see how it unfolded. But there's a sudden commotion and I see that the girl, Mimi, has spilled her glass of wine. The crimson liquid has spattered over the rug, up one leg of the sofa.

No one moves for a second. Maybe, like me, the other two are watching as the dark liquid soaks into the fabric and feeling grateful that it wasn't them.

The girl's face is a livid, beetroot red. "*Merde,*" she says.

"It's all right," Sophie says. "*Pas de problème.*" But her voice is steel.

Mimi

PUTAIN. I WANT TO LEAVE right now but that would cause another scene so I can't. I have to just sit here and take it while they all stare at me. While *she* stares at me. The white noise in my head becomes a deafening roar.

Suddenly I can feel the sickness rising inside me. I have to leave the room. It's the only way. I feel like I'm not quite in control of myself. The wine glass . . . I'm not even sure whether it was an accident or whether I did it on purpose.

I jump up from the sofa. I can still feel her watching me. I stumble down the corridor, find the bathroom.

Get a grip, Mimi. *Putain de merde.* Get a fucking grip.

I vomit into the toilet bowl and then look in the mirror. My eyes are pink with burst blood vessels.

For a moment I actually think I see him; appearing behind me. That smile of his, the way it felt like a secret shared just between the two of us.

I COULD WATCH him for hours. Those hot early-autumn nights while he worked at his desk with all the windows open and I lay on my bed with the fan blowing cool air onto the back of my neck and the lights off so he couldn't see me in the shadows. It was like watching him on a stage. Sometimes he walked about shirtless. Once with just a towel wrapped around his waist so I could see the dark shadow of hair on his chest, that line of hair that arrowed from his stomach down beneath the towel: a man, not a boy. He hardly ever remembered to close the shutters. Or maybe he left them open on purpose.

I got out my painting materials. He was my new favorite subject. I'd never painted that well before. I'd never covered the canvas so quickly. Normally I had to stop, check, correct my mistakes. But with him I didn't need to. I imagined that one day, perhaps, I would ask him to sit for me.

Sometimes I could hear his music drifting out across the courtyard. It felt like he wanted me to hear it. Maybe he was even playing it for me.

One night he looked up and caught me watching.

My heart stopped. *Putain.* I'd watched him for so long I forgot that he could see me too. It was so embarrassing.

But then he raised his hand to me. Like he did on that first day, when we saw him arriving in the Uber. Except then he was just saying hi, and it was to Camille too: mainly to Camille, probably, in her tiny bikini. But this time it was different. This time it was just to me.

I raised mine back.

It felt like a private sign to each other.

And then he smiled.

I know I have this tendency to get a little fixated. A little obsessed. But I reckoned he was obsessive too; Ben. He sat there and typed until midnight, sometimes later. Sometimes with a cigarette in his mouth. Sometimes I smoked one too. It felt almost like we were smoking together.

I watched him until my eyes burned.

* * *

NOW, IN THE bathroom I splash cold water on my face, rinse the sourness of the vomit from my mouth. I try to breathe.

Why did I agree to come this evening? I think of Camille, throwing her little wicker basket over her arm, tripping out in the city earlier to hang out with friends, not a care in the world. Not trapped here like me, friendless and alone. How badly I longed to trade places with her.

I can hear him speaking, suddenly. As clearly as if he were standing behind me whispering in my ear, his breath warm against my skin: "You're strong, Mimi. I know you are. So much stronger than everyone thinks you are."

Jess

THERE'S A LONG SILENCE AFTER Mimi disappears. I take a sip of my wine.

"So," I say at last. "How do you all—"

I'm interrupted by the sound of a knock on the door. It seems to echo endlessly in the silence. Sophie Meunier gets up to answer it. Antoine and I are left facing each other. He stares at me, unblinking. I think of him smashing that bottle in his apartment while I watched through the spyhole, how violent it seemed. I think of that scene with his wife in the courtyard.

And then, under his breath, he hisses at me: "What are you doing here, little girl? Haven't you got the message yet?"

I take a sip from my glass. "Enjoying some of this nice wine," I tell him. It doesn't come out as flippant as I'd hoped: my voice wavers. I like to think I'm not scared of much. But this guy scares me.

"Nicolas," I hear Sophie say, using the French pronunciation of the name. And then, in English: "Welcome. Come and join us—would you like a drink?"

Nick! Part of me feels relieved at his being here, that I'm not going to be stuck alone with these people. At the same time I wonder: what is he doing here?

A few moments later he appears around the bookcase behind Sophie Meunier, holding a glass of wine. Apparently living in Paris has given him more style than the average British guy: he's in a crisp white shirt, open at the neck and setting off his tan perfectly, and navy trousers. His curling, dark gold hair is pushed back from his brow. He looks like someone from a perfume ad: beautiful, aloof—I catch myself. What am I doing . . . lusting after this guy?

"Jess," Sophie says, "this is Nicolas."

Nick smiles at me. "Hey." He turns back to Sophie. "Jess and I know each other."

There's a slightly awkward pause. Is this just something rich people who live in apartments like this do, all hang out together? It's not like any neighbors I've ever had. But then again I haven't exactly lived in very *neighborly* places.

Sophie gives a wintry smile. "Perhaps, Nicolas, you could show Jess the view from the roof garden?"

"Sure." Nick turns to me. "Jess, you want to come and have a look?"

I feel like Sophie's trying to get rid of me, but at the same time it's a chance to talk to Nick without the others listening. I follow him back past the bookcase, up another flight of stairs.

He pushes open a door. "After you."

I have to step past him as he holds open the door, close enough that I can smell his expensive cologne, the faint tang of his sweat.

A blast of freezing air hits me first. Then the night sky, the lights below. The city spread out beneath me like an illuminated map, bright ribbons of streets snaking away in all directions, the blurry red glow of taillights . . . for a second it feels like I've stepped out into thin air. I reel back. No: not quite thin air. But there's not much separating me from the streets five floors down beside a flimsy-looking iron rail.

Suddenly uplighters are humming on all around us: they must be on some kind of sensor. Now I can see shrubs and even trees in big stoneware pots, a big rose bush which still has some white blooms attached to it, statues not unlike the one that got smashed to pieces in the courtyard.

Nick steps up onto the terrace behind me. Because I've been rooted to the spot, staring, I haven't given him any space; he has to stand pretty close behind me. I can feel the warmth of his breath on the back of my neck, such a contrast to the freezing air. I have a sudden crazy impulse to lean back against him. What would his reaction be if I did? Would he pull away? But at the same time I have an equally crazy urge to dive forward into the night. It feels like I could swim in it.

When you're this high up, do you ever get the urge to jump?

"Yes," Nick says, and I realize I must have spoken the question out loud.

I turn to him. I can barely make him out, just a dark silhouette stitched against the glow from the lights behind him. He's tall, though. Standing this close I'm aware of the difference between our heights. He takes a tiny step back.

I look beyond him and notice that there's an extra layer of building above us: the windows dark and small and dust-smeared, ivy wound all over them, like something from a fairytale. I wouldn't be surprised to see a ghostly face appearing behind the glass.

"What's up there?"

He follows my gaze. "Oh, it'll be the old *chambres de bonne*— where the former maids' quarters were." That must be where the wooden ladder leads. Then he gestures back out at the city. "Pretty good view from up here, isn't it?"

"It's insane," I say. "How much do you reckon a place like this costs? A couple million? More than that?"

"Er . . . I've got no idea." But he must have some sort of idea; he must know what his own apartment is worth. It probably makes him feel awkward. I suspect he's too classy to talk about this sort of thing.

"Have you heard anything?" I ask him. "From that guy at the police station? Blanchot?"

"Unfortunately not." It's strange, not being able to see his expression. "I know it's frustrating. But it's only been a few hours. Let's give it time."

I feel a swoop of despair. Of course he's right, of course it's too soon. But I can't help panicking that I'm no closer to finding Ben. And no closer to working any of these people out.

"You all seem pretty friendly in there," I say, trying to keep my tone light.

Nick gives a short laugh. "I wouldn't say that."

"But do you all get together often? I've never had drinks with my neighbors."

I can hear his shrug. "No—not that often. Sometimes. Hey, do you want a cigarette?"

"Oh, sure. Thanks."

I hear the click of his lighter and when the flame sparks I see his face lit up from beneath. His eyes are black holes, blank as that statue's in the courtyard. He passes me my cigarette and I feel the quick warm touch of his fingers, then his breath on my face as I lean closer for him to light the tip. A shiver of something in the air between us.

I take a drag. "I don't think Sophie likes me much."

He shrugs. "She doesn't like anyone much."

"And Jacques? Her husband? The one in that massive portrait. What's he like?"

He screws up his face. "A bit of a cunt, to be honest. And she's definitely just with him for his money."

I almost choke on my cigarette smoke. It was so casual; the way he said it. But with a real emphasis on the "cunt." I wonder what he has against the couple. And if he's clearly not a fan, what on earth is he doing coming for drinks in their apartment?

"How about that guy from the downstairs flat? Antoine?" I ask. "I can't believe she'd invite him up here. I'm surprised she even lets him sit on her couch. And when I first arrived he told me to fuck off—talk about hostile."

Nick shrugs. "Well . . . it's no excuse but his wife just left him."

"Yeah?" I say. "If you ask me she had a pretty lucky escape."

"Look," he says, pointing beyond me, "you can see the Sacré-Coeur, over there." Clearly he doesn't want to talk about his neighbors any more. We gaze together at the cathedral: illuminated, seeming to float above the city like a big white ghost. And in the distance . . . yes—there—I can see the Eiffel Tower. For a few seconds it lights up like a giant Roman candle and a thousand moving lights shimmer up and down its height. I'm suddenly aware of how huge and unknowable this city is. Ben's out there somewhere, I think, I hope . . . Again, that feeling of despair.

I give myself a mental shake. There must be something else I can learn, some new angle to this I haven't explored. I turn to Nick. "Ben never mentioned what he was looking into, did he?" I ask. "The thing he was writing? The investigative piece?"

"He didn't say anything to me about it," Nick says. "As far as I knew, he was still working on restaurant reviews, that kind of thing. But then that's typical of him, isn't it?" I think I hear a note of bitterness.

"What do you mean?"

"Well, you have to ask whether anyone really knows the real Benjamin Daniels." You're telling me, I think. Still, I wonder exactly what he means by it. "Anyway, it's what he always wanted to do." He sounds different now, more wistful. "Investigative stuff. That or write a novel. I remember him saying that he wanted to write something that would have made your mum proud. He talked all about it on the trip."

"You mean the one you took after uni?" The way he said "the trip" made it sound important. The Trip. I think of that screen-saver. Some instinct tells me to press him on it. "What was it like? You went all across Europe, right?"

"Yeah." His tone is different again: lighter, excited. "We spent a whole summer doing it. Four of us: a couple of other guys, Ben and me. I mean, we were really roughing it. Grotty trains with no air-con, blocked loos. Days, weeks, of sleeping sitting up in hard plastic seats, eating stale bread, hardly washing our clothes. And then when we did we had to use launderettes."

He sounds thrilled. Babe, I think, if you think that's roughing it you don't know you're born. I think of his minimalist apart-ment: the Bang & Olufsen speakers, the iMac, all that stealth wealth. I kind of want to hate him for it, but I can't. There's something melancholy about the guy. I remember the oxycodone I found in his bathroom.

"Where did you go?" I ask.

"All over," he says. "We'd be in Prague one day, Vienna the next, Budapest a few days later. Or sometimes we'd just spend a whole week lying on the beach and hitting the clubs every night—like we did in Barcelona. And we lost a whole weekend to food poisoning in Istanbul."

I nod, like I know what he's talking about, but I'm not sure I could point to all those places on a map.

"So that's what Ben was up to," I say. "Sounds a long way from a one-bed in Haringey."

"Where's Haringey?"

I give him a look. He even pronounced it wrong. But of course a rich kid like him wouldn't have heard of it. "North London? It's where we come from, Ben and I. Even then he couldn't wait to escape, to travel. Actually, it reminds me of something—"

"What?"

"My mum, she used to leave us on our own quite a lot, while she went out. She did shift work and she'd lock us in from about six, so we couldn't get up to any trouble—it can be a rough part of town—and we'd be so bored. But Ben had this old globe . . . you know, one of those light-up ones? He'd spend hours spinning it round, pointing out the places we might go. Describing them to me—spice markets, turquoise seas, cities on mountaintops . . . God knows how he knew any of that. Actually, he probably made it all up." I pull myself out of the memory. I'm not sure I've spoken to anyone else about all of that. "Anyway. It sounds like you had a ball. The photo on your screensaver, that was Amsterdam, right?"

I look at Nick but he's staring out into the night. My question is left hanging in the chill autumn air.

Concierge

THE LOGE

I'M WATCHING THE ROOF TERRACE from my position in the courtyard. I saw the lights come on a few moments ago. Now I see someone step close to the rail. I catch the sound of voices, the faint strains of music floating down. Rather a contrast with the sounds coming from a few streets away, the whine of police sirens. I heard it just now on the radio: the riots are beginning again in earnest tonight. Not that any of them up there will know or care.

The radio was a gift from him, actually. And only a few weeks ago I watched him up there on the roof terrace, too, smoking a cigarette with the wife of the drunk on the first floor.

As the figure next to the rail turns I realize it's her, the girl staying in his apartment. She has somehow gained access to the penthouse. Invited in? Surely not. If she is anything like her brother I can imagine she may have invited herself.

In a couple of days she has gained access to parts of this building that I have never entered, despite working here for so many years. This is only to be expected. I am not one of them, of course. In all the time I have worked here I can only recall the great Jacques Meunier looking at me twice, speaking to me once. But of course to a man like that I am barely human. I am something less than visible.

But this girl is an outsider, too. Just as much as I am—maybe more so. Also apparently given to climbing, like her brother. Insinuating herself. Does she really know what she has got herself into here? I think not.

I see another figure appear behind her. It's the young man from the second floor. I snatch in a breath. She really is very close to the rail. I only hope she knows what she is doing. Climbing so high, so quickly: it only makes for further to fall.

Nick

TELLING JESS ABOUT IT HAS brought it back—that thrill. The buzz of shunting between different cities, playing endless rounds of poker with a battered old deck of cards, drinking warm cans of beer. Talking shit, talking about the deep stuff—often a mixture of both. Something real. All my own. Something money couldn't buy. It's why I leapt at the chance to reunite with Ben, in spite of everything. It's not the first time I've longed to go back there, to that innocence.

I catch myself. Talk about rose-tinted glasses. Because it wasn't all innocent, was it?

Not when our mate Guy nearly OD-d in a Berlin nightclub and we found him pouring water into his face, had to save him from basically drowning himself.

Not when we had to pass a bribe to a Hungarian train guard, because our tickets had expired and he was threatening to dump us in the middle of a vast pine forest.

Not when we nearly got our throats slit by a gang in a back alley in Zagreb after they'd stolen all our remaining cash.

Not in Amsterdam.

I watch Jess now as she takes a drag on her cigarette. I remember Ben telling me about her in a Prague beer hall: "My half sister, Jess . . . She was the one who found Mum. She was only a kid. The bedroom door was locked, but I'd taught her how to trip a lock with a piece of wire . . . An eight-year-old should never have to see something like that. It . . . *fuck*—" I remember how his voice broke a little, "it eats me up, that I wasn't there."

I wonder what that would do to you. I study Jess, think of finding her yesterday, about to steal that bottle of wine. Or appearing in this apartment tonight, uninvited. There's something reckless about her—it feels as though she might do anything. Unpredictable. Dangerous. And given this morning's outing she's clearly got issues with the police.

"I've never been anywhere outside the UK," she says, suddenly. "Apart from here, of course. And look how well this is turning out."

I stare at her. "What—this is the first time you've been abroad?"

"Yeah." She shrugs. "Haven't had any reason to go before. Or the cash, for that matter. So . . . what was Amsterdam like?"

I think back to it. The stink of the canals in the heat. We were a group of young guys so of course we went straight to the red-light district. De Wallen, it's called. The neon glow of the windows: orange, fuchsia pink. Girls in lingerie, pressing themselves against the glass, signaling that there was more to see if you were happy to pay. And then a sign: LIVE SEX SHOW IN BASEMENT.

The others wanted to do it: of course they wanted to. We were basically still horny kids.

Down a tunnel, down some stairs. The light growing dimmer. Into a small room. Smell of stale sweat, stale cigarette smoke. Harder to breathe, like the air was getting thinner, like the walls were pressing closer. A door opening.

"I can't do this," I said, suddenly.

The others looked at me like I'd lost it.

"But this is what you *do* in Amsterdam," Harry said. "It's just for fun. You're not telling me you're scared of a bit of snatch? And anyway, it's legal here. So it's not like we'll get in any trouble, if that's what you're worried about."

"I know," I said. "I know but I just . . . I can't. Look, I'll—I'll hang around . . . and meet all of you afterward."

I could tell they thought I was a pussy, but I didn't care. I couldn't do it. Ben looked at me then. And even though he couldn't know, I felt like somehow he got it. But that was Ben all over. Our de facto leader. The grown-up of our little group: somehow more worldly than the rest of us. The one who could talk his way into any nightclub, any hostel that claimed to be full—and out of situations too: he was the one who passed that bribe. I was so envious of that. You can't learn or buy that sort of charm. But I had wondered if maybe just a little of that confidence, that sureness, might rub off on me.

"I'll come with you, mate," he said. Howls of disappointment from the others: "It'll be weird if it's just the two of us," and "What's wrong with you both? Fuck's sake."

But Ben slung an arm around my shoulders. "Let's leave these losers to their cheap thrills," he said. "How about we go find a weed café?"

We walked out into the street and instantly I felt like I could breathe easier. We wandered to a spot a couple of streets away. Sat down with our ready-rolled joints.

He leaned forward. "You all right, mate?"

"Yeah . . . fine." I inhaled greedily, hungry for the weed haze to descend.

"What freaked you out so much?" he asked, a moment later, "about that place back there?"

"I don't know," I said. "It's not something I want to talk about. If that's OK."

We'd started with the weaker stuff. It didn't seem to do all that much at first. But as it kicked in I felt something shift.

Actually, now I think about it, maybe it wasn't so much the weed. It was Ben.

"Look," he said. "I get that you don't want to talk. But if you need to get anything off your chest, you know?" He put up his hands. "No judgment here."

I thought of that place, the girls. I'd kept it inside me for so long, my grim little secret. Maybe it would be a kind of catharsis. I took a deep breath. A long pull of my joint. And then I started talking. Once I started I didn't want to stop.

I told him about my sixteenth birthday present. How my dad had told me it was time for me to become a man. His gift to me. Best of the best, for his son. He wanted to give me an experience I'd never forget.

I remember the staircase leading downward. Opening that door. Telling him I didn't want that.

"What?" My dad had stared at me. "You think you're too good for this? You're going to throw this back in my face? What's wrong with you, boy?"

I told Ben how I stayed. Because I had to. And how I left that place a changed person—barely a man yet. How it left its stain on me.

All of a sudden it was just spilling out of me, all my secrets, shit I had never told anyone, like this putrid waterfall. And Ben just sat listening, in the dark of the café.

"Christ," he said, his pupils large. "That's seriously fucked-up." I remember that, clearly.

"I haven't told anyone else about it," I said. "Don't—don't tell the others, yeah?"

"It's safe with me," Ben said.

After that we started on the stronger stuff. Egging each other on. That was when it really hit. We'd look at each other and just giggle, even though we didn't know why.

"We didn't see all that much of the city," I tell Jess, now. "So I'm not exactly what you'd call an expert. If you want a good weed café I could probably tell you that much."

If only the night had ended there. Without what came next. Without the darkness. The black water of the canal.

Jess

"HANG ON," I SAY. "YOU told me you and Ben hadn't seen each other for over a decade when you guys bumped into each other again?"

"Yes."

"And that was after that trip, right?"

"Yeah. I hadn't seen him since then."

I let it sit a little, wait for him to continue, to explain the long stretch of time. Silence.

"I have to ask," I say, "what on earth happened in Amsterdam?" I mean it as a joke—mainly. But it feels like there's something there. The way his voice changed when he spoke about it.

For a moment Nick's face is a mask. Then it's like he remembers to smile. "Ha. Just boys being boys. You know."

A gust of icy wind hits us, ripping leaves from the shrubs and tossing them into the air.

"Jesus!" I say, wrapping my arms around myself.

"You're shivering," Nick says.

"Yeah, well—this jacket's not really designed for the cold. Primarni's finest." Though I highly doubt Nick knows what Primark is.

He stretches a hand out toward me, such a sudden motion that I jerk backward.

"Sorry!" he says. "I didn't mean to startle you. You've got a leaf caught in your hair. Wait a second, I'll get it out."

"There's probably all sorts in there," I say, casting around for a joke. "Food, cigarette butts, the lot." I can feel the warmth of his breath on my face, his fingers in my hair as he untangles the leaf.

"Here—" he plucks it out and shows it to me: it's a dead brown ivy leaf. His face is still very close to mine. And in the way you do just know with these things, I think he might be about to kiss me. It's a very long time since I've been kissed by anyone. I find myself letting my lips open slightly.

Then we're plunged into darkness again.

"Shit," Nick swears. "It's the sensors—we've been too still."

He waves an arm and they come back on. But whatever was just happening between us has been shattered. I blink spots of light from my eyes. What the hell was I thinking? I'm trying to find my missing brother. I don't have time for this.

Nick takes a step away from me. "Right," he says, not meeting my eyes. "Shall we go back down?"

We climb back down into the apartment. "Hey," I say. "I think I'll just find a bathroom." I need to pull myself together.

"You want me to show you the way?" Nick asks. Clearly he's familiar with this apartment, I note, despite what he says about not doing this often.

"No, I'm good," I tell him. "Thanks."

He goes back to join the others. I wander down a dimly lit corridor. Thick carpet beneath my feet. More artworks hanging on the walls. I push open doors as I go: I don't know exactly what I'm looking for, but I do know I've got to find something that might tell me more about these people, or what Ben had to do with any of them.

I find two bedrooms: one very masculine and impersonal, like I imagine a room in a swanky business hotel might be, the other more feminine. It looks as though Sophie and Jacques Meunier sleep in different rooms. Interesting, though maybe not surprising. Off Sophie's bedroom is a room-sized wardrobe, with rows of high heels and boots in sensible shades of black and tan and camel, hanging racks of dresses and silk shirts, expensive-looking sweaters with tissue interleaved between them. In one corner is an ornate dressing table with a spindly antique-looking chair and a big mirror. I thought only the Kardashians and people in films had rooms like this.

I find the bathroom too, big enough to hold a yoga class in, with a huge sunken bath encased in marble, his-and-hers sinks. The next door opens onto the toilet: if you're rich I suppose you probably don't wee in the same place that you bathe in your scented oils. A quick poke around in the cabinets, but I don't find much beyond some very posh-looking wrapped soaps from somewhere called Santa Maria Novella. I pocket a couple.

The room opposite the toilet seems to be some sort of study. It smells like leather and old wood. A huge antique-looking desk with a burgundy leather top squats in the center. There's a big black and white picture opposite it which I think is some abstract image at first but then suddenly—like a magic eye—realize is actually a photograph of a woman's torso: breasts, belly button, vee of pubic hair between her legs. I stare at it for a moment, taken aback. It seems like quite an odd thing to hang in your study, but then I suppose you can do what you like if you work from home.

I try the drawers to the desk. They're locked, but these kinds of locks are pretty easy to pick. I've got the first open in a minute or so. The first thing I find is a couple of sheets of paper. It looks like the top sheet must be missing, because these are numbered "2" and "3" at the bottom. Some sort of price list, it looks like. No: accounts. Wines, I think: I see "Vintage" at the top of one column. The number of bottles bought—never more than about four, I notice. A price next to each wine. Jesus. Some of these single bottles seem to be going for more than a thousand euros.

And then what looks like a person's name next to each of these entries. Who spends that much money on wine?

I reach right to the back of the drawer, to see if there's anything else in there. My fingers close around something small and leathery. I pull it out. It's a passport. A pretty old one, by the looks of things. On the front it has a gold circular design and some foreign-looking letters. Russian, maybe? It looks pretty old, too. I open it up and there's a black and white photograph of a young woman. I have the same feeling I did when I looked at that portrait over the fireplace. That I know this person from somewhere . . . though I can't place her. Her cheeks and lips full, her hair long and wild and curling, her eyebrows plucked into thin half-moons. All at once it hits me. Something about the set of the mouth, the tilt of the chin. It's Sophie Meunier, only about thirty years younger. I look at the front cover again. So she's actually Russian or something—not French. Odd.

I shut the drawer. As I do, something falls with a thud off the desk and onto the floor. Shit. I snatch it up: not broken, thank God. A photograph in a silver frame. A posh, formal-looking one. I don't know how I didn't notice it before: I must have been so focused on the drawers. There are several people in it. I recognize the man first. It's Jacques Meunier, Sophie's husband: the guy in the painting. And there's Sophie Meunier next to him, somewhere between the age she is now and in that passport photo, wearing what's probably meant to be a smile on her face instead of a chilly grimace. And then three kids. I frown, squinting at the faces, then tilt the photograph toward me, try and see it better under the dim lights. Two teenagers—boys—and a little girl.

The younger-looking boy, with his mop of golden hair. I've seen him before. And then I remember. I saw him in a photograph in Nick's flat, next to a sailing boat, a man's hand on his shoulder. The younger boy is Nick.

Hang on. Hang on, this doesn't make any sense. Except it does, suddenly, make a terrible kind of sense. That older boy with the darker hair and the scowl, nearly a man—I think that's Antoine. This tiny girl with the dark hair . . . I peer at it more closely. There's something about the startled expression that's familiar. It's Mimi. The people in this photograph are—

It's then I hear my name being called. How long have I been in here? I put the photograph down with a clatter, my hands suddenly clumsy. I scuttle across the room to the door, peek out through the crack into the corridor. The door at the end is still closed but as I watch it begins to open. While there's still time not to be seen I scurry across the hallway, into the toilet.

I hear Nick's voice saying, "Jess?"

I open the door to the toilet again and step into the corridor with my best expression of innocent surprise. My heart is hammering somewhere up near my throat.

"Hey!" I say. "All good?"

"Oh," Nick says. "I just—well, Sophie wanted me to make sure you hadn't got lost." He smiles that nice guy smile and I think: I do not know this person at all.

"No," I say. "I'm fine." My voice, incredibly, sounds almost normal. "I was just coming back to join you."

I smile.

And all the time I'm thinking: *they're a family, they're a family.* Nice guy Nick and frosty Sophie and drunken Antoine and quiet, intense Mimi.

What the actual fuck.

Sophie

THEY'VE ALL LEFT. MY JAW is stiff with the effort of maintaining a mask of serenity. The girl turning up here completely derailed my plans for the evening. I haven't managed to achieve anything I wanted to with the others.

The bottle of wine is left open on the table. I have drunk far more than I would have had Jacques been here. He would be appalled to see me have much more than a glass. But then I have also spent many evenings alone here over the years. I suppose I'm not unlike other women of my social standing. Left to rattle around in their huge apartments while their husbands are away—with their mistresses, caught up in their work.

When I married Jacques I understood it as an exchange. My youth and beauty for his wealth. Over the years, as is the way with this particular kind of contract, my worth only diminished as his increased. I knew what I was getting into, and for the most part I do not regret my choice. But maybe I hadn't reckoned with the loneliness, the empty hours. I glance over at Benoit, sleeping in his bed in the corner. Small wonder that so many women like me have dogs.

But being alone is better than the company of my stepsons. I see how they look at me, Antoine and Nicolas.

I reach for the bottle and pour the remainder into a glass. The liquid reaches to the very rim. I drink it down. It's a very fine burgundy but it doesn't taste good like this. The acid stings the back of my throat and nostrils like vomit.

I open a new bottle and start drinking that too. I drink it straight from the neck this time, tipping the bottle vertical. The wine rushes out too fast for me to gulp it down; I cough. My throat is burning, raw. The wine pours over my chin, down my neck. The cool of it is strangely refreshing. I feel it sinking into the silk of my shirt.

I SAW HIM in the courtyard the morning after our drinks, talking to Mimi's flatmate, Camille, in a puddle of sunlight. Jacques once told me he approved of that girl living with our daughter. A good influence. Nothing to do with that little pink pout, the delicate upturned nose, the small high breasts, I am sure.

She was leaning toward Benjamin Daniels as a sunflower in a Provençal field tilts toward the sun, Vichy-check top slipping off brown shoulders, white shorts so brief that half a bronzed buttock was visible beneath each hem. The two of them together were beautiful, just as he and Dominique had been beautiful; impossible not to see it.

"*Bonjour Madame Meunier,*" Camille trilled. A little wave as she shifted her weight from one leg to the other. The "Madame" calculated, no doubt, to make me feel all the cruel power of her youth. Her phone trilled. She read whatever had arrived, a smile forming as though she were reading some secret message from a lover. Her fingers went to her lips. The whole thing was a display for him, perhaps: meant to entice, intrigue. "I have to go," she said. "*Salut* Ben!" She turned and blew him a kiss.

And then it was just me and Benjamin Daniels in the courtyard. And the concierge, of course. I was certain she would be watching all of this from her cabin.

"You've made it beautiful out here," he said.

How did he know it was all my work? "It's not looking its best," I told him. "This time of year—everything is almost over."

"But I love the rich colors," he said. "Tell me, what are those—over there?"

"Dahlias. Agapanthus."

He asked me about several of the borders. He seemed genuinely interested, though I knew he was just humoring me. But I didn't stop. I was enjoying telling him—telling somebody—about the oasis I had created. For a moment I almost forgot my suspicion of him.

And then he turned to face me. "I've been meaning to ask you. Your accent intrigues me. Are you originally from France?"

"Excuse me?" I fought not to lose control of my expression, felt the mask slipping.

"I noticed that you don't always use the definite article," he said. "And your consonants: they're a little harder than a native speaker's." He made a pinch with his thumb and forefinger. "Just a little. Where are you from originally?"

"I—" For a moment, I couldn't speak. No one had ever commented on my accent, not even the French—not even the Parisians, who are the worst snobs of all. I had begun to flatter myself that I had perfected it. That my disguise was complete, foolproof. But now I realized that if he had guessed, and he wasn't even French, it meant others would have done too, of course they would. It was a chink, an opening in the shell through which my former self might be glimpsed. Everything I had carefully put in place, all I had worked so hard at. With that one question he was saying: *you don't fool me.*

* * *

"I DON'T LIKE him," I told Jacques, later. "I don't trust him."

"What on earth do you mean? I was impressed by him last night. You can feel the ambition coming off him. Perhaps he'll be a good influence on my wastrel sons."

What could I tell him? *He made a comment about my accent? I don't like the way he seems to watch all of us? I don't like his smile?* It sounded so weak.

"I don't want him here," I said. It was all I could think to say. "I think you should ask him to leave."

"Oh really?" Jacques said, quite pleasantly. Too pleasantly. "You're going to tell me, now, are you, who I may and may not have in my own house?"

And that was that. I knew not to say anything more on the matter. Not for the time being. I would just have to think of another way to rid this place of Benjamin Daniels.

THE NEXT MORNING a new note arrived.

I know you, Sophie Meunier. I know the shameful secrets hiding beneath that bourgeois exterior. We can keep this between us, or the rest of the world can learn them too. I ask just a small fee for my service of silence.

The amount my blackmailer was asking for had doubled.

I suppose a few thousand euros should sound like small fry to someone living in an apartment worth several million. But the apartment is in Jacques' name. The money tied up in Jacques' accounts, his investments, his business. Ours has always been an old-fashioned arrangement; at any given time I have only had what has been handed out to me for housekeeping, for my wardrobe. I did not realize before I became a part of this world how invisible the grease—the money—that moves its wheels really is. It is all squirreled away, invested, liquid or fixed, so little of it available in ready cash.

Still, I did not tell Jacques. I knew how badly he would react, which would only make things worse. I knew that by telling him I would make this thing real, would dredge up the past. And it would only further underscore the imbalance of power that existed between my husband and me. No, instead I would find a way to pay. I still felt able to handle it on my own. Just. I chose a diamond bracelet, this time: an anniversary gift.

The next morning, I dutifully left another wedge of grubby notes in a cream-colored envelope beneath the loose step.

NOW, I LOOK at myself in the mirror across the room. The spreading crimson stain of the wine. I'm transfixed by the sight of it. The red sinking into the pale silk of the shirt. Like spilled blood.

I rip the shirt from me. It tears so easily. The mother of pearl buttons explode from the fabric, skitter to the corners of the room. Next, the trousers. The fine soft wool is tight, clinging. A moment later I am on the ground, kicking them from me. I am sweating. I am panting like an animal.

I look at myself in my lingerie, bought at great expense by my husband but so seldom seen by him. Look at this body, denied so much pleasure, still so well-honed from the years of dieting. The xylophone of my décolletage, the wishbone of my pelvis. Once my body was all curves and ripeness. A thing to provoke lust or contempt. To be touched. With a great effort I changed it into something to be concealed, upon which to hang the garments made for a woman of my standing.

My lips are stained by the wine. My teeth, too. I open my mouth wide.

Holding my own gaze in the mirror I let out a silent scream.

Jess

I MADE MY EXCUSES TO leave the penthouse as quickly as I could. I just wanted to get out. There was a moment, sensing them all watching, when I wondered if one of them might try and stop me. Even as I opened the door I thought I might feel a hand on my shoulder. I walked back down the stairs to Ben's apartment quickly, the back of my neck prickling.

They're a family. They're a family. And this isn't Ben's apartment: not really. Right now I'm sitting here inside someone's family home. Why on earth didn't Ben tell me this? Did it not seem important? Did he somehow not know?

I think of how impressed I was with Nick's fluent French in the police station. Of course he's bloody fluent: it's his first language. I'm trying to think back to our first conversation. At no point, as far as I can recall, did he actually tell me he was English. That stuff about Cambridge, I just assumed—and he let me.

Although he *did* lie to me about something. He pretended his surname was Miller. Why pick that in particular? I remember the results I got when I searched for him online: did he simply choose it because it's so generic? I march to Ben's bookshelf, pull out his dog-eared French dictionary, flip through to "M." This is what I find:

meunier (mønje, jɛR) **masculine noun**: miller

Miller = Meunier. He gave me a translation of his surname.

One thing I can't work out, though. If Nick has got some other, hidden agenda, why was he so keen to help? Why did he come to the police station with me, speak to Commissaire Blanchot? It doesn't fit. Maybe he has another more innocent reason for keeping all of this from me. Maybe they're just a really private family as they're so rich. Or maybe I've been taken for a complete fool . . .

A chill goes through me as I think of them tonight at the drinks party. Observing me like an animal at the zoo. I think how it didn't make sense that such a random group of people should choose to hang out together. That they seemed to have nothing in common. But a family . . . that's different. You don't have to have anything in common with your family; the thing that binds you is your shared blood. I mean, I assume that's how it is. I've never had much of a family. And I wonder whether that's why I didn't spot the truth. I couldn't read the signs, the important little clues. I don't know how families work.

I go to put the dictionary back on the shelf. As I do, a sheet of paper comes loose and falls out onto the floor. I think it's one of the pages of the book at first, because it's such a ratty old thing, until I pick it up. It takes me a moment to work out why I recognize it. I'm sure it's the top sheet of those accounts I found in the desk drawer in the penthouse apartment. Yes: there's a "1" at the bottom of the page. The same sort of thing: the vintages, the prices paid, the surnames of the people who have bought them, all with a little "M." in front of them. But what *is* interesting is what's printed at the top of the sheet of paper. The symbol of a firework exploding, in raised gold emboss. Just like the strange metal card Ben had in his wallet: the one I've lent to Theo, yesterday. And what's also interesting is that Ben—in the same scrawl he'd used in his notebook—has written something in the margin:

Numbers don't make sense. Wines surely worth much less than these prices.

Then, underneath, underlined twice: *ask Irina.*

My heart starts beating a little faster. This is a connection. This is something important. But how on earth am I going to work out what it means? And who the hell is Irina?

I take out my phone, snap a photo. Piggybacking off Nick's Wifi again, I send it to Theo.

Found this in Ben's stuff. Any ideas?

I think of our meeting in the café. I'm not sure I entirely trust the guy. I'm not even convinced I'll hear back from him. But he's literally the only person I've got left—

My thumb freezes on the phone. I go very still. I just heard something. A scratching sound, at the apartment's front door. I wonder briefly if it's the cat, before I realize it's lying stretched out on the sofa. My chest tightens. There's someone out there, trying to get in.

I get up. I feel the need for something to defend myself with. I remember the very sharp knife in Ben's kitchen, the one with the Japanese characters on it. I go and get it. And then I approach the door. Fling it open.

"You."

It's the old woman. The concierge. She takes a step back. Puts her hands up. I think she's holding something in her right fist. I can't tell what it is, the fingers are clenched too tightly.

"Please . . . Madame . . ." Her voice a rasp, as though it's rusty from lack of use. "Please . . . I did not know you were here. I thought—"

She stops abruptly, but I catch her involuntary glance upward.

"You thought I was still up there, right? In the penthouse." So she's been keeping an eye on my movements around this place.

"So you thought . . . what? You'd come and have a snoop around? What's that in your hand? A key?"

"No, Madame . . . it's nothing. I swear." But she doesn't open her fingers to show me.

Something occurs to me. "Was that *you* last night? Sneaking in here? Creeping around?"

"Please. I do not know what you are talking about."

She is cringing backward. And suddenly I don't feel good about this at all. I might not be big, but she's even smaller than me. She's an old woman. I lower the knife: I hadn't even realized I was pointing it at her. I'm a little shocked at myself.

"Look, I'm sorry. It's OK."

Because how harmless can she be, really? A little old lady like that?

ALONE AGAIN, I think about my options. I could confront Nick about all this, see what he says. Ask him what the hell he thought he was doing, giving me a fake name. Get him to explain himself. But I reject this pretty quickly. I have to pretend to know nothing. If he knows I've discovered his secret—their secret— that will make me a threat to him and to whatever else he might be trying to hide. If he thinks I still don't know anything, then perhaps I can keep digging—invisible in plain sight. When I look at it like this, my new knowledge gives me a kind of power. From the beginning, from the moment I stepped foot in this building, the others have held all the cards. Now I've got one of my own. Just one, but maybe it's an ace. And I'm going to use it.

Mimi

WHEN I GET BACK TO the apartment I just want to go to my room and pull the covers over my head, crawl deep down into the darkness with Monsieur Gus the penguin and sleep for days. I'm exhausted by the drinks upstairs, the effort it all took. But when I try to open the front door I find my way blocked with crates of beer, bottles of spirits and MC Solaar blaring out of the speakers.

"*Qu'est-ce qui se passe?*" I call. "What's going on?"

Camille appears in a pair of men's boxers and lace camisole, dirty blond hair piled up on top of her head in an unraveling bun. A lit spliff dangles from one hand. "Our Halloween party?" she says, grinning. "It's tonight."

"Party?"

She looks at me like I'm crazy. "Yeah. Remember? Nine thirty, down in the *cave*, for the spooky atmosphere—then maybe bring a few people up here for an afterparty. You said before that your papa would probably be away this week."

Putain. I totally forgot. Did I really agree to this? If I did it feels like a lifetime ago. I can't have people here, I can't cope—

"We can't have a party," I tell her. I try to sound firm, assertive. But my voice comes out small and shrill.

Camille looks at me. Then she laughs. "Ha! You're joking, of course." She strides over and ruffles my hair, plants a kiss on my cheek, wafting weed and Miss Dior. "But why the long face, *ma petite chou?*" Then she stands back and looks at me properly. "Wait. *Es-tu sérieuse?* What the *fuck*, Mimi? You think I can just cancel it now, at what, eight thirty?" She's staring now, looking at me properly—as though for the first time. "What's wrong with you? What's going on?"

"*Rien,*" I say. *Nothing.* "It's fine. I was only joking. I'm—uh—really looking forward to it, actually." But I'm crossing my fingers behind me like I did as a little kid, hiding a lie. Camille is looking closely at me now; I can't hold her gaze.

"I just didn't sleep well last night," I say, shifting from one foot to the other. "Look, I . . . I have to go and get ready." I can feel my hands trembling. I clench them into fists. I want to stop this conversation right now. "I need to get my costume together."

This distracts her, thank God. "Did I tell you I'm going as one of the villagers from *Midsommar?*" She asks. "I found this amazing vintage peasant dress from a stall at Les Puces market . . . and I'm going to throw a load of fake blood over it too—it'll be super cool, *non?*"

"Yeah," I say, hoarsely. "Super cool."

I rush into my room and close the door behind me, then lean against it and breathe out. The indigo walls envelop me like a dark cocoon. I look up at the ceiling, where when I was small I stuck a load of glow-in-the-dark stars and try to remember the kid who used to stare at them before she fell asleep. Then I glance at my Cindy poster on the opposite wall and I know it is only my imagination but suddenly she looks different: her eyes wild and frightened.

I've always loved this time of year, Halloween especially. The chance to wallow in darkness after all the tedious cheerfulness and heat of the summer. But I've never been into parties, even at the best of times. I'm tempted to try and hide up here. I glance at the shadowy space under the bed. Maybe I could climb under there like I did as a child—when Papa was angry, say—and just wait for it all to be over . . .

But there's no point. It will only make Camille more suspicious, more persistent. I know I don't have any other option except to go out there and show my face and get so drunk I can't remember my own name. With a stubby old eyeliner I try to draw a black spider-web on my cheek so Camille won't say I've made no effort but my hands are shaking so much I can't hold the pencil steady. So I smudge it under my eyes instead, down my cheeks, like I've been crying black tears, rivers of soot.

When I next look in the mirror I take a step back. It's kind of spooky: now I look how I feel on the inside.

Concierge

SHE CAUGHT ME. IT'S NOT like me to be so sloppy. Well. I'll just have to watch and wait and try again when the opportunity presents itself.

I'm back in my cabin. The buzzer for the gate goes again and again. Each time I hesitate. This is my tiny portion of power. I could refuse them entry if I wanted. It would be so easy to turn the party guests away. Of course, I do not. Instead I watch them streaming into the courtyard in their costumes. Young, beautiful; even the ones who aren't truly beautiful are gilded by their youth. Their whole lives ahead of them.

A loud whoop—one boy jumps on another's back. Their actions show they are children, really, despite their grown bodies. My daughter was the same age as them when she came to Paris. Hard to believe, she seemed so adult, so focused, compared to these youths. But that's what being poor does to you; it shortens your childhood. It hardens your ambition.

I talked to Benjamin Daniels about her.

At the height of the September heat wave he knocked on the door of my cabin. When I answered, warily, he thrust a cardboard box toward me. On the side was a photograph of an electric fan.

"I don't understand, Monsieur."

He smiled at me. He had such a winning smile. "*Un cadeau.* A gift: for you."

I stared at him, I tried to refuse. *"Non, Monsieur*—it's too generous. I cannot accept. You already gave me the radio . . ."

"Ah," he said, "but this was free! I promise. A two-for-one offer at Mr. Bricolage—I bought one for the apartment and now I have this second, going spare. I don't need it, honestly. And I can tell it must get pretty stifling in there"—with a nod to my cabin. "Look, do you want me to set it up for you?"

No one ever comes into my home. None of the rest of them have ever been inside. For a moment I hesitated. But it *was* stifling in there: I keep all the windows shut for my privacy, but the air had grown stiller and hotter until it was like sitting inside an oven. So I opened the door and let him in. He showed me the different functions on the fan, helped me position it so I could sit in the stream of air while I watched through the shutters. I could see him glancing around. Taking in my tiny bureau, the pull-down bed, the curtain that leads through to the washroom. I tried not to feel shame; I knew at least that it was all tidy. And then, just as he was leaving, he asked about the photographs on my wall.

"Who's this, here? What a beautiful child."

"That is my daughter, Monsieur." A note of maternal pride; it had been a while since I had felt that. "When she was younger. And here, when she was a little older."

"They're all of her?"

"Yes."

He was right. She had been such a beautiful child: so much so that in our old town, in our homeland, people would stop me in the street to tell me so. And sometimes—because that's the way in our culture—people would make the sign against the evil eye, tell me to take care: she was too beautiful, it would only bring misfortune if I wasn't careful. If I was too proud, if I didn't hide her away.

"What's her name?"

"Elira."

"She was the one who came to Paris?"

"Yes."

"And she still lives here too?"

"No. Not any more. But I followed her here; I stayed after she had gone."

"She must be . . . what—an actress? A model? With looks like that—"

"She was a very good dancer," I said. I couldn't resist. Suddenly, hearing his interest, I wanted to talk about her. It had been such a long time since I had spoken about my family. "That was what she came to Paris to do."

I remembered the phone call, a month in. Not much email, back then, or texting. I would wait weeks for a call that would be cut short by the bleeping that would tell us she was running out of coins.

"I found a place, Mama. I can dance there. They'll pay me good money."

"And you're sure it's all right, this place? It's safe?"

She laughed. "Yes, Mama. It's in a good part of town. You should see the shops nearby! Fancy people go there, rich people."

NOW I WATCH as one of the partygoers staggers over to the nearby flowerbed, the one that has just been replanted, and relieves himself right there on the soil. Madame Meunier would be horrified if she knew, though I suspect she has rather more pressing matters to concern herself with at the moment. And usually the thought of her precious border being soaked with urine would give me a dark kind of pleasure. But this is not a normal time. Right now I am more anxious about this invasion of the building.

These people shouldn't be here. Not now. Not after everything that has happened in this place.

Jess

I'M PACING THE APARTMENT. WONDERING: are the rest of them still up there, in the penthouse, drinking wine? Laughing at my stupidity?

I open the windows to try and draw in some fresh air. In the distance I can hear the faint wailing of police sirens—Paris sounds like a city at war with itself. But otherwise it's eerily quiet. I can hear every creak of the floorboards under my feet, even the scuttle of dry leaves in the courtyard.

Then a scream rips through the silence. I stop pacing, every muscle tensed. It came from just outside—

Then another voice joins it and suddenly there's loads of noise coming from the courtyard: whoops and yells. I open the shutters and see all these kids piling in through the front gate, streaming across the cobbles and into the main building, carrying booze, shouting and laughing. Clearly there's some sort of party going on. Who the hell is having a party, here? I take in the pointed hats and flowing capes, the pumpkins carried under their arms, and the penny drops. It must be Halloween. It's kind of hard to believe there's a world, time passing, outside the mystery of this apartment and Ben's disappearance. If I were still in Brighton I'd be dressed as a "sexy cat" right now, serving Jägerbombs to stag dos down from London. It's not much over forty-eight hours since I left that life but already it feels so far away, so long ago.

I see one bloke stop and pee in one of the flowerbeds while his friends look on, cackling. I slam the shutters closed, hoping that'll help block out some of the noise.

I sit here for a moment, the sounds beyond the windows muffled but still audible. Something has just occurred to me. There's a chance someone going to that party might know Ben; he's been living here for a few months, after all. Maybe I can learn more about this family. And frankly anything is better than sitting here, feeling surrounded and spied upon, not knowing what they might be planning for me.

I don't have a costume, but surely I can make use of something here. I stride into the bedroom and while the cat watches me curiously, sitting tucked into its haunches on top of Ben's chest of drawers, I tug the sheet off the bed. I find a knife in the drawer, stab some eye-holes into it and then chuck the thing over my head. I march into the bathroom to have a look, trying not to trip over the edges of the sheet. It's not going to win any prizes, but now I've got an outfit and a disguise in one, and frankly it's a hell of a lot better than a sodding sexy cat, the basic bitch of Halloween costumes.

I open the door to the apartment, listen. It sounds as though they're heading into the basement. I creep down the spiral staircase, following the music and the stream of guests down the stairwell into the *cave*, the thump of the bass getting louder and louder until I can feel it vibrating in my skull.

Nick

I'M ON MY THIRD CIGARETTE of the evening. I only took up smoking when I came back here; the taste disgusts me but I need the steadying hit of the nicotine. All those years of clean living and now look at me: sucking on a Marlboro like a drowning man taking his last breaths. I look down from my window as I smoke, watch the kids streaming into the courtyard. I almost kissed her this evening, up on the terrace. That moment, stretching out between the two of us. Until it seemed like the only thing that made sense.

Christ. If the lights hadn't gone off and shocked me out of my trance, I would have done. And where would I be now?

His sister. His *sister*.

What was I thinking?

I wander into the bathroom. Stub out the cigarette in the sink where it fizzles wetly. Look in the mirror.

Who do you think you are? my reflection asks me, silently. More importantly, *who does* she *think you are?*

The good guy. Eager to help. Concerned about his mate.

That's what she sees, isn't it? That's what you've let her believe.

You know, I read somewhere that sixty percent of us can't go more than ten minutes without lying. Little slippages: to make ourselves sound better, more attractive, to others. White lies to avoid causing offense. So it's not like I've done anything out of the ordinary. It's only human. But, really, the important thing to stress is I haven't actually lied to her. Not outright. I just haven't told her the whole truth.

It's not my fault she assumed I was British. Makes sense. I've honed my accent and my fluency pretty well over the years; made a big effort to do so when I was at Cambridge and didn't want to be known as "that French guy". Flattening my vowels. Hardening my consonants. Perfecting a kind of London drawl. It's always been a point of pride for me, a little thrill when Brits have mistaken me for one of them—just like she did.

The second thing she assumed was that the people in this building are nothing more than neighbors to one another. That was all her, honestly. I just didn't stand in the way of her believing it. To tell the truth, I liked her believing in him: Nick Miller. A normal guy, nothing to do with this place beyond the rent he paid on it.

Look. Can anyone say they've really never wished their family were less embarrassing, or different in some way? That they've never wondered what it might be like to be free of all those familial hang-ups? That baggage. And this family has rather more baggage than most.

I've heard from Papa this evening, incidentally. *Everything OK, son? Remember I'm trusting you to take care of things there.* The "son" was affectionate for him. He must really want me to do his bidding. But then my father excels at getting others to do his bidding. The second part is classic Papa, of course. *Ne merdes pas.* Do not mess this up.

I think of that dinner, during the heat wave. All of us summoned up to the roof terrace. The light purplish, the lanterns glowing among the fig trees, the warm scent of their leaves. The streetlamps coming on below us. The air thick as soup, like you had to swallow it rather than inhale.

Papa at one end of the table, my stepmother beside him in eau-de-nil silk and diamonds, cool as the night was hot, profile turned toward the skyline as though she were somewhere else entirely—or wished she were. I remember the first time Papa introduced us to Sophie. I must have been about nine. How glamorous she seemed, how mysterious.

At the other end of the table sat Ben: both guest of honor and fatted calf. Papa had invited him personally. He had made quite an impression at the drinks party.

"Now Ben," my father said, walking over with a new bottle of wine. "You must tell me what you think of this. It's clear you have an excellent palate. It's one of those things that cannot be learned, no matter how much of the stuff you drink."

I looked over at Antoine, well into his second bottle by now and wondered: had he caught the barb? Our father never says anything accidentally. Antoine is his supposed protégé: the one who's worked for him since he left school. But he's also Papa's whipping boy, even more so than I am—especially because he's had to take all the flak in the years I've been absent.

"Thank you, Jacques." Ben smiled, held out his glass.

As Papa poured a crimson stream into one of my mother's Lalique glasses he put a paternal hand on Ben's shoulder. Together they represented an ease that Papa and I had never had, and looking at them I felt a kind of ridiculous envy. Antoine had noticed, too. I saw his scowl.

But maybe this could work to my advantage. If my father liked Ben this much, someone I had invited into this house, into our family, perhaps there was some way he would finally accept me, his own son. A pathetic thing to hope, but there you have it. I've always had to hunt for scraps where paternal affection's concerned.

"I see that peevish expression of yours, Nicolas," my father said—using the French word, *maussade*—turning to me suddenly in that unnerving way of his. Caught out, I swallowed my wine too fast, coughed and felt the bitterness sting my throat. I don't even particularly like wine. Maybe the odd biodynamic variety— not the heavy, old-world stuff. "Quite incredible," he went on. "Same look exactly as your sainted dead mother. Nothing ever good enough for her."

Beside me I felt Antoine twitch. "That's her fucking wine you're pouring," he muttered, under his breath. My mother's was an old family: old blood, old wine from a grand estate: Château Blondin-Lavigne. The cellar with its thousands of bottles was part of her inheritance, left to my father on her death. And since her death, my brother, who has never forgiven her for leaving us, has been working his way through as many of them as possible.

"What was that, my boy?" Papa said, turning to Antoine. "Something you'd care to share with the rest of us?"

A silence expanded, dangerously. But Ben spoke into it with the exquisite timing of a first violin entering into his solo: "This is delicious, Sophie." We were eating my father's favorite (of course): rare fillet, cold, sautéed potatoes, a cucumber salad. "This beef might be the best I've ever tasted."

"I didn't cook it," Sophie said. "It came from the restaurant." No fillet for her, just cucumber salad. And I noticed that she didn't look at him, but at a point just beyond his right shoulder. Ben hadn't won her over, it seemed. Not yet. But I noticed how Mimi snatched furtive glances at him when she thought no one was looking at her, almost missing her mouth with her fork. How Dominique, Antoine's wife, gazed at him with a half-smile on her face, as though she'd prefer him to the meal before her. And all the while Antoine gripped his steak knife like he was planning to ram it between someone's ribs.

"Now, of course you've known Nicolas since you were boys," my father said to Ben. "Did he ever do any work at that ridiculous place?"

That ridiculous place meaning: Cambridge, one of the top universities in the world. But the great Jacques Meunier hadn't needed a college education, and look where he'd got himself. A self-made man.

"Or did he just piss away my hard-earned cash?" Papa asked. He turned to me. "You're pretty good at doing that, aren't you, my boy?"

That stung. A short while ago I invested some of that "hard-earned cash" in a health start-up in Palo Alto. Anyone who knew anything was buzzed about it: a pin-prick of blood, the future of healthcare. I used most of the money Papa had settled on me when I turned eighteen. Here was a chance to prove my mettle to him; prove my judgment in my own field was just as good as his . . .

"I can't speak for how hard he worked at uni," Ben said, with a wry grin in my direction—and it was a relief to have him cut the tension. "We took different courses. But we pretty much ran the student paper together—and a group of us traveled all over one summer. Didn't we, Nick?"

I nodded. Tried to match his easy smile but I had the feeling, suddenly, of sighting a predator in the long grass.

Ben went on: "Prague, Barcelona. Amsterdam—" I don't know if it was a coincidence, but our eyes met at that moment. His expression was impossible to read. Suddenly I wanted him to shut the fuck up. With a look I tried to convey this. *Stop. That's enough.* This was not the time to be talking about Amsterdam. My father could never find out.

Ben glanced away, breaking eye contact. And that was when I realized how reckless I had been, inviting him here.

Then there was a sound so loud it felt like the building itself might be collapsing under us. It took me a couple of seconds to realize it was thunder, and immediately afterward a streak of lightning lit the sky violet. Papa looked furious. He might control everything that happens in this place, but even he couldn't order the weather what to do. The first fat drops began to fall. The dinner was over.

Thank Christ.

I remembered to breathe again. But something had shifted.

Later that night, Antoine stormed into my room. "Papa and your English pal. Thick as thieves, aren't they? You know it would be just like him, right? Disinherit us and leave it all to some random fucking stranger?"

"That's insane," I said. It was. But even as I said it I could feel the idea taking root. It would be just like Papa. Always telling us, his own sons, how useless we were. How much of a disappointment to him. But would it be like Ben?

What had always made my mate intriguing was his very unknowability. You could spend hours, days, in his company—you could travel across Europe with him—and never be sure you'd got to the real Benjamin Daniels. He was a chameleon, an enigma. I had no idea, really, who I had invited under this roof, into the bosom of my family.

I REACH INTO the cabinet under the sink and grab the bottle of mouthwash, pour it into the little cup. I want to wash away the rank taste of the tobacco. The cabinet door is still open. There are the little pots of pills in their neat row. It would be so easy. So much more effective than the cigarettes. So helpful to feel a little less . . . present right now.

The fact of the matter is that while I've been pretending to Jess, I could almost pretend to myself: that I was a normal adult, living on his own, surrounded by the trappings of his own success. An apartment he paid the rent on. Stuff he'd bought with his own hard-earned cash. Because I want to be that guy, I really do. I've tried to be that guy. Not a thirty-something loser forced back to his father's house because he lost the shirt off his back.

Trust me—as much as I've tried to kid myself, it doesn't make a difference having a lock on the front door and a buzzer of your own. I'm still under his roof; I'm still infected by this place. And I regress, being here. It's why I escaped for a decade to the other side of the world. It's why I was so happy in Cambridge. It's why I went straight to meet Ben in that bar when he got in touch, despite Amsterdam. Why I invited him to live here. I thought his presence might make my sentence here more bearable. That his company would help me return to a different time.

So that's all it was, when I let her think I was someone and something else. A little harmless make-believe, nothing more sinister than that.

Honest.

Jess

THE VOICES ARE A ROAR of sound over the top of the music. I can't believe how many people are packed into the space down here: it must be well over a hundred. Fake cobwebs have been draped from the ceiling and candles placed along the floor, illuminating the rough walls. The scent of the burning wax is strong in the tight, airless space. The reflection of the dancing flames gives the impression that the stone is moving, wriggling like something alive.

I try to blend into the crowd. My costume is by far the worst one I can see. Most of the guests have gone all out. A nun in a white habit drenched in blood is kissing a woman who has painted her entire semi-naked body red and is wearing a pair of twisted devil horns. A plague doctor dressed from head to toe in a black cloak and hat lifts up the long, curved beak of his mask to take a drag from a cigarette and then lets the smoke blow out of the eyeholes. A tall tuxedo-clad figure with a huge wolf's head sips a cocktail through a straw. Everywhere I look there are mad monks, grim reapers, demons and ghouls. And a strange thing: the surroundings make all these figures seem more sinister than they would up above ground, in proper lighting. Even fake blood somehow looks more real down here.

I'm trying to work out how to insert myself into one of these groups of people and start a conversation about Ben. I also desperately need a drink.

Suddenly I feel my sheet wrenched off my head. A dead cowboy puts up his hands: "Oops!" He must have tripped over the trailing fabric. Crap, it's already grimy from the ground, wet with spilled beer. I scrunch it up into a dirty ball. I'll just have to do it without the disguise. There are so many people here I'm hardly going to stand out.

"Oh, *salut!*"

I turn to see a stupidly pretty girl wearing a huge flower crown and a floaty white peasant dress splattered with blood. It takes me a moment to place her: Mimi's flatmate. Camille: that was it.

"It's you!" she says. "You're Ben's sister, right?" So much for trying to blend in.

"Um. I hope this is OK? I heard the music—"

"*Plus on est de fous, plus on rit*, you know? The more the merrier! Hey, such a shame Ben isn't here." A little pout. "That guy seems to love a party!"

"So you know my brother?"

She wrinkles her tiny freckled nose. "Ben? *Oui, un peu.* A little."

"And they all like him? The Meuniers, I mean? The family?"

"But of course. Everyone loves him! Jacques Meunier likes him a lot, I think. Maybe even more than his own children. Oh—" She stops, like she's remembered something. "Antoine. He doesn't like him."

I remember the scene in the courtyard that first morning. "Do you think there might have been something . . . well, between my brother and Antoine's wife?"

The smile vanishes. "Ben and Dominique? *Jamais.*" A fierceness to the way she says it. "They flirted. But it was nothing more than that."

I try a different tack. "You said you saw Ben on Friday, talking to Mimi on the stairs?"

She nods.

"What time was that? What I mean is . . . did you see him after that? Did you see him that night at all?"

A tiny hesitation. Then: "I wasn't here that night," she says. Now she seems to spot someone over my shoulder. "*Coucou Simone!*" She turns back to me. "I must go. Have fun!" A little wave of her hand. The carefree party girl seems to be back. But when I asked her about the night Ben disappeared, she didn't seem quite so happy-go-lucky. She suddenly seemed very keen to stop talking. And for a moment I thought I saw the mask slip. A glimpse of someone totally different underneath.

Mimi

FOURTH FLOOR

BY THE TIME I GET down to the *cave* there are already so many people crammed inside. I'm never good with crowds at the best of times, with people invading my space. Camille's friend Henri has brought his decks and a massive speaker and is playing "La Femme" at top volume. Camille's greeting newcomers at the entrance in her *Midsommar* dress, the flower crown wobbling on her head as she jumps up and throws her arms around people.

"Ah, *salut* Gus, Manu—*coucou* Dédé!"

No one pays me much attention even though it's my place. They've come for Camille, they're all her friends. I pour ten centimeters of vodka into a glass and start drinking.

"*Salut* Mimi."

I look down. *Merde*. It's Camille's friend LouLou. She's sitting on some guy's lap, drink in one hand, cigarette in the other. She's dressed as a cat; a headband with black lace ears, silk leopard-print slip dress falling off one shoulder. Long brown hair all tangled like she just got out of bed and her lipstick smudged but in a sexy way. The perfect Parisienne. Or like those Instagram cretins in their Bobo espadrilles and cat-eye liner doing fuck-me eyes at the lens. That's how people think French girls should look. Not like me with my home-cut mullet and pimples round my mouth.

"I haven't seen you for so long." She waves her cigarette—she's also one of those girls who lights cigarettes outside cafés but doesn't actually inhale, just holds them and lets the smoke drift everywhere while she gestures with her pretty little hands. Hot ash lands on my arm. "*I* remember," she says, her eyes widening. "It was at that bar in the park . . . August. *Mon Dieu*, I've never seen you like that. You were *crazy*." A cute little giggle for weirdo Mimi.

At this moment the music changes. And I can barely believe it but it's that song. "Heads Will Roll," by the Yeah Yeah Yeahs. It feels like fate. And suddenly I'm back there.

IT WAS TOO hot to be inside so I suggested to Camille we go to this bar, Rosa Bonheur, in the Parc des Buttes-Chaumont. I hadn't told Camille but knew Ben might be there. He was writing a piece on the bar; I'd heard him talking to his editor through the apartment's open windows.

Since he lent me that Yeah Yeah Yeahs record I'd Googled the lead singer, Karen O. I'd tried dressing like her and when I did I felt like someone else. I'd spent the afternoon cutting my hair into her short, jagged style. And that evening I put on my Karen O outfit: a thin white tank top, painted my lips red, ringed my eyes in black eyeliner. At the last moment I took off my bra.

"*Waouh!*" Camille breathed, when I came out. "You look so . . . different. Oh my God . . . I can see your *nénés*!" She grinned. "Who's this for?"

"*Va te faire foutre.*" I told her to fuck off because I was embarrassed. "It's not *for* anyone." And it was hardly anything compared to what she was wearing: a loose-knit gold mesh dress that stopped just below her *chatte*.

Outside the streets were so hot you could feel the burning pavement through the soles of your shoes and the air was shimmering with dust and exhaust fumes. And then the most horrible coincidence: just as we were leaving through the front gate there was Papa, coming in the other direction. Despite the heat I felt cold all over. I wanted to die. I knew the exact moment when he saw me; his expression shifting dangerously.

"*Salut*," Camille said, a little wave. He smiled at her—always a smile for Camille; like every other guy on earth. She was wearing a jacket buttoned over her dress so you couldn't see that she was pretty much naked beneath. I've noticed that she has this way of being exactly what men want her to be. With Papa she has always been so demure, so innocent, all "*oui Monsieur*" and "*non Monsieur*" from beneath her lowered eyelashes.

Papa turned from Camille to me. "What are you wearing?" he asked, his eyes glittering.

"I . . ." I stammered. "It's so hot, I thought . . ."

"*Tu ressembles à une petite putain.*" That's what he said. I remember it so clearly because I felt the words like they were being burned into me: I can still feel the sting of them now. *You look like a little slut.* He'd never spoken to me like that before. "And what have you done to your hair?"

I put my hand up, touched my new Karen O fringe.

"I'm ashamed of you. Do you hear me? Never dress like this again. Go and change."

His tone scared me. I nodded. "*D'accord, Papa.*"

We followed him back into the building. But as soon as he had disappeared into the penthouse, Camille grabbed my hand and we ran out of there and along the street to the Metro and I tried to forget about it, tried to be just another carefree nineteen-year-old out for the night.

The park felt like a jungle, not part of the city: steam rising up off the grass, the bushes, the trees. A big crowd around the bar. This buzz, this wild energy. I could feel the beat of the music deep under my rib cage, vibrating through my whole body. There were people wearing way less than me, less than Camille even: girls in tiny bikinis who'd probably spent the day sunbathing on the Paris Plages, those artificial beaches by the river they construct in the summer. The air smelled like sweat and suntan lotion and hot, dry grass and the sticky sweet of cocktails.

I drank my first Aperol Spritz like it was lemonade. I still felt sick about the look on Papa's face. *A little slut.* The way he spat out the words. I drank the second one quickly too. Then I didn't care so much.

The girl at the decks turned the music up and people started dancing. Camille took my hand and dragged me into the crowd. There were some friends of ours—no, hers—from the Sorbonne. There were pills going round from a little plastic baggie. That's not me. I drink but I never take drugs.

"*Allez Mimi*," LouLou said, after she'd placed the tab on her tongue and swallowed it. "*Pourquoi pas?*" Come on, Mimi. Why not? "Just a half?"

And maybe I really had turned into someone else because I took the little half of the tab she held out to me. I kept it on my tongue for a second, let it dissolve.

After that it got blurry. Suddenly I was dancing and I was right in the middle of the crowd and I just wanted to carry on forever in the middle of all those sweaty bodies, these strangers. It seemed like everyone was smiling at me, love just pouring out of them.

People were dancing on tables. Someone lifted me up onto one. I didn't care. I was someone different, someone new. Mimi was gone. It was wonderful.

And then the song came on: "Heads Will Roll." At the same moment I looked over and I saw him. Ben. Down there, in the middle of the crowd. A pale gray T-shirt and jeans, despite the heat. A bottle of beer in his hand. It was like something from a film. I'd spent so much time watching him in his apartment, watching him across the table at dinner, it felt so weird to see him in the real world, surrounded by strangers. I had started to feel like he belonged to me.

And then he turned, like the pressure of my eyes had been enough for him to know I was there, and he raised a hand and smiled. There was a current running through me. I went to step toward him. But suddenly I was falling; I had forgotten about the table, and the ground was rushing up to meet me—

"Mimi. Mimi? Who are you here with?"

I couldn't see the others. All the faces that had seemed to be smiling before weren't now. I could see them looking and I could hear laughter and it seemed like I was surrounded by a pack of wild animals, teeth gnashing, eyes staring. But he was there; and I felt like he would keep me safe.

"I think you need some air." He put out his hand. I grasped hold of it. It was the first time he had touched me. I didn't want to let go, even after he had pulled me up. I didn't ever want to let go. He had beautiful hands, the fingers long, elegant. I wanted to put them in my mouth, to taste his skin.

The park was dark, so dark, away from the lights and sounds of the bar. Everything was a million miles away. The farther we went the more it felt like none of the rest of it was real. Just him. The sound of his voice.

We went down to the lake. He made to go and sit on a bench but I saw a tree right next to the water, roots spreading beneath the surface. "Here," I said. He sat down beside me. I could smell him: clean sweat and citrus.

He passed me an Evian bottle. Suddenly I was thirsty, so thirsty. "Not too much," he said. "Steady on—that's enough." He took the bottle away from me. We sat there for a while in silence. "How do you feel? Want to go back and find your friends?"

No. I shook my head. I didn't want that. I wanted to stay here in the dark with the hot breeze moving the tall trees above us and the lapping of the lake water against the banks.

"They're not my friends."

He took out a cigarette. "You want one? I suppose it might help . . ."

I took one, put it between my lips. He went to pass me the lighter. "You do it," I said.

I loved watching his fingers working the lighter, like he was casting some spell. The tip lit, glowed. I sucked in the smoke.

"*Merci,*" I said.

Suddenly the shadows under the next tree along seemed to move. There was someone there. No . . . two people. Tangled together. I heard a moan. Then a whisper: "*Je suis ta petite pute.*" *I'm your little whore.*

Normally I would have looked away. I would have been so embarrassed. But I couldn't take my eyes off them. The pill, the darkness, him sitting so close—that most of all—it loosened something inside me. Loosened my tongue.

"I've never had that," I whispered, looking toward the couple under the tree. And I found myself telling him my most embarrassing secret. That while Camille brought back different guys every week—sometimes girls, too—I'd never actually had sex with anyone. Except right then I didn't feel embarrassed; it felt like I could say anything.

"Papa's so strict," I said. I thought of how he had looked at me earlier. *A little slut.* "He said this horrible thing this evening . . . about how I looked. And sometimes I get this feeling, like he's ashamed, like he doesn't really like me that much. He looks at me, talks to me, like I'm an . . . an imposter, or something." I didn't think I was explaining very well. I'd never said any of this to anyone. But Ben was listening and nodding and, for the first time, I felt heard.

Then he spoke. "You're not a little girl any longer, Mimi. You're a grown woman. Your father can't control you anymore. And what you just described? The way he makes you feel? Use it, to drive yourself. Use it for inspiration in your art. All true artists are outsiders." I looked at him. He'd spoken so fiercely. It felt like he was talking from experience. "I'm adopted," he said then. "In my opinion, families are overrated."

I looked toward him, sitting so close in the darkness. It made sense. It was part of that connection between us, the one I'd felt since the first time I saw him. We were both outsiders.

"And you know what?" he said—and his voice was still different than usual. More raw. More urgent. "It's not about where you came from. What kind of shit might have happened to you in the past. It's about who *you* are. What you do with the opportunities life presents to you."

And then he put his hand gently on my arm. The lightest touch. The pads of his fingertips were hot against my skin. The feeling seemed to travel straight from my arm right to the very center of me. He could have done anything to me right there in the dark and I'd have been his.

And then he smiled. "It looks good, by the way."

"*Quoi?*"

"Your hair."

I put my hand up to touch it. I could feel where the hair was sticking to my forehead with sweat.

He smiled at me. "It suits you."

And that was the moment. I leaned over and I grabbed hold of his face in both hands and kissed him. I wanted more. I half-clambered on top of him, tried to straddle him.

"Hey," he laughed, pulling back, pushing me gently away, wiping his mouth. "Hey, Mimi. I like you too much for that."

I got it, then. Not here; not like this: not for the first time. The first time between us had to be special. Perfect.

Maybe you could say it was the pill. But that was the moment I felt myself fall in love with him. I thought I had been in love once before but it didn't work out. Now I knew how false the other time had been. Now I understood. I'd been waiting for Ben.

THE SONG ENDS and the spell is broken. I'm back in the *cave*, surrounded by all these idiots in their stupid Halloween costumes. They're playing Christine and the Queens now, everyone howling along to the chorus. People shoving past me, ignoring me, like always.

Wait. I've just spotted a face in the crowd. A face that has no business being at this party.

Putain de merde.

What the hell is *she* doing here?

Jess

I MOVE THROUGH THE CAVE, deeper into the crowd of masked faces and writhing bodies. The party's getting wild; I'm pretty sure I spot a couple up against a wall having sex or something close to it and a little way on a small group doing lines. I wonder if the room full of wine has been locked. I reckon this many people could put quite a dent in those racks of bottles.

"*Veux-tu un baiser de vampire?*" a guy asks me. I see that he's dressed as Dracula in a plasticky cape and some fake fangs—it's almost as crap a costume as my ghost outfit was.

"Erm . . . sorry, what?" I say, turning toward him.

"A Vampire's Kiss," he says in English, with a grin. "I asked if you want one?" For a moment I wonder if he's suggesting we make out. Then I look down and realize he's holding out a glass swimming with bright red liquid.

"What's in it?"

"Vodka, grenadine . . . maybe some Chambord." He shrugs. "Mostly vodka."

"OK. Sure." I could do with some Dutch courage. He hands it over. I take a sip—Jesus, it's even more grim than it looks, the metallic hit of the vodka beneath the sticky sweet of the syrup and raspberry liqueur. It tastes like something we might have served at the Copacabana, and that's not a good thing. But it's worth it for the vodka, even if I'd really prefer to take it neat. I take another long glug, braced this time for the sweetness.

"I've never met you before," he says, sounding almost more French now he's speaking English. "What's your name?"

"Jess. You?"

"Victor. *Enchanté.*"

"Er . . . thanks." I get straight to the point. "Hey, do you know Ben? Benjamin Daniels. From the third floor?"

He makes a face. "*Non, désolé.*" He looks genuinely sorry to have let me down. "I like your accent," he adds. "It's cool. You're from London, *non?*"

"Yup," I say. It's not exactly true, but then where am I from, really?

"And you're a friend of Mimi's?"

"Er—yes, I suppose you could say that." As in: I've met her precisely twice and she's never seemed exactly delighted to see me, but I'm not going to go into particulars.

He raises his eyebrows in surprise, and I wonder if I've made some sort of mistake.

"It's just . . . most people here are friends of Camille. No one really knows Mimi. She—how do you say it in English?—keeps herself to herself. Kind of intense. A bit—" He makes a gesture that I take to mean: "cuckoo."

"I don't know her *that* well," I say, quickly.

"Some people don't get why Camille's friends with Mimi. But I say—you just have to look at Mimi's apartment to know why. Mimi's got rich parents. You know what I'm saying?" He points up toward the apartment. "In this part of town? Seriously expensive. That is some *sick crib.*" He attempts to do the last two words in a kind of American accent.

In other circumstances I could almost feel sorry for Mimi. That people would assume someone's only friends with you because of your money: that's rough. I mean, it's never a problem I've had to deal with, but still.

"So what are you?" he asks.

"What?" A beat, and then I realize he means my costume.

"Oh—right." Shit. I look down at my outfit: jeans and old bobbly sweater. "Well, I was a ghost but now I'm just an ex-barmaid who's sick of everyone's shit."

"*Quoi?*" He frowns.

"It's—er, a British thing," I tell him. "It might not translate."

"Oh right." He nods. "Cool."

An idea hits me. If Camille and Mimi are down here then no one is up there, in the apartment. I could take a look around.

"Hey," I say, "Victor—could you do me a favor?"

"Tell me."

"I really need to pee. But I don't think there's an, er—*toilette*—down here?"

He looks suddenly uncomfortable: clearly French boys get as embarrassed about such matters as their British counterparts.

"Could you ask Camille if we can borrow the key to the place?" I smile my most winning smile, the one I'd use on the big tippers at the bar. Little hair flip. "I'd be *so* grateful."

He grins back. "*Bien sûr.*"

Bingo. Maybe Ben's not the only one with the charm.

I sip my drink while I wait: it's growing on me, now. Or maybe that's the vodka kicking in. Victor comes back a few minutes later, holds up a key.

"Amazing," I say, holding out my hand.

"I'll come with you," he says, with a grin. Crap. I wonder what he thinks is going to come out of this. But maybe it helps me look less suspicious if we go together.

I follow Victor up out of the *cave*, up the dark staircase. We take the lift—his suggestion—and we end up pressed against each other as there's barely room for one person. I can smell his breath— cigarettes and vodka, not a totally unappealing combination. And he's not bad-looking. But too pretty for my liking; you could cut a lemon on his jawline. Besides, he's basically a child.

I have a sudden flashback to Nick and me a couple of hours ago on the roof terrace. That moment, after he'd taken the leaf out of my hair—when he didn't move away as quickly as he should have. That snatched piece of time, just before the lights went out, when I was convinced he was going to kiss me. What would have happened if it hadn't suddenly gone dark? If I hadn't gone sneaking into the rest of the apartment and found that photograph? Would we have gone back to his apartment, fallen into his bed together—

"You know, I've always wanted to be with an older woman," Victor says, earnestly, jolting me back into the real world.

Steady on, mate, I think. And besides, I'm only twenty-eight.

The lift grinds to a halt on the fourth floor. Victor unlocks the door to the apartment. There are a load of bottles and crates of beer stacked in the main room—must be extra party supplies.

"Hey," I say. "Why don't you fix us a couple more drinks while I go and pee? This time big on the vodka please, less of the red stuff."

There's a corridor leading off the main room with several doors. The layout reminds me a little of the penthouse flat, only everything here is more cramped and instead of original artworks on the walls there are peeling posters—CINDY SHERMAN: CENTRE POMPIDOU and a tour list for someone called DINOS. The first room I come to is an absolute tip: the floor scattered with clothes, lace lingerie in bright sorbet colors and shoes—bras and thongs tangled around the sharp points of heels. A dressing table covered in makeup, about twenty mashed lipsticks all missing their lids. The air's so heavily scented with perfume and cigarette smoke it gives me an instant headache. A huge poster on one wall of Harry Styles in a tutu and, on the opposite, Dua Lipa in a tux. I think of Mimi and her scowl, her jagged, grungy fringe. I'm pretty sure this isn't her vibe. I close the door.

The next room has to be Mimi's. Dark walls. Big black and white angry prints on the walls—one of a freaky, blank-eyed woman—lots of serious-looking arty tomes on the bookshelf. A record player with a load of vinyls in a special case next to it. The one on the turntable is by the Yeah Yeah Yeahs: *It's Blitz!*

I creep across to the window. It turns out that Mimi's got a perfect diagonal view into the main living space of Ben's apartment, across the courtyard. I can see his desk, the sofa. Interesting. I think of her dropping her wine glass earlier when I spoke about Ben. She's hiding something, I know it.

I open the cupboard, search through drawers of clothes. Nothing to note. It's all so neat, almost anally so. But the problem is I don't know what I'm looking for—and I suspect I don't have much time before Victor starts wondering why I'm taking so long.

I get on my knees and grope around under the bed. My hand connects with what feels like material wrapped around something harder, wood maybe, and I just know I've found something significant. I get a hold of the whole lot, pull it toward me. A piece of gray material falls open to reveal a ragged pile of artists' canvases, slashed and torn into pieces. So much mess and chaos compared to the rest of the room.

I look more closely at the material they were wrapped in. It's a gray T-shirt with Acne on the label, an exact match for the ones in Ben's cupboard. I'm sure it's one of his. It even smells like his cologne. Why has Mimi been keeping her art stuff in one of Ben's T-shirts? More importantly: why has she got one of Ben's T-shirts at all?

"Jessie?" Victor calls. "Are you OK, Jessie?"

Shit. It sounds like he's getting closer.

I start trying to fit some of the scraps of canvas back together as quickly as I can. It's like doing a really messy jigsaw puzzle. Finally I've pieced enough pieces of the first one together to see the picture. I stand back. It's a really good likeness. She's even managed to get his smile, which others have called charming but I'd definitely tell him makes him look like a smarmy git. Here he is, right in front of me. Ben. Just as he is in life.

Except for one terrible, terrifying difference. I lift a hand to my mouth. His eyes have been removed.

"Jessie?" Victor calls again, "*où es-tu*, Jessie?"

I fit the next image together, and the next. Jesus. They're all of him. There's even one of him lying down and—Christ alive, that's way more of my brother than I ever needed to see. In every single one the eyes have been destroyed, punched or torn out with something.

I had a feeling Mimi was lying about knowing him the first time I met her. I suspected she was hiding something as soon as her wine glass hit the floor in Sophie Meunier's apartment. But I never expected anything like this. If these are anything to go by—if that nude painting is any clue—she knows Ben very well indeed. And feels strongly enough about him to have done some pretty serious damage to these paintings: those tears in the fabric could only have been made with something really sharp, or with a lot of force—or both.

I stand up but as I do a strange thing happens. It's like the whole room tilts with the movement. Whoa. I go to steady myself against the nightstand. I try to blink away the dizziness. I take a step backward and it happens again. As I stand, trying to get my balance, it feels like the ground is rolling around under my feet and everything around me is made of jelly, the walls collapsing inward.

I stagger out of the bedroom, into the corridor. I have to keep a hand out on both sides to stop myself from keeling over. And then Victor appears, at the end of the passage.

"Jessie—there you are. What were you doing?" He's walking toward me down the dark corridor. He smiles and his teeth are very white—just like a real vampire. My only way out is past him; he's blocking my escape. Even with my brain turned to syrup I know what this is. You don't work in twenty different divey bars and not know what this is. The drink some guy's offered to buy you, the freebie that is anything but. I never, ever fall for that shit. What the hell was I thinking? How could I have been so stupid? It's always the pretty ones, the seemingly harmless ones, the so-called nice guys.

"What the fuck was in that drink, Victor?" I ask.

And then everything goes black.

Mimi

FOURTH FLOOR

MORNING. I'M SITTING ON THE balcony watching the light seep into the sky. The joint I stole from Camille hasn't helped me relax: it's just making me feel sick and even more jittery. I feel . . . I feel like I'm trapped inside my own skin. Like I want to claw my way out.

I hurry out of the apartment and run down the twisting stairway to the *cave*, not wanting to meet anyone on the way. It's full of the detritus from the party last night: broken glass and spilled drinks and dropped accessories from people's costumes—wigs and devil's forks and witches' hats. I normally like it better down here, in the dark and the quiet: another place to hide away. But right now I can't be here either because his Vespa is there, leaning against the wall.

I don't—can't—look at it as I pull my bicycle from the rack beside it.

He always went out on that Vespa. I wanted to know about his life, I wanted to follow him into the city, see where he went, what he did, who he met with, but it was impossible because he used that bike to go everywhere. So one day I went down into the *cave* and I stabbed a small hole into the front wheel with the very sharp blade of my canvas-cutting knife. That was better.

He wouldn't be able to use it for a few days. I only did it because I loved him.

That afternoon I saw him leave on foot. My plan had worked. I went after him, followed him into the Metro and got onto the next carriage. He got off in this really shitty part of town. What the hell was he doing there? He went and sat down in this greasy-looking kebab place. I sat in a shisha bar across the road and ordered a Turkish coffee and tried to look like I fitted in among all the old guys puffing away on their rose-scented tobacco. Ben was making me do things I never normally would, I realized. He was making me brave.

Ten minutes or so later a girl came and joined Ben. She was tall and thin, a hood up over her head, which she only took down once she was sitting opposite him. I felt my stomach turn over when I saw her face. Even from across the street I could see that she was beautiful: dark chocolate hair with a sharp fringe that looked so much better than my home-cut one, a model's cheek-bones. And young: probably only my age. Yes, her clothes were bad: a fake-looking leather jacket with that hoodie underneath and cheap jeans, but they somehow made her seem even more beautiful by contrast. As I watched them together I could actually feel my heart hurting, a hot coal burning behind my rib cage.

I waited for him to kiss her, to touch her face, her hand, to stroke her hair—anything—waited for the worse pain I knew would come when I saw him do it. But nothing happened. They just sat there talking. I realized it seemed quite formal. Like they didn't actually know each other that well. There was definitely nothing between them to suggest they might be lovers. Finally he passed her something. I tried to see. It looked like a phone or a camera, maybe. Then she got up and left, and he did too. They went in different directions. I still couldn't work out why he'd been talking to her, or what he might have given her, but I was so relieved I could have cried. He hadn't been unfaithful to me. I knew I shouldn't have doubted him.

Later, back in my room, I thought of that night in the park, how we'd shared that cigarette. The two of us in the dark by the lake. The taste of his mouth when I'd kissed him. I thought about it when I lay in bed at night, fingers exploring. And I whispered those words I heard in the darkness by the lake. *Je suis ta petite pute.* I'm your little whore.

This was it, I knew it. This was why I'd waited so long. I was different from Camille. I couldn't just screw around with random guys. It had to be something real. *Un grand amour.* I had thought I'd been in love before. The art teacher, Henri, at my school—Les Soeurs Servantes du Sacré Coeur. I'd known we had a connection from the beginning. He'd smiled at me in that first lesson, told me how talented I was. But later, when I sent him the paintings I had made of him, he took me aside and told me they weren't appropriate—even though I'd worked so hard on them, on getting the proportions right, the tone: just like he'd taught us. And when I sent them to his wife instead, but cut up into little pieces, they made some kind of formal complaint. And then—well, I don't want to go into all that. I heard they left for another school abroad.

I didn't know where this part of me had been hiding. The part that could fall in love. Actually: I did. I'd been keeping it locked away. Deep down inside me. Terrified that sort of weakness would make me vulnerable again. But I was ready now. And Ben was different. Ben would be loyal to me.

DOWN IN THE *cave*, I tear my eyes away from his Vespa. I feel like there's a metal band around my ribs stopping me from taking in enough air. And in my ears still this horrible rushing sound, the white noise, the storm. I just need to make it stop.

I yank my bike free and haul it up the stairs. I can feel the pressure building inside me as I wheel it across the courtyard, as I push it along the cobbled street . . . all the way down to the main road where the morning rush-hour traffic is roaring past. I jump onto the saddle, look quickly in each direction through the tears blurring my eyes, push straight out into the street.

There's a screech of brakes. The blare of a horn. Suddenly I'm lying on my side on the tarmac, the wheels spinning. My whole body feels bruised and torn. My heart's pounding.

That was so close.

"You stupid little bitch," the van driver screams, hanging out of his open window and gesturing at me with his cigarette. "What the fuck were you doing? What the hell were you thinking, pulling out into the road without looking?"

I yell back, my language even worse than his. I call him *un fils de pute*, son of a whore, *un sac a merde*, a bag of shit . . . I tell him he can go fuck himself. I tell him he can't drive for shit.

Suddenly the front door of the apartment building clangs open and the concierge is running out. I've never seen that woman move so fast. She always seems so old and hunched. But maybe she moves more quickly when you're not looking. Because she's always there when you least expect to see her. Appearing around corners and out of shadows, lurking in the background. I don't know why we even have a concierge. Most places don't have them any longer. We should have just installed a modern intercom system. It would be much better than having her around, snooping on everyone. I don't like the way she watches. Especially how she watches me.

Without saying anything she puts out her hands, helps me to stand up. She's much stronger than I ever would have guessed.

Then she looks at me closely; intensely. I feel like she's trying to tell me something. I look away. It makes me think she knows something. Like maybe she knows everything.

I throw off her hand. "*Ça va,*" I say. *I'm OK.* "I can get up on my own."

My knees are still stinging like a kid's who has taken a tumble in the playground. And my bike chain has come off. But that's the worst of it.

It could have ended so differently. If I hadn't been such a coward. Because the truth is, I *was* looking. That was the point.

I knew exactly what I was doing.

It was so close. Just not close enough.

Sophie

I DESCEND THE STAIRCASE WITH Benoit trotting at my heels. As I pass the third floor I pause. I can feel her there behind the door, like something poisonous at the heart of this place.

It was the same with him. His presence upset the building's equilibrium. I seemed to see him everywhere after that dinner on the terrace: in the stairwell, crossing the courtyard, talking to the concierge. We never talk to the concierge beyond issuing instructions. She is a member of staff, that sort of divide must be respected. Once I even saw him following her into her cabin. What could they be speaking about in there? What might she be telling him?

When the third note came, it wasn't left in the letterbox. It was pushed beneath the door of the apartment, at a time when I suppose my blackmailer knew Jacques would be out. I had returned from the boulangerie with Jacques' favorite quiche, which I have bought for him every Friday for as long as I can remember. When I saw the note I dropped the box I was holding. Pastry shattered across the floor. It sent a thrill through me that I knew had to be fear but for a moment felt almost like excitement. And that was just as disturbing.

I had been invisible for so long, any currency spent long ago. But these notes, even as they frightened me, felt like the first time in a very long while that I had been seen.

I knew I could not stay in the building for a moment longer.

Outside the streets were still white with heat, the air shimmering. At the cafés tourists clustered at pavement tables and sweated into their *thé glacés* and *citron pressés* and wondered why they didn't feel refreshed. But in the restaurant it was dim and cool as some underwater grotto, as I had known it would be. Dark paneled walls, white tablecloths, huge paintings upon the walls. They had given me the best table, of course—Meunier SARL has supplied them with rare vintages over the years—and the air-conditioning sent an icy plume down the back of my silk shirt as I sipped my mineral water.

"Madame Meunier." The waiter came over. "*Bienvenue.* The usual?"

Every time I have eaten there with Jacques I have ordered the same. The endive salad with walnuts and tiny dabs of Roquefort. An aging wife is one thing; a fat wife is another.

But Jacques was not there.

"*L'entrecôte,*" I said.

The waiter looked at me as though I had asked for a slab of human flesh. The steak has always been Jacques' choice.

"But Madame," he said, "it is so *hot*. Perhaps the oysters—we have some wonderful *pousses en Claire*—or a little salmon, cooked *sous vide* . . ."

"The steak," I repeated. "Blue."

The last time I ate steak was when a gynecologist, all those years ago, prescribed it for fertility; doctors here still recommend red meat and wine for many ailments. Months of eating like a caveman. When that didn't work came the indignity of the treatments. The injections into my buttocks. Jacques' glances of vague disgust. I had inherited two stepsons. What was this obsession with having a child? I could not explain that I simply wanted someone to love. Wholehearted, unreserved, requited. Of course, the treatments didn't work. And Jacques refused to adopt. The paperwork, the scrutiny into his business affairs—he would not stand for it.

The steak came and I cut into it. Watched as the blood ran thin and palest pink from the incision. It was then that I looked up and saw him, Benjamin Daniels, in the corner of the restaurant. He had his back to me, though I could see his reflection in the mirror that ran along the wall. Something elegant about the line of his back: the way he sat, hands in his pockets. The posture of someone very comfortable in their own skin.

I felt my pulse quicken. What was he doing here?

He glanced up and "caught" me watching him in the mirror. But I suspected he knew I was there all along, had been waiting for me to notice him. His reflection raised the glass of beer.

I looked away. Sipped my mineral water.

A few seconds later, a shadow fell across the table. I looked up. That ingratiating smile. He wore a crumpled linen shirt and shorts, legs bare and brown. His clothes were entirely inappropriate for the restaurant's formality. And yet he seemed so relaxed in the space. I hated him for it.

"Hello Sophie," he said.

I bristled at the familiarity, then remembered I had asked him not to call me "Madame." But the way he said my name: it felt like a transgression.

"May I?" He indicated the chair. To do anything other than agree would have been rude. I nodded, to show I didn't care either way what he did.

It was the first time I had been so close to him. Now I saw that he wasn't handsome, not in the traditional sense. His features were uneven. His confidence, charisma: that was what made him attractive.

"What are you doing here?" I asked.

"I'm reviewing the place," he said. "Jacques suggested it at dinner. I haven't eaten yet but I'm already impressed by the space—the atmosphere, the art."

I glanced at the painting he was looking at. A woman on her knees: powerfully built, almost masculine. Strong limbs, strong jaw. Nothing elegant about her, only a kind of feral strength. Her head thrown back, howling at the moon like a dog. The splayed legs, the skirt rucked . . . it was almost sexual. If you could get close enough to sniff it, I imagined it wouldn't be paint you smelled but blood. I felt suddenly very aware of the sweat that might have soaked into the silk beneath my arms on the walk over here, hidden half-moons of damp in the fabric.

"What do you think?" he asked. "I love Paula Rego."

"I'm not sure I agree," I said.

He pointed to my lip. "You have a little—just there."

I put the corner of the napkin up to my mouth and dabbed. Took it away and saw that the thick white linen was stained with blood. I stared at it.

He coughed. "I sense—look, I just wanted to say that I hope we haven't got off on the wrong foot. The other day—when I commented on your accent. I hope I didn't seem rude."

"*Mais non,*" I said. "What would make you think that?"

"Look, I took French studies at Cambridge, you see, I'm just fascinated by such things."

"I was not offended," I told him. "*Pas du tout.*" Not at all.

He grinned. "That's a relief. And I enjoyed the dinner on the roof terrace so much. It was kind of you to invite me."

"I didn't invite you," I said. "That dinner was all Jacques' idea." Perhaps it sounded rude. But it was also true. No invitation would be offered without Jacques' say-so.

"Poor Jacques, then," he said, with a rueful smile. "The weather that night! I've never seen anyone so furious. I actually thought he was going to try and take the storm on, like Lear. The look on his face!"

I laughed. I couldn't help it. I should have been appalled, offended. No one made a joke at my husband's expense. But it was the surprise of it. And he'd pulled such an accurate impression of Jacques' outraged expression.

Trying to regain my composure I reached for my water, took a sip. But I felt lighter than I had in a very long time.

"Tell me," he said, "what is it like being married to a man like Jacques Meunier?"

The sip caught in my throat. Now I was coughing, my eyes watering. One of the waiters ran forward to offer assistance: I waved him away with a hand. All I could think was: what did Ben know? What could Nicolas have told him?

"Sorry." He gave a quick smile. "I don't think my question came out quite right. Sometimes I can be so clumsy in French. What I meant was: being married to such a successful businessman. What's it like?"

I didn't answer. The look I gave him by way of reply said: *you don't frighten me*. Except I was frightened. He was the sender of the notes, I was certain of it now. He was the one collecting those envelopes of cash I left beneath the loose step.

"I just meant," he said, "that should you ever want to give an interview, I'd be so interested to talk to you. You could talk about what it is to run such a successful business—"

"It's not my business."

"Oh, I'm sure that isn't true. I'm sure you must—"

"No." I leaned across the table to emphasize the point, tapped out each word with a fingernail on the tablecloth. "The business is nothing to do with me. *Comprenez-vous?*" *Do you understand?*

"OK. Well." He looked at his watch. "The offer still stands. It could be . . . more of a lifestyle piece. On you as the quintessential Parisienne, something like that. You know where I am." He smiled.

I just looked at him. Perhaps you don't understand who you're dealing with, here. There are things I have had to do to get to where I am. Sacrifices I have had to make. People I have had to climb over. You are nothing compared to all that.

"Anyway," he stood. "I better be going. I have a meeting with my editor. I'll see you around."

When I was sure he had gone I called the waiter over. "The 1998."

His eyes widened. He looked as though he was about to offer an alternative to such a heavy red in that heat. Then he saw my expression. He nodded, scurried away, returned with the bottle.

As I drank I remembered a night early in my marriage. The Opéra Garnier, where we watched *Madame Butterfly* beneath Chagall's painted ceiling and sipped chilled champagne in the bar in the interval and I hoped Jacques might show me the famous reliefs of the moon and the sun painted in pure gold on the domed ceilings of the little chambers at each end. But he was more interested in pointing out people, clients of his. Ministers for certain governmental departments, businessmen, significant figures from the French media. Some of them even I recognized, though they didn't know me. But they all knew Jacques. Returning his nod with tight little nods of their own.

I knew exactly what sort of man I was marrying. I went into the whole thing clear-eyed. I knew what I'd be getting out of it. No, our marriage would not always be perfect. But what marriage is? And he gave me my daughter, in the end. I could forgive anything for that.

* * *

NOW, I PAUSE for a moment on the landing outside the third-floor apartment. Stare at the brass number 3. Remember standing in this exact spot all those weeks ago. I'd spent the rest of the afternoon at the restaurant, drinking my way through the 1998 vintage as all the waiters no doubt watched, appalled. *Madame Meunier has gone mad.* As I drank I thought about Benjamin Daniels and his impertinence, about the notes, the horrible power they had over me. My rage blossomed. For the first time in a long time I felt truly alive. As though I might be capable of anything.

I came back to the apartment as dusk was falling, climbed the stairs, stood on this same spot and knocked on his door.

Benjamin answered it quickly, before I had a chance to change my mind.

"Sophie," he said. "What a pleasant surprise."

He was wearing a T-shirt, jeans; his feet were bare. There was music playing on the record player behind him, a record spinning round lazily. An open beer in his hand. It occurred to me that he might have someone there with him, which I hadn't even considered.

"Come in," he said. I followed him into the apartment. I suddenly felt as though I was trespassing, which was absurd. This was my home, he was the intruder.

"Can I get you a drink?" he asked.

"No. Thank you."

"Please—I have some wine open." He gestured to his beer bottle. "It's wrong—my drinking while you don't."

Somehow he had already managed to wrong-foot me, by being so gracious, so charming. I should have been prepared for it.

"No," I said. "I don't want any. This is not a social visit." Besides, I could still feel my head swimming from the wine I had drunk in the restaurant.

He grimaced. "I apologize," he said. "If this is about the

restaurant—my questions—I know that was presumptuous of me. I realize I crossed a line."

"It's not that." My heart was beating very fast. I had been carried here by my anger, but now I felt afraid. Voicing this thing would bring it into the light, would finally make it real. "It's you, isn't it?"

He frowned. "What?" He hadn't expected this, I thought. Now it was his turn to be on the back foot. It gave me the confidence I needed to go on.

"The notes."

He looked nonplussed. "Notes?"

"You know what I'm talking about. The notes—the demands for payment. I have come to tell you that you do not want to threaten me. There is little I will not do to protect myself. I will . . . I will stop at nothing."

I can still hear his awkward, apologetic laugh. "Madame Meunier—Sophie—I'm so sorry but I have literally no idea what you're talking about. What notes?"

"The ones you have been leaving for me," I said. "In my letter-box. Under my door."

I watched his face so carefully, but I saw only confusion. Either he was a consummate actor, which I wouldn't have put past him, or what I was saying really didn't mean anything to him. Could it be true? I looked at him, at his bemused expression, and I realized, in spite of myself, that I believed him. But it didn't make sense. If not him, then who?

"I—" The room seemed to tilt a little: a combination of the wine I had drunk and this new realization.

"Would you like to sit down?" he asked.

And I did sit, because suddenly I wasn't sure that I could stand.

He poured me a glass of wine without asking, this time. I needed it. I took the offered glass and tried not to hold the stem so tightly that it snapped.

He sat down next to me. I looked at him—this man who had been a thorn in my side since he arrived, who had occupied so much space in my thoughts. Who had made me feel seen—with all the discomfort that came with that—just when I thought I had become invisible for good. Invisible had been safe, if occasionally lonely. But I had forgotten how exciting it could feel to be seen.

I was in a kind of trance, perhaps. All the wine I had drunk before coming here to face him. The pressure that had been building in me for weeks as my blackmailer taunted me. The loneliness that had been growing for years in secrecy and silence.

I leaned over and I kissed him.

Almost immediately I pulled away. I could not believe what I had done. I put a hand up to my face, touched my hot cheek.

He smiled at me. I hadn't seen this smile before. This was something new. Something intimate and secret. Something just for me.

"I—I need to leave." I put my wine glass down and as I did I knocked his beer bottle to the ground. "Oh, *mon Dieu*. I'm sorry—"

"I don't care about the beer." And then he cradled my head in his hands and pulled me toward him and kissed me back.

The scent of him, the foreignness of it, the alien feel of his lips on mine, the loss of my self-control: these were all a surprise. But not the kiss itself, not really. In some part of myself I had known I wanted him.

"Ever since that first day," he said, as though he were echoing my own thoughts, "when I saw you in the courtyard, I've wanted to know more about you."

"That's ridiculous," I said, because it was. But what made it feel less so was the way he was looking at me.

"It's not. I've been hoping to do that ever since that night at your drinks party. When it was just the two of us in your husband's study—"

I thought of the outrage I had felt, finding him in there looking at that photograph. The fear. But fear and desire are so tangled up in one another, after all.

"That's absurd," I said. "What about Dominique?"

"Dominique?" He seemed genuinely confused.

"I saw you two together at the drinks."

He laughed. "She could eye-fuck a statue. And it was convenient for me to be able to distract your husband from the fact that I was lusting after his wife."

He reached out and pulled me toward him again.

"This can't happen . . ."

But I think he heard my lack of conviction because he grinned. "I hate to say it. But it already *is* happening."

"We have to be careful," I whispered a few minutes later as I began unbuttoning my shirt. As I revealed the lingerie that had been bought at great expense but hardly ever seen by eyes other than my own. Revealed my body, denied so much pleasure, kept and kempt for a man who barely glanced at it.

He dropped to his knees in front of me, as though worshipping at my feet. Pushed down the tight wool of my trousers, finding the thin lace of my knickers with his lips, opening his mouth against me.

Nick

I DIDN'T SLEEP WELL LAST night, and not just because of the bass from the party in the *cave* thumping up the stairwell all night. In the bathroom I shake two more little blue pills into my hand. They're about the only thing keeping me functioning right now. I toss them back.

I wander out into the apartment. As I pass the iMac the screen flickers to life. Did I jolt it? If so I didn't notice. But there it is. The photograph of Ben and me. I stand frozen in place in front of it. Drawn to it in the same way, I suppose, that a self-harmer is drawn to run the razor blade over the skin of their wrist.

After that dinner on the rooftop everything was different. Something had shifted. I didn't like the way Papa had favored Ben. I didn't like the way Ben's eyes slid away from mine when he talked about our Europe trip. I also very much didn't like the fact that every time I suggested we go for a drink, he was too busy. Had to rush off to see his editor, to review some new restaurant. Avoiding my calls, my texts, avoiding my eye when we met on the stairs.

This wasn't how it was supposed to be. It wasn't what I'd planned when I had offered him the apartment. He had been the one to get in touch with me. His email had blown open the past. I had taken a huge risk, inviting him here. I had assumed we had an unspoken agreement.

I walk across to the wall behind my iMac, run my hands over the surface. Feel the thin crack in the plaster. There's a second staircase here. A hidden one. Antoine and I used to play in it when we were kids. Used it to hide from Papa, too, when he was in one of his dangerous moods. I am ashamed to admit this, but there were a couple of times when I used it to watch Ben, peering into his apartment, into his life. Trying to work out what he was up to. Wondering what he could be writing so busily on his laptop, who he was calling on his mobile—I strained to hear the words, but caught nothing.

Though he snubbed me, it seemed he did have time for the other residents of this place. I found them in the *cave* one afternoon when I came down to do my washing. Heard the laughter, first. Then Papa's voice: "Of course, when I inherited the business from their mother it was a mess. Had to make it profitable. Have to be creative now, with a wine business. Especially when the estate's no longer producing and it'll all turn to vinegar soon. Have to find ways to diversify."

"What's going on?" I called. "A private tasting?"

They stepped out of the wine cellar like two naughty schoolboys. Papa holding a bottle in one hand, two glasses in the other. Ben's teeth when he smiled were tinted from the wine he'd drunk. He held one of the few remaining magnum bottles of the 1996 vintage. A gift from my father, it seemed.

"Nicolas," Papa drawled. "I suppose you've come to break up the party?"

Not: *Would you like to join us, son? Care for a glass?* In all the time I have lived under his roof my father has never suggested the two of us do anything like their cozy little wine tasting. It was salt in the wound. The first proper betrayal. I'd told Ben what sort of man my father really is. Had he forgotten?

* * *

BEN GRINS OUT at me from the photograph on the screensaver. And there I am grinning away next to him, like the fool that I was. July, Amsterdam. The sun in our eyes. Talking to Jess has brought it all back. That evening Ben and I spent in the weed café. Telling him all about my birthday, the "gift" from Papa. How it was like a catharsis. How I felt cleansed, purged of it all.

Afterward, Ben and I wandered out into the darkening streets. Just kept walking, chatting. I wasn't sure where we were going; I don't think he had a clue either. Somewhere along the way we'd left the touristy part of town and the crowds behind: these canals were quieter, more dimly lit. Elegant old houses with long windows through which you could see people inside: talking over glasses of wine, eating dinner, a guy typing at a desk. This was somewhere people actually lived.

You couldn't hear anything other than the lapping of the water against the stone banks. Black water, black as ink, the lights from the houses dancing on it. And the smell, like moss and mold. An ancient smell. No queasy clouds of weed to walk through, here. I was sick of the reek of it. Sick, too, of the crush of other people's bodies, the chatter of other people's conversation. I was sick even of the two other guys: their voices, the stink of their pits, their sweaty feet. We'd spent too long together that summer. I'd heard every joke or story they had to tell. With Ben it was different, somehow—though I couldn't put my finger on why.

This quiet: I felt like I wanted to drink it in like a cold glass of water. It felt magical . . . And telling Ben all that stuff about my dad—you know when you've eaten something bad and after you vomit you feel empty but also kind of cleansed, almost better than before in some indefinable way?

"Thanks," I said again. "For listening. You won't tell anyone, will you? The other guys?"

"No, of course not," he said. "This is our secret, mate. If you like."

We were walking along a part of the canal now that was even darker; I think a couple of the lamps had stopped working. It was deathly quiet.

You know those moments in life that seem to happen so smoothly it feels like they've been scripted in advance? This was like that. I don't remember any conscious decision to move toward him. But the next thing I knew, I was kissing him. It was definitely me that made the first move, I know that—even if it was like my body moved before my brain had worked out what it was going to do.

I'd kissed plenty of people. Girls, I mean. Only ever girls. At house parties, or drunk after a formal, a college ball. Fooled around. And it wasn't unpleasant. But it had never felt any more intimate or exciting than, I don't know, a handshake. It didn't disgust me, exactly, but the whole time it was happening I'd found myself thinking about the logistical things—like whether I was using my fingers and tongue right, feeling a little queasy about how much saliva was being passed back and forth between us. It felt like a sport I was practicing, maybe trying to get better at. It never felt like something exciting, something that made my pulse quicken.

But this—this was different. It was as innate as breathing. It was strange how firm his mouth seemed after the softness of the girls' I'd kissed—I wouldn't have thought there would be a difference. And it seemed so right, somehow. Like it was the thing I had been waiting for, the thing that made sense.

I took hold of the chain around his neck, the one I had watched so many times appear and disappear beneath the line of his shirt, the one with the little figure of the saint hanging from it. I gave it a little tug, pulled him closer to me.

And then we were moving backward into the darkness—I

was pushing him into some secret corner, falling to my knees in front of him, again every movement so fluid, like it had all been written out in advance, like it was meant to be. Unzipping his fly and taking him in my mouth, the warmth and hardness, the secret scent of his skin. My knees stung where I knelt on the rough cobblestones. And even though I had never allowed myself to think about this, I must have thought about it, somewhere in my subconscious, somewhere in my deepest thoughts hidden even from myself, because I knew exactly what I was doing.

He smiled, afterward. A sleepy, lazy, stoned smile.

But for me, after that rush of euphoria, there was an immediate descent. I've never had a comedown like it. My knees hurt, my jeans were damp from something I'd knelt in.

"Fuck. Fuck—I don't know what happened there. Shit. I'm just . . . I'm so wasted." Which was a lie. I had been stoned, yes. But I'd never felt more clear-headed in my life. I'd never felt more alive, either—electric, wired—so many different things.

"*Mate*," he said, with a smile. "It's nothing to be worried about. We were a bit pissed, a lot stoned." He gestured around us, shrugged. "And it's not like anyone saw."

I couldn't believe how relaxed he was about it. But maybe at the back of my mind I'd known this about him; this side of him. I'd once heard someone at Cambridge describe him as an "omnivore"; wondered what that meant.

"Don't tell anyone," I told him. I was light-headed with fear, suddenly. "Look, you don't understand. This—it has to stay just between us. If it somehow got back . . . look, my dad, he wouldn't get it." The thought of him finding out was like a punch to the gut, it winded me just thinking about it. I could see his face, hear his voice. Could still remember what he'd said when I told him I didn't want that birthday gift, what was in that room: *What's wrong with you, son? Are you a* faggot? The disgust in his voice.

He actually might kill me, I thought. If he suspected. He'd probably prefer that to having a son like me. At the very least, he'd disinherit me. And while I didn't know how I felt about taking his money, I wasn't ready to give it up just yet.

AFTER AMSTERDAM I decided I never wanted to see Benjamin Daniels again. We drifted apart. I had a string of girlfriends. I left for the States for nearly a decade, didn't look back. Yeah, there were a couple of guys there: the freedom of thousands of miles of land and water—even if I still always seemed to hear my father's voice in my head. But nothing serious.

It doesn't mean I didn't think about that night later. In a way, I know I've been thinking about it ever since; trying not to. And then, all those years later: Ben's email. It had to mean something, him getting in touch like that, out of the blue. It couldn't just be a casual catch-up.

Except after that dinner on the terrace, when he'd so impressed Papa, I barely saw or spoke to him other than in passing. He even had time for the concierge, for God's sake, but not me—his old friend. He was ensconced here practically rent-free. He'd taken what he needed and then cut loose. I began to feel used. And when I thought about how shifty he was each time I approached him I felt a little frightened, too, though I couldn't put my finger on why. I thought of Antoine's words about Papa disinheriting us on a whim. It had seemed like madness at the time. But now . . . I began to feel that I didn't want Ben here after all. I began to feel that I wanted to take back the invitation. But I didn't know how to do it. He knew too much. Had so much he could use against me. I had to find another way to make him leave.

THE COMPUTER'S TIMER must have run out; the screen of my iMac goes black. It doesn't matter. I can still see the image. I have been haunted by it for over a decade.

I think about how I nearly kissed his sister last night. The sudden, shocking, wonderful resemblance to him when she turned her head just so, or frowned, or laughed. And also the resemblance of the moment: the darkness, the stillness. The two of us held apart from the rest of the world for just a beat.

That night in Amsterdam. It was the worst, most shameful thing I had ever done.

It was the best thing that had ever happened to me. That was how I used to see it, anyway. Until he came to stay.

Jess

I WAKE IN DARKNESS. THERE'S a heavy weight on my chest, a horrible taste in my mouth, my tongue dry and heavy like it doesn't belong to me. For a few long moments, everything that happened to me before now is a total blank. It feels like peering forward and staring into a black hole.

I grope around, trying to make out my surroundings. I seem to be lying on a bed. But which bed? Whose?

Fuck. What happened to me?

Gradually I remember: the party. That disgusting drink. Victor the vampire.

And then I see something I recognize. Some little green digits, glowing in the blackness. It's Ben's alarm clock. Somehow I'm back here, in the apartment. I blink at the numbers. 17:38. But that can't be right. That's the afternoon. That would mean I've been asleep for—Jesus Christ—the whole day.

I try to sit up. I make out two huge, glowing, slit-pupiled eyes a few inches from my nose. The cat is sitting on me—so that's the weight on my chest. It starts kneading its claws into my throat in painful little darts. I push it away: it hops off the bed. I look down at myself. I'm fully clothed, thank God. And I remember now, in flashes of memory: Victor was the one who got me down here after I blacked out in Mimi's apartment. Not the date-raping predator I suddenly thought he might be. In fact he'd seemed scared by the state I was in—left as quick as he could. I suppose at least he tried to help.

A flicker of memory. I found something last night. Something that felt important. But at first everything that happened only comes back to me in hazy, disjointed fragments. There are big missing patches like holes in a jigsaw. I know my dreams were really trippy. I recall an image of Ben shouting at me through a pane of glass; but I couldn't see his face clearly, the glass seemed warped. He was trying to warn me of something—but I couldn't hear what he was saying. And then suddenly I could see his face clearly but that was much, much worse. Because he didn't have any eyes. Someone had scratched them out.

Now I remember the paintings under Mimi's bed. Jesus Christ. That's what I found last night. Those tears in the canvas, like she'd ripped them all apart in some kind of frenzy. The slashes, the holes where the eyes should have been. And Ben's T-shirt, wrapped around them.

I haul myself out of bed, stumble into the main room. My head throbs. I might be small, but I'm not a cheap date—one drink is not enough to get me in that much of a state. It might not have been Victor, but I'm pretty sure of one thing: someone did this to me.

A loud trilling, so loud in the silence it makes me jump. My phone. Theo's name flashes up on the screen.

I pick up. "Hello?"

"I know what that card is." No niceties, no preamble.

"What?" I ask. "What are you talking about?"

"The card you gave me. The metal one, with the firework on it. I know what it is. Look, can you meet me at quarter to seven? So—in about an hour? The Palais Royal Metro station; we can walk from there. Oh, and try and look as smart as possible."

"I don't—"

But he's already hung up.

Mimi

I PUT THE STUFF IN her drink last night. It was so easy. There was ketamine going around and I got hold of some, shook the powder into her glass until it dissolved and asked one of Camille's friends to give it to the British girl with the red hair. He seemed only too pleased to do it: she's quite pretty, I suppose.

I had to do it. I couldn't have her there. But that doesn't mean I don't feel bad about it . . . I've been so careful my whole life about drugs—apart from that night in the park. And then to inflict them on someone else without them even knowing. That wasn't cool. It's not her fault she made the mistake of coming to this place. That's the worst part. She's probably not even a bad person.

But I know I am.

Camille comes out of her room wearing a silk slip, black rings of smudged makeup around her eyes. This is the first time she's surfaced all day.

"Hey. Last night was craaaazy. People really enjoyed it, don't you think?" She looks at me closely. "*Putain*, Mimi, you look like shit. What happened to your knees?" They still hurt from where I hit the tarmac in front of that van; the concierge insisted on dabbing some antiseptic onto the grazes. She grins. "Someone had a good night, *non*?"

I shrug. "*Oui.* I suppose so." Actually it was probably one of the worst nights of my life. "But I didn't . . . sleep well." I didn't sleep at all.

She looks at me more closely. "Ohhh. Was it *that* kind of no sleep?"

"What do you mean?" I wish she'd stop looking at me so intently.

"You know what I mean! Your mystery guy?"

My heart's suddenly beating too fast in my chest. "Oh. No. It wasn't anything like that."

"Wait," she grins at me. "You never told me. Did it work?"

"What do you mean, did it work?" I feel like she's crowding me, the smell of Miss Dior and stale cigarette smoke suddenly overpowering. I need her out of my space.

"The stuff we picked out. Mimi!" She raises her eyebrows. "You can't have forgotten? It was only, like, two weeks ago!"

ALREADY IT FEELS like it happened to someone else. I see myself like a character in a film, knocking on the door to Camille's room. Camille sitting on the bed painting her toenails, the room stinking of nail polish and weed.

"I want to buy some lingerie," I told her.

Maman always bought all my underwear. We went together, every season, to Eres and she would buy me three simple sets: black, white, nude. But I wanted something different. Something I had picked myself. Only I didn't have any idea where to go. I knew Camille would.

Camille's eyebrows shot up. "Mimi! What's happened to you? That new look and now . . . *lingerie*? Who is he?" She smiled slyly. "Or she? *Merde*, you're so mysterious I don't even know if you actually prefer girls." A smirk. "Or maybe you're like me and it depends what mood you're in?"

Could she really not know who it was? To me it seemed so obvious. Not just that I was into him, but that he and I had a special connection. It felt like it was obvious to the outside world, to everyone who saw us.

"Come," she said, jumping up, throwing her foam toe dividers to one side. "We're going now."

She dragged me into Passage du Desir in Châtelet. It's a sex shop—one of a chain—on a big busy shopping street alongside shoe and clothes shops because, I guess, this is France and screwing is, like, a thing of national pride. You see couples coming out carrying bags over their arms, smiling secret smiles at each other, women striding in there on their lunch breaks to buy vibrators. I'd never gone into one before. In fact every time I'd passed one of their stores I'd blushed at the window displays and looked away.

I felt like everyone in there was looking at me, wondering what this blushing loser virgin was doing among all that latex fetish wear and lube. I lowered my head, trying to hide behind my new fringe. I had horrific images of Papa walking past and somehow spotting me inside, dragging me out by my hair: calling me *une petite salope* in front of the whole street.

Camille dug out boxes with things called "love kits" in: whole lingerie and suspender sets for ten euros. But I shook my head; they weren't sophisticated enough. She grabbed a huge, bright pink dildo with obscene protruding veins, waved it in front of me. "Maybe you should get one of *these* while we're here."

"Put it back," I hissed, ready to die of shame. Yeah, we have that expression in French too: *mourir de honte.*

"Masturbating is healthy, *chérie*," Camille said, way louder than she needed to. She was enjoying this, I could tell. "You know what's not healthy? *Not* masturbating. I bet that school your papa sent you to told you it's a sin."

I've told Camille about the school, just not why I had to leave. "*Va te faire foutre*," I said, giving her a shove.

"Ah, but that's exactly what you need to do. Go fuck *yourself*."

I dragged her out of there. We went into a classier place where the shop assistants with their chignons and their perfect red lipstick looked at me sideways. My men's shirts, my big boots, my home-cut fringe. A security guard tailed us. That would be enough normally. I'd leave. But I needed to do this. For him.

"I want to pick out something too," Camille told me, holding a silk harness up against herself.

"You own more stuff than this entire shop."

"*Oui*. But I want something more sophisticated, you know?"

"Who's it for?" I asked her.

"Someone new." She gave a secretive smile. That was weird. Camille's never mysterious about anything. If she has a new fuck-buddy on the scene the whole world has normally heard about it about thirty minutes after their first screw.

"Tell me," I said. But still she refused to say. I didn't like this new, mysterious Camille. But I felt too high with the thrill of my purchase to think much about it. I couldn't wait.

Next to shelves of designer sex toys we browsed through racks of lace and silk, felt the fabric between our fingers. The lingerie had to be perfect. Some of it was too much: crotchless, buckles and straps, leather. Some of it Camille rejected as "stuff your maman would buy": flowers and silk in pastel colors—pink, pistachio, lavender.

Then: "I've found it, the one for you." She held it up to me. It was the most expensive set of all the ones we'd looked at. Black lace and silk so fine you could hardly feel it between your fingers. Chic but still sexy. Grown-up.

In a changing room with velvet drapes I tried the set on. I held up my hair and half closed my eyes. I was feeling less embarrassed now. I'd never looked at myself like this before. I thought I'd feel stupid, gauche. I thought I'd worry about my small tits, my slight pot belly, my bow legs.

But I didn't. Instead I imagined revealing myself to him. I pictured the look on his face. Saw him sliding it off me.

Je suis ta petite pute.

After I'd changed I took it over to the desk and told the shop assistant to ring it up. I liked how she tried to hide her surprise as I took out my credit card. *Yeah: fuck you, bitch. I could buy everything in here if I wanted.*

All the way back to the apartment I thought about the bag over my arm. It weighed nothing, but suddenly it was everything.

For the next few nights I watched him through the windows. They'd got later and later, these writing sessions: fueled by the pots of coffee he'd make on his stove and drink looking out of the windows onto the courtyard. It was something important, I could tell. I could see how fast he typed, hunched over the keyboard. Maybe he'd let me read it one day soon. I'd be the first person he shared it with. I watched him bend down and stroke the cat's head and I imagined I was that cat. I imagined one day I would lie there on his sofa with my head in his lap and he would stroke my hair like he did that cat's fur. And we'd listen to records and we'd talk about all the plans we'd make. I saw the image of us there together in his apartment so clearly it was like I was watching it. So clearly that it felt like a premonition.

Nick

A HAMMERING ON THE DOOR of my apartment. I jump with shock.

"Who is it?"

"*Laissez-moi entrer.*" *Let me in.* More hammering. The door shudders on its hinges.

I go to open it. Antoine shoves his way past me into the room in a cloud of booze and stale sweat. I take a step back.

He pushed his way in here like this only two weeks ago: "Dominique's cheating on me. I know she is. The little slut. She comes back smelling of a different scent. I called her yesterday in the stairwell and I heard her ringtone coming from somewhere in this building. Second time I rang she'd switched it off. She'd told me she was having a pedicure in Saint-Germain. It's him, I know it. It's that English *connard* you invited to live here . . ."

And me thinking: could it be true? Ben and Dominique? Yes, there had been flirtation at that drinks, on the roof terrace. I hadn't read anything into it. Ben flirted with everyone. But could this be an explanation for why he had been avoiding my eye, avoiding my calls? Why he had been *so busy*?

Now Antoine snaps his fingers in front of my face. "Wakey wakey, *petit frère*!" He doesn't say it affectionately. His eyes are bloodshot, breath rank with wine. I couldn't believe the change when I came back after those years away. When I left, my brother was a happy newlywed. Now he's an alcoholic mess whose wife has left him. That's what working for our father does to you. "What are we going to do about her?" he demands. "The girl?"

"Just calm down—"

"*Calm down?*" He stabs the air in front of me with a finger. I take another step back. He may be a mess but I'll always be the younger brother, ready to duck a punch. And he's so like Papa when he's angry. "You know this is all your fault, don't you? All your mess? If you hadn't invited that cunt to live here. Coming here and thinking he could just . . . just help himself. You know he used you, right? But you couldn't see that, could you? You couldn't see any of it." He frowns, mock-thoughtful. "In fact, now I think about it, the way you looked at him—"

"*Ferme ta gueule.*" *Shut your mouth.* I take a step toward him. The anger is sudden, blinding. And when I'm next aware of what I'm doing I realize my hand is around his throat and his eyes are bulging. I loosen my fingers—but with an effort, as though some part of me resists the instruction.

Antoine puts up a hand, rubs at his neck. "Hit a nerve there, didn't I, little bro?" His voice is hoarse, his eyes a little frightened, his tone not as flippant as he'd probably like it. "Papa wouldn't like that, would he? No, he wouldn't like that at all."

"I'm sorry," I say. Ashamed. My hand aches. "Shit, I'm sorry. This isn't helping anything, us fighting like this."

"Oh look at you. So grown-up. Embarrassed about your little hissy fit because you like pretending that you're sorted, don't you? But you're just as fucked-up as I am." When he says the word "fucked"—a harsh *foutu* in French—a huge gob of spit lands on my cheek. I put my hand up, wipe it off. I want to go and wash my face, scrub at it with hot water and soap. I feel *infected* by him.

When Jess spoke about Antoine last night I saw him through a stranger's eyes. I was ashamed of him. She's right. He is a mess.

But I hated her saying it. Because he's also my brother. We can do our family members down as much as we like. But the second an outsider insults them our blood seethes. At the end of the day I don't like him—but I love him. And I see my own failures in him. For Antoine it's the booze, for me it's the pills, the self-punishing exercise. I might be a little more in control of my addictions. I might be less of a mess—in public anyway. But is that really something to boast about?

Antoine's grinning at me. "Bet you wish you'd never come back here, huh?" He takes another step closer. "Tell me, if it was all so great rubbing shoulders with the high-flyers in Silicon Valley, why did you come back? Ah, *oui* . . . because you're no better than the rest of us. You try and pretend you are, that you don't need him, his money. But then you came crawling back here, like we all do, wanting to suck a little more from the paternal teat—"

"Just shut the fuck up!" I shout, hands forming fists.

I take a long breath: in for four, out for eight, like my mindfulness app tells me. I'm not proud of myself losing my temper like this. I'm better than this. I am not this guy. But no one can get under my skin like Antoine. No one else knows exactly what to say and how to say it for maximum impact. Except my father, of course.

But the worst part is that my brother's right. I came back. Back to the paterfamilias like some seasonal bird returning to the same poisoned lake.

"You've come home, son," Papa told me, as we sat together up on the roof terrace on my first night back. "I always knew you would. We'll have to make a trip to the Île de Ré, take the boat out one weekend."

Maybe he'd changed. Mellowed. He didn't taunt me over the money I'd lost on the investment—not yet. He even offered me a cigar, which I smoked, though I loathe the taste. Maybe he'd missed me.

It was only later that I realized it wasn't that at all. It was just more proof of his power. I had failed at finding a life apart from him.

"If you want any more of my money," he told me, "you can come back under my roof so I can keep an eye on you. There'll be no more gallivanting around the world. I want a return on my investment. I want to know you're not pissing it all up the wall. *Tu comprends?* Do you understand?"

Antoine is pacing up and down in front of me. "So what are we going to do about her?" he asks, with drunken belligerence.

"Keep your voice down," I say. "She might understand something." The walls have ears in this place.

"Well what the fuck is she still doing here?" He kicks at the doorframe. "What if she goes to the police?"

"I've handled that."

"What do you mean?"

"It helps to have friends in high places."

He understands. "But she needs to go." He's muttering to himself now: "We could lock her out. It would be so easy. All we'd need to do is change the combination on the front gate—she wouldn't be able to get in then."

"No," I say, "that wouldn't—"

"Or we could make her leave. Little girl like that? Wouldn't be hard."

"No. If anything we'd just force her into going to the police again on her own . . ."

Antoine lets out something between a roar and a groan. He's a total liability. Family, huh? Because blood is always thicker than water, in the end. Or, as we say in French: *la voix du sang est la plus forte.* The voice of blood is the strongest. Summoning me back here to this place.

"It's better that she stays here," I say, sharply. "You must see that. It's better that we can keep an eye on her. For the time being we simply have to hold our nerve. Papa will know what to do."

"Have you heard from him?" Antoine says. "Papa?" His tone has changed. Something needy in it. When he said "Papa" for a second he sounded like the little boy he once was, the little boy who sat outside his mother's bedroom as Paris' best physicians came and went, unable to make sense of the illness eating away at her.

I nod. "He got in touch this morning."

I hope you're holding the fort there, son. Keep Antoine under control. I'll be back as soon as I can.

Antoine scowls. He's Papa's right-hand man in the family business. But right now, for the time being, I'm the trusted one. That must hurt. But that's the way it's always been, our father pitting the two of us against each other in a struggle for scraps of parental affection. Except on the few occasions we unite against a common enemy.

Seventy-Two Hours Earlier

SHE WATCHES THROUGH THE SHUTTERS as he is carried from the building. Just as she watches everything in this place. Sometimes from her cabin in the garden, sometimes from the recesses of the building where she can spy on them unnoticed.

The body in its improvised shroud is visibly heavy. Already stiffening perhaps, unwieldy. A dead weight.

The lights in the third floor apartment have been on up until now, blazing out into the night. Now they are extinguished and she sees the windows become dark blanks, masking everything inside. But it will take more than that to expunge the memory of what has occurred within.

Now the light in the courtyard snaps on. She watches as they set to work, hidden from the outside world behind the high walls, doing everything that needs to be done.

Seeing him, she thought she would feel something, but there was nothing. She smiles slightly at the thought that his blood will now be part of this place, its dark secret. Well, he liked secrets. His stain will be here forever now, his lies buried with him.

Something terrible happened here tonight. She won't talk about what she saw, not even over his dead body. No one in this building is entirely innocent. Herself included.

A new light blinks on: four floors up. At the glass she glimpses a pale face, dark hair. A hand up against the pane. Perhaps there is one innocent in this, after all.

Jess

I'M HUNTING THROUGH BEN'S CLOSET in case there's an outfit an old girlfriend left behind, something I could borrow. Before Theo hung up on me I was going to tell him that I don't have anything smart to wear this evening. And no time or money to get something—he's barely given me any warning.

Just for a moment I pause my riffling through Ben's shirts and pull one of them against my face. Try, from the scent, to conjure him here, to believe that I will see him standing in front of me soon. But already the smell—of his cologne, his skin—seems to have faded a little. It feels somehow symbolic of our whole relationship: that I'm always chasing a phantom.

I drag myself away. Choose the one of my two sweaters that doesn't have any holes and brush my hair: I haven't washed it since I arrived, but at least it's less of a bird's nest now. I chuck on my jacket. Thread another pair of cheap hoop earrings through my earlobes. I look in the mirror. Not exactly "smart," but it'll have to do.

I open the door to the apartment. The stairwell's pitch-black. I fumble around for the light switch. There's that whiff of cigarette smoke, but even stronger than usual. It smells almost like someone's smoking one right now. Something makes me glance up to my left. A sound, perhaps, or just a movement of the air.

And then I catch sight of something out of place: a tiny glowing red dot hovering overhead in the blackness. It takes a moment before I understand what it is. I'm looking at the end of a cigarette butt, held by someone hidden in darkness just above me.

"Who's there?" I say, or try to say, because it comes out as a strangled bleat. I fumble around for the light switch near the door and finally make contact with it, the lights stuttering on. There's no one in sight.

MY HEART'S STILL beating double time as I walk across the courtyard. Just as I reach the gate to the street, I hear the sound of quick shuffling footsteps behind me. I turn.

It's the concierge, emerging once more from the shadows. I try to take a step away and when my heel hits metal I realize I'm already backed right up against the gate. She only comes up to my chin—and I'm not exactly big—but there's something threatening about her nearness.

"Yes?" I ask. "What is it?"

"I have something to say to you," she hisses. She glances up at the encircling apartment building. She reminds me of a small animal sniffing the air for a predator. I follow her gaze upward. Most of the windows are dark blanks, reflecting the gleam of the streetlamps across the road. There's only one light on upstairs, in the penthouse apartment. I can't see anyone watching us—I'm sure this is what she's checking for—but then I don't think I'd necessarily be able to spot them if they were.

Suddenly she snatches out a hand toward me. It's such a swift, violent action that for a moment I really think she's going to hit me. I don't have time to step away, it's too fast. But instead she grabs a hold of my wrist in her claw-like hand. Her grip's surprisingly strong; it stings.

"What are you doing?" I ask her.

"Just come," she tells me—and with such authority I don't dare disobey her. "Come with me, now."

I'm going to be late for meeting Theo now but he can wait.

This feels important. I follow her across the courtyard to her little cabin. She moves quickly, in that slightly stooped way of hers, like someone trying to duck out of a rainstorm. I feel like a child in a storybook being taken to the witch's hut in the woods. She looks up at the apartment building several more times, as though scanning it for any onlookers. But she seems to decide that it's worth the risk.

Then she opens the door and ushers me in. It's even smaller inside than it looks on the outside, if that's possible. Everything is crammed into one tiny space. There's a bed attached to the wall by a system of pulleys and currently raised to allow us to stand; a washstand; a minuscule antique cooking stove. Just to my right is a curtain that I suppose must lead through to a bathroom of some sort—simply because there's nowhere else for it to be.

It's almost scarily neat, every surface scrubbed to a high shine. It smells of bleach and detergent—not a thing out of place. Somehow I would have expected nothing less from this woman. And yet the cleanness, the neatness, the little vase of flowers, somehow make it all the more depressing. A little mess might be a distraction from how cramped it is, or from the damp stains on the ceiling which I'm fairly sure no amount of cleaning could remove. I've lived in some dives in my time, but this takes the biscuit. And what must it feel like to live in this tiny hovel while surrounded by the luxury and space of the rest of the apartment building? What would it be like to live with the reminder of how little you have on your doorstep every day?

No wonder she hated me, swanning in here to take up residence on the third floor. If only she knew how out of place I am here too, how much more like her than them I really am. I know I can't let her see my pity: that would be the worst insult possible. I get the impression she's probably a very proud person.

Behind her head and the tiny dining table and chair I see several faded photographs pinned to the wall. A little girl, sitting on a woman's lap. The sky behind them is bright blue, olive trees in the background. The woman has a glass in front of her of what looks like tea, a silver handle. The next is of a young woman. Slim, dark-haired, dark-eyed. Maybe eighteen or nineteen. Not a new photograph: you can tell from the saturated colors, the fuzziness of it. But at the same time it's definitely too recent to be of the old woman herself. It must be a loved one. Somehow it's impossible to imagine this elderly woman having a family or a past away from this place. It's impossible, even, to imagine her ever having been young. As though she has always been here. As though she is a part of the apartment building itself.

"She's stunning," I say. "That girl on the wall. Who is she?"

There's a long silence, so long that I think maybe she didn't understand me. And then finally, in that rasping voice, she says: "My daughter."

"Wow." I take another look at her in light of this, her daughter's beauty. It's hard to see past the lines, the swollen ankles, the clawed hands—but maybe I can see a shadow of it, after all.

She clears her throat. "*Vous devez arrêter,*" she barks, suddenly, cutting into my thoughts. *You have to stop.*

"What do you mean?" I ask. "Stop what?" I lean forward. Perhaps she can tell me something.

"All your questions," she says. "All of your . . . *looking.* You are only making trouble for yourself. You cannot help your brother now. You must understand that—"

"What do you mean?" I ask. A chill has gone right through me. "What do you mean, I cannot help my brother now?"

She just shakes her head. "There are things here that you cannot understand. But I have seen them, with my own eyes. I see everything."

"What?" I ask her. "What have you seen?"

She doesn't answer. She simply shakes her head. "I am trying to help you, girl. I have been trying since the beginning. Don't you understand that? If you know what is good for you, you will stop. You will leave this place. And never look back."

Sophie

THERE'S A KNOCK ON THE door. I go to answer it and find Mimi standing there on the other side.

"Maman." The way she says the word. Just like she did as a little girl.

"What is it, *ma petite*?" I ask, gently. I suppose to others I may seem cold. But the love I feel for my daughter; I'd challenge you to find anything close to it.

"Maman, I'm frightened."

"Shh." I step forward to embrace her. I draw her close to me, feeling the frail nubs of her shoulder blades beneath my hands. It seems so long since I have held her like this, since she has *allowed* me to hold her like this, like I did when she was a child. For a time I thought I might never do so again. And to be called "Maman." It is still the same miracle it was when I first heard her say the word.

I have always felt she is more mine than Jacques'. Which I suppose makes a kind of sense: because in a way she was Jacques' greatest gift to me, far more valuable than any diamond brooch, any emerald bracelet. Something—someone—I could love unreservedly.

ONE EVENING—ROUGHLY A week after the night I had knocked on Benjamin Daniels' door—Jacques was briefly home for supper.

I presented him with the quiche Lorraine I had bought from the boulangerie, piping hot from the oven.

Everything was as it should be. Everything following its usual pattern. Except for the fact that a few nights before I had slept with the man from the third-floor apartment. I was still reeling from it. I could not believe it had happened. A moment—or rather an evening—of madness.

I placed a slice of quiche on Jacques' plate. Poured him a glass of wine. "I met our lodger on the stairs this evening," he said as he ate, as I picked my way through my salad. "He thanked us for supper. Very gracious—gracious enough not to mention the disaster with the weather. He sends you his compliments."

I took a sip of my wine before I answered. "Oh?"

He laughed, shook his head in amusement. "Your face— anyone would think this stuff was corked. You really don't like him, do you?"

I couldn't speak.

I was saved by the ringing of Jacques' phone. He went into his study and took a call. When he returned his face was clouded with anger. "I have to go. Antoine made a stupid mistake. One of the clients isn't happy."

I gestured to the quiche. "I'll keep this warm for you, for when you come back."

"No. I'll eat out." He shrugged on his jacket. "Oh, and I forgot to say. Your daughter. I saw her on the street the other night. She was dressed like a whore."

"*My* daughter?" I asked. Now that she had done something to displease him she was "my" daughter?

"All that money," he said, "sending her to that Catholic school, to try and make her into a properly behaved young woman. And yet she disgraced herself there. And now she goes out dressed like a little slut. But then, perhaps it's no surprise."

"What do you mean?"

But I didn't need to ask. I knew exactly what he meant.

And then he left. And I was all alone in the apartment, as usual.

For the second time in a week, I was filled with rage. White hot, powerful. I drank the rest of the bottle of wine. Then I stood up and walked down two flights of stairs.

I knocked on his door.

He opened it. Pulled me inside.

This time there was no preamble. No pretense of polite conversation. I don't think we spoke one word. We weren't respectful or gentle or cautious with one another now. My silk shirt was torn from me. I gasped against his mouth like someone drowning. Bit at him. Tore the skin of his back with my nails. Relinquished all control. I was possessed.

Afterward, as we lay tangled in his sheets, I finally managed to speak. "This cannot happen again. You understand that, don't you?"

He just smiled.

Over the next few weeks we became reckless. Testing the boundaries, scaring ourselves a little. The adrenaline rush, the fear—so similar a feeling to the quickening of arousal. Each seemed to heighten the other, like the rush of some drug. I had behaved so well for so long.

The secret spaces of this building became our private playground. I took him in my mouth in the old servants' staircase, my hands sliding into his trousers, expert, greedy. He had me in the laundry room in the *cave*, up against the washing machine as it thrummed out its cycle.

And every time I tried to end it. And every time I know we both heard the lie behind the words.

* * *

"MAMAN," MIMI SAYS now—and I am jolted, abruptly, guiltily, out of these memories. "Maman, I don't know what to do."

My wonderful miracle. My Merveille. My Mimi. She came to me when I had given up all hope of having a child. You see, she wasn't always mine.

She was, quite simply, perfect. A baby: only a few weeks old. I did not know exactly where she had come from. I had my ideas, but I kept them to myself. I had learned it was important, sometimes, to look the other way. If you know that you aren't going to like the reply, don't ask the question. There was just one thing I needed to know and to that I got my answer: the mother was dead. "And illegal. So there's no paper trail to worry about. I know someone at the *mairie* who will square the birth certificate." A mere formality for the grand and powerful house of Meunier. It helps to have friends in high places.

And then she was mine. And that was the important thing. I could give her a better life.

"Shh," I say. "I'm here. Everything will be OK. I'm sorry I was stern last night, with the wine. But you understand, don't you? I didn't want a scene. Leave it all with me, *ma chérie.*"

It was—is—so fierce, that feeling. Even though she didn't come out of my body, I knew as soon as I saw her that I would do anything to protect her, to keep her safe. Other mothers might say that sort of thing casually. But perhaps it is clear by now that I don't do or say anything casually. When I say something like that, I mean it.

Jess

I COME UP OUT OF the Palais Royal Metro station. I almost don't recognize the tall, smartly dressed guy waiting at the top of the steps until he starts walking toward me.

"You're fifteen minutes late," Theo says.

"You didn't give me any time," I say. "And I got caught up—"

"Come on," Theo says. "We can still make it if we're snappy about it." I look him over, trying to work out why he looks so different from the last time I met him. Only a five o'clock shadow now, revealing a sharp jawline. Dark hair still in need of a cut but it's had a brush and he's swept it back from his face. A dark blazer over a white shirt and jeans. I even catch a waft of cologne. He's definitely scrubbed up since the café. He still looks like a pirate, but now like one who's had a wash and a shave and borrowed some civilian clothes.

"That's not going to cut it," he says, nodding at me. Clearly, he's not having the same charitable thoughts about my outfit.

"It's all I had to wear. I did try to say—"

"It's fine, I thought that might be the case. I've brought you some stuff."

He thrusts a Monoprix bag-for-life toward me. I look inside: I can see a tangle of clothes; a black dress and a pair of heels.

"You *bought* this?"

"Ex-girlfriend. You're roughly the same size, I'd guess."

"Ew. OK." I remind myself that this might all somehow help me find out what's happened to Ben, that beggars can't be choosers about wearing the haunted clothes of girlfriends past. "Why do I have to wear this sort of stuff?"

He shrugs. "Them's the rules." And then, when he sees my expression: "No, they actually are. This place has a dress code. Women aren't allowed to wear trousers, heels are mandatory."

"That's nice and sexist." Echoes of The Pervert insisting I keep the top four buttons of my shirt undone "for the punters": *You want to look like you work in a kindergarten, sweetheart? Or a branch of fucking McDonald's?*

Theo shrugs. "Yeah, well, I agree. But that's a certain part of Paris for you. Hyper-conservative, hypocritical, sexist. Anyway, don't blame me. It's not like I'm taking you to this place on a date." He coughs. "Come on, we don't have all night. We're already running late."

"For what?"

"You'll see when we get there. Let's just say you're not going to find this place in your Lonely Planet guide."

"How does this help us find Ben?"

"I'll explain it when we get there. It'll make more sense then."

God, he's infuriating. I'm also not completely sure I trust him, though I can't put my finger on why. Maybe it's just that I still can't work out what his angle is, why he's so keen to help.

I hurry along next to him, trying to keep up. I didn't see him standing up at the café the other day—I'd guessed he was tall, but now I realize he's well over a foot taller than me and I have to take two steps for every one of his. After a few minutes of walking I'm actually panting.

To the left of us I catch sight of a huge glass pyramid, glowing with light, looking like something that's just landed from outer space. "What is that thing?"

He gives me a look. It seems I've said something stupid. "That's the Pyramide? In front of the Louvre? You know . . . the famous museum?"

I don't like being made to feel like an idiot. "Oh. The *Mona Lisa*, right? Yeah, well, I've been a bit too busy trying to find my missing brother to take a nice tour of it yet."

We push through crowds of tourists chattering in every language under the sun. As we walk, I tell him about what I've discovered: about them all being a family. One united front, acting together—and probably against me. I keep thinking about stumbling into Sophie Meunier's apartment, all of them sitting together like that—an eerie family portrait. The words I'd heard, crouching outside. *Elle est dangereuse.* And Nick discovering that he wasn't the ally I thought he was—that part still stings.

"And just before I left to come here the concierge gave me a kind of warning. She told me to 'stop looking.'"

"Can I tell you something I've learned in my long and not especially illustrious career?" Theo asks.

"What?"

"When someone tells you to stop looking, it normally means you're on the right track."

I CHANGE QUICKLY in the underground toilet of a chi-chi bar while Theo buys a *demi* beer upstairs so the staff don't chuck us out. I shake out my hair, study my reflection in the foxed glass of the mirror. I don't look like myself. I look like I'm playing a part. The dress is figure-hugging but classier than I'd expected. The label inside reads *Isabel Marant*, which I'm guessing might be a step up from my usual Primark. The shoes—*Michel Vivien* is the name printed on the footbed—are higher than anything I'd wear but surprisingly comfortable; I think I might actually be able to walk in them. So I guess I'm playing the part of Theo's ex-girlfriend; not sure how I feel about that.

A girl comes out of the stall next to me: long shining dark hair, a silky dress falling off one shoulder underneath an over-sized cardigan, wings of black eyeliner. She starts outlining her lips in lipstick. That's what I need: the finishing touch.

"Hey." I lean over to her, smile my most ingratiating smile. "Could I borrow some of that?"

She frowns at me, looks slightly disgusted, but hands it over. "*Si tu veux.*"

I put some on a finger, dab it onto my lips—it's a dark vampiric red—and pass it back to her.

She puts up a hand. "*Non, merci.* Keep it. I have another." She tosses her gleaming hair over one shoulder.

"Oh. Thanks." I put the lid back on and it closes with a satisfying magnetized click. I notice it has little interlocking "C"s stencilled on the top.

Mum had a lipstick like this, even though she definitely didn't have spare cash to spend on expensive makeup. But then that was Mum all over: blow it on a lipstick and be left with nothing for dinner. Me, sitting on a chair, legs dangling. Her pressing the waxy stub of it against my lips. Turning me to face the mirror. *There you go, darling. Don't you look pretty?*

I look at myself in the mirror now. Pout just like she asked me to do all those years—a million years, a whole lifetime—ago. There; done. Costume complete.

I HEAD BACK upstairs. "Ready," I tell Theo. He downs the dregs of his stupidly tiny glass of beer. I can feel him running a quick eye over the outfit. His mouth opens and for a moment I think he might say something nice. I mean, part of me wouldn't know what to do with a compliment right now, but at the same time it might be nice to hear. And then he points to my mouth.

"Missed a bit," he says. "But yeah, otherwise that should do."

Oh fuck off. I rub at the edge of my lips. I hate myself for even having cared what he thought.

We leave the bar, turn onto a street thronged with very well-dressed shoppers. I could swear the air around here smells of expensive leather. We pass the glittering windows of rich people shops: Chanel, Celine, and aha!—Isabel Marant. He leads me away from the crowds into a much smaller side street. Gleaming cars flank the pavements. In contrast to the crowded shopping boulevard there's no one in sight and it's darker here, fewer streetlamps. A deep hush over everything.

Then Theo stops at a door. "Here we are." He looks at his watch. "We're definitely a little late. Hopefully they'll let us in."

I look at the door. No number, but there's a plaque with a symbol I recognize: an exploding firework. Where *are* we?

Theo reaches past me—a trace of that citrus cologne again—and presses a doorbell I hadn't noticed. The door swings open with a click. A man appears, dressed in a black suit and bow tie. I watch as Theo fishes a card from his pocket, the same one I found in Ben's wallet.

The doorman glances at the card, nods his head toward us. "*Entrez, s'il vous plaît.* The evening is about to start."

I try and peer past the doorman to get a glimpse of what lies beyond. At the end of the corridor I see a staircase leading downward, dimly lit by sconces with real candles burning in them.

Theo plants a hand in the small of my back and, with a little push, steers me forward. "Come on," he says. "We don't have all night."

"*Arrêtez*," the doorman says, barring our entry with a hand. He looks me over. "*Votre mobile, s'il vous plaît.* No phone allowed—or camera."

"Er—why?" I glance back at Theo. It occurs to me again that I know absolutely nothing about this guy beyond what it says on his business card. He could be anyone. He could have brought me anywhere.

Theo gives a tiny nod, gestures: *don't make a fuss. Do what the guy says.* "O—K." I hand my phone over, reluctantly.

"*Vos masques.*" The man holds up two pieces of material. I take one. A black mask, made of silk.

"Wha—"

"Just put it on," Theo murmurs, near my ear. And then louder: "Let me help, darling." I try to act natural as he smooths down my hair, ties the mask behind my head.

The doorman beckons us through.

With Theo close behind me, I begin to descend the stairs.

Jess

AN UNDERGROUND ROOM. I SEE dark red walls, low lighting, a small crowd of dimly lit figures sitting in front of a stage veiled by a wine-colored velvet curtain. Masked faces turn to look as we descend the final few steps. We're definitely the last to turn up at the party.

"What the hell is this place?" I whisper to Theo.

"*Shh.*"

An usher in black tie meets us at the bottom of the stairs, beckons us forward. We pass walls decorated with stylized gold dancing figurines, then weave among little booths with masked figures sitting behind tables, more faces turning in our direction. I feel uncomfortably exposed. Luckily the table we're taken to is tucked into a corner—definitely the worst view of the stage.

We slide into the booth. There really isn't very much room in here, not with Theo's long legs, which he has to pull up against himself, his knees hard against the wooden surround. He looks so uncomfortable that in different circumstances it might give me a laugh. The tiny amount of seat left means I have to sit with my thigh pressed right up against his.

I look about. It's hard to tell whether this place is actually old or just a clever imitation. The others around us are all very well-heeled; judging by their clothes they could be out for an evening at the theatre. But the atmosphere is wrong. I lean back in my chair, trying to look casual, like I fit in here among the tailored suits, the jewel-encrusted earlobes and necks, the rich person hair. A weird, hungry hum of energy is coming off them, coiling through the room—an intense note of excitement, of anticipation.

A waiter comes over to take our drinks order. I open the leather-bound menu. No prices. I glance at Theo.

"A glass of champagne for my wife," he says, quickly. He turns to me wearing a smile of fake adoration—so convincing it gives me a chill. "Seeing as we're celebrating, darling." I really hope he's paying. He looks down the menu. "And a glass of this red for me."

The waiter is back in a minute, brandishing two bottles in white napkins. He pours a stream of champagne into a glass and passes it to me. I take a sip. It's very cold, tiny bubbles electric on the tip of my tongue. I can't think when I've ever had the real stuff. Mum used to say she was "a champagne girl" but I'm not sure she ever had it either: just cheap, sweet knock-offs.

As the waiter pours Theo's red the napkin slips a little and I notice the label.

"It's the same wine," I whisper to Theo, once the waiter's left us. "The Meuniers have that in their cellar."

Theo turns to look at me. "What was that name you just used?" He sounds suddenly excited.

"The Meuniers. The family I was telling you about."

Theo lowers his voice. "Yesterday I submitted a request to see the *matrice cadastrale*—that's like the Land Registry—for this place. It's owned by one Meunier Wines SARL."

I sit up very straight, everything sharpening into focus. A feeling like a thousand tiny pin-pricks across the surface of my skin.

"That's them. That's the family Ben's been living with." I try to think. "But why was Ben interested in this place? Could he have been reviewing it? Something like that?"

"He wasn't reviewing it for me. And I'm not sure, being so exclusive, that it's the sort of place that exactly courts press coverage."

The lights begin to dim. But just before they do a figure in the crowd catches my eye, oddly familiar despite the mask they're wearing. I try to shift my gaze back to the same spot but the lights are dimming further, voices lowering and the room falling into darkness.

I can hear the smallest rustle of people's clothing, the odd sniff, their intakes of breath. Someone coughs and it sounds deafening in the sudden hush.

Then the velvet curtain begins to roll back.

A figure stands on the stage against a black background. Skin lit up pale blue. Face in shadow. Completely naked. No—not naked, a trick of the light—two scraps of material covering her modesty. She begins to dance. The music is deep, throbbing— some sort of jazz, I think . . . no melody to it, but a kind of rhythm. And she's so in sync with it that it feels almost as if the music is coming from her, like the movements she is making are creating it, rather than following it. The dance is strange, intense, almost menacing. I'm torn between staring and tearing my eyes away; something about it disturbs me.

More girls appear, dressed—or undressed—in the same way. The music gets louder and louder, beating until it's so overpowering that the pulse of it is like the sound of my own heartbeat in my ears. With the blue light, the shifting, undulating bodies on stage, I feel as though I'm underwater, as though the outlines of everything are rippling and bleeding into one another. I think of last night. Could there be something in the champagne? Or is it just the effect of the lighting, the music, the darkness? I glance over at Theo. He shifts in his seat next to me; takes a sip of wine, his eyes locked on the stage. Is he turned on by what's happening on stage? Am *I*? I'm suddenly aware of how close we are to each other, of how tightly my leg is pressed up against his.

The next act is just two women: one dressed in a close-fitting black suit and bow tie, the other in a tiny slip dress. Gradually they remove each other's clothes until you can see that without them they're almost identical. I can feel the audience sitting forward, drinking it in.

I lean toward Theo. Whisper: "What *is* this place?"

"A rather exclusive club," he murmurs back. "Its nickname, apparently, is La Petite Mort. You can't get in unless you have one of those cards. Like the one you found in Ben's wallet."

The lights dim again. Silence falls on the crowd. Another nearly naked girl—this one wearing a kind of feathered head-dress rather than a mask—is lowered from the ceiling on a sus-pended silver hoop. Her act is all confined to the hoop: she does a somersault, a kind of backflip, lets herself fall and then catches herself with the flick of an ankle—the audience gasps.

Theo leans in close. "Careful now, but look behind you," he whispers, breath tickling my ear. I start to swivel round. "No— Jesus, more subtly than that."

God, he's patronizing. But I do as he says. Several times I take small, sly glances behind me. And as I do I notice a series of booths hidden in the shadows at the back, their occupants shielded from the view of the regular punters by velvet curtains and attended by a constant flow of waiters carrying bottles of wine and trays of canapés. Every so often someone leaves or enters, and I notice that it always seems to be a man. All of a similar type and age: elegant, suited, masked, an air of wealth and importance about them.

Theo leans over, as though he's whispering another sweet nothing. "Have you noticed?"

"How they're all men?"

"Yes. And how every so often one of them goes through that door over there."

I follow the direction of his gaze.

"But I'd stop looking now," he murmurs. "Before we start to draw attention to ourselves."

I turn back to the stage. The girl has stepped off the hoop. She smiles out at the audience, taking us all in in a sweeping glance. When she gets to me, she stops. I'm not imagining it: she freezes. She is staring at me in what looks like horror. I feel a thrill go through me. The sharp brown fringe, the height, even the little mole beneath her left eye which I can make out now under the spotlight. I know her.

Sophie

PENTHOUSE

THEY FILE INTO THE APARTMENT. Nicolas, Antoine, Mimi. Take up the same positions on the sofas they occupied last night, when the girl interrupted us. Nick's foot is tapping a frantic rhythm on the Ghom rug. As I watch I am certain I can make out a tiny black scorch mark just beneath his toe. One of several burned into the priceless silk. But you'd only spot them if you knew what you were looking for.

Suddenly I am assaulted by memories. It was my greatest transgression, inviting him up here. We stole a bottle from Jacques' cellar: one of the finest vintages. Had each other there on the rug, Paris glittering nosily in at us through the vast windows. We lay tangled together afterward, warmed by the cashmere throw I had pulled around our naked bodies. If Jacques had come back unexpectedly . . . But wasn't there some part of me that wanted to be caught? Look at me, who you have left here alone all these years. Wanted. Desired.

As we lay there I stroked his hair, enjoying the dense velvety softness of it between my fingers. He lit a cigarette that we passed back and forth like teenage lovers, hot ash scattering, sizzling into the silk of the rug. I didn't care. All that mattered was that with him here the apartment suddenly seemed warm, full of life and sound and passion.

"My mum used to stroke my hair."

I pulled my hand away, sharply.

"I didn't mean it like that," he said, quickly. "I just meant I hadn't realized how much I missed it." And when he turned to look across at me I saw in his expression something undefended and frail, something that had hidden beneath all the charm. I thought I saw my own loneliness reflected there. But in the next moment he smiled and it had vanished.

A minute or so later he sat up, taking in the empty apartment around us. "Jacques is away a lot in the evenings, isn't he?"

I nodded. Was he already planning our next encounter? "He's very busy."

His gaze seemed to sweep over the paintings on the walls, the furnishings, the richness of the place. "I suppose that must mean business is flourishing."

I froze. He'd said it lightly. Too lightly? It brought me back to myself: the madness of what we were doing, all that was at stake. "You should go," I told him, suddenly angry at him . . . at myself. "I can't do this." This time I really believed I meant it. "I have too much to lose."

I close my eyes. Open them again and focus on my daughter's face. She does not meet my eye. All the same, it has brought me back to myself. To what is important. I take a steadying sip of my wine. Force down the memories. "So," I say to them all. "Let us begin."

Nick

MY STEPMOTHER HAS CALLED US all to order. We're sitting upstairs in the penthouse apartment. A dysfunctional little family conference. Like the one we'd been going to have last night before Jess turned up unannounced and set the cat among the pigeons. I was always a keen student of English idioms. We have a French one like it, actually: *jeter un pavé dans la mare*—throw a paving stone in the pond. And maybe that's a more accurate description of what happened when she arrived here. She has displaced everything.

I look at the others. Antoine knocking back the wine—he might as well have picked up the whole bottle. Mimi white-faced and looking ready to bolt from the room. Sophie sitting rigid and expressionless. She's not looking quite herself, my stepmother. I can't work out what's different about her at first. Her shining black bob doesn't have a strand out of place, her silk scarf is knotted expertly at her throat. But there's something off. Then it hits me: she's not wearing lipstick. I don't know if I've ever seen her without it. She looks diminished, somehow. Older, frailer, more human.

Antoine speaks first. "That stupid little cunt is at the club." He turns to me. "Still suggest we do nothing, little bro?"

"I . . . I think the important thing is we all pull together," I say. "A united front. As a family. That's the most important thing. We can't fall apart now."

But I realize, looking at their faces, that they're all unknown quantities to me. I don't feel like I know these people. Not really. I was away for so long. And we're all so estranged from one another that we don't look and feel like the real thing. Even to one another.

"Yes, because you've been such a key player in this family up until now," Antoine says, making me feel even more of an imposter, a fraud. He gestures toward Sophie. "And you're not going to catch me playing the adoring stepson to that *salope*."

"Hey," I say. "Let's just—"

"Watch your mouth," Sophie says caustically, turning to Antoine. "You're sitting in my apartment."

"Oh it's your apartment, is it?" He gives a mock bow. "I'm so sorry, I hadn't realized. I thought you were just a parasite living off Papa's money—I didn't know you'd *earned* any of it yourself."

I was only eight or nine when Papa married the mysterious new woman who had materialized in our lives but Antoine was older, a teenager. Maman had been an invalid for so long, languishing in her rooms on the third floor. This newcomer seemed so young, so glamorous. I was a little besotted. Antoine took it rather differently. He's always had it in for her.

"Just stop it," Mimi says suddenly, her hands over her ears. "All of you. I can't take any more—"

Antoine turns to Mimi with a horrible smile on his face. "*Ah*," he slurs at her now, "and as for you, well you're not really part of this family, are you, *ma petite soeur*—"

"Stop that," Sophie says to Antoine, her voice ice-cold: the lioness protecting her cub.

At her feet the whippet startles and gives a sharp bark.

"Oh, I think she can give as good as she gets," Antoine says. "What about all that stuff at her school, with the teacher? Papa had to make a pretty hefty donation and agree to remove her to keep that one quiet. But perhaps it's no surprise, huh?" He turns to Mimi. "When you consider where she comes from."

"Don't you dare speak to her like that," Sophie says. Her tone is dangerous.

I glance over at Mimi. She's just sitting there, staring at Antoine, her face even paler than usual.

"OK," I say. "Come on, let's all just—"

"And can I just say," Antoine says, "that it's just typical that our darling père has decided to fuck off for all of this. Isn't it?"

All of us glance instinctively at the portrait of my father on the wall. I know it must be my imagination or a trick of the light, but it looks as though his painted frown has deepened slightly. I shiver. Even when he's miles away you can still feel his presence in this apartment, somehow, his authority. The all-seeing, all-powerful Jacques Meunier.

"Your father," Sophie says to Antoine now, sharply, "has his own business to be taking care of. As you well know. It would only complicate things further if he returns. We must all hold the fort for him in his absence."

"What a surprise, he's not here when the shit hits the fan." Antoine gives a laugh, but there's no humor in it.

"He trusts you to be able to handle the situation on your own," Sophie says. "But perhaps that is simply too much to ask. Look at you. You're a forty-year-old man still living under his roof, leeching off his money. He has given you everything. You've never had to grow up. You've had everything handed to you by your father on a silver platter. You're both useless hothouse flowers, too weak for the outside world. Unable to fly the nest." That stings. "For God's sake," she says. "Show your father some respect."

"Oh yeah?" Antoine gives her a nasty smile. "Are you really going to talk to me about respect, *putain*?" The last word hissed under his breath.

"How dare you speak to me like that?" She rounds on him, a surge of real anger breaching the icy façade.

"Oh, how dare I?" Antoine gives her a sly-looking grin. "*Vraiment?* Really?" He turns to me. "You know what she is? You know what our very elegant stepmother really is? You know where she comes from?"

I've had my suspicions. As I grew older, they grew too. But I've barely even allowed myself to think them, let alone voice them aloud, for fear of my father's wrath.

Antoine stands up and walks out of the room. A few moments later he comes back carrying something in a large frame. He turns it around so that all of us can see it. It's a black and white photograph, a large nude: the one from my father's study.

"Put that back," says Sophie, her voice dangerous. Her hands are clenched into fists. She looks over at Mimi who is sitting stock still, her eyes wide and scared.

Antoine sits back in the chair looking pleased with himself, propping the photograph beside him like a child's science project. "Look at her," he says, gesturing to the image, then at Sophie. "Hasn't she done well? The Hermès scarves, the trench coats. *Une vraie bourgeoise.* You'd never know it, would you? You'd never know that she was really a—"

A crack, loud as a pistol shot. It happens too quickly to understand what's going on: she moved so fast. Then Antoine is sitting there holding his hand to his face and Sophie is standing over him.

"She hit me," Antoine says—but his voice is small and scared as a little boy's. It isn't the first time he's been hit like this. Papa always was pretty free with his fists and Antoine, the eldest, seemed to get the worst of it. "She fucking hit me." He takes his hand away and we all see the mark of her hand on his cheek, the imprint of it a livid pink.

Sophie continues to stand over him. "Think what your father would say if he heard you talking to me like that."

Antoine looks up at Papa's portrait again. Tears his eyes away with an effort. He's a big guy but he seems almost to shrink into himself. We all know that he would never dare speak to Sophie like this in Papa's presence. And we all know that when Papa gets back there'll be hell to pay if he hears about it.

"Can we please just focus on what's important?" I say, trying to gain some control. "We have a bigger problem to focus on here."

Sophie gives Antoine another venomous stare, then turns to me and nods, tightly. "You're right." She sits back down and in a moment that chilly mask is back in place. "I think the most important thing is that we can't let her find out any more. We have to be ready for her, when she returns. And if she goes too far? Nicolas?"

I nod. Swallow. "Yes. I know what to do. If it comes to it."

"The concierge," Mimi says suddenly, her voice small and hoarse.

We all turn to look at her.

"I saw that woman, Jess, going into the concierge's cabin. She was on her way to the gate and the concierge ran out and grabbed her. They were in there for at least ten minutes." She looks at all of us. "What . . . what could they have been talking about for all that time?"

Jess

I STARE AT THE GIRL on the stage. It's her, the girl who followed me two days ago, the one I chased onto the Metro train. She stares back. The moment seems to stretch. She looks as terrified as she did when that train pulled away from the platform. And then, as if she's coming out of a trance, she swings her gaze back to the audience, smiles, climbs back onto the hoop as it starts to rise upward—and is gone.

Theo turns to me. "What was that?"

"You saw it too?"

"Yeah, I saw it. She was staring right at you."

"I met her," I say. "Just after I spoke to you for the first time at the café." I explain it all: catching her following me, chasing her into the Metro. My heart is beating faster now. I think of Ben. The family. The mystery dancer. They all feel like parts of the same puzzle . . . I know they are. But how do they all fit?

After the show ends the audience members drain the remainders from their glasses and surge up the staircase, heading out into the night.

Theo gives me a nudge. "Come on then, let's go. Follow me."

I'm about to protest—surely we're not just going to leave?—but I stop when I see that rather than continuing up the stairs with the rest of the paying customers, Theo has shoved open a door on our left. It's the same one we noticed earlier, during the performance, the one through which those suited men kept disappearing.

"Let's try and talk to your friend," he murmurs.

He slips through the door. I follow close behind. Beneath us is a dark, velvet-lined staircase. We begin to descend. I can hear sounds coming from below, but they're muted, like they're coming from underwater. I hear music, I think, and the hum of voices and then a sudden, high-pitched cry that might be male or female.

We have almost reached the bottom of the stairs. I hesitate. I thought I heard something. Another set of footsteps beside our own.

"Stop," I say. "Did you hear that?"

Theo looks at me questioningly.

"I'm sure I heard footsteps."

We listen for a couple of moments in silence. Nothing. Then a girl appears at the bottom of the stairs. One of the dancers. Up close she's so made-up it looks like she's wearing a mask. She stares at us. For a moment I have the impression that there's a scared little girl looking out at me behind the thick foundation, fake eyelashes, and glossy red lips.

"We're looking for a friend," I say, quickly. "The girl who did that act on the swing? It's about my brother, Ben. Can you tell her we're looking for her?"

"You cannot be here," she hisses. She looks terrified.

"It's OK," I say, trying to sound reassuring. "We're not going to stay for long."

She hurries past us, up the stairs, without a backward glance. We keep going. At the end of the corridor there's a door. I put my shoulder against it but there's no give. I suddenly have a sense of how far underground we are: at least two floors deep. The thought makes it harder to breathe. I try to swallow down my fear.

"I think it's locked," I say.

The sounds are louder now. Through the door I hear a kind of groan that sounds almost animal.

I try the handle again. "It's definitely locked. You have a go—"

But Theo doesn't answer me.

And I know, before I turn, that there's someone behind us. Now I see him: the doorman who met us at the entrance, his huge frame filling the corridor, his face in shadow.

Shit.

"*Qu'est-ce qui se passe?*" he asks, dangerously, quietly, as he begins moving toward us. "What are you doing down here?"

"We got lost," I say, my voice cracking. "I . . . was looking for the toilets."

"*Vous devez partir,*" he says. And then he repeats it in English: "You need to leave. Both of you. Right now." His voice is still quiet, all the more menacing than if he were shouting. It says, *absolutely do not fuck with me.*

He takes a hold of my upper arm in one of his huge hands. His grip burns. I try to pull away. He grips tighter. I get the impression he's not even putting much effort in.

"Hey, hey—that's not necessary," Theo says. The doorman doesn't answer, or let go. Instead he takes hold of Theo's arm too, in his other hand. And Theo, who up until now I'd thought of as a large guy, looks suddenly like a child, like a puppet, held in his grip.

For a moment the doorman stands stock-still, his head cocked to one side. I look at Theo and he frowns, clearly as confused as I am. Then I hear a tinny murmur and realize that he is listening. Someone is feeding him instructions through an earpiece.

He straightens up. "Please, Madame, Monsieur." Still that scarily polite tone, even as his hand tightens further around my bicep, burning the skin. "Do not make a scene. You must come with me, now." And then he is steering us, with more than a little force, along the corridor, back up the first flight of stairs, back into the room with the tables, the stage. Most of the lights have been turned off and it's completely empty now. No, not completely. Out of the corner of my eye I think I catch sight of a tall figure standing quite still, watching us from the shadowy recesses in one corner. But I don't manage to get a proper look because now we're being manhandled up the next flight of steps, up to ground level.

Then the front door is opened and we're thrust out onto the street, the doorman giving me such a hard shove in the back that I trip and fall forward onto my knees.

The door slams behind us.

Theo, who has managed to keep his balance, puts out a hand and hauls me up. It takes a long time for my heartbeat to return to normal. But as I manage to gain some control over my breathing I realize that though my knees hurt and my arm feels badly bruised, it could have been so much worse. I feel lucky to be back out here gulping freezing lungfuls of air. What if the voice in the doorman's ear had given different instructions? What might be happening to us now?

It's this thought rather than the cold that makes me shiver. I pull my jacket tighter around me.

"Let's get away from here," Theo says. I wonder if he's thinking along the same lines: *let's not give them a chance to change their minds.*

The street is almost silent, completely deserted: just the blink of the security lights in shop windows and the echo of our feet on the cobblestones.

And then I hear a new sound: another pair of feet, behind us and moving quickly, quicker, growing louder as my heart starts beating faster. I turn to see. A tall figure, hood pulled up. And as the light catches her face just so, I see that it's her. The girl who followed me two nights ago, the girl on the hoop, who stared at me in the audience this evening like she'd come face to face with a nightmare.

Concierge

THE LOGE

I AM DUSTING, UP ON the top floor. Normally I do the hallways and staircases at this time of day—Madame Meunier is very particular about that. But this evening I have trespassed onto the landing. It is the second risk I have taken; the first was speaking to the girl earlier. We might have been seen. But I was desperate. I tried to put a note under her door yesterday evening, but she caught me there, threatened me with a knife. I had to find another way. Because I saw who she was the first night she arrived, coming to that woman's aid, helping her put the clothes back into her suitcase. I could not stand back and let another life be destroyed.

They are all in there, in the penthouse: all apart from him, the head of the family. I could have taken the back staircase—I use it sometimes to keep watch—but the acoustics are much better from here. I can't hear everything they're saying but every so often I catch hold of a word or a phrase.

One of them says his name: Benjamin Daniels. I press a little closer to the door. They are talking about the girl now, too. I think about that hungry, interested, bright way about her. Something in her manner. She reminds me of her brother, yes. But also of my daughter. Not in looks, of course: no one could match my daughter in looks.

* * *

ONE DAY, WHEN the heat had begun to dissipate I invited Benjamin Daniels into my cabin for tea. I told myself it was because I had to show my gratitude for the fan. But really I wanted company. I had not realized how lonely I had been until he showed an interest. I had lost the shame I had felt at first about my meager way of living. I had begun to enjoy the companionship.

He glanced again at the photographs on the walls as he sat cradling his glass of tea. "Elira: have I got that right? Your daughter's name?"

I stared at him. I could not believe he had remembered. It touched me. "That's correct, Monsieur."

"It's a beautiful name," he said.

"It means 'the free one.'"

"Oh—in what language?"

I paused. "Albanian." This was the first thing I trusted him with. From this detail he might have been able to guess my status here, in France. I watched him carefully.

He simply smiled and nodded. "I've been to Tirana. It's a wonderful city—so vibrant."

"I have heard that . . . but I don't know it well. I'm from a small village, on the Adriatic coast."

"Do you have any pictures?"

A hesitation. But what harm could it do? I went to my tiny bureau, took out my album. He sat down in the seat across from me. I noticed he took care not to disturb the photographs as he turned the pages, as though handling something very precious.

"I wish I had something like this," he said, suddenly. "I don't know what happened to the photos, from when I was small. But then again I don't know if I could look—"

He stopped. I sensed some hidden reservoir of pain. Then, as though he had forgotten it—or wanted to forget it—he pointed at a photograph. "Look at this! The color of that sea!"

I followed his gaze. Looking at it I could smell the wild thyme, the salt in the air.

He glanced up. "I remember you said you followed your daughter to Paris. But she isn't here any longer?"

I saw his gaze flicker around the cabin. I heard the unspoken question. It wasn't as though I had left poverty at home for a life of riches here. Why would a person abandon their life for this?

"I did not intend to stay," I said. "Not at first."

I glanced up at the wall of photographs. Elira looked out at me—at five, at twelve, at seventeen—the beauty growing, changing, but the smile always the same. The eyes the same. I could remember her at the breast as an infant: dark eyes looking up at me with such brightness, an intelligence beyond her years. When I spoke it was not to him but to her image.

"I came here because I was worried about her."

He leaned forward. "Why?"

I glanced at him. For a moment I had almost forgotten he was there. I hesitated. I had never spoken to anyone about this. But he seemed so interested, so concerned. And there was that pain I had sensed in him. Before, even when he had shown me the little kindnesses and attentions, I had seen him as one of them. A different species. Rich, entitled. But that his pain made him human.

"She forgot to call when she said she would. And when I eventually heard from her she didn't sound the same." I looked at the photographs. "I—" I tried to find a way to describe it. "She told me she was busy, she was working hard. I tried not to mind. I tried to be happy for her."

But I knew. With a mother's instinct, I knew something was wrong. She sounded bad. Hoarse, ill. But worse than that she sounded vague; not like herself. Every time we had spoken before I felt her close to me, despite the hundreds of miles between us. Now I could feel her slipping away. It frightened me.

I took a breath. "The next time she called was a few weeks later."

All I could hear at first were gasps of air. Then finally I could make out the words: "I'm so ashamed, Mama. I'm so ashamed. The place—it's a bad place. Terrible things happen there. They're not good people. And . . .' The next part was so muffled I could not make it out. And then I realized she was crying; crying so hard she could not speak. I gripped the phone tight enough that my hand hurt.

"I can't hear you, my darling."

"I said . . . I said I'm not a good person, either."

"You are a good person," I told her, fiercely. "I know you: and you're mine and you're good."

"I'm not, Mama. I've done terrible things. And I can't even work there any longer."

"Why not?"

A long pause. So long that I began to wonder if we had been cut off. "I'm pregnant, Mama."

I thought I hadn't heard her properly at first.

"You're . . . pregnant?" Not only was she unmarried; she hadn't mentioned any partner to me; anyone special. I was so shocked I couldn't speak for a moment. "How many months?"

"Five months, Mama. I can't hide it any longer. I can't work."

After this, all I could hear was the sound of her crying. I knew I had to say something positive.

"But I'm—I'm so happy, my darling," I told her. "I'm going to be a grandmother. What a wonderful thing. I'll start getting some money together." I tried not to let her hear my panic, about how I would do this quickly enough. I would have to take on extra work—I would have to ask favors, borrow. It would take time. But I would find a way. "I'll come to Paris," I told her. "I'll help you look after the baby."

I looked at Benjamin Daniels. "It took some time, Monsieur. It was not cheap. It took me six months. But finally I had the money to come here." I had my visa, too, which would allow me to stay for a few weeks. "I knew that she would already have had the baby, though I hadn't heard from her for several weeks." I had tried not to panic about this. I had tried, instead, to imagine what it would be like to hold my grandchild for the first time. "But I would be there to help her with the care; and to care for her: that was the important thing."

"Of course." He nodded in understanding.

"I had no home address for her, when I arrived. So I went to her place of work. I knew the name; she had told me that much. It seemed such an elegant, refined place. In the rich part of town, as she had said.

"The doorman looked at me in my poor clothes. "The entrance for the cleaners is round the back," he said.

"I was not offended, it was only to be expected. I found the entrance, slipped inside. And, because I looked the way I did, I was invisible. No one paid me any attention, no one said I should not be there. I found the women—the girls—who had worked with my daughter, who knew her. And that was when—"

For a moment I could not speak.

"When?" he prompted, gently.

"My daughter died, Monsieur. She died in childbirth nineteen years ago. I came to work here and I have stayed ever since."

"And the baby? Your daughter's baby?"

"But Monsieur. Clearly you have not understood." I took the photograph album from him and shut it back in the bureau with my relics, my treasures. The things I have collected over the years: a first tooth, a child's shoe, a school certificate. "My granddaughter is here. It's why I came here. Why I have worked here for all these years, in this building. I wanted to be close to her. I wanted to watch her grow up."

A WORD, FROM behind the penthouse door, and suddenly I am wrenched back into the present. I have just distinctly heard one of them say: "Concierge." I step backward into the gloom, treading carefully to avoid the creaking floorboards. An instinct: I should not be here. I need to get back to my cabin. Now.

Mimi

I BURST BACK INTO THE apartment. I go straight to my room, straight to the window, stare out through the glass. It was hell, sitting up there with all of them. Talking, shouting at each other. I just wanted it to stop. I wanted so badly to be alone.

Mimi. Mimi. Mimi.

It takes a moment for me to work out where the sound is coming from. I turn around and see Camille standing there in my doorway, hands on her hips.

"Mimi?" She walks toward me, clicks her fingers in front of my face. "Hello? What are you doing?"

"*Quoi?*" *What?* I stare at her.

"You were just staring out of the window. Like some sort of zombie." She does an impression: eyes wide, jaw hanging open. "What were you looking at?"

I shrug. I hadn't even realized. But I must have been looking into his apartment. Old habits die hard.

"*Putain*, you're scaring me, Mimi. You've been acting so . . . so weird." She pauses. "Even weirder than normal." Then she frowns, like she's working something out. "Ever since the other night. When I came back late and you were still up. What is it?"

"*Rien*," I say. *It's nothing.* Why won't she just leave me alone?

"I don't believe you," she says. "What happened here, before I got back that night? What's going on with you?"

I shut my eyes, clench my fists. I can't cope with all these questions. All this probing. I feel like I'm about to explode. With as much control as I can manage, I say: "I just . . . I need to be on my own right now, Camille. I need my own space."

She doesn't take the hint. "Hey—was it something to do with that guy you were being so mysterious about? Did it not work out? If you'd just tell me, maybe I could help—"

I can't take any more. The white noise is buzzing in my head. I stand up. I hate the way she's looking at me: the concern and worry in her expression. Why can't she just get it? I suddenly feel like I don't want to see her face any more. Like it would be much better if she weren't here at all.

"Just shut up! *Fous le camp!*" *Fuck off.* "Just—just leave me alone."

She takes a step back.

"And I'm sick of you bugging me," I say. "I'm sick of all your mess around the place, everywhere I look. I'm sick of you bringing your, your . . . fuck-buddies back here. I might be a weirdo— yes, I know all of your friends think that—but you . . . you're a disgusting little slut."

I think I've done it now. Her eyes are wide as she steps farther away from me. Then she disappears from the room. I don't feel good, but at least I can breathe again.

I hear sounds coming from her bedroom next door, drawers being pulled open, cupboard doors slamming. A few moments later she appears with a couple of canvas bags over each arm, stuff spilling out of them.

"You know what?" she says. "I might be a disgusting little slut, but you are one crazy bitch. I can't be bothered with this any more, Mimi, I don't need this. And Dominique's got her own place now. No more sneaking around. I'm out of here."

There's only one person I know with that name. That doesn't make any sense. "Dominique—"

"Yeah. Your brother's ex. And all that time he thought she was flirting with Ben." A little smile. "That was a good decoy, right? Anyway. This is different. This is the real deal. I love her. It's one woman for me now. No more Camille the—what was it you called me?—disgusting little slut." She hoists her bag higher on her shoulder. "*Bof.* Whatever. I'll see you around, Mimi. Good luck with whatever the fuck is going on with you."

A couple of minutes later she's gone. I turn back to the window. I watch her striding across the courtyard, bags over her arm.

For a moment I actually feel better, calmer, freer. Like maybe I'll be able to think more clearly with her gone. But now it's too quiet. Because it's still here; the storm in my head. And I don't know whether I'm more frightened of it—or of what it's drowning out.

I lift my gaze from the courtyard. I look back into his apartment. A few days ago, I let myself in there with the key I stole from the concierge's cabin. I've been going into that cabin since I was a little girl, sneaking in while I was sure the old woman was on one of the top floors cleaning. It used to fascinate me: it was like the cabin in the woods from a fairytale. She has all these mysterious photographs on the walls, the proof she actually had another life before she came here, as hard as it is to believe. A beautiful young woman in so many of them: like a princess from the same fairytale.

Now I'm older, of course, I know that there's nothing magical about the cabin. It's just the tiny, lonely home of a poor old lady; it's depressing. But I still remembered exactly where she kept the master set of keys. Of course, she's not allowed to use them. They're in case of emergencies, if there was a flood in one of the apartments, say, while we're away on holiday somewhere. And she doesn't have a set for my parents' apartment: that's off-limits.

It was early evening, dusk. I waited, watched him go out

through the courtyard, like I watched Camille just now. He was only in a shirt and it was cold, so I didn't think he was going far. Perhaps just a few streets over to buy some cigarettes from the *tabac*, which still gave me enough time to do what I needed.

I ran down the single flight of steps and let myself into the third-floor apartment.

Underneath my clothes I was wearing the new lingerie I had bought with Camille. I could feel the secret, rustling slipperiness of it against my skin. I felt like someone braver. Bolder.

I was going to wait for him until he came back. I wanted to surprise him. And this way I would be the one in control of the situation.

I'd watched him so many times from my bedroom. But to stand in his apartment was different, I could *feel* his presence there. Smell the scent of him beneath the strange, musty, old-lady odor of the place. I wandered around for a while, just breathing him in. The whole time his cat stalked after me, watching me. Like it knew I was up to no good.

I opened his fridge and I riffled through his cupboards. I looked through his records, his collection of books. I went into his bedroom and lay down on his bed, which still had the imprint of his body in it, and I inhaled the scent of him on the pillows. I looked through the toiletries in his bathroom, opened the caps. I sprayed his lemon-scented cologne down the front of my shirt and in my hair. I opened his closet and buried my face in his shirts, but better were the shirts in his laundry basket—the ones he'd worn, the ones that smelled like his skin and sweat. Better even than that were the short hairs I found around the sink where he'd shaved and hadn't managed to wash them all away. I collected several on a finger. I swallowed them.

If I'd watched myself, I might have said I looked like someone in the grip of an *amour fou*: an obsessive, mad love. But an *amour fou* is usually unrequited. And I *knew* that he felt the same way: that was the important thing. I just wanted to become a part of it, this world, his world. I'd had thousands of conversations with him in my head. I'd told him about my brothers. How horrible Antoine has always been to me. How Nick is really just a big loser who lives off Papa's money and I honestly didn't get why Ben was friends with him. How the second I graduated, I'd be out of here. Off to travel the world. We could go together.

I found a glass in the kitchen and poured myself some of his wine, drank it down like it was a glass of grenadine. I needed to be drunk enough to do this. Then I took off my clothes. I lay down on his bed: waiting like a present left there on the pillow. But after a while I felt stupid. Maybe the wine was wearing off. I was a little too cold. This wasn't how I'd planned it in my head. I'd thought he'd have come back sooner.

Half an hour ticked by. How long was he going to be?

I wandered over to his desk. I wanted to read what he was writing so late into the night—scribbling notes, typing on his laptop.

I found a notebook. A Moleskine, just like I use for my sketching. Another sign that we were meant to be: twinned souls, soulmates. The music, the writing. We were so similar. That was what he was telling me that night when we sat in the darkened park together. And before that, when he gave me the record. Outsiders, but outsiders together.

The book was full of notes for restaurant reviews. Little doodles in between the writing. Cards for restaurants tucked between the pages. It made me feel so close to him. His handwriting: beautiful, clever, a little spiky. Exactly as I would have imagined. Elegant like the fingers that had touched my arm that night in the park. I fell a little deeper in love, seeing that writing.

And then, on the last page, there was a note that had my name written there. A question mark after it, like this:

Mimi?

Oh my God. He'd been writing about me.

I had to know more, had to find out what this meant. I opened his laptop. It asked me for the password. *Merde.* I hadn't a chance of getting in. It could be literally anything. I tried a couple of things. His surname. His favorite football team—I'd found a Manchester United shirt hanging in his closet. No luck. And then I had an idea. I thought of that necklace he always wore, the one he said came from his mum. I typed in: StChristopher.

No: it bounced back at me. It was just a blind guess, so I wasn't surprised. But just because I could I tried again, with numbers substituted for some of the letters, a tighter encryption: 5tChr1st0ph3r.

And this time, when I pressed enter, the password box closed and his desktop opened up.

I stared at the screen. I couldn't believe I had guessed it. That *had* to mean something too, didn't it? It felt like a confirmation of how well I knew him. And I know writers are private about their work, in the same way that I'm private about my art, but it now felt almost like he wanted whatever was on here to be found and read by me.

I went to his documents; to "Recent." And there it was at the top. All the others had the names of restaurants, they were obviously reviews. But this one was called: *Meunier Wines SARL.* According to the little time stamp this was what he had been working on an hour ago. I opened it.

Merde, my heart was beating so fast.

Excited, terrified, I began to read.

But as soon as I did I wanted to stop; I wished I had never seen any of it.

I didn't know what I had expected, but this was not it.

It felt like my whole world was caving in around me.

I felt sick.

But I couldn't stop.

Jess

THE GIRL STEPS FORWARD INTO the light of the streetlamp. She appears totally different from how she did in her act. She wears a cheap-looking fake-leather jacket and jeans with a hoodie underneath—but it's also that she's taken off all that thick makeup. She looks a lot less glamorous and at the same time much more beautiful. And younger. A *lot* younger. I didn't get a proper look at her in the darkness near the cemetery that time—if you'd asked me I might have guessed late twenties. But now I'd say somewhere closer to eighteen or nineteen, the same sort of age as Mimi Meunier.

"Why did you come?" she hisses at us, in that thick accent. "To the club?"

I remember how she turned and sprinted away the first time we met. I know I have to tread very carefully here, not spook her.

"We're still looking for Ben," I say, gently. "And I feel like you might know something that could help us. Am I right?"

She mutters something under her breath, the word that sounds like "*koorvah*." For a moment I think she might be about to turn and sprint away again, like she did the first time we met. But she stays put—even steps a little closer.

"Not here," she whispers. She looks behind her, nervous as a cat. "We must go somewhere else. Away from this place."

AT HER LEAD we walk away from the posh streets with the fancy cars and the glitzy shop windows. We walk through avenues with red-and-gold-fronted cafés with wicker seats outside, like the one I met Theo in, signs advertising *Prix Fixe* menus, groups of tourists still mooching about aimlessly. We leave them behind too. We walk through streets with bars and loud techno, past some sort of club with a long queue snaking around the corner. We enter a new neighborhood where the restaurants have names written in Arabic, in Chinese, other languages I don't even recognize. We pass vape shops, phone shops that all look exactly the same, windows of mannequins wearing different style wigs, stores selling cheap furniture. This is not tourist Paris. We cross a traffic intersection with a bristle of flimsy-looking tents on the small patch of grass in the middle, a group of guys cooking stuff on a little makeshift stove, hands in their pockets, standing close to keep warm.

The girl leads us into an all-night kebab place with a flickering sign over the door and a couple of small metal tables at the back, rows of strip lights in the ceiling. We sit down at a greasy little Formica table in the corner. It's hard to imagine anywhere more different from the low-lit glamor of the club we've just left. Maybe that's exactly why she's chosen it. Theo orders us each a carton of chips. The girl takes a huge handful of hers and dunks them, all together, into one of the pots of garlic sauce then somehow crams the whole lot hungrily into her mouth.

"Who's he?" she mumbles through her mouthful, nodding at Theo.

"This is Theo," I say. "He works with Ben. He's helping me. I'm Jess. What's your name?"

A brief pause. "Irina."

Irina. The name is familiar. I remember what Ben had scribbled on that sheet of wine accounts I found in his dictionary. *Ask Irina.*

"Ben said he would come back," she says suddenly, urgently.

"He said he would come back for me." There's something in her expression I recognize. Aha. Someone else who has fallen in love with my brother. "He said he would get me away from that place. Help find a new job for me."

"I'm sure he was working on it," I say cautiously. It sounds quite like Ben, I think. Promising things he can't necessarily deliver. "But like I said before, he's disappeared."

"What has happened?" she asks. "What do you think has happened to him?"

"We don't know," I tell her. "But I found a card for the club in his stuff. Irina, if there's anything you can tell us, anything at all, it might help us find him."

She sizes both of us up. She seems confused by being in this unfamiliar position of power. And frightened, too. Glancing over her shoulder every few seconds.

"We can pay you," I say. I look across at Theo. He rolls his eyes, pulls out his wallet.

When we've agreed on an amount of cash Irina is happy with—depressingly small, actually—and after she's finished the chips and used up both of our pots of garlic sauce, she draws one leg up against the table protectively, the skin of her knee pale and bruised in one spot through the ripped denim. For some reason this makes me think of playground scrapes, the child she was not so long ago.

"You have a cigarette?" she asks Theo. He passes her one and she lights up. Her knee is juddering against the table, so hard that the little salt and pepper shakers are leaping up and down.

"You were really good by the way," I say, trying to think of something safe to begin with. "Your dancing."

"I know," she says, seriously, nodding her head. "I'm very good. The best at La Petite Mort. I trained as a dancer, before, where I come from. When I came for the job, they said it was for dancing."

"It seemed like the audience really enjoyed it," I say. "The show. I thought your performance was very . . ." I try and think of the right word. "Sophisticated."

She raises her eyebrows, then makes a kind of *ha* sound without any humor in it.

"The show," she mutters. "That's what Ben wanted to know about. It seemed like he knew some things already. I think someone told him some of it, maybe."

"Told him some of what?" I prompt.

She takes a long drag on her cigarette. I notice that her hand is shaking. "That the show, all of it: it's just—" She seems to be searching for the right words. "Window . . . looking. No. Window shopping. Not what that place is really about. Because afterward they come downstairs. The special guests."

"What do you mean?" Theo says, sitting forward. "Special guests?"

A nervous glance out through the windows at the street. Then suddenly she's fumbling the roll of notes Theo gave her back out of her jacket pocket, thrusting it at him.

"I can't do this—"

"Irina," I say, quickly, carefully, "we're not trying to get you in any trouble. Trust me. We won't go blabbing to anyone. We're just trying to find out what Ben knew, because I think that might help us find him. Anything you can tell us might be useful in some way. I'm . . . really scared for him." As I say it my voice breaks: it's no act. I lean forward, begging her. "Please. Please help us."

She seems to be absorbing all this, deciding. I watch her take a long breath. Then, in a low voice, she begins to talk.

"The special guests pay for a different kind of ticket. Rich men. Important men. Married men." She holds up her hand for emphasis, touches her ring finger. "We don't know names. But we know they are important. With—" she rubs her thumb and forefinger together: *money*. "They come downstairs. To the other rooms, below. We make them feel good. We tell them how handsome they are, how sexy."

"And do they," Theo coughs, "buy . . . anything?"

Irina stares at him blankly.

I think his delicacy might have been lost in translation.

"Do they pay for sex?" I ask, lowering my voice to a murmur—wanting to show we have her back. "That's what he means."

Again she glances at the windows, out at the dark street. She's practically hovering in her seat, looking like she's ready to leg it at any moment.

"Do you want more money?" I prompt. I kind of want her to ask for more. I'm sure Theo can afford it.

She nods, quickly.

I nudge Theo. "Go on then."

A little reluctantly he pulls another couple of notes out of his pocket, slides them across the table to her. Then, almost like she's reading from some sort of script, she says: "No. It is illegal in this country. To pay."

"Oh." Theo and I look at each other. I think we must both be thinking the same thing. *In that case, then what . . . ?*

But she hasn't finished. "They don't buy *that*. It's clever. They buy wine. They spend *big* money on wine." She spreads her hands to demonstrate this. "There's a code. If they ask for a 'younger' vintage that's the kind of girl they want. If they ask for one of the 'special' vintages it means they'd like . . . extras. And we do everything they want us to. We do whatever they ask. We're theirs for the night. They choose the girl—or girls—they want, and they go to special room with a lock on the door. Or we go somewhere with them. Hotel, apartment—"

"Ah," Theo says, grimacing.

"The girls at the club. We don't have family. We don't have money. Some have run from home. Some—many—are illegal." She sits forward. "They have our passports, too."

"So you can't leave the country," I say, turning to Theo. "That's fucking dark."

"I can't go back there anyway," she says, suddenly, fiercely. "To Serbia. It wasn't—it wasn't a good situation back home." She adds, defensively: "But I never thought—I never thought that would be where I'd end up, a place like that. They know we won't go to the police. One of the clients, some girls say he *is* police. Important police. Other places get shut down all the time. But not that place."

"Can you actually prove that?" Theo asks, sitting forward.

At this, she checks over her shoulder and lowers her voice. Then she nods. "I took some photos. Of the one they say is police."

"You've got photos?" Theo leans forward, eagerly.

"They take our phones. But when I started speaking to Ben he gave me a camera. I was going to give this to your brother." A hesitation. Her eyes dart between us and the window. "More money," she says.

Both of us turn to Theo, wait as he finds some more cash and puts it on the table between us.

She fumbles her hand into the pocket of her jacket, then takes it back out, fist clenched, knuckles showing white. Very carefully, like she's handling something explosive, she places a memory card on the table and pushes it toward me. "They're not such good photos. I had to be so careful. But I think it's enough."

"Here," Theo says, reaching out a hand.

"No," Irina says, looking at me. "Not him. You."

"Thank you." I take it, slide it into my own jacket pocket. "I'm sorry," I say, because it seems suddenly important to say it. "I'm sorry this has happened to you."

She shrugs, hunches into herself. "Maybe it's better than other things. You know? At least you're not going to end up murdered at the end of an alley or in the Bois de Boulogne, or raped in some guy's car. We have more control. And sometimes they buy us presents, to make us feel good. Some of the girls get nice clothes, jewelry. Some go on dates, become girlfriends. Everybody's happy."

Except she looks anything but happy.

"There's even a story—" She leans closer, lowers her voice.

"What?" Theo asks.

"That the owner's wife came from there."

I stare at her. "What, from the club?"

"Yes. That she was one of the girls. So I guess it worked out OK for some."

I'm trying to process this. Sophie Meunier? The diamond earrings, the silk shirts, the icy stare, the penthouse apartment, the whole vibe of being better than everyone else . . . she was one of *them*? A sex worker?

"But it's not rich husbands for everyone. Some guys—they refuse to wear anything. Or they take it off when you're not looking. Some girls get, you know . . . sick."

"You mean STIs?" I ask.

"Yes." And then in a small voice: "I caught something." She makes a face, a grimace of disgust and embarrassment. "After that, I knew I had to leave. And some girls get pregnant. It happens, you know? There's a story too, about a girl a long, long time ago—maybe it's just a rumor. But they say she got pregnant and wanted to keep it, or maybe it was too late to do something . . . anyway, when she went into—" She mimes doubling over with pain.

"Labor?"

"Yes. When that happened she came to the club; she had no other place to go. When you're illegal, you're scared to go to hospital. She had the baby *in* the club. But they said it was a bad birth. Too much blood. They took her body away, no one ever knows she existed. No problem. Because she wasn't official."

Jesus Christ. "And you told all this to Ben?" I ask her.

"Yes. He said he would make sure I was safe. Help me out. A new start. I speak English. I'm clever. I want a normal job. Waitressing, something like that. Because—" Her voice wavers. She puts up a hand to her eyes. I see the shine of tears. She swipes at them with the heel of her hand, almost angrily, like she doesn't have time for crying. "It's not what I came to this country for. I came for a new life."

And even though I never cry I feel my own eyes pricking. I hear her. Every woman deserves that. The chance of a new life.

Mimi

I SIT HERE ON MY bed, staring into the darkness of his apartment, remembering. On his laptop, three nights ago, I read about a place with a locked room. About what happened in that room. About the women. The men.

About how it was—is—connected to this place. To this family.

I felt sick to my stomach. It couldn't be right, what he'd written. But there were names. There was detail. So much horrible detail. And Papa—

No. It couldn't be true. I refused to believe it. It had to be lies—

And then I saw my own name, like I had in his notebook, when it had been so exciting. Only now it filled me with fear. Somehow I was connected to that place, too. There were horrible things my older stepbrother had said. I had always thought they were just random insults. Now I wasn't sure. I didn't think I could bring myself to read it, but I knew I had to.

What I saw next . . . I felt my whole life fall apart. If it was true, it would explain exactly why I had always felt like an outsider. Why Papa had always treated me the way he had. Because I wasn't really theirs. And there was more: I glimpsed a line, something about my real mother, but I couldn't read it because my eyes had blurred with tears—

I froze. Then I heard footsteps outside, approaching the door. *Merde.* I slammed the laptop closed. The key was turning in the lock. He was back.

Oh God. I couldn't face him. Not now. Not like this. Everything was changed between us, broken. Everything I believed in had just been shattered. Everything I had ever known was a lie. I didn't even know who I was any more.

I ran into the bedroom. There was no time . . . The closet. I yanked the doors open, slipped inside, crouched down in the darkness.

I heard him put a record on the player in the main room and the music streamed out, just like the music I had heard every hot summer night, floating to me across the courtyard. As though he had been playing it for me.

It felt like my heart was breaking.

It couldn't be true. It couldn't be true.

Then, over the sound of my own breathing, I heard him entering the room. Through the keyhole I saw him moving around. He pulled off his sweater. I saw his stomach, that line of hair I had noticed on the first day. I thought about that girl I had been, the one who had watched him from the balcony. I hated her for being such a clueless little idiot. A spoiled brat. Thinking *she* had issues. She had no idea. But at the same time I was grieving for the loss of her. Knowing I could never go back to her.

He paced close to the closet—I cringed back into the shadows—and then moved away again, stepping into the bathroom. I heard him turn on the shower. All I wanted, now, was to get out of there. This was my moment. I pushed the door open. I could hear him moving around in the bathroom, the shower door opening. I began to tiptoe across the floor. Quiet as I could. Then there was a knock on the front door to the apartment. *Putain.*

Back I ran, back to the closet, crouching down in the darkness.

I heard the shower stop. I heard him go to answer it, greeting whoever it was at the door.

And then I heard the other voice. I knew it straightaway, of course I did. They talked for a while, but I couldn't hear what they were saying. I opened the closet door a crack, trying to hear.

Then they were coming into the bedroom. Why? What were they doing in the bedroom? Why would those two come in here? I could just make them out through the keyhole. Even in those snatched glimpses I could see there was something strange about their body language—something I couldn't quite work out. But I knew that something was wrong . . . something was not how it should be.

And then it happened. I saw them move together, the two of them. I saw their lips meet. It felt like it was happening in slow motion. I was digging my nails so hard into my palms I thought I might be about to draw blood. This couldn't be happening. This couldn't be real. I sank down into the darkness, fist in my mouth, teeth biting into my knuckles to stop myself from screaming.

A few moments later I heard the shower start again. The two of them going into the bathroom, closing the door. Now was my chance. I didn't care about the risk, that they might catch me. Now nothing mattered as much as getting out of there. I ran like I was running for my life.

BACK IN MY room, back in the apartment, I fell to pieces. I was sobbing so hard I could hardly breathe. The pain was too much; I couldn't bear it. I thought of all the plans I had made for the two of us. I knew he had felt it too, what had been between us in the park that night. And now he'd broken it. He'd ruined it all.

I took out the paintings I'd made of him and forced myself to look at them. Grief became rage. Fucking bastard. Fucking lying *fils de pute*. All those horrible, twisted, lying words on his computer. And then he and Maman, the two of them together like that—

I stopped, remembered what I'd seen on his computer. I had called her Maman, but after everything I had read I wasn't even sure what she was to me now—

No. I couldn't think about that. I wouldn't, couldn't believe it. It was all too painful. I could only focus on my anger: that was pure, uncomplicated. I took out my canvas-cutting knife, the blade so sharp you can cut yourself just by touching it to your thumb. I held it to the first canvas and I sliced through it. All the time I felt like he was watching me with those beautiful eyes, asking what I was doing, so I punched holes through them so I couldn't see his eyes any longer. And then I ripped into all of them, stabbing through the canvas with the blade, enjoying hearing it tear. I pulled at the fabric with my hands, the canvas rasping as his face, his body, was torn to pieces.

Afterward I was trembling.

I looked at what I'd done, the mess, the violence of it. Knowing that it had come from me. I felt like I had an electric current running through me. A feeling that was kind of like fear, kind of like excitement. But it wasn't enough.

I knew what I had to do.

Jess

"I HAVE TO GO," IRINA says. A nervous glance out at the dark, empty street beyond the windows. "We've been too long, talking like this."

I feel bad just letting her wander off into the city on her own. She's so young, so vulnerable.

"Will you be OK?" I ask her. She gives me a look. It says: I've been looking after myself for a very long time, babe. I trust myself to do that better than anyone else. And there's something proud about her as she walks away, a kind of dignity. The way she holds herself, so upright. A dancer's posture, I suppose.

I think how Ben promised to take care of her. I could make promises, too. But I don't know if I can keep them. I don't want to lie to her. But I make a vow to myself, in this moment, that if I can find a way, I will.

AS THEO AND I walk toward the Metro I'm reeling, running through everything Irina told us. Do they all know? The whole family? Even "nice guy" Nick? The thought makes me feel nauseous. I think of how he told me that he was "between jobs," how it clearly didn't make much odds to him. I suppose it wouldn't if you don't need an income, if your lifestyle is being bankrolled by a load of girls selling themselves.

And if the Meunier family knew that Ben had found out the truth about La Petite Mort, what might they have done to prevent a secret like that from getting out?

I turn to Theo. "If Ben's story had printed the police would have to act, wouldn't they? It wouldn't matter if the Meuniers have some high-up contacts. Surely there'd be public pressure to investigate."

Theo nods, but I sense he's not really listening. "So he really was onto something, after all," he mutters quickly, almost to himself. He sounds very different from his usual sardonic, downbeat self. He sounds . . . I try to put my finger on it. Excited? I glance at him.

"It's going to be a huge scoop," he says. "It's big. It's really big. Especially if establishment figures are involved. It's like the President's Club but way, way darker. It's the sort of thing that wins awards . . ."

I stop dead. "Are you taking the piss?" I can feel anger pulsing through me. "Do you even care about Ben at all?" I stare at him. "You don't, do you?" Theo opens his mouth to say something but I don't want to hear another word. "Ugh. You know what? Fuck you."

I march away from him, as fast as I can in these ridiculous heels. I'm not completely sure where I'm going, and of course my stupid phone ran out of data, but I'll work it out. Far better than having to spend literally another second in his company.

"Jess!" Theo calls.

I'm half jogging now. I turn left onto another street. I can't hear him anymore, thank God. I think this is the way. But the problem is that all the crappy phone shops look exactly the same, especially with their lights off and grilles down, no one about. There's an odd smell coming from somewhere, acrid, like burning plastic.

What a bastard. I seem to be crying. Why the hell am I crying? I always knew I couldn't trust him, really; I suspected he'd had some angle the first time we met. So it's not like it's a big surprise. It must be everything, the stress of the last few days. Or

Irina: the horror of everything she just told us. Or simply the fact that, even though I half saw it coming, I'd kind of hoped I was wrong, just this once.

And now here I am alone, again. Like always.

I turn onto a new street. Hesitate. I don't think I recognize this. But there seem to be Metro stops everywhere in this city. If I walk for another couple of blocks I'm sure I'll find one. Over the churn of angry thoughts in my head I'm vaguely aware of some sort of commotion nearby. Yelling and shouting: a street party? Maybe I should head in that direction. Because I've just realized there's a lone guy walking in my direction from the other end of the street, hands in his pockets, and I'm sure he's fine, but I don't really want to test it.

I turn off, head toward the noise. And way, way too late I realize this is no street party. I see a mass of people surging in my direction, some of them wearing balaclavas and swim goggles and ski masks. Huge plumes of black smoke are mushrooming into the air. I can hear screaming, shouting, the sound of metal being struck.

Heat roars toward me in a powerful wave and I see the fire in the middle of the street: the flames as high as the second-floor windows of the buildings opposite. In the middle you can just make out the blackened skeleton of a police van that has been turned on its side and lit ablaze.

Now I can make out the police approaching the protestors in riot gear, helmets and plastic visors, waving batons in the air. I hear the whiplash crack of the batons as they make contact. And mixing with the black smoke is another kind of vapor: grayish, spilling in all directions—coming toward me. For a moment I stand, frozen, watching. People are running in this direction, slaloming around me. Pushing, yelling, desperate, holding scarves and T-shirts over their mouths. A guy next to me turns and lobs something—a bottle?—back in the direction of the police.

I turn and follow, trying to run. But there are too many bodies and the gray vapor is catching up with me, swirling all around. I start coughing and can't stop; I feel like I'm choking. My eyes are stinging, watering so much I can hardly see. Then I collide—smack!—into another body, someone who's just standing still in the middle of the stampede. I ricochet back, winded by the impact. Then look up, squinting through the tears.

"Theo!"

He grabs hold of the arm of my jacket and I cling onto him. Together we turn and half-run, half-stumble, coughing and wheezing. Somehow we find a side street, manage to break free from the torrent of people.

A few minutes later we shove through the door of a nearby bar. My eyes are still streaming: I look at Theo and see his are red-rimmed too.

"Tear gas," he says, putting his forearm up to rub at them. "Fuck."

People are turning on their bar stools to stare at us.

"We need to wash this stuff out of our eyes," Theo says. "Straightaway."

The barman points us wordlessly in the right direction.

It's a single, largish bathroom. We get the tap running and splash water onto our faces, leaning together over the small sink. I can hear ragged breathing. I'm not sure if it's mine or his.

I blink. The water has helped to ease the stinging a little. It's now, as my pulse returns to normal, that I remember: I don't want to be in this guy's company at all. I grope for the door.

"Jess," Theo says. "About before . . ."

"No. Nope. Fuck off."

"Please, hear me out." He does, at least, look a little ashamed. He puts up a hand, mops his eyes. The fact that the tear gas makes him look like he's been crying is an odd addition. He starts speaking, quickly, like he's trying to get it all out before I can cut him off: "Please let me explain. Look. This job is a total pain in the arse, it pays absolutely nothing, it broke up my last relationship—but every so often something like this comes along and you get to expose the bad guys and suddenly it all seems worthwhile. Yeah—I realize that's no excuse. I got carried away. I'm sorry."

I look down at the floor, my arms crossed.

"And if I'm truthful, no, I didn't really care about your brother. One key skill as a journalist is being able to read people. And can I be really, brutally honest now? Ben always seemed totally self-interested. Always out for numero uno."

I hate him for saying it, not least because there's a part of me that suspects he may be right. "How dare—"

"No, no. Let me speak. When he initially told me about his big scoop, I was skeptical. He's also a bit of a bullshit merchant, no? But when you played me that voicemail, I thought: yeah, actually there might be a story here. Maybe he did get tangled up in something nasty. It might be worth seeing where this all leads after all. So no, I didn't care about your brother. But you know what, Jess? I want to help you."

"Oh f—"

"No, listen. I want to help you because I think you deserve a break and I think you're pretty bloody brave and I also think you don't have a bad bone in your body."

"Ha! Then you *really* don't know me at all."

"Christ, does anyone really know anyone? But I'm not a bad guy, Jess. To be fair, I'm not an entirely good one, either. But—" He coughs, looks down at the floor.

I glance at him. Is he bullshitting me? My eyes have started streaming again: I really don't want him to think they're tears.

"Ow. Jesus," I wince as I rub at them.

He steps toward me. "Hey. Can I take a look?"

I shrug.

He reaches out a hand and tilts my chin upward. "Yeah—they're still pretty red. But I think we only got a little of it, thank God. It should wear off soon."

His face is very close to mine. And I'm not quite sure how it happens, but one moment he's holding my jaw and peering at me, his touch surprisingly gentle; the next I appear to be kissing him and he tastes like cigarettes and the wine from the club, which is suddenly one of the better tastes I can imagine, and he's a lot taller than me so my neck is cricked but actually I don't care, in fact I kind of like it, because this is hot—it's really fucking hot—and also wrong in so many different ways, not least because I'm wearing his ex-girlfriend's clothes.

And even though he's so much bigger than me I'm the one pushing him back against the sink and he's letting me and one of his big hands is tangling in my hair and then I'm taking his other hand and pulling it under this stupid, tiny dress. And it's only now that we remember we should probably lock the door.

Sophie

THE OTHERS HAVE LEFT THE penthouse. I sent Mimi to her apartment, to wait. I don't want her to witness any of what's to come. My daughter is so fragile. Our relationship, too. We have to find a new way of being with one another.

I walk into the bathroom, gaze at myself in the mirror, grip the sides of the sink. I look pale and drawn. I look every one of my fifty years. If Jacques were here right now he would be appalled. I smooth my hair. I spray scent behind my ears, on the pulse points of my wrists. Powder the shine off my forehead. Then I pick up my lipstick and apply it. My hand falters only once; otherwise I am as precise as ever.

Then I walk back to the main room of the apartment. The bottle of wine is still there on the table. Another glass, just to help me think—

I start as I realize I am not alone. Antoine stands by the floor-to-ceiling windows, watching me: a malignant presence. He must have stayed behind after the other two left.

"What are you doing here?" I ask him. I try to keep my voice controlled, even though my pulse is fluttering up somewhere near my throat.

He steps forward, under the spotlights. The mark of my hand is still pink on his cheek. I'm not proud of myself for that loss of restraint. It happens so rarely; I have become good at keeping my emotions in check over the years. But on those very rare occasions when the provocation is great enough, I seem to lose all sense of proportion. The rage takes over.

"It's been fun," he says, coming nearer still.

"What has been fun?"

"Oh." The grin he gives me now makes him look quite deranged. "But surely you have guessed by now? After that whole thing with the photograph in Papa's study? You know. Leaving those little notes for you in your postbox, under your door. Waiting to collect my cash. I really do like how you package it up like that for me. Those nice cream envelopes. Very discreet."

I stare at him. I feel as though everything has just been turned on its head. *"You?* It's been you all along?"

He gives a little mock-curtsy. "Are you surprised? That I got it together enough? A 'useless hothouse flower' like me? I even managed to keep it all to myself . . . up till now. Didn't want my darling brother to try and get in on the action too. Because, as you well know, he is just as much of a—what was the word you used again?—*leech* as I am. He's just more hypocritical about it. Hides it better."

"You don't need money," I tell him. "Your father—"

"That's what you think. But you see, I had an inkling a few weeks ago that Dominique might be about to try and leave. Just as I suspected, she's trying to fleece me for everything I've got. She's always been a greedy little bitch. And darling Papa is so fucking tight-fisted. So I've wanted a little extra cash, you know? To squirrel away."

"Did Jacques tell you?"

"No, no. I worked it all out on my own. I found the records. Papa keeps very precise notes, did you know that? Of the clients, but also of the girls. I always had my suspicions about you, but I wanted proof. So I went deep into the archives. I found the details of one Sofiya Volkova, who used to "work"—he puts the word in air quotes—"at the club nearly thirty years ago."

That name. But Sofiya Volkova no longer exists. I left her back there, shut up in that place with the staircase leading deep underground, the velvet walls, the locked room.

"Anyway," Antoine says. "I'm more switched on than people realize. I see a great deal more than everyone thinks." That manic grin again. "But then you knew that part already, didn't you?"

Jess

THEO AND I WALK TO the Metro together. Funny, how after you've slept with someone (not that you'd call what we just did up against the sink "sleeping") you can suddenly feel so shy, so unsure of what to say to each other. I feel stupid, thinking about the time we might have just wasted. Even if, admittedly, neither of us took that much time. It also feels almost like it just happened to someone else. Especially now I've changed back into my normal clothes.

Theo turns to face me, his expression solemn. "Jess. You obviously can't go back to that place. Back into the belly of the beast? You'd be bloody mad." His tone no longer has that drawling, sardonic edge to it: there's a softness there. "Don't take this the wrong way. But you strike me as the kind of person who could be a little . . . reckless. I know you probably think it's the only way you can help Ben. And it's really . . . commendable—"

I stare at him. "*Commendable*? I'm not trying to win some kind of bloody school prize. He's my brother. He's literally the only family I have in the entire world."

"OK," Theo says, putting his hands up. "That was clearly the wrong word. But it's way, way too dangerous. Why don't you come to mine? I have a couch. You'd still be in Paris. You'll be able to keep looking for Ben. You could speak to the police."

"What, the same police who supposedly know about that place and haven't done anything about it? The same police who might well actually be in on it? Yeah, fat lot of good that would do."

We head down the steps to the Metro together, down onto the

platform. It's almost totally empty, just some drunk guy singing to himself on the opposite side. I hear the deep rumble of a train approaching, feel it behind my breastbone.

Then I have a sudden, definite feeling that something is wrong, though I can't work out what. A kind of sixth sense, I suppose. Then I hear something else: the sound of running feet. Several pairs of running feet.

"Theo," I say, "look, I think—"

But before I've even got the words out it's happening. Four big guys are tackling Theo to the ground. I realize that they're in uniform—police uniforms—and one of them is triumphantly holding a baggie full of something white in the air.

"That's not mine!" Theo shouts. "You've planted that on me— fuck's s—"

But his next words are muffled, then replaced by a groan of pain as one policeman slams his face into the wall, while another clips cuffs on him. The train is pulling into the platform: I see the people in the nearest carriage staring from the windows.

Then I see that another man is approaching us from the stairs onto the platform: older, wearing a smart suit beneath an equally smart gray coat. That cropped steel-gray hair, that pitbull face. I know him. It's the guy Nick took me into the police station to meet. Commissaire Blanchot.

Now, thinking wildly back, I make another connection. The figure I thought I recognized in the audience at the club, just before the lights went down. It was him. He must have been following us all night.

The two policemen who aren't so preoccupied with holding Theo start toward me now: it's my turn. I know I only have a few seconds to act. The train doors are opening. Suddenly a whole crowd of protestors are pouring from the carriage, carrying signs and makeshift weapons.

Theo manages to turn his head toward me. "Jess," he calls through a split lip, his voice slurred. "Get on the bloody train." The guy behind him knees him in the back; he crumples onto the platform.

I hesitate. I can't just leave him here . . .

"Get on the fucking train, Jess. I'll be fine. And don't you dare go back there."

The nearest policeman lunges for me. I step quickly out of his way, then turn and shove my way through the oncoming crowd. I leap up into the carriage just before the doors close.

Sophie

"WELL," ANTOINE SAYS. "MUCH AS I have enjoyed our little chit-chat, I'd like my cash now, please." He puts out his hand. "I thought I'd come and collect it in person. Because I've been waiting for three days now. You've always been so prompt in the past. So diligent. And I've let a day go by for extenuating circumstances, you know . . . but I can't wait forever. My patience does have limits."

"I don't have it," I say. "It is not as easy as you think—"

"I think it's pretty fucking easy." Antoine gestures about at the apartment. "Look at this place."

I unclasp my watch and hand it to him. "Fine. Take this. It's a Cartier Panthère. I'll—I'll tell your father it has gone for mending."

"Oh, *mais non*." He puts up a hand, mock-affectedly. "I'm not getting my hands dirty. I'm Papa's son, after all, you must know that about me, surely? I would like another pretty cream-colored envelope of cash, please. It's so very like you, isn't it? The elegant exterior, the cheap grubby reality inside."

"What have I done to make you hate me so much?" I ask him. "I've done nothing to you." Antoine laughs. "You're telling me that you really don't know?" He leans in a little closer and I can smell the stink of the alcohol on his breath. "You are nothing, *nothing*, compared to Maman. She was from one of the best families in France. A truly great French line: proud, noble. You know the family thinks he killed her? Paris' best physicians and they couldn't work out what was making her so sick. And when she died he replaced her with what—with you? To be honest I didn't need to see those records. I knew what you were from the moment I met you. I could *smell* it on you."

My hand itches to slap him again. But I won't allow another loss of control. Instead I say: "Your father will be so disappointed in you."

"Oh, don't try with the 'disappointment' card. It doesn't work for me any longer. He's been disappointed in me ever since I came out of my poor mother's *chatte*. And he's given me fucking nothing. Nothing, anyway, that hasn't been tied up with guilt and recrimination. All he's given me is his love of money and a fucking Oedipal complex."

"If he hears about this—you threatening me, he'll . . . he'll cut you off."

"Except he won't hear about it, will he? You can't tell him because that's the whole point. You can't let him find out. Because there's so much I *could* tell. Other things that have gone on inside these apartment walls." He pulls a thoughtful expression. "How does that saying go, again? *Quand le chat n'est pas là, les souris dansent . . ." While the cat's away, the mice dance.* He takes out his phone, waves it back and forth in front of my face. Jacques' number, right there on the screen.

"You wouldn't do it," I say. "Because then you wouldn't get your money."

"Well isn't that exactly the point? Chicken and egg, *ma chère belle-mère.* You pay, I don't tell. And you really don't want me to tell Papa, do you? About what else I know?"

He leers at me. Just as he did when I left the third-floor apartment one evening, and he emerged out of the shadows on the landing. Looked me up and down in a way that no stepson should look at their stepmother. "Your lipstick, *ma chère belle-mère*," he said, with a nasty smile. "It's smudged. Just there."

"No," I tell Antoine, now. "I'm not going to give you any more."

"Excuse me?" He cups a hand behind his ear. "I'm sorry, I don't understand."

"No, you're not getting your money. I'm not going to give it to you."

He frowns. "But I'll tell my father. I'll tell him the other thing."

"Oh no, you won't." I know that I am in dangerous territory. But I can't resist saying it. Calling his bluff.

He nods at me, slowly, like I'm too stupid to understand him. "I assure you, I absolutely will."

"Fine. Message him now."

I see a spasm of confusion cross his face. "You stupid bitch," he spits. "What's wrong with you?" But suddenly he seems uncertain. Even afraid.

I TOLD BENJAMIN Daniels about Sofiya Volkova. That was my most reckless act. More than anything else I did with him. We had showered together that afternoon. He had washed my hair for me. Perhaps it was this simple act—far more intimate than the sex, in its way—that released something in me. That encouraged me to tell him about the woman I thought I had left behind in a locked room beneath one of the city's better-heeled streets. In doing so I felt suddenly as though I was the one in control. Whoever my blackmailer was, they would no longer hold all of the cards. I would be the one telling the story.

"Jacques chose me," I said. "He could have had his pick of the girls, but he chose me."

"But of course he chose you," Ben said, as he traced a pattern on my naked shoulder.

He was flattering me, perhaps. But over the years I had also come to see what the attraction must have been for my husband. Far better to have a second wife who could never make him feel inferior, who came from somewhere so far beneath him that she would always be grateful. Someone he could mold as he chose. And I was so happy to be molded. To become Madame Sophie Meunier with her silk scarves and diamond earrings. I could leave that place far behind. I wouldn't end up like some of the others. Like the poor wretch who had given birth to my daughter.

Or so I thought. Until that first note showed me that my past hung over my life like a blade, ready at any moment to pierce the illusion I had created.

"And tell me about Mimi," Ben murmured, into the nape of my neck. "She's not yours . . . is she? How does she fit into all this?"

I went very still. This was his big mistake. The thing that finally shocked me out of my trance. Now I knew I wasn't the only one he was speaking to. Now I realized how stupid I had been. Stupid and lonely and weak. I had revealed myself to this man, this stranger—someone I still didn't really know, in spite of all our snatched time together. In hindsight, perhaps even as he had told me about his childhood he had been selecting, editing— part of him slipping away from me, ever unknowable. Giving me choice morsels, just enough that I would unburden myself to him in return. He was a journalist, for God's sake. How could I have been so foolish? In talking I had handed him the power. I hadn't just risked everything I had built for myself, my own way of life. I had risked everything I wanted for my daughter, too.

I knew what I had to do.

Just as I know what I have to do now. I steel myself, give Antoine my most withering stare. He may be taller than me but I feel him cringing beneath it. I think he has just understood that I am beyond bullying.

"Message your father or not," I say. "I don't care. But either way, you aren't getting another euro from me. And at this moment I think we all have more important matters to focus on. Don't you? You know Jacques' position on this. The family comes first."

Jess

I'M BACK HERE. BACK IN this quiet street with its beautiful build-ings. That familiar feeling settles over me: the rest of the city, the world, seems so far away.

I think of Theo's words: *"You strike me as the kind of person who could be a little . . . reckless."* It made me angry, when he said it, but he was right. I *know* there is a part of me that is drawn to danger, even seeks it out.

Maybe it's madness. Maybe if Theo hadn't just been arrested, I'd have gone back to his place like he said I should. Crashed on his sofa. Maybe not. But as it stands I don't have anywhere else to go. I know I can't go to the police. I also know that if I want to find out what happened to Ben, this place is the only option. The building holds the key, I'm sure of it. I won't find any answers running away.

I had a gut feeling that day with Mum, too. She was acting weirdly that morning. Wistful. Not herself. Her smile dreamy, like she was already somewhere else. Something told me I shouldn't go to school. Fake a sick note, like I had before. But she wasn't sad or frightened. Just a little checked out. And it was sports day and once upon a time I was good at sports and it was summer and I didn't want to be around Mum when she was like that. So I went to school and completely forgot Mum even existed for a few hours, that anything existed except my friends and the three-legged race and the sack race and all that stupid stuff.

When I got home at ten to four I knew. Before I even got to the bedroom. Before I even unpicked that lock and opened that door. I think maybe she'd changed her mind, remembered she had kids who needed her more than she needed to leave. Because she wasn't lying peacefully on the bed. She was lying like a snapshot of someone doing a front crawl, frozen in the act of swimming toward the door.

I'll never ignore a gut feeling again.

If they've done something to Ben, I know I've got the best chance of finding it out. Not the police in their pay. No one but me. I've got nothing to lose, really. If anything, I feel a kind of pull toward this place now. To crawl, as Theo put it, back into the belly of the beast. I'd thought it sounded melodramatic when he said it but, when I stand at the gate and look up at it, it feels right. Like this place, this building, is some huge creature ready to swallow me whole.

THERE'S NO SIGN of anyone about when I enter the apartment building, not even the concierge. All the lights are off in the apartments up above. It seems as deathly quiet as it did the night I arrived. It's late, I suppose. I tell myself it must just be my imagination that lends the silence a heavy quality, like the building has been waiting for me.

I move toward the stairwell. Strange. Something draws my eye in the dim light. A large, untidy pile of clothes at the bottom of the stairs, strewn across the carpet. What on earth is that doing there?

I reach for the light switch. The lights stutter on.

I look back at the pile of old clothes. My stomach clenches. I still can't see what it is but in an instant I know, I just know. Whatever is there at the bottom of the stairs is something bad. Something I don't want to see. I move toward it as though I'm pushing through water, resisting, and yet knowing I have to go and look. As I get closer I can make it out more clearly. There's a solid shape visible inside the softness of the material.

Oh my God. I'm not sure if I whisper this out loud or if it's only in my head. I can see now with horrible clarity that the shape is a person. Lying face down, spread-eagled on the flagstones. Not moving. Definitely not moving.

Not again. I've been here before. The body in front of me, so horribly still. *Oh my God oh my God.* I can see little spots dancing in front of my eyes. *Breathe,* Jess. *Just breathe.* Every part of me wants to scream, to run in the opposite direction. I force myself to crouch down. There's a chance she could still be alive . . . I bend down, put out a hand—touch the shoulder.

I can feel bile rising in my throat, gagging me. I swallow, hard. I roll the concierge over. Her body moves as though it really is just a loose collection of old clothes, too fluid, too senseless. A couple of hours ago she was warning me to be careful. She was frightened. Now she's—

I put a couple of fingers to her neck, sure there'll be nothing . . .

But I think I feel something. Is that?—yes, beneath my fingertips: a stuttering, a pulse. Faint, but definite. She is still alive, but only just.

I look up at the dark stairwell, toward the apartments. I know this wasn't an accident. I know one of them did this.

Jess

"CAN YOU HEAR ME?" CHRIST, I realize I don't even know the woman's name. "I'm going to call an ambulance."

It seems so pointless. I'm sure she can't hear me. But as I watch her lips begin to part, as though she's trying to say something.

I reach into my pocket for my phone.

But there's nothing there. My jacket pocket is empty. What the hell—

I scrabble in my jeans pockets. Not in there either. Back up to my jacket. But it's definitely not here. No phone.

And then I remember. I handed it over to that doorman in the club, because he wouldn't let us in otherwise. We got thrown out before I had a chance to collect it—and I'm certain he wouldn't have handed it over anyway.

I close my eyes, take a deep breath. OK, Jess: think. *Think*. It's fine. It's fine. You don't need your phone. You can just go onto the street and ask someone else to call an ambulance.

I shove open the door, run through the courtyard to the gate. Pull at the handle. But nothing happens. I pull harder: still nothing. It doesn't move a millimeter. The gate is locked; it's the only explanation. I suppose the same mechanism that allows it to be opened with the key code can also be used to lock it shut. I'm trying to think rationally. But it's difficult because panic is taking over. The gate is the only way out of this place. And if it's locked, then I'm trapped inside. There is no way out.

Could I climb it? I look up, hopefully. But it's just a sheet of steel, nothing to get a toehold on. Then there are the anti-climb spikes along the top and the shards of glass along the wall either side that would shred me to pieces if I tried to climb over.

I run back into the building, into the stairwell.

When I return I see the concierge has managed to sit up, her back against the wall near the bottom of the staircase. Even in the gloom I can make out the cut at her hairline where she must have hit her head on the stone floor.

"No ambulance," she whispers, shaking her head at me. "No ambulance. No police."

"Are you mad? I have to call—"

I break off, because she has just looked up at the staircase behind me. I follow her gaze. Nick is standing there, at the top of the first flight of stairs.

"Hello Jess," he says. "We need to talk."

Nick

"YOU ANIMAL," SHE SAYS. "YOU did this to her? Who the fuck are you?"

I put up my hands. "It—it wasn't me. I just found her."

It was Antoine, of course. Going too far, as usual. An old woman, for God's sake: to shove her like that.

"It must have been a . . . a terrible accident. Look. There are some things I have to explain. Can we talk?"

"No," she says. "No, I don't want to do that, Nick."

"Please, Jess. Please. You have to trust me." I need her to stay calm. Not do anything rash. Not force me to do something I'll regret. I'm also still unsure whether or not she has a phone on her.

"Trust you? Like I trusted you before? When you took me to meet that shady cop? When you hid from me that you were a family?"

"Look, Jess," I say, "I can explain everything. Just—come with me. I don't want you to get hurt. I really don't want anyone else to get hurt."

"What," she gestures to the concierge. "Like her? And Ben? What have you done to Ben? He's your friend, Nick."

"No!" I shout it. I've been trying to be so calm, so controlled. "He was not my friend. He was never my friend." And I don't even try to keep the bitterness at bay.

* * *

THREE NIGHTS AGO my little sister Mimi came and told me what she had found on his computer.

"It said . . . it said our money doesn't come from wine. It says . . . it says it's girls. Men buying girls, not wine . . . this horrible place, this club—*ce n'est pas vrai* . . . it can't be true, Nick . . . tell me it's not true." She was sobbing as she tried to speak. "And it says . . ." she fought for breath, "it says I'm not really theirs . . ."

I suppose we always knew about Mimi, Antoine and I. I suppose all families have these kind of secrets, these commonly agreed deceptions that are never spoken of aloud. Frankly, we were too afraid. I remember how, when we were little more than kids, Antoine made some comment that our father overheard—some insinuation. Papa backhanded him across the room. It has never properly been mentioned again. Just another skeleton thrown to the back of the closet.

Ben had clearly been very, very busy. It sounded as though he had discovered more about Papa and his business than I even knew myself. But then I haven't wanted to know all the deplorable particulars. I've kept as much distance, as much ignorance, as possible over the years. Still, it was all tied up with the thing I had told him in strictest confidence ten years before in a weed café in Amsterdam. The confession he had promised me, hand on heart, never to share with another soul. The secret at the very heart of my family. My main, terrible, source of shame.

I can still remember my father's words when I was sixteen, outside that locked door at the bottom of the velvet staircase. Taunting: "Oh, you think this is something you can just turn your nose up at, do you? You think you're above this? What do you think really paid for that expensive school? What do you think paid for the house you live in, the clothes you wear? Some dusty old bottles? Your sainted mother's precious inheritance?

No, my boy. *This* is where it comes from. Think you're immune now? Think you're too good for all of it?"

I knew all too well what Mimi had felt, reading about it on Ben's computer. Learning about the roots of our wealth, our identity. Discovering it was sullied money that had paid for everything. It's like a disease, a cancer, spreading outward and making all of us sick.

But at the same time you can't choose your blood. They are still the only family I have.

When Mimi told me what she had read, all of it—Ben's casual text message months ago, our meeting in the bar, the move into this building—suddenly revealed itself to be not the workings of happy coincidence, but something far more calculated. Targeted. He had used me to fulfil his own ambitions. And now he would destroy my family. And in the process, he apparently didn't care that he would also destroy me.

I thought again of that old French saying about family. *La voix du sang est la plus forte*: the voice of blood is the strongest. I didn't have a choice.

I knew what I had to do.

Just as I know what I have to do now.

Jess

"PLEASE JESS," NICK SAYS IN a reasonable tone. "Just hear me out. I'll come down there and we can chat."

For a moment I think: just because they're a family, it doesn't mean they're all responsible for what's happened here. I remember how Nick briefly referred to his father as "a bit of a cunt": clearly they don't all see eye to eye. Maybe I've jumped to conclusions—maybe she really did fall. An old woman, frail, slipping on the stairs late at night . . . no one to hear her because it's late. And maybe the front gate is locked because it's late, too—

No. I'm not going to take my chances. I turn to look back at the concierge, slumped on the floor and grimacing in pain. And as I do, I see the door to the first-floor apartment opening. I watch as Antoine steps out onto the landing to stand next to his brother—the two of them so much more alike than I had realized. He smiles down at me, a horrible grin.

"Hello, little girl," he says.

Where to run? The front gate is locked. I refuse to be the girl in the horror film who flees into the basement. Both brothers are advancing toward me down the stairs now. I don't have any time to think. Instinctively I step into the lift. I press the button for the third floor.

The lift clanks upward, the mechanism grinding. I can hear Nick running up the stairs below: through the metal grille I can see the top of his head. He's chasing me. The gloves are off now.

Finally I reach the third floor. The lift clanks into place agonizingly slowly. I open the metal gate and dash across the landing, shove the keys into the door to Ben's apartment and fling it open, slam it shut behind me, lock the door, my chest heaving.

I try to think, panic making me stupid, just when I need my thoughts to be as clear as possible. The back staircase: I could try and use that. But the sofa's in the way. I run to it, start trying to tug it away from the door.

Then I hear the unmistakable sound of a key beginning to turn in the lock. I back away. He has a key. Of course he has a key. Could I pull something in front of the door? No: there's no time.

Nick starts advancing toward me across the room. The cat, seeing him, streaks past and jumps up onto the kitchen counter to his right, mewing at him—perhaps hoping to be fed. Traitor.

"Come on, Jess," Nick says, coaxingly, still that chillingly reasonable tone. "Just, just stay where you are—"

This new menace in Nick is so much more frightening than if he hadn't worn that nice-guy mask before. I mean, his brother's violence has always seemed to simmer just beneath the surface. But Nick—this new Nick—he's an unknown quantity.

"So what?" I ask him. "So you can do the same thing to me that you've done to Ben?"

"I didn't do anything—"

There's a strange emphasis on the way he says this. A stress on the "I": "*I* didn't."

"Are you saying someone else did? One of the others?" He doesn't answer. Keep him talking, I tell myself, play for time. "I thought you wanted to help me, Nick," I say.

He looks pained now. "I did want to, Jess. And it's all my fault. I set this whole thing in motion. I invited him here . . . I should have known. He went digging into stuff he shouldn't have . . . fuck—" He rubs at his face with his hands and when he takes them away I see that his eyes are rimmed with red. "It's my fault . . . and I'm sorry—"

I feel a coldness creeping through me. "What have you done to Ben, Nick?" I meant it to sound tough, authoritative. But my voice comes out with a tremor.

"I haven't . . . I didn't . . . I haven't done anything." Again that emphasis: "*I* didn't, *I* haven't."

The only way out is past Nick, through that front door. Just by the door is the kitchen area. The utensil pot's right there; inside it is that razor-sharp Japanese knife. If I can just keep him talking, somehow grab the knife—

"Come on, Jess." He takes another step toward me.

And suddenly there's a streak of movement, a flash of black and white. The cat has leapt from the kitchen counter onto Nick's shoulders—the same way it greeted me the very first time I entered this apartment. Nick swears, puts his hands up to tear the animal away. I sprint forward, yank the knife out of the pot. Then I lunge past him for the door, wrench it open, and slam it behind me.

"Hello little girl."

I turn: fuck—Antoine stands there, he must have been waiting in the shadows. I lunge the knife toward him, slashing so violently at the air with the blade that he staggers backward and falls down the flight of stairs, collapsing in a heap on the next landing. I peer at him through the gloom, my chest burning. I think I hear a groan but he's not moving.

Nick will be out any moment. There's only one way to go.

Up.

I'm clearly outnumbered here, one of me: four of them. But perhaps there's somewhere I can hide, to try and buy some time.

Come on, Jess. Think. You've always been good at thinking yourself out of a tight spot.

Mimi

FOURTH FLOOR

"WHAT'S GOING ON OUT THERE? Maman?" After everything I have learned the word still feels strange, painful.

"Shh," she says, stroking my hair. "Shh, *ma petite*."

I'm crouched on the bed, trembling. She came down to check on me. I've allowed her to sit beside me, to put an arm around my shoulders.

"Look," she says. "Just stay in here, yes? I'm going to go out there and see what's going on."

I grab hold of her wrist. "No—please don't leave me." I hate the neediness in my voice, my need for her, but I can't help it. "Please," I say. "*Maman*."

"Just for a couple of minutes," she says. "I just have to make sure—"

"No. Please—don't leave me here."

"Mimi," she says, sharply. "Let go of my arm, please."

But I keep hanging onto her. In spite of everything I don't want her to leave me. Because then I'd be left alone with my thoughts—like a little girl afraid of the monsters under the bed.

Jess

I SPRINT UP THE STAIRS, taking them two at a time. Fear makes me run faster than I've ever done in my life.

Finally I'm on the top floor, opposite the door to the penthouse apartment, the wooden ladder up to the old maids' quarters in front of me. I begin to climb, ascending into the darkness. Maybe I can hide out here long enough to gather my thoughts, work out what the hell I'm going to do next. I'm already pulling the hoop earrings from my ears, bending them into the right shape, making my rake and my pick. I grab for the padlock, get to work. Normally I'm so quick at this but my hands are shaking—I can feel that one of the pins inside the lock is seized and I just can't get the pressure right to reset it.

Finally, finally, the lock pops open and I wrench it off and push open the door. I close it again quickly behind me. The open padlock is the only thing to give me away; I'll just have to pray they won't immediately guess I've come in here.

My eyes start to adjust in the gloom. I'm looking into a cramped attic space, long and thin. The ceiling slopes down sharply above me. I have to crouch so I don't knock my head on one of the big wooden beams.

It's dark but there's a dim glow which I realize is the full moon, filtering in through the small, smeared attic windows. It smells of old wood and trapped air up here and something animal: sweat or something worse, something decaying. Something that stops me from breathing in too deeply. The air feels thick, full of dust motes which float in front of me in the bars of moonlight. It feels as though I have just pushed open a door into another world, where time has been suspended for a hundred years.

I move forward, looking around for somewhere to hide.

Over in the dim far corner of the space I see what looks like an old mattress. There appears to be something on top of it.

I have that feeling again, like I did downstairs when I found the concierge. I don't want to step any closer. I don't want to look.

But I do, because I have to know. Now I can see what it is. Who it is. I see the blood. I understand.

He's been up here all along. And I forget that I am meant to be hiding from them. I forget everything apart from the horror of what I'm looking at. I scream and scream and scream.

Mimi

A SCREAM TEARS THROUGH THE apartment.

"He's dead. He's dead—you've fucking killed him."

I let go of my mother's arm.

The storm in my head is growing louder, louder. It's a swarm of bees . . . then like being crashed underwater by the waves, now like standing in the middle of a hurricane. But it still isn't loud enough to shut out the thoughts that are beginning to seep in. The memories.

I remember blood. So much blood.

You know how when you're a kid you can't sleep because you're afraid of the monsters under the bed? What happens if you start to suspect that the monster might be you? Where do you hide?

It's like the memories have been kept behind a locked door in my mind. I have been able to see the door. I have known it's there, and I have known that there is something terrible behind it. Something I don't want to see—ever. But now the door is opening, the memories flooding out.

The iron stink of the blood. The wooden floor slippery with it. And in my hand, my canvas-cutting knife.

I remember them pushing me into the shower. Maman . . . someone else, too, maybe. Washing me down. The blood running dilute and pink into the drain, swirling around my toes. I was shivering all over; I couldn't stop. But not because the shower was cold; it was hot, scalding. There was a deep coldness inside me.

I remember Maman holding me like she did when I was a little girl. And even though I was so angry with her, so confused, all I wanted, suddenly, was to cling to her. To be that little girl again.

"Maman," I said. "I'm frightened. What happened?"

"Shh." She stroked my hair. "It's OK," she told me. "I'm not going to let anything happen. I'll protect you. Just let me take care of all of this. You aren't going to get into any trouble. It was his fault. You did what had to be done. What I wasn't brave enough to do myself. We had to get rid of him."

"What do you mean?" I searched her face, trying to understand. "Maman, what do you mean?"

She looked closely at me then. Stared hard into my eyes. Then she nodded, tightly. "You don't remember. Yes, yes, it's best like that."

Later, there was something crusted under my fingernails, a reddish-brown rust color. I scrubbed at it with a toothbrush in the bathroom until my nail beds started bleeding. I didn't care about the pain; I just wanted to be rid of whatever it was. But that was the only thing that seemed real. The rest of it was like a dream.

And then she arrived here. And the next morning she came to the door. She knocked and knocked until I had to open it. Then she said those terrible words:

"My brother—Ben . . . he's . . . well, he's kind of disappeared."

That was when I realized it could have been real, after all.

I think it might have been me. I think I might have killed him.

Sophie

PENTHOUSE

"HE'S DEAD. HE'S DEAD—YOU'VE FUCKING killed him."

"I have to go, *chérie*," I tell Mimi. "I have to go and deal with this." I step onto the landing, leaving her in the apartment.

I look upward. It has happened. The girl is in the *chambres de bonne*. She's found him.

I remember pushing open the door to his apartment that terrible night. My daughter, covered in blood. She opened her mouth as though to speak, or scream, but nothing came out.

The concierge was there, too, somehow. But then of course she was: she sees, knows, everything—moving around this apartment building like a specter. I stood looking at the scene before me in a state of utter shock. Then a strange sense of practicality took over.

"We need to wash her," I said. "Get rid of all this blood." The concierge nodded. She took Mimi by the shoulders and led her toward the shower. Mimi was muttering a stream of words now: about Ben, about betrayal, about the club. She knew. And for some reason she had not come to me.

When she was clean the concierge took her away, back to her apartment. I could see my daughter was in a state of shock. I wanted to go with her, comfort her. But first I had to deal with the consequences of what she had done. The thing, in all honesty, that I had considered doing myself.

I found and used every tea towel in the apartment. Every towel from the bathroom. All of them, soaked through crimson. I wrenched the curtains down from the windows and wrapped the body in them, tied it carefully with the curtain cords. I hid the weapon in the dumbwaiter, in its secret cavity inside the wall, and wound the handle so it traveled up to a space between the floors.

The concierge brought bleach; I used it to clean up after I'd washed the blood away. Breathing through my mouth so as not to smell it. I pressed the back of my hand to my mouth. I couldn't vomit, I had to stay in control.

The bleach stained the floor, leached the varnish out of the wood. It left a huge mark, even larger than the pooling blood. But it was the best I could do, better than the alternative.

And then—I don't know how much later—the door opened. It wasn't even locked, I had forgotten that in the face of the task ahead of me.

They stood there. The two Meunier boys. My stepsons. Nicolas and Antoine. Staring at me in horror. The bleach stain in front of me, blood up to my elbows. Nick's face drained of all color.

"There's been a terrible accident," I said.

"Jesus Christ," Nicolas said, swallowing hard. "Is this be-cause—"

There was a long pause, while I tried to think of what to say. I would not speak Mimi's name. I decided that Jacques could take the blame, as a father should. This was, after all, really his mess. I settled on: "Your father found out what Ben had been work-ing on—"

"Oh Jesus." Nick put his face in his hands. And then he howled, like a small child. A sound of terrible pain. His eyes were wet, his mouth gaping. "This is all my fault. I told Papa. I told him what Mimi had found, what Ben had been writing. I had no idea. If I'd known, oh Jesus—"

For a moment, he seemed to sway where he stood. Then he rushed from the room. I heard him vomiting, in the bathroom.

Antoine stood there, arms folded. He looked equally sickened, but I could see he was determined to tough it out.

"Serves him right, the *putain de bâtard*," he said, finally. "I'd have done it myself." But he didn't sound convinced.

A few minutes later, Nick returned, looking pale but determined.

The three of us stood there, staring at one another. Never before had we been anything like a family. Now we were oddly united. No words passed between us, just a silent nod of solidarity. Then we got to work.

Jess

EVEN IN MY DARKEST MOMENTS over the last couple of days, even learning what Ben had got himself into, I haven't allowed myself to imagine it. Not finding my brother like this, how I found Mum.

I sink to my knees.

It doesn't look like my brother, the body on the mattress. It isn't just the pale, waxy color of the skin, the sunken eye-sockets. It's that I've never seen him so still. I can't think of my brother without thinking of his quick grin, his energy.

I take in the dark, rusted crimson color of his T-shirt. I can see that elsewhere the fabric is pale. It's a stain. It covers his entire front.

He must have been up here all along, all this time, while I've been scurrying around following clues, tying myself in knots. Thinking I was helping him somehow. And to think I'd seen that locked attic door on my first morning here.

Crouched here beside him, I rock back and forth as the tears begin to fall.

"I'm so sorry," I say. "I'm so bloody sorry."

I reach down to take a hold of his hand. When was the last time we held hands, my brother and I? That day in the police station, maybe. After Mum. Before we went our separate ways. I squeeze his fingers tight.

Then I almost drop his hand in shock.

I could have sworn I felt his fingers twitch against mine. I know it's my imagination, of course. But for a moment, I really thought—

I glance up. His eyes are open. They weren't open before . . . were they?

I get to my feet, stand over him. Heart thundering.

"Ben?"

I'm sure I just saw him blink.

"Ben?"

Another blink. I didn't imagine it. I can see his eyes attempting to focus on mine. And now he opens his mouth, but no sound comes out. Then—"Jess." It's little more than an exhalation, but I definitely heard him say it. He closes his eyes again, as though he's very, very tired.

"Ben!" I say. "Come on. Hey. Sit up." It suddenly seems very important to get him upright. I put my arms under his armpits. He's almost a dead weight. But somehow I manage to haul him into a sitting position. He half slumps forward and his eyes are cloudy with confusion, but they are open.

"Oh, Ben." I take hold of his shoulders—I don't dare hug him in case he's too badly hurt. Tears are streaming down my face now; I let them fall. "Oh my God, Ben: you're alive . . . you're alive." I hear a door slam behind me. It's the door to the attic. For a moment I had genuinely forgotten about anything and anyone else.

I turn around, slowly.

Sophie Meunier stands there. Behind her: Nick. And even though I'm reeling from everything that's just happened, I'm still able to make out that there's a big difference in their expressions. Sophie's face is an intense, terrifying mask. But Nick's, as he looks at Ben, shows surprise, horror, confusion. In fact, Nick looks—and this is the only way I can think to describe it—as though he has seen a ghost.

Nick

I FEEL DREAD CREEPING THROUGH me as I take in the scene in the attic. I ran up here when I heard the screaming, after dragging Antoine, semi-conscious, to the sofa in my apartment.

He's here. Ben is here. He doesn't look well, but he is sitting up. And he is alive.

This can't be right. It doesn't make any sense. It's not possible.

Ben is dead. He's been dead since Friday night. My one-time friend, my old university mate, the guy I fell for on that warm summer night in Amsterdam over a decade ago and have been thinking about ever since.

He died and it was my fault and in the days since I have been trying to live with the guilt and the grief of it: walking around feeling only barely alive myself.

I look to my stepmother, expecting to see my own shock reflected in her expression. It isn't there. This doesn't seem to have come as a surprise to her. She knows. It's the only explanation. Why else would she be so calm?

Finally I manage to speak. "What is this?" I ask, voice hoarse. "What is this? What the fuck is happening?" I point to Ben. "This isn't possible. He's dead."

You see, I know it for a fact. I had plenty of time to take it all in: the unspeakable horror of that lifeless shape in its makeshift shroud. The undeniable fact of it. Of the blood, too, spilled across the floorboards and soaked into the towels: far more blood than anyone could lose and live. But it's more than that. Three nights ago, Antoine and I carried his body down the stairs and dug a shallow trench and buried him in the courtyard garden.

Mimi

IT HAS ALL GONE SO quiet now, after the scream up above. What is going on? What has she found?

This is the part I remember. After this there is nothing, until the blood.

It was late and I was tired from all the thoughts whirring around my brain, but couldn't sleep. I couldn't stop thinking about what I had read. What I saw. Ben—and my mother. I'd destroyed my paintings of him. But it didn't feel like enough. I could see him over there in his apartment, working away at his computer. But it was all different now. I knew what he was writing about and the thought of it made me feel sick, all over again. I could never un-know it. Even if I tried not to believe it. But I think I do. I think I do believe it. The hushed tones everyone uses when they talk about Papa's business. Things I've heard Antoine say. It was all beginning to make a horrible kind of sense.

Ben came to the window and looked out. I ducked out of sight, so he wouldn't spot me. Then I went back to watching.

He moved back to his desk, looking at his phone, holding it to his ear. But then he looked up. Turned his head. He began to stand. The door was opening. Someone was stepping into the room.

Oh—merde.

Putain de merde.

What was he doing there?

It was Papa.

He wasn't meant to be home.

When did he get back? And what was he doing in Ben's apartment?

Papa had something in his hands. I recognized it: it was the magnum of wine he had given Ben as a present only a few weeks earlier.

He was going to—

I couldn't bear to keep looking. But at the same time I couldn't look away. I watched as Ben crumpled to his knees. As Papa raised the bottle again and again. I watched as Ben staggered backward, as he collapsed onto the floor, as blood began to soak into the front of his pale T-shirt, turning the whole thing red. And I knew it was all my fault.

Ben crawled toward the window. I watched as he raised his hand, hit his palm against the glass. And then he mouthed a word: *Help.*

I saw my father raise the bottle again. And I knew what was going to happen. He was going to kill him.

I had to do something. I loved him. Ben had betrayed me. He had destroyed my whole world. But I loved him.

I reached for the nearest thing at hand. And then I ran down the stairs so quickly it felt as though my feet weren't even touching the ground. The door to Ben's apartment was open and Papa was standing over him and I just had to make him stop—I had to make him stop and at the same time maybe there was a little voice inside me saying: he's not really your papa, this man. And he's not a good man. He's done some terrible things. And now he's about to become a killer too.

Ben was on the ground and his eyes were closed. And then I was behind Papa—he hadn't seen me, hadn't heard me creep into the room—and I had my canvas cutting knife in my hand and it's small but the blade is sharp, so very sharp, and I raised it above my head . . .

And then nothing.

And then the blood.

Later, I thought I heard the sound of voices in the courtyard. I heard the scrape of shovels. It didn't make any sense. Maman likes to garden, but it was dark, nighttime. Why was she doing it now? It couldn't be real: it had to be a dream. Or some kind of nightmare.

Nick

SECOND FLOOR

I REMEMBER LEAVING PAPA'S STUDY after I had told him what Ben had been up to, what he was writing about. I had called him home, told him there was something he needed to hear. As I descended the staircase I thought about the look on his face. The barely controlled rage. A charge of fear that returned me to childhood; when he wore that expression it was time to make yourself scarce. But at the same time I felt a frisson of perverse pleasure, too. At bursting the Benjamin Daniels bubble. At showing Papa that his famous judgment wasn't always as sound as he thought, tarnishing the golden boy he had briefly seemed to hold closer than his own sons. I had betrayed Ben, yes, but in a much smaller way than he had betrayed me and my family's hospitality. He had it coming.

Any feeling of triumph soured quickly. Suddenly I wanted to be numb. I went and took four of the little blue pills and lay in my apartment in an oxycodone haze.

Maybe I was aware of some kind of commotion upstairs, I don't know—it was like it was happening in another universe. But after a while, as the pills began to wear off, I thought perhaps I should go and see what was going on.

I met Antoine on the stairs. Could smell the booze on him: he must have been passed out in yet another drunken stupor.

"What the fuck's happening?" he asked. His tone was gruff, but there was something fearful in his expression.

"I have no idea," I said. This wasn't quite true. Already, an unnameable suspicion was forming in my mind. We climbed to the third floor together.

The blood. That was the first thing I saw. So much of it. Sophie in the middle of it all.

"*There's been a terrible accident.*" That was what she told us.

I knew in an instant that this was my fault. I had set all of this in motion. I knew what kind of man my father was. I should have known what he might be driven to do. But I had been so blinded by my own anger, my sense of betrayal. I had told myself I was protecting my family. But I also wanted to lash out. To hurt Ben somehow. But this . . . the blood, that terrible, inert form wrapped in the curtain shroud. I could not look at it.

In the bathroom I vomited as though I could expel the horror like something I had eaten. But of course it did not leave me. It was part of me now.

Somehow I pulled myself together. Ben was beyond help. I knew I had to do this, now, for the survival of the family.

The terrible weight of the body in my arms. But none of it felt real. Part of me thought that if I looked at Ben's face it would make it real. Perhaps that was important, for some sort of closure. But in the end I couldn't bring myself to do it. To undo all that tight binding, to confront what lay beneath.

So you see, this is what happened. Three nights ago Ben died—and we buried him.

Didn't we?

Sophie

FROM THE MOMENT I SAW her, covered in blood—my husband's blood—I acted so quickly, almost without thought. Everything I did was to protect my daughter. It is possible that I was in shock too but my mind seemed very clear. I have always been single-minded, focused. Able to make the best out of a bad situation. It's how I ended up with this life, after all.

I knew that if I were to have the cooperation of his sons, their help in this, Jacques would have to be alive. I knew that it had to be Benjamin who had died. Before I wrapped the body I had held Jacques' phone up to his face, unlocked it, changed the passcode. I have kept it on me ever since, messaging Antoine and Nicolas as their papa. The longer I could keep Jacques "alive," the more I could get out of his sons.

After I had done what I could for Benjamin—stemming the blood with a towel, cleaning the wounds—the concierge and I brought him up here to the *chambres de bonne*. He was too con-cussed to struggle; too badly injured to try and free himself. Here I've been keeping him alive—just. I've been giving him water, scraps of food: the other day a quiche from the boulange-rie. All until I could decide what to do with him. He was so badly wounded that it might have been easier to let nature take its course. But we had been lovers. There was still that reminder of what we had briefly been to each other. I am many things: a whore, a mother, a liar. But I am not a killer. Unlike my beloved daughter.

"Jacques has gone away for a while," I told my stepsons, when they arrived. "It is best that no one knows he was here in Paris tonight. So as far as you know, should anyone ask, he has been away the entire time on one of his trips. Yes?"

They nodded at me. They have never liked me, never approved of me. But in their father's absence they were hanging on my every word. Wanting to be told what to do, how to act. They have never really grown up, either of them. Jacques never allowed them to.

I think of the gratitude that I'd felt to Jacques in the beginning, for "rescuing" me from my previous life. I didn't realize at the time how cheaply I had been bought. I didn't free myself when I married my husband, as I'd thought. I didn't elevate myself. I did the exact opposite. I married my pimp: I chained myself to him for life.

Perhaps my daughter did the very thing I hadn't had the courage to do.

Jess

I GRIP THE KNIFE, READY to defend Ben—and myself—should either of them come closer. Strangely, they don't seem so threatening right now. The air feels less charged with tension. Nick is looking from Sophie to Ben and back; his eyes wild. Something else is going on here, something I can't understand. And yet still I grip the knife. I can't let my guard down.

"My husband is dead," Sophie Meunier says. "That is what happened." At these words I watch Nick stagger backward. *He didn't know?*

"*Qui?*" he says, hoarsely. "*Qui?*" I think he must be asking who.

"My daughter," Sophie Meunier says, "she was trying to protect Ben. I have been keeping your brother here," she gestures in our direction, "I have kept him alive." She says it like she thinks she deserves some sort of credit. I can't find the words to answer.

I look from one to the other, trying to work out how to play this. Nick is a shrunken figure: crouched down, head in his hands. Sophie Meunier is the threat here, I'm sure. I'm the one with the knife but I wouldn't put anything past her. She steps toward me. I raise the knife but she barely seems fazed.

"You are going to let us go," I say: trying to sound a lot more assertive than I feel. I might have a knife, but she has us trapped here: the outside gate is locked. I'm quickly realizing there's no way we're getting out of this place unless she agrees to it. I doubt Ben can stand without a lot of help and there's the whole building between us and the outside world. She's probably thinking the same thing.

She shakes her head. "I cannot do that."

"Yes. You have to. I need to take him to a hospital."

"No—"

"I won't tell them," I say, quickly. "Look . . . I won't say how he got the injuries. I'll . . . I'll tell them he fell off his moped, or something. I'll say he must have come back to his apartment—that I found him."

"They won't believe you," she says.

"I'll find a way to convince them. I won't tell." I can hear desperation in my voice now. I'm begging. "Please. You can take my word for it."

"And how can I be sure of that?"

"What other choice do you have?" I ask. "What else can you do?" I take a risk here. "Because you can't keep us here forever. People know I'm here. They'll come looking." Not exactly true. There's Theo, but he's presumably banged up in a cell right now and I never told him the address: it would take him some time to find out. But she doesn't need to know this. I just need to sell it. "And I know you aren't a killer, Sophie. As you say, you kept him alive. You wouldn't have done that if you were."

She watches me levelly. I have no idea if any of this is working. I sense I need something more.

I think of how she said, "My daughter," the intensity of feeling in it. I need to appeal to that part of her.

"Mimi is safe," I say. "I promise you that much. If what you're saying is true, she saved Ben's life. That means a lot—that means everything. I will never tell anyone what she did. I swear to you. That secret is safe with me."

Sophie

PENTHOUSE

CAN I TRUST HER? DO I have any other choice?

"I will never tell anyone what she did." Somehow she has managed to guess my greatest fear.

She is right: if I wanted to kill them, I would have done so already. I know that I cannot trap the two of them here indefinitely. Nor do I want to. And I don't think my stepsons will cooperate with me now. Nicolas appears to be falling apart at the realization of his father's death; Antoine has helped so far only because he thought he was doing his father's bidding. I dread to think what his reaction will be when he learns the truth. I will have to work out what to do with him, but that's not my main problem now.

"You will not tell the police," I say. It isn't a question.

She shakes her head. "The police and I don't get along." She points to Nicolas. "He'll back me up on that." But Nicolas barely seems to hear her. So she keeps talking, her voice low and urgent. "Look. I'll tell you something, if it helps. My dad was a copper, actually. A real fucking hero to everyone else. Except he made my mum's life hell. But no one would believe me when I told them about it: how he treated her, how he hit her. Because he was a 'good guy,' because he put bad guys in jail. And then . . ." she clears her throat, "and then one day it got too much for my mum. She decided it would just be easier to stop trying. So . . . no. I don't trust the police. Not here, not anywhere. Even before I met your guy—Blanchot. You have my word that I am not going to go and tell them about this."

So she knows about Blanchot. I had wondered about calling him for help here. But he has always been Jacques' man, I do not know if his loyalties would extend to me. I cannot risk him learning the truth.

I size the girl up. I realize that, almost in spite of myself, I believe her. Partly because of what she's just told me, about her father. Partly because I can see it in her face, the truth of it. And finally, because I'm not sure I have any other choice but to trust her. I have to protect my daughter at all costs: that is all that matters now.

Nick

I AM NUMB. I KNOW that feeling will return at some point, and that no doubt when it does the pain will be terrible. But for now there is only this numbness. There is a kind of relief in it. Perhaps I do not yet know what to feel. My father is dead. I spent a childhood terrorized by him, my whole adult life trying to escape him. And yet, God help me, I loved him, too.

I am acting on pure instinct, like an automaton, as I help to lift Ben, to carry him down the stairs. And though I am numb I am still aware of the strange and terrible echo of three nights ago, when I carried another body, so stiff and still, out into the courtyard garden.

For a moment, our eyes meet. He seems barely conscious, so perhaps I am imagining it . . . but I think I see something in his expression. An apology? A farewell? But just as quickly it is gone, and his eyes are closing again. And I know I wouldn't trust it anyway. Because I never knew the real Benjamin Daniels at all.

Jess

WE SIT IN SILENCE ACROSS the Formica table, my brother and I. Ben knocks back the espresso in its little paper cup. I tear one end from my croissant and chew. This may be a hospital café but it's France, so the pastries are still pretty good.

Finally, Ben speaks. "I couldn't help myself, you know? That family. Everything we never had. I wanted to be part of it. I wanted them to love me. And at the same time, I wanted to destroy them. Partly for living off women who might have been Mum, at one stage in her life. But also, I suppose, just because I could."

He's looking bloody awful: half his face covered in dark green bruising, the skin above his eyebrow stapled together, his arm in a cast. When we sat down the woman next to us gave a little start of shock and glanced quickly away. But knowing Ben he'll have an attractive scar to show for it soon enough, one he'll work into his charm offensive.

I brought him to the hospital in a taxi: with cash from his wallet, naturally. Explained that he'd had a fall on his moped near his apartment, got a pretty bad head injury. Said he'd made it back to his place and collapsed there, totally out of it, until I turned up and saved the day. It raised a few eyebrows—crazy English tourists—but they've treated him.

"Thanks," he says, suddenly. "I can't believe what you went through. I knew I should have told you not to come and stay—"

"Well, thank God you didn't, right? Because I wouldn't have been able to save your life."

He swallows. I can tell he doesn't like hearing it. It's uncomfortable, acknowledging that you need people. I know this.

"I'm sorry, Jess."

"Well, don't expect me to rescue you next time."

"Not just for that. For not being there when you needed me. For not being there the one time it really mattered. You shouldn't have had to find her alone."

A long silence.

Then he says, "You know, in a way I've always been jealous of you."

"For what?"

"You got to see her one last time. I never got to say goodbye." I can't think of anything to say to this. I couldn't have imagined anything worse than finding her. But maybe a part of me understands.

Ben glances up.

I follow his gaze and see Theo in a dark coat and scarf, hand raised, on the other side of the windows. I might have lost my phone but luckily I still had his business card in my stuff. With his split lip he now looks like a pirate who's been in some sort of duel. He looks good, too.

I turn back to Ben. "Hey," I say. "Your article. You still have it, right?"

He raises his eyebrows. "Yes. Christ knows what they did to my laptop, but I'd already backed it up to my Cloud. Any writer worth their salt knows that."

"It needs to come out," I say.

"I know, I was thinking the same thing—"

"But," I hold up a finger. "We have to do it right. If it publishes, the police will have to look into the club. And those girls who work there—most of them will get deported, right?"

Ben nods.

"So it'll be even worse for them than it is now,' I say. I think of Irina. *I can't go back . . . it wasn't a good situation.* I think of how she spoke about wanting a new life. I promised that if I found Ben, I would find a way to help her. I'm definitely not going to be responsible for her being sent home. If we get this wrong, only the vulnerable will get screwed, I know this.

I look at Ben and then at Theo as he crosses the room to join us. "I have an idea."

Sophie

THE CREAM-COLORED ENVELOPE TREMBLES IN my grip. Hand-delivered to the apartment building's postbox this morning.

I tear it open, slide out a folded letter. I have never seen this handwriting before—a rather untidy scrawl.

> *Madame Meunier,*
> *There was something we didn't get a chance to discuss. I think we both had other things on our minds? Anyway, I made you a promise: I haven't talked to the police and I won't. But Ben's article about La Petite Mort will publish in two weeks' time, whether you do anything or not.*

I catch my breath.

> *But, if you help, it'll have a different emphasis. Either you can be part of the story, take its starring role. Or he'll make sure you aren't named, that you're left out of it as far as possible. And your daughter won't be mentioned at all.*

I grip the letter tighter. Mimi. I've sent her away to the South of France, to paint, to recuperate. This went against every maternal instinct; I didn't want to be separated from her, knowing how vulnerable she was, how angry. But I knew she couldn't stay here, with the shadow of death hanging over this place. But before she left I explained it all to her, in my own words. How much she was wanted when she came into my life. How much she is loved. How I have never thought of her as anything other than my very own. My miracle, my wondrous girl.

I have also tried to make her see that in the circumstances she did the only thing she could that night. That she saved a life as well as taking one. That she, too, acted out of love. I did not tell her I might have done the same. That for a brief time he was almost everything to me, too. But I suspect she knows, somehow, about the affair—if that is what one can call those snatched few weeks of selfish, reckless, glorious insanity.

I know that things may never again be the same between my daughter and I. But I can hope. And love her. It is all I can do.

I, too, would leave this place and join her—given the choice. But my late husband is buried in the garden. I have to stay. It is something I have made my peace with. This may be a gilded cage, but it is the life I have chosen.

I keep reading.

Nick won't be mentioned either. Maybe he's not a bad guy, underneath it all. I think he just made some questionable choices. (P.T.O.)

Nicolas has also left, along with the few possessions he kept here. I don't think he'll be back. I think it will be good for him to leave this place. To stand on his own two feet.

My other stepson remains here and while he isn't the most congenial of neighbors it is better having him where I can keep an eye on him. And he is a less threatening presence now. I don't think I'll be receiving any more of his little notes. He seems diminished by everything, by the grief he feels for a father who was rarely anything other than cruel to him. In spite of myself I feel for him.

I turn the letter over. Read on:

Here's what I'm asking you to do. Those girls? The ones at the club? The ones who are your daughter's age, who are being screwed by rich, important guys so that all of you can live in that place? You're going to do right by them. You're going to give every one of them a nice big chunk of cash.

I shake my head. "There's no way—"

I suppose you'll say the building, all that, is in your husband's name. But what about those pictures on the walls? What about those diamonds in your ears, that cellar of wine downstairs? I'm not exactly an expert, but even by my modest estimate you're sitting on quite a fortune. I'm telling you now that you should sell it to someone who doesn't want a paper trail. Someone who pays cash.

I'll give you a couple of weeks. It'll give the girls a chance to sort themselves out, too. But then Ben's story has to go to print. He's got an editor who's expecting it, after all. And that place needs to disappear. La Petite Mort needs to die its own little death. The police will have to investigate, then. Maybe not as hard as they might do, considering they're probably tied up in it.

I'm asking you to do all of this as a mother, as a woman. Besides, something tells me you wouldn't mind being completely free of that place yourself. Am I right?

I fold the letter again. Slide it back into the envelope.
And then I nod.
I glance up, feeling watched. My gaze goes straight to the cabin in the corner of the courtyard. But there's no one inside. I looked for her that night. I searched the building from top to

bottom, thinking that she couldn't possibly have gone far with her injuries. I even looked in her cabin. But there was no sign. Along with the photographs on the wall, several of the smallest and yet most valuable items from the apartment—that little Matisse, for example—and also my silver whippet, Benoit, the concierge was gone.

AN ARTICLE IN THE *PARIS GAZETTE*

It would appear that the owner of La Petite Mort, Jacques Meunier, has vanished in the wake of the sensational allegations about the exclusive nightclub. The police are now attempting to conduct a full-scale investigation, though this is reportedly hampered by the fact that there are no witnesses available for questioning. Every dancer formerly employed by the club has apparently disappeared.

This may come as something of a relief for the former patrons of the club's alleged illegal activities. However, an anonymized website has recently published what it claims is a list of accounts from La Petite Mort's records, listing dozens of names from the great and good of the French establishment.

In addition, a high-ranking police official, Commissaire Blanchot, has tendered his resignation following the circulation of explicit images purporting to show him *in flagrante* with several women in one of the club's basement rooms.

As has previously been reported, Meunier's son, Antoine Meunier (allegedly his father's right-hand man), shot himself with an antique firearm at the family property in order to avoid being taken into custody.

Jess

I TRUNDLE MY SUITCASE ACROSS the concourse at Gare de l'Est, the broken wheel catching every few steps; I really do need to get it fixed. I look up at the screen to find my train.

There it is: the night service to Milan, where I'll change before going on to Rome. In the early hours of the morning we'll travel along the shore of Lake Geneva and apparently when it's clear you can see the Alps. Sounds pretty good to me. I thought it was time for my own European tour, of sorts. Ben's staying here to make a name for himself as an investigative journalist. So for perhaps the first time ever, I'm the one leaving him. Not running from anything or anyone. Just traveling, in search of the next adventure.

I've even got a place waiting for me. A studio, which is actually a fancy word for a tiny room where you can reach everything from the bed. Funnily enough, it's a conversion of an old maids' quarters at the top of an apartment block. And apparently it has a view of St. Peter's, if you squint. It probably won't be much bigger than the concierge's cabin. But then I don't have that much to put in it: the contents of one broken suitcase.

Anyway, it's all mine. No, not *mine* mine . . . I didn't buy it— are you crazy? Even if I did somehow have the cash, I wouldn't want my name on the deeds for anything. Wouldn't want to be tied down. But I did put down the deposit on it and paid the first month in advance. I took a cut of the money the girls at the club were getting. A kind of finder's fee, if you like. I'm not a saint, after all.

As for the girls—the women, I should say—of course I couldn't hold each of their hands and make sure it was all going to be OK. But it's nice to know that they've been given the same thing I have. That it'll buy them time. A little breathing room. Maybe even the opportunity to do something else.

Twenty minutes before my train leaves. I look around for somewhere to grab a snack. And as I do I glimpse a figure moving through the crowd. Small, with a familiar, crouching, shuffling gait. A silk headscarf. A silver whippet on a lead. Joining the queue of people waiting to board a train—I look up at the screen above the platform—to Nice, in the South of France. And then I glance away, and don't look again until the train is pulling out of the platform. Because we're all entitled to that, aren't we?

The chance of a new life.

ACKNOWLEDGMENTS

I LOVED WRITING THIS BOOK. At the same time, it was the hardest of my books to write: partly because it was the most complicated structure and premise I've attempted yet . . . and partly because it was written first while I was very pregnant and then with a new baby in tow. *And* during a pandemic, though on that score I know how lucky I am to have a job where I can easily work from home, unlike so many, especially those incredibly brave key workers.

Anyway, I'm so proud of this book and of releasing it into the world. It's not very British to say it, but I am! At the same time, it feels so, so important to stress that none of it would have been possible without the hard work of some very kind, dedicated, and talented people. There really should be multiple names on that front cover: this book has been a huge team effort!

Thank you to the phenomenal Cath Summerhayes, for your endless wit and wisdom and sage counsel, and for being such fun to work with and to go for lunch with and for cocktails with . . . and for always being there on the end of the phone. I am so lucky to have you and so grateful for everything you do.

Thank you to the incredible Alexandra Machinist, for your unfailingly excellent advice and unbelievable negotiating skills. And though for the time being our planned Parisian adventures have fallen foul of the winter vomiting virus, I know we'll be having a glass of champagne on the *terrasses* soon—I can't wait to toast your brilliance!

Thank you to Kim Young, for being the most patient and supportive of editors, for championing this book from its first inception and (frankly fairly ropey) first draft. You always know how to coax my best work from me—you inspire me with your belief in me and my writing! Thank you for holding my hand throughout this whole process—and for always being ready to jump on the phone to discuss a mad new plot idea!

Thank you to Kate Nintzel, for your masterly editorial counsel—for your razor-sharp eye and overall publishing wizardry. I still can't quite believe what you have achieved with *The Guest List* in the U.S., bringing my dark little British book to well over a million readers! I am so lucky to have you as my champion.

Thank you to the utterly brilliant Charlotte Brabbin. You are such a talented, dedicated editor. I am so grateful for all your hard work and advice, tact and creativity, and for always being ready and willing for a brainstorm—however small or silly the query, whatever time of day or night!

Thank you to Luke Speed, for all your kindness and wisdom . . . and for your endless patience in explaining the magical and mystifying world of film to me! And thank you at the same time for being such fun to work with. You and Cath are the dream team! May there be many more lunches . . . and cinema dates!

Thank you to Katie McGowan, Callum Mollison, and Grace Robinson, for your incredible work in finding my books so many publishers around the world. It's such a thrill to think of them being translated into other languages and finding so many new readers globally. I'm in awe of what you do.

Thank you to the fabulous Harper Fiction family: to Kate Elton, Charlie Redmayne, Isabel Coburn, Abbie Salter, Hannah O'Brien, Sarah Shea, Jeannelle Brew, Amy Winchester, Claire Ward, Roger Cazalet, Izzy Coburn, Alice Gomer, Sarah Munro, Charlotte Brown, Grace Dent, and Ben Hurd. I am so lucky to be published by you all. I'm so hoping we all get to raise a glass together soon!

Thank you to the brilliant team at William Morrow: Brian

Murray, Liate Stehlik, Molly Gendell, Brittani Hilles, Kaitlin Harri, Sam Glatt, Jennifer Hart, Stephanie Vallejo, Pam Barricklow, Grace Han, and Jeanne Reina. Thank you so much for your tireless work and dedication and for championing my books stateside. I can't wait to visit you all in New York and celebrate together!

Thank you to the wonderful wider Curtis Brown A-Team: to Jonny Geller, Jess Molloy, and Anna Weguelin.

Thank you to my darling friend Anna Barrett, for doing such a fantastic early read-through and edit of *The Paris Apartment* when I was too scared to show it to anyone else—for hugely boosting my confidence in the book with your encouragement and suggestions. I highly recommend Anna if you're looking for an independent edit of your novel—she's at www.the-writers-space.com.

Last, but very much not least . . . thank you to my family:

Thank you to the Foley, Colley, and Allen clans, for all your support.

Thank you to my wonderful siblings, Kate and Robbie (again—thank God!—nothing like the siblings in this book!). I'm so proud of you both and so lucky to have you.

Thank you to my parents, for your pride in me and for the endless, unflagging support. Thank you for forgiving me for turning up to stay only to dump the wee man on you with no warning and disappear behind my laptop. For being such kind and loving grandparents, feeding and playing and looking after the little guy so lovingly and uncomplainingly while I've been mired in copyedits and proofreads. Thank you for encouraging me in my storytelling since I was a little girl telling Farmer Pea tales in the back seat!

Thank you to Al, for quite literally making all of this possible. For holding the baby; for putting stuff on hold to help me; for talking me through plot crises at three A.M. and on walks and drives and over dinners we've gone out for and holidays we've taken to *get away* from the book . . . for your wisdom; your support; your belief; your encouragement. For reading through almost as many drafts of this book as I have myself, biro in hand—even when knackered from a day's work or baby wrangling . . . or both. You say twenty percent—I say I owe you everything.

B & N EXCLUSIVE MATERIAL:
A NOTE ON INSPIRATION

I HAD THE IDEA FOR *The Paris Apartment* while working on another book—my previous murder mystery, *The Guest List*. Rather than going on specific writing retreats, I like to rent an apartment in a foreign city, somewhere away from all the distractions of home life, so I can focus on my draft (and go for walks and long coffee breaks). Where better than Paris, which has held a particular magic for me ever since I first visited it as a little girl?

I found a place in a beautiful old building with a slightly faded grandeur to it. I think my apartment must have been in the family, unchanged, for generations: the cooking appliances, as well as the furniture, were, let's just say, antique. The windows looked onto the ivy-tangled courtyard of the building, and there was something deliciously voyeuristic about it: as I sat at the elegant little desk, I could see my neighbors coming and going—the elderly lady with her dog on the ground floor, the young guy who lived upstairs—and, of course (because it's what I do and because I wanted an escape from the latest set of edits), I'd invent little backstories for them.

I also noticed that first thing in the morning and last thing at night I could hear something odd from the apartment above me: the sound of something heavy being dragged across wooden floorboards. A piece of furniture? . . . A *body*?! If there is one specific moment in which a book sparks into life, this was that moment for *The Paris Apartment*. I knew there was a story to be told here and I knew I wanted to be the one to tell it . . .

CHRISTINE 21

4 rue Christine

THIS IS A TINY cinema in Saint Germain and I'm almost loath to share it, because it's one of my favorite Parisian haunts. It shows old films in English: lots of noir, lots of Hitchcock. I first watched *Rear Window*, *The Third Man*, and *Stage Fright* there—all of which, in some way, now I come to think of it, inspired me in writing *The Paris Apartment*. It's a wonderful place to while away a couple of free hours on a rainy autumn afternoon, and somehow the tiny screening rooms and eclectic clientele—usually several fur coat–clad elderly ladies and the odd amorous couple—only enhance the atmosphere.

ROSA BONHEUR

Parc des Buttes-Chaumont, 2 avenue de la Cascade

THIS BAR APPEARS IN *The Paris Apartment* in one of Mimi's recollections. I had to have it in the book because it's one of my favorite Parisian addresses—I've spent some very memorable nights there! Named after a female French artist, it's tucked away inside the Parc des Buttes-Chaumont: by day it's a cafe, families stopping there with kids to grab a pizza. But by night the music ramps up and the disco ball and stripper pole come into their own (the gloriously wacky decor has to be seen to be believed), and everyone chats and drinks and dances into the small hours of the morning. The park itself, too, is worth a visit: much less formal than the classic Parisian park (the Jardin du Luxembourg or the Tuileries, say), with grottoes and undulating hills and a lake in the middle, where to my amazement I once spotted a turtle.

SHAKESPEARE & COMPANY
37 rue de la Bûcherie

THIS IS HARDLY A secret Parisian spot, but as a book lover I have to include it here. The utterly delightful Shakespeare & Company bookstore on the left bank of the Seine is a treasure trove of books in English. It's a slice of history too: Allen Ginsberg, James Baldwin, and Lawrence Durrell were all early habitués, and it's named after the original Shakespeare & Company, which closed during the Second World War but was frequented by Ernest Hemingway, James Joyce, and F. Scott Fitzgerald. I have spent many happy hours browsing its shelves—and was thrilled, on a recent visit, to find copies of my own books there! While I was in Paris for research, I'd pop in to discover more Simenon novels for my collection: each slender Maigret book (involving Simenon's Parisian detective Inspector Maigret) is a wonderful exploration of twentieth-century Paris and its dark underbelly. That glimpse beneath the gilded facade of the city was a huge source of inspiration when I was writing *The Paris Apartment*.

THE CATACOMBS

NOT EXACTLY A WELL-KEPT secret, the catacombs being a prime Parisian tourist destination! But with good reason: there's nothing quite like them anywhere in the world. It's a breathtaking, sobering experience to descend beneath the streets and witness this vast memento mori: the bones of millions of the city's dead arranged in silent, dim corridors of earth. The catacombs inspired *The Paris Apartment*'s exploration of the unseen, the darkness beneath the surface. I even wrote a scene in which Jess and Nick visit them together, which sadly hit the cutting room floor!

I love the fact that, despite their popularity, the catacombs have retained their mystique. The section open to the public is apparently a tiny fraction of the entire network, and when I was researching the book I lost myself in stories of the "cataphiles"—urban explorers who illegally access the hidden spaces, sometimes risking life and limb—and of the restaurants, bars, and even cinemas(!) that have popped up and then disappeared again in the many secret subterranean caverns.